RANGE OF *MOTION*

RANGE OF
MOTION

a novel

BRIAN TRAPP

ACRE
CINCINNATI 2025

Acre Books is made possible by the support of the Robert and Adele Schiff Foundation and the Department of English at the University of Cincinnati.

Copyright © 2025 by Brian Trapp
All rights reserved
Printed in the United States of America

Designed by Barbara Neely Bourgoyne
Cover art: AdobeStock/hyam (boar); AdobeStock/TilasBR (wolf)
Interior art: AdobeStock/hyam (wolf)

ISBN-13 (pbk): 978-1-946724-96-0
ISBN-13 (ebook): 978-1-946724-97-7

No part of this work may be reproduced or transmitted in any form or by any means, electronic or mechanical, including photocopying and recording, or by any information storage or retrieval system, without express written permission, except in the case of brief quotations embodied in critical articles and reviews.

This book is a work of fiction. Names, characters, businesses, places, events, and incidents are either products of the author's imagination or used in a fictitious manner. Any resemblance to actual persons, living or dead, or actual events is purely coincidental.

The press is based at the University of Cincinnati, Department of English and Comparative Literature, Arts & Sciences Hall, Room 248, PO Box 210069, Cincinnati, OH, 45221–0069.
www.acre-books.com

Acre Books titles may be purchased at a discount for educational use. For information please email business@acre-books.com.

For Danny

I would carry that boy's mind like a bowl picked up in the dark; you don't know what's in it. He feeds on odd remnants that we have not priced; he eats a sleep that is not our sleep. There is more in sickness than the name of that sickness. In the average person is the peculiar that has been scuttled, and in the peculiar the ordinary that has been sunk; people always fear what requires watching.

—Djuna Barnes, *Nightwood*

RANGE OF *MOTION*

AUGUST 2002

It was late morning on their third day at Camp Cheerful, right before lunch, and it was unclear if Sal was having fun.

Michael had prepped Sal on a beach towel under the shaded green awning. He pulled on Sal's tube socks so he wouldn't scuff his feet on the pool tiles. He fastened Sal's life vest, which was made of hard yellow foam and framed his head, making him look as if he were in the stocks or some other very relaxing torture device.

Now Sal was submerged, his head held aloft above the water. The vest made Sal so light in the pool that with Sal deep enough, Michael could let go, let Sal touch his tube-socked toes to the bottom. He could let Sal float by himself. "Look at you standing," Michael said.

Sal smiled just barely. Then his smile disappeared, and he said it: "Mom-ma."

"Momma?" Michael said. "What do you mean 'Momma'? Here. Forget about her. Dance with me." Michael made techno music with his mouth as he moved Sal's hands up and down. Sal's skinny legs scissored back and forth under the water. His feeding tube floated—taped shut—waggling from his belly in the pool current.

"Mike-a," Sal said.

Michael leaned in, still dancing. "Yeah buddy?"

"Mom-ma," he said again into his brother's face.

"Come on. Camp isn't that bad. A little brotherly quality time. A little sibling R-and-R."

Sal sputtered his lips.

Okay," Michael said. "Now you're just hurting my feelings."

This was supposed to be a special place for special people. That's what the brochure said in bright balloon letters, why Michael and Sal's mother had sent them here for the last week of summer. "I'm not special," Michael told his mother, but she said, "You watch your mouth. Don't you ever say that," even though she knew full well Sal was "special" in the way the brochure meant: severe cerebral palsy and mental disabilities. He could barely control his own powerchair. He needed Michael, his twin, to tag along as his attendant—his escort in fun, personal hygiene, and not dying—before the brothers, aged eighteen, went their separate ways.

So far, Camp Cheerful seemed to be mostly about singing. You sang for your breakfast. You sang for your lunch. When you tried to fall asleep, good luck. Someone was singing. The morning they drove across the bridge and into camp, the very first activity was to gather around the flagpole and sing about baby sharks and a-bear-way-up-there and the spelling out of b-a-n-a-n-a. The camp had a distinct feel of a cult, with lyrics designed to break the will. Sal had bunched up his lips to his incisors, made "squirrel teeth," his patent look of displeasure. Michael had whispered, "Where did Mom send us?" and Sal caught Michael's eye like *We are in hell*.

The first day, the Art Leader, a German woman in dreadlocks, forced the campers to rub crayons over leaves to, as she said, "Reveal vein" until someone yelled "Ants!" and everyone started slapping. The second day, during Nature, they tried to fish off the bridge into the creek's deep pool using the only two functional fishing rods, but Jerry, one of their campers, ate all the bait—an entire package of hotdogs—and when someone pulled up a rod too quick, Sal almost got hotdog-hooked in the face.

Sal not having fun wasn't all the camp's fault. Michael was also fucking up. The first mistake Sal had found funny. Michael put Sal's AFOs, his hard plastic ankle-foot braces, on the wrong feet and had trouble stuffing them into his shoes. The braces probably hurt, but Sal seemed to enjoy Michael being an idiot much more. Sal liked less the red slashes on the tops of his ears, wrists, and knees, where Michael had missed with the SPF 50. No wonder his mother rubbed that stuff on like Sal was trying to pass as an albino. The fuckups continued: While Michael was scoping possible ladies for Sal during dinner, his feeding tube catheter slipped out. Sal said "Mike-a" repeatedly, but Michael thought Sal was just doing his torture-you-with-your-name routine and ignored him until he saw the damp circle ballooning on Sal's shorts. Then, this morning, Sal was so stiff it was difficult to thread his arms through his sleeves. Michael pulled too hard, and Sal said, "Eh-eh!" like *Careful! I have nerve endings.* And when Michael lifted Sal to his chair and Sal clicked the joystick down, nothing happened; Michael had forgotten to plug it in, so they had to sit in the cabin charging his battery while everyone else went to sing for their breakfast. Every time Michael messed up, he felt Sal saying with a furrowed caterpillar brow: *You're incompetent. You're no replacement for Mom.*

They were stuffed into a twelve-bunk cabin, with only a small cubby to hold Sal's several trash bags full of clothes. Their cabin mates were grown men, some in wheelchairs, some not. Michael had looked at their charts, which cataloged their disabilities, their likes and dislikes. Michael met the person first, in all their messiness, and then saw the label, the neat pathology. They had Gill, who every morning did fifteen pull-ups on a cabin beam (Deaf); Claude, a Black man who talked smack from his wheelchair (CP); and Jerry, the hot dog eater (Down syndrome). Then there were Boom Boom and Ron: two mentally disabled men who worked together in a packing plant and were mostly concerned about sneaking cigarettes behind the cabin. And Vince, who had a traumatic brain injury and a pencil-thin red mustache and talked like an enraged father, yelling from his manual wheelchair at Boom Boom and Ron for smoking too close to the cabin: "Get away from the windows, you bastards!"

The only one with serious behaviors was Terrance, who had autism. Terrance didn't talk much and took a pill that gave him tremors. He was a natural scowler and could have passed for a street tough. He'd clamp on to weaker campers' arms with a vise grip, and say in a schoolmarm reprimand: "No no no . . . No no no." Terrance dragged around a beige plastic helmet with a clear visor in case of self-harm. It gave him the air of a superhero, as if at the first sign of damsel in distress, he would snap on his helmet and transform. The only thing that seemed to calm him was his giant headphones and listening to NPR.

Michael's mother had said, "I thank God Sal doesn't have any behaviors." She was right, in a way. Sal did not, for example, eat dirt or slap himself or bite his own hand. He did not have to be reminded about hands to himself or public masturbation. There was a minimum of bellowing. When Sal bit Michael or went after a shin with his powerchair, he usually had good reason. He was a (mostly) responsible powerchair driver with a clean record. Michael thought his brother was predictable. You could assume what he would do, which was not much. He might go the other way, not behaving, not responding, withholding himself so much that you were desperate for him to show up inside his own body.

But there were moments when Michael was sure Sal was enjoying himself. He smiled during Barn, where he pet rabbits, those beady-eyed balls of fur. He beamed during archery, when they'd tied Sal via string to the adaptive crossbow trigger and he backed up his powerchair enough to punch the arrow into the target with a *thwack*. And he laughed during Rec when they floated up a giant parachute and Sal gunned it to the other side until the fabric softly came down and swallowed him. And Sal joy-screamed yesterday in the pool when Michael raced him against Claude, helping him talk shit: "Sal is a high-octane watercraft! Do not challenge him!" They played drunk boating, Sal shaking with laughter as Michael crashed him into unsuspecting swimmers, whispering, "Who should we get next? Who's on your hit list?"

Sal also enjoyed their twin schtick, when campers and counselors would ask them if they were really twins and Sal said, "Eh-eh," like *I barely even know this guy*, and Michael became mock-outraged, put his hand to his chest and gasped like a Southern belle: "Sal, I can't believe you. That's it! I'm telling Mom!" Sal laughed so hard he'd forget how to breathe, and he'd tear up and get red-faced as his chest heaved. They'd even started calling Michael "the Aide" because if he wasn't Sal's twin, who was this guy?

Sal had fun at his brother's expense, and Michael was happy to pay the bill—because for as much as Michael fucked up, he'd also gotten Sal right. He combed the kinks out of Sal's dyed blond hair and made tasteful wardrobe suggestions that would broadcast Sal's cool—*this surfing shirt is dope; these cargo shorts hide your Skeletor knees*. At feeding time, besides the leaking incident, Michael had efficiently handled Sal's tube, priming the pump with distilled water, ensuring the pump was set to *click click click* slow enough so Sal didn't puke, confirming his formula was neither too cold nor too warm, and providing moderately entertaining commentary during their long shifts at the cafeteria table. Michael even got Sal eating orally, taking a few actual bites of ice cream, something he rarely did since the feeding tube. And Michael expertly changed his diaper, plucking the turd out of Sal's butt with a clean section of the diaper, and thoroughly dabbing his nether regions with wet wipes, with an extra *pffft* of baby powder to ward away diaper rash. And come bedtime, Michael put the pillows under Sal's every gap and wedged in the stuffed animals between the bars so expertly that when Michael asked for a kiss before lights out, Sal grudgingly scraped his bottom lip against his teeth, like *Okay. Not bad.* Michael hadn't even felt the need to smoke the weed he'd smuggled in his pocket along with his one-hitter. Because if Michael were being honest, he felt closer to Sal here at this camp—away from all the distraction and drama of home—than he had in years.

But then, when everything was going right, Sal would pull away and do his black-hole routine. He'd say "Momma," which was not what Michael needed. Soon they'd go back across the bridge to whatever was waiting for them. Sal off to the facility, Michael off to his little college on the other side of the country. Michael needed Sal to have the time of his life.

Michael looked at the pool deck under the green awning, at the pool noodles drooping in a plastic bin like underwatered flowers. A row of nonswimmers—both men and women—sat in their wheelchairs and patio furniture, bored and baking in the sun. Sebastian, one of three counselors in Michael and Sal's cabin, was sitting in his sunchair, his body in blob-formation, a knob of lotion on his nose. He had Asperger's, a former camper turned counselor, and constantly mumbled into his walkie-talkie, searching, as he said, "for signs of intelligent life."

A foam ball skidded across the water, right near Sal's face. "Watch it," Michael yelled.

"Sorry, dude," said Jim, another counselor. With his shock of red hair and skinny pale bod, he looked like a victim of the potato famine. He pointed to Gill, wearing his hearing aids and fighter pilot sunglasses on the pool deck. "Gill, watch the gun."

Gill flexed his biceps. "My bad," he said.

"Close one," Michael said to Sal.

"Mmmmm," Sal said.

Michael looked beyond the fence at the concrete bridge leading out of camp, heard the faint whooshing of cars heading down Route 42. Only four more days left. He tried not to count, wondered if Sal was counting too. He eyed the life-vested camper Jim was holding in the water. "You want to race Claude again?"

"Eh-eh," Sal said.

"Yes, you do. Come on." Michael pulled Sal over to Jim and Claude. "Rematch," he said.

Claude had divots in his head and talked shit in a slow drawl: "You ... want ... some ... more? I ... don't ... give ... a ... care ... for ... that ... boy. I'm ... the ... fast ... est ... man ... on ... the ... water." He laughed with an abrupt halt in the back of his throat: "Ahh-hek!"

"Let's do this," Jim said, and then they were off to the other side of the pool, wading fast over the sharp tiles. Jim's legs were longer, and Michael crashed Sal's specialized life vest onto the wall a second too late. Sal just floated there, glaring in defeat.

Claude was ecstatic. "That ... s ... right ... fools. Do ... not ... mess ... with ... the ... best!"

"Ohhh," Jim said. "Sal's a sore loser. What's wrong, Sally? Not having fun?"

"Eh-eh," Sal said.

"He's joking," Michael said.

Darren, the last counselor in their cabin, scooted by, holding a kickboard on which Jerry, the hot dog eater, was floating, slapping the water with his feet. Jerry kept snapping his yellow teeth open and shut. Every day he was something different: a cowboy, a ninja, a secret agent. Right now he was a shark. "Easy, Shark Man," Darren said. Darren was their cabin's team leader, even though Michael thought he was the laziest one. He had California blond hair and wrestling muscles. He wore a ratty hemp necklace and wrote esoteric poetry on the Great Hall whiteboard, mostly about birds. His latest: "The grackle pecks / the rusty Ford / in the used-car lot / its beak remembering." He was about to start his second year at Stanford. Michael was sure he worked at the camp just to put it on his med-school application. Darren eyed Sal pouting in the water and said, "I don't know, Aide. Your brother looks pretty miserable. Maybe he wants to get out."

"Thanks for your color commentary," Michael said. "Don't you have work you should be pretending to do?"

"If I had to rely on you," Darren said, "I'd be pissed too. Okay, Shark Man. Resume the hunt." Jerry growled and snapped his teeth as he splashed away.

Michael looked down at his brother. "What's wrong, Sally?" Sal didn't answer. Maybe it was the chlorine. There seemed to be a dangerous amount in the pool, even to guard against the occasional turd submarine. *He couldn't know about the facility. He didn't.*

Their mother had told Michael about the facility right before they left for camp. She pulled him into the dining room while Sal lay oblivious in his bedroom, his punk rock cranked. She said this day had been coming for a while.

"So you're just going to give him away?"

"Michael. Stop. Don't put it like that. I've thought a lot about this."

Sal's health had been worse since he got the feeding tube, sure, but enough to make his mother quit? "Oh," he said. "I know what this is. You're trying to guilt me into staying."

"I would never ask you to do that," she said.

"But you want me to."

"I want you to have your own life."

Michael looked toward Sal's bedroom, where Joey Ramone was singing about his wish to be sedated. "Does he know?"

She shook her head. "You know how he gets. I don't want to tell him until I have to. I don't want to ruin your last week."

Michael came back to the present when the lifeguard announced, "Count your campers!"

The counselors poked the air, tallying their campers, but Michael only had to count to one: Sal, stick in the mud. Sal, refusing to have fun.

There was still time for Sal to get with the program. Because Michael was having fun, if he was being honest, spending twenty-four-seven with Sal. He'd found himself falling back into old habits, interpreting Sal's every word, every facial expression, studying him like scripture. Sometimes he felt like he knew what his twin brother was thinking. He'd forgotten how much he missed him—this version of Sal, this version of himself.

The next morning, Michael vowed to do everything right. He unplugged Sal's chair from the charger, which he'd remembered to plug in. He changed Sal's soaked diaper and played an extra-long round of Pick the Right T-Shirt before Sal settled on a dinosaur skateboarding. He got Sal out the cabin door in time for them to make flagpole, where he held Sal's hand during morning songs of "Mr. Sun, Sun, Mr. Golden Sun" and "Head, Shoulders, Knees and Toes." After breakfast, they went to Barn, where Sal indulged in another round of "pet those rabbits." And still, Sal wouldn't stop with the "Momma."

Michael expected more resistance as they headed for Art. The art cabin had stained-glass windows of smiling cartoon suns, like a church with the most annoying religion. The room was trashed, with paint tins stacked in the sink and boxes of broken crayons and pencils lining the walls. The Art Leader walked around the room stacking plastic squeeze bottles full of non-toxic paint onto white paper sheets. She asked in her German accent, "You know the great American artist Jackson Pollock? Who does the drip?" When everyone said no, she ordered them to splatter on the paper anyway.

The campers grabbed the paint bottles and squeezed them with abandon, but Sal just stared at the table. "You want to paint?" Michael asked, but Sal said, "Eh-eh," like *I'll pass*.

Only three more days, Michael thought. But then a female counselor walked up to them, followed by her camper in a powerchair. "Hey, Aide," she said. It was Melissa, the cute college girl with shapely soccer legs who always wore a bandana over her auburn hair. She had the dreamy affect of someone stoned in movies. Her camper had blond chunky bangs, a gap between her two front teeth, and high cheekbones, all of which made her look French. They were both pretty enough to be featured on Camp Cheerful promotional materials. Melissa thumbed back at her camper. "Maya here wants to know if you guys are . . . like . . . really twins."

Maya covered her eyes with her neon-pink hand-splint, blushing and embarrassed. God, would they get this question all week? Maybe they'd look more like twins if Sal hadn't dyed his hair blond while Michael stuck with the brown. And if Michael had at least some cerebral palsy. Sucking at sports didn't count. And now Michael expected Sal to say, "Eh-eh," like *I don't even know this guy*, but Sal held back. He glanced at Michael. He wanted to do something different.

"Of course we are," Michael said. "What you should ask, Maya, is who's the evil twin. There's one in every pair. So guess."

Maya uncovered her eyes and glanced back and forth between them. But before she could answer, Sal ran his wheelchair into Michael's shin.

"Ow!" Michael yelped. "Sal, don't give it away, you evil bastard."

They all cracked up. Sal had timed it perfectly, and he knew it. His chest shook with laughter, his eyes watering. He could hardly breathe.

"You guys are trouble," said Melissa, still laughing as they went back to their table.

After they left, Michael said, "Maya's cute. Tomorrow's the camp dance. Maybe she'll save a dance for you?"

Sal stole a glance at her like *Maybe*.

Everything came easier after that. "What color do you want to start with? This one?" Michael held up the blue bottle. Sal's bottom lip jutted out pensively as he scanned his other choices, settling back on the blue. "Eh" he said, like *Let's do it*. Together they squeezed a slash of blue onto the paper with a percussive *shart*.

Sal smirked like *Okay. That sound = hilarious*.

Michael picked another bottle, lime-green this time. "How about this one?"

"Eh," Sal said. That's right. He knew the one Sal wanted. *I'm his twin and know him best*.

Sal toggled his joystick forward and ran his wheels over the picture, his back tires making ragged rows of green and blue. He drove his chair off the composition and turned around, creating smooth, lined bands of red with his front wheel's tread. Sal looked down at the paper. A string of drool dripped onto his chest strap, and he smiled, flashing his crooked teeth like *Ta da*. There he was. There was his brother. It was controlled chaos with Sal's own wheeled stamp. Like Sal was saying: *Dude. Look. I did it myself.*

The next day was Messy Olympics. Michael asked Jim, "What's messy about it?" and Jim said, "Oh ho ho. Everything." Each cabin gathered behind the Great Hall, where manicured lawn gave way to shabbily mowed field. Before them lay rolls of toilet paper, endless cartons of eggs, a kiddie pool, and—inexplicably—a Slip 'N Slide. Michael was glad he'd dressed Sal in a trash bag with a hole cut for his head. It might save him a shower.

The campers were pumped, already talking shit to each other.

"You going down," Boom Boom said to the next cabin, sweating through his Marlboro t-shirt.

"In your dreams, bitch," said another camper.

Sebastian announced into his walkie-talkie, "We've got some smack talking over here."

After one round of Count Your Campers, the games began. There was stand-on-one-foot and water-balloon toss. There was spoon-egg relay, where Sal gave them an advantage, resting the egg on a spoon in his lap as he ferried it to Michael. There was Make-a-Mummy, where they encased Jim in rolls of toilet paper as he moaned like the non-verbal un-dead. There was dizzy base running, where the campers spun and stumbled around the sandbags, drunk on vertigo.

The camp director announced it was time for egg firing range.

"Who should we nominate?" Darren asked.

Sal took a deep breath and said it first: "Mike-a!"

"The Aide!" the cabin shouted.

They pushed Michael out fifteen feet and lined him up with other unfortunates, while the kitchen ladies placed a small battery of egg cartons in front of each line of campers.

"Shouldn't you be farther away?" Michael asked.

No one responded.

Sal was first to throw, with Darren whispering in his ear. They seemed to be talking about more than how hard to hurl the eggs, like Darren was saying: *This is for all he's done and didn't do. This is your revenge.* Sal smiled with his tongue stuffed between his teeth. Darren brought the egg close to Sal's lips, and what did Sal do? He raked his bottom lip against his front teeth. He blew it a kiss.

The director barked into the megaphone, and the barrage commenced. Michael saw Darren wind up and then felt the *thwack* of egg shatter against his sternum. *Gaw*. Did Darren play varsity baseball too? Why couldn't a beanpole autistic throw first, or a wild-pitch CP? Then came Boom Boom, Ron, and Gill, who in their aim and mechanics and velocity, were clearly products of excellent special-ed PE programs. Egg shattered on Michael's cheek, cut against his neck. His chest burned, and he gulped air. Jim threw Vince's egg, which landed with a pop on Michael's gut as Vince shouted, "Take that, you bastard!" Terrance tossed a floater that cracked at Michael's feet. There was only Jerry left, thank God, but Jerry knew his own limitations and just ran up with a shirt full of eggs and smashed each one against Michael's torso. "We missed a spot," he said, crushing one into Michael's ribs. He was out of character, without his cowboy hat or ninja bandana. "What are you supposed to be now?" Michael asked, and Jerry said, "The angel of death." And then they all rushed the cartons.

As an egg exploded against Michael's orbital lobe, his twin brother Chewbacca-screamed: "Ahhhh-rah-ahhhhh! Mike-aaa!" like, *Now this is fun!*

Michael didn't worry about college or the facility or anything else on the other side of the bridge. He was in pain, and in camp, and inside the moment. He was covered in eggs, ritually humiliated, and reborn. He raised his fists and roared.

After Messy Olympics, most of the campers rested in their bunks. Michael and Sal went behind the cabin with Boom Boom and Ron. Boom Boom banged a new hard pack of Marlboros against his broad and callused palm, and ripped out the foil like it was a throat. He fingered the filters until he came to the one he liked, flipped it around, and blessed it. "Lucky," he said.

Boom Boom passed out the cigarettes, leaving Sal out. He lit his Zippo and held it in the center of the circle, waiting for everyone to dip their tips into the flame.

"Eh," Sal said, nodding his head up like *Excuse me?*

"You smoke, Sal?" asked Ron.

"Yeah," he said softly, like *Sort of.*

Michael clarified. "It's usually secondhand from our dad." Michael thought about saying Sal couldn't smoke, not with his bout of pneumonia last year. But as soon as he opened his mouth, he realized whose words he'd be using: his mother's. It was just like her to baby Sal, to hold him back from the world. Camp was all about adapting, participating, no matter what the activity. "Here, Sal," he said. "You can share mine." Michael took three deep drags, enough to feel lightheaded, and then put the burning cigarette between Sal's cracked lips, where it hung slanting down and wafting smoke.

"Whoa," Boom Boom said. "James Dean."

"Clint Eastwood," Ron said.

"Sid Vicious," Michael said.

Sal moaned like *Mmmmm. Cancer.* He coughed and the cig fell into his lap, and Michael scrambled to pick it up before Sal's purple Umbros went up in flames.

Jim came around the corner with Vince. "Did I see a cigarette in Sal's mouth?"

"Yup," Ron said. "We're corrupting youth." He turned to Vince. "What do *you* want?"

Jim said, "He wants to yell at you guys in person."

"Stay away from the windows!" Vince yelled. "You bastards!"

Boom Boom asked Vince if he lived in Crawford House, a group home on the West Side. "Didn't I see you at a UCP dance a few months ago? With some girl on your arm?"

"Don't try to sweet talk me," Vince said.

"Relax," Boom Boom said. "Tell us about yourself. Cigarettes are bad for your health but good for conversation."

Vince looked from Boom Boom to Sal, tightened his arms and thrust up his trunk, said, "Just step away from the windows. I'm looking out for the others. My fiancée, she hates smoke. She was the one on my arm."

Everyone took a step back from the windows.

Ron said, "Your fiancée? What's she like?"

"She's great," Vince said. "She has curly hair and a real job in an office and her own apartment. We want to have five kids."

Michael was surprised that someone like Vince had a fiancée. Five kids? How fat were these social security checks? But why would he doubt that Vince could find someone to love him, to create five little Vinces he could yell at and call bastards? Maybe because Michael doubted he'd find someone to love himself. For the first time he wondered if the facility might be a good thing, if Sal would find love there.

"What's your group home like?" he asked Boom Boom and Ron.

Boom Boom said it wasn't too bad. They could have friends and family visit. They cooked their own meals. They went to Cedar Point and rode the rollercoasters with a special pass that let them cut to the front of the line. The staff was sometimes lazy but otherwise helpful, though they needed to mind their own freaking business.

Ron smiled. "We can have girls over."

"I can," Boom Boom said.

"Shut up," Ron said.

Michael said, "It sounds sort of nice." They nodded. Michael watched Sal's face. At the mention of "group home," he got extra stiff, his lips clamped shut, his arms curled tight. *He couldn't know. He didn't.* But after a moment, he settled. Michael took a drag of their cigarette. Maybe it was just a spasm.

After dinner, the whole camp rushed back to their cabins to get ready for the dance. As Sal lay on his hospital bed, Michael combed his brother's hair and blasted his armpits with spray deodorant. After a quick diaper change (number one . . . whew), he rumbled an electric shaver over Sal's face. Michael gave him a sniff. "Not terrible. Let me see the dimple."

Sal smiled.

"Deadly." He turned to Jim. "What's the dress code again?"

"Toga," Jim said.

"I don't know," said Michael. "You'll get cold."

Sal thrust his head up and said "Eh," like *But I want to.*

"Fine, but you're also putting on a t-shirt and shorts."

Michael dressed Sal in a white undershirt and a fresh pair of Umbros and lifted him into his powerchair. After he put on Sal's braces and shoes, he took one of Sal's baby-blue bedsheets (did he really need three?) and stuffed an end between the wheelchair seat and back, arranging the sheet across Sal's chest and down his lap and leg divider, covering his shorts, pressing it all together with the chest strap and seat belt. He was ready.

"Maya's not gonna stand a chance," Michael said. "A Greek God. What's the disabled one's name again?"

"Hephaestus," Darren said.

"Of course you know that," Jim said.

Darren shrugged. "I don't watch TV."

As Michael was about to rip off his own bedsheet, Jim reached under his bunk and retrieved an industrial-sized roll of Saran Wrap.

"Look what I stole from the kitchen," he said.

"For what?" Michael asked.

"For us. I'm thinking we leave a little less to the imagination. You in?"

"I don't know."

"It's the last dance of the summer. Come on, Aide. You're one of us now."

"I wouldn't go that far," Darren said.

"Counselors, aides," Jim said. "Strip down to your boxers."

Michael disrobed, and Jim helped him create a toga of plastic wrap, layer upon layer around his shoulder and groin and thighs until he had a tight garment already growing sticky with sweat. Michael had forgotten about his baby fat, which bulged against the sides of the plastic, and his weird left nipple, which was exposed. They could see through the toga to his little ducky boxers. What if he got a boner? He tried not to think about it burrowing through the plastic. *Baseball. Baseball. Baseball.* He took a step forward. His outfit creaked.

Sal stared at him like *You freak.*

"What?" Michael asked as he creaked around the cabin. "I'm fitting in." He pulled up his socks to just below the knee. In any other place, he would be mortified. But this was camp.

As they walked over, Michael remembered a different dance. At his own prom, he'd refused to take Sal along and felt so guilty he drank too much, freaked out his date, and had to get his stomach pumped. He wanted this night to be different. He wanted a redo.

At the Great Hall, music was blasting out of the open door. The DJ on the stage announced in an upbeat baritone: "Hey, everybody! It's a toga par-ty!" He had a thick dark mane combed straight back and a gold chain underneath his double chin, topped off with a Hawaiian shirt so bright it made it hard to see the rest of him. He worked pro bono. He seemed insane with happiness. He stabbed at his console, and from the speakers came a prison-alarm sound effect. "Jail break!" he yelled. He played Duran Duran's "Hungry Like the Wolf" and double-pointed to a middle-aged woman in a powerchair who started having a spaz attack as she drove in circles. *For you*, he mouthed, and blew her a kiss. Other campers joined in, dancing in the middle of the hall. Who knew what kind of life this man had? But on this side of the bridge, he was a celebrity.

Michael and Sal took their places against the wall and watched the campers file in with every type of bedsheet toga: Snoopy, Power Rangers, Mickey Mouse, moon and stars, navy-blue, floral, argyle.

"Oooh," Michael said, pointing to a very nice sheet on a woman bent over a walker. "What do you think is the thread count on that one?"

Sal rolled his eyes. Michael searched for Maya and Melissa but didn't see them.

The last cabin walked through the door. The campers, all male, had decided to wear not togas but dresses. They'd raided the attic for costume jewelry. A camper with a gray beard wore a shimmering sequin gown. A large man had draped a feathered boa around his neck and painted his nails neon pink. A fellow in a wheelchair wore a tube top with gray chest hair peeking over the brim. Their counselors sashayed in high heels and sundresses borrowed from a female cabin. Klaus, the camp's only out counselor, shouted, "I've corrupted them!"

Jim said to Michael, "Man, they might have us beat." Jim adjusted his Saran and went to hug each of them. "Look at you guys!" he shouted. "So fabulous!"

Michael and Sal stared in wonder at everyone in bedsheets and women's eveningwear. This was not how Michael imagined a camp for disabled people. This was not in the brochure.

The DJ called into his microphone: "Hello, ladies!" He scanned the lines of people against the walls. "Too much standing around. I'll fix you," he said, and pressed another button. From the speakers came Michael Jackson's "Thriller." Then, not far away, Michael spotted Melissa and Maya in their togas, dancing in a circle with their cabin mates.

"Come on," Michael said. "There's Maya." He pressed Sal's joystick forward, thrusting him out a few feet. Sal pinched his hand and put himself back. Why wasn't he letting Michael make it up to him? Why didn't he want to have the time of his life? "Fine," Michael shouted. "Be that way!" He walked rhythmically onto the dance floor by himself.

The cling wrap was starting to irritate his skin. He could feel the hives breaking out. He was sweating profusely. A cold drop ran down his waist. He felt ridiculous.

But they were on the other side of the bridge. Here, on this side, people didn't care who was watching, or if their bodies matched the beat.

He started moving to the music in whatever way his body wanted.

Melissa took one look at his plastic-wrap getup and doubled over in laughter. "Did Jim put you up to this?" she yelled over the music. "That dude is seriously S&M."

She shimmied her hips as Maya toggled right-to-left. Michael pumped his hand high above his head because that's what his hand wanted to do.

Michael realized that no one had stared at his brother all week. He hadn't felt the usual low-grade anxiety walking around with his twin, the eyes either staring or looking away, the sympathetic smiles like: *Such a good brother to that poor disabled boy.* At camp, there was too much singing, sure, but the air did not have that extra charge.

Did it take one song or two? All he knew was that they were dancing in a circle when a wheelchair cut in, and he recognized those shoes. Sal had finally driven out from the wall and was toggling his chunky white Nikes back and forth to the music. Then Maya sidled up next to him, and suddenly they were dancing, their hands locked over their wheelchair armrests, dancing, just them.

Michael found himself jumping up and down as far as his calves would carry him, up and down. The DJ called for another round of "Count . . . those . . . campers!" *One*, Michael thought. Sal. Brother. Twin. Who was driving farther out onto the dance floor for the next song, looking back for Michael to follow.

He felt that lightness again, the same feeling he was chasing at the Messy Olympics, in his best moments with his brother. For one week, he and Sal could feel it. They could feel what it was like to be true twins again. They had been in a world without buildings Sal couldn't get into, without schools he couldn't attend, without events he wasn't invited to, without conversations he couldn't join. They were a twin comedy duo, making people laugh with Michael's setups, Sal driving home the jokes. They moved through life in tandem, as Sal–Michael, him first, Michael just behind.

They waited until the bathhouse was empty. Michael peeled himself out of his Saran wrap, soggy with sweat. He walked to the largest shower stall and turned on the water, the floor cold and wet and teeming with athlete's foot. He unwedged Sal's sheet and took off his shoes and braces. He transferred Sal from his wheelchair to the padded changing table, where he stripped Sal of his t-shirt and shorts and wet diaper. He lifted his brother into the wheeled recliner with a frame of PVC pipes and blue mesh backing. The night had grown chilly, and after a moment, Sal was shivering, his arms curved in and his hands flexed down. Michael tested the water with the inside of his wrist (too hot) and adjusted the temp. He turned the detachable spray nozzle on his brother and let the warm water hit him. As the spray ran over Sal's chest, Michael unwrapped the bar of Irish Spring soap from its sandwich baggie and worked up a green lather in his hands. He rubbed Sal's bony chest, the wisps of black hair around his nipples. He lathered the bulge of the baclofen pump, the small hockey puck under Sal's skin that dripped muscle relaxers into his spine, and gave it a little knock for good luck. He lathered the pink flesh around his g-tube, the rest of Sal's tight belly. He soaped the crook of his collarbone, the back of his neck, the hairs under his chin that Michael had missed with the shaver. As he jerked his tight arms loose to get inside the caverns of his armpits, Michael thought: *This could be the last time I shower you. This could be the last time I touch you like this.*

Michael soaped Sal's hairy chicken legs and bony knees, the white surgical scar on his hip and the soft flesh of his hamstrings. He lathered his warped feet and yellow layered toenails, his patterned ankles and calves, the skin puckered from his tube socks. He grasped Sal's neck and tilted his upper half off the mesh, cleaning his sway back, the crooked nubs of his spine.

"Okay," Michael said. "I'm sorry. It's time." For this he used the loofah. Sal's black pubes were matted from being crushed inside a diaper all day. While Michael scrubbed, he sang their usual shower song: "Just washin' . . . just washin' . . . just washin' my bro-ther's penis." And Sal shouted, "Ahhhhhhhh!" —a complicated heckle like *God, you are such an idiot* that doubled for *It's freaking cold.*

Michael looked at his twin half-covered in the green lather. He looked at his tube, the disk of his pump, the white lines on his skin where they'd cut tendons, inserted pins. Michael looked down at his own body and marveled at its every working part: the arm he was washing with, the muscled legs to balance on, his coordinated throat, his swift and lying tongue. There were no extra holes in him that you could see. It wasn't fair, but it never had been. In his college application essay, he'd written: "My brother taught me to be thankful for what I have." But that was bullshit. He was not thankful. He couldn't shake the feeling that he was wasting this body, this clumsy thing, and that Sal would do better if given a chance. What was this great future that Michael was hurtling toward but Sal was not? Working nine-to-five for some corporate overlord? Raising kids who'd grow up to resent him? Getting weird hobbies to outrun the emptiness? Sal could have it. They could play the twin trick. They could trade places and see who would notice.

"Mike-a," Sal said, calling him back, teeth chattering again like *Okay. Get on with it.*

Michael sprayed him clean as the lather fell in ropes and swirled to the drain. Michael worked the yellow Johnson & Johnson tear-free shampoo into Sal's hair, massaging his scalp as Sal's eyes grew heavy. Before Michael rinsed, he sealed his finger and thumb over Sal's caterpillar brow, keeping the water from his eyes and mouth, so he didn't think he was drowning.

Next week, Sal would go to the facility. Would they know how to seal his brow? Would they give his baclofen pump a good-luck knock? Who would touch him like this?

In the morning, their last full day, Sal acted like he hadn't slept, even though he'd been passed out with his Darth Vader snore when Michael crawled into bed.

Sal said, "Eh-eh" as Michael stripped off his pajamas and changed his diaper. Sal had a morning gift—a major dump, a ten-wet-wiper at least. Thank God. That would be his mother's first question: How much did he poop? For Michael, the answer was always *Too much*.

Michael pretended to be outraged as he cleaned. "You couldn't hold it one more day?" But even then Sal didn't smile. Their father was always in an excellent mood after a morning bowel movement, practically kicking back the carpet like their dog did the grass, but Sal fell far from the tree. "Someone's cranky," Michael said as he breathed through his mouth. Then Sal refused to pick a t-shirt, making them late for flagpole. And as Michael sang into Sal's face, Sal did not join in with *Ahhhhhhhs* but instead flashed his squirrel teeth like *I'm in hell*, the same hell they were in on the first day, as if Sal's painting and Messy Olympics and the camp dance never happened.

In the Great Hall, as Sal *click click click*-ed his breakfast, his mood improved. Maybe all he needed was a little formula in his belly. Everyone ate their pancakes and sausage in unusual silence, like they were all hungover.

Jim rubbed his neck. "I should not have headbanged. I'm missing serious brain cells."

"You guys were crazy last night," Boom Boom said.

"We're feeling it," Michael said. Maybe that was it. Sal was just overstimulated, tired from all the activity, and needed to go slower.

They sat in the cabin during Barn. They lay in their bunks during Rec. They emerged briefly for lunch and afternoon meds, for Michael to wolf down a ham sandwich and for Sal's formula to *click click click* into his gut. Michael felt like he was watching the march of time, wet sand emptying into Sal inch by inch from his hanging bag. He knew Sal was in no mood to eat orally, so he didn't even try his luck with ice cream at the snack stand.

Back in the cabin, Sal wanted to sulk again. Michael laid him on the bed with one condition: He was coming to the camp luau, tonight's evening activity, the week's grand finale. Michael was desperate for his brother to come back, to show up inside his own body again. "Think about Melissa and Maya in their bathing suits. It's our last chance."

Sal smirked like *You perv.*

"So you're coming?" he asked, and Sal said, "Yeah," like *If you'll shut up.*

At 4:45, he got Sal dressed for pool, slid Sal's electric guitar–themed bathing suit over a clean diaper, and applied a fresh layer of SPF 50. Was it possible to get zinc poisoning? Sal would see. Michael rubbed his brother's nose, the row of freckles next to his eyebrow, the tops and folds of his ears, his bony wrists and chest. There were little angry slashes of red where Michael had missed with the sunblock early in the week, but he covered those too. "This time I won't let any sun through, okay?"

Sal stared up at him from the bed. He smiled, said "Mike-a" softly like *Thank you.*

At five p.m., the bell rang, and the campers started their march to the pool. The counselors had staked bamboo tiki torches along the fence, the flames whipping in the breeze. The boy band on the boom box had been replaced by a sweet, choppy ukulele with a mellow slide guitar humming up and down. And after Michael and Sal walked through the gate, after the director blessed them with "Aloha!" and matching blue leis, after Sal parked himself poolside under the emerald-green awning and Michael fetched Sal's adaptive yellow life vest, ready to clamp it onto his brother's neck and walk him into the pool for the first round of drunk boating, Sal said, "Eh-eh." He did not want to swim on this last day of camp.

Michael could see the campers wading down the ramp and into the blue water, see Jerry already motoring his feet on a kickboard, see a camper working up his courage for a cannonball, see the fine honeys in their bathing suits, all ready for Sal to have fun. "What do you mean, 'Eh-eh?'" Michael asked.

"Eh-eh," Sal said.

Michael dropped the life vest on the deck. "Fine. We'll sit. But only for a little."

Michael pulled up a deck chair, and they watched Gill collect foam balls, gathering ammunition for the evening. They watched Boom Boom and Ron staked out by the water traps, their hands riding waves to the Hawaiian slide guitar. They watched Melissa in her sleek black one-piece, as tight as seal skin, pulling Maya lounging in an innertube. They watched nearly the whole camp descend the ramp into the warm water while Sal sat with the line-up of party poopers: Sebastian shuffling his Uno deck, a woman in deep conversation with a purple ribbon, Terrance rocking with his headphones, the helmet at his feet.

"Come on, Sally," Michael said into Sal's zinc-caked ear. "What's wrong? You want to talk about it?" but Sal wouldn't respond, just sat there open-mouthed, doing his zombie routine, waiting for a fly to move in, put in carpet.

Tomorrow camp was over, and everything would change. They were growing up. Michael had meant to give Sal the best week of his life, and here his brother was, brooding in the dying light, staring into a dark puddle on the pool deck like it was an abyss he'd like to fall through.

And in the last few moments they had together, Sal was icing him, was his black-hole self. Michael thought they'd felt it for a moment, felt what it was like to be true twins again, but now his brother was turning away.

It didn't have to end like this. This was Camp Cheerful. They could get with the program. Sal could jump in that warm Camp Cheerful water right now and let its chlorine go to work. Sal needed to race Claude and go drunk boating. He needed to hang with Ron and Boom Boom by the water traps. He needed to flirt with Maya in her innertube.

Michael stood up. "That's it," he said. "You're going in." He released Sal's chest strap and threw it overboard, unbuckled Sal's seat belt and flung it apart. He relieved Sal of his head strap and peeled back the Velcro holding Sal's feet.

"Eh-eh," Sal said like *Get away* and tried to reverse his chair, but Michael lifted his hand off the joystick.

"You need this, buddy," Michael said. "You want this." He stripped Sal of his blue lei and red surfing shirt. Sal bit the shirt on the way off, but Michael ripped it out of his mouth with more force than he'd meant to. He released Sal's headrest and hooked the foam flotation device around his neck, clasping it under Sal's chin. Sal was stiff and thrashing in his chair, trying to pull his jaw back through the hole in the flotation device. Why was he making this so difficult? "Come on," Michael said, burrowing his arms under Sal's neck and knees. As Sal moaned and gnashed his teeth, Michael peeled him from his chair. The flotation device was a convenient bite guard, keeping Sal's teeth away from Michael's skin. Finally, Michael stood up straight, holding Sal to his chest. "You're going," he said. "And you're having fun."

He took one step with Sal in his arms, but when he looked out into the pool, no one was swimming. They were frozen and staring up at Michael holding Sal. They were watching Sal's red face and barred teeth, his eyes wide with terror, his arms tremoring, his trunk thrashing. They were listening to Sal make an awful sound, screaming, "Ahhhhhhh-ehhh-ahhhh!"

Michael did not need to be Sal's twin to catch his meaning, but he heard him loud and clear: "Get away from me! Leave me alone! I hate you! I hate you! I fucking hate you!"

Michael stopped. Maybe he'd gotten too much sun. Maybe he was overtired. Maybe he really had done too much headbanging the night before. Or maybe he was finally losing his mind. Because he'd heard Sal, actually heard him, as clearly as when they were little. He turned around and put Sal back in his wheelchair, placing him gently into his seat. He unlatched Sal's flotation device and tugged his t-shirt back on. He rebuckled Sal's seat belt and refastened his chest strap. He raked his fingers through his brother's blond hair, smoothing it back down. "There," he said.

Michael sat in the deckchair. The pool was back in action, the campers splashing and floating. Gill hurled a waterlogged foam ball at Jim's head. A female camper commandeered the inflatable alligator. Melissa cupped water over Maya's head in the innertube. Jerry jumped off the diving board and belly-flopped into the water.

A few counselors sat on the deck, overseeing the non-swimmers. Sebastian had a good game of Uno going with three campers. Maybe all Sal wanted was a little space. Michael looked out at the pool, at all the campers. In the water, they were short-staffed. If Sal didn't need him, the campers did. He felt possessed by this wild need to help someone, anyone. He needed to be reborn again, even if it had to be without his brother. If Sal wouldn't let him help, he needed to give himself to someone else.

Michael asked his brother, "Is it all right if I go in for a while?"

"Yeah," Sal said.

Michael got up, went to the ramp, and walked into the pool. He fell to his knees and felt the water climb up to his neck. He grabbed Vince floating in a life vest from Jim and cradled him in his arms. "Here," he said. "Let me help."

On the deck near the deep end, a woman danced in her grass skirt, her arms undulating like cresting waves. Gill nailed Darren with a foam ball. Jerry waded through the shallows, gripping a kickboard above his head like it held the Ten Commandments. Boom Boom and Ron still soaked near the filter, bobbing their heads to the ukulele. A woman in a bathing cap splashed a man with spina bifida, who yelled, "Don't make me. *Do not make* me!" A goggled camper got a running start, shouted "Cannonball!" and the lifeguard blew his whistle but too late. Everyone blinked against the splash.

The head counselor on the pool deck screamed, "Count your campers!"

Ha, ha. Very funny. That's the first thing Michael thought when he saw the empty space where Sal was supposed to be. He imagined his twin brother making a slow-mo getaway, his joystick cranked forward, topping out at four mighty miles per hour. Charlie Chaplin in a power wheelchair. Michael stood on his tiptoes in the water and scanned the fence around the pool, expecting to see Sal hiding with a counselor, an able-bodied co-conspirator. But Michael looked in every direction. His brother had disappeared.

How long had he left him alone? Fifteen minutes? Twenty? What had Michael been doing? He'd given Vince a pinball tour around the pool, crashing him into other swimmers, pulling him in the same reckless manner he'd meant to pull Sal, whispering: "Who should we get next? Who's on your hit list?" He'd danced with Boom Boom and Ron near the water trap. "The sweet life?" they'd asked, puffing imaginary Cubanos, and Michael agreed, "The sweet life." He'd joked with Melissa and Maya: "Just taking a little break from my evil twin . . . ha ha," even though he'd felt like the evil one. He'd dipped his head under the water, holding his eyes open against the burn.

It was just a little break. When he came up for air, he heard the head counselor's plaintive cry: "Count your campers!"

He craned his neck, searching for Sal beyond the gate. The gate to the pool area was shut, but campers closed and opened that thing all the time on the way to the bathhouse.

Still, Sal wouldn't. He'd never done anything like that before. He didn't have "behaviors." The more likely scenario was that Sal had help disappearing, that this was a practical joke, a classic camp prank designed to test Michael's cardiovascular system: Hide his twin and watch him lose his shit. So Michael smiled, played it cool.

"Does everyone have everyone?" the head counselor asked, red in the face. Michael thought she, like him, was in line for an early heart attack.

Michael saw Darren by the pool steps talking to Melissa, who had Maya in her innertube. They glanced at him and flashed a smile. They seemed to be holding something in, about to explode with laughter.

"Okay," Michael said to them. "You got me. Camp prank of the century. Joke's over. Where's Sal?"

Melissa knitted her eyebrows. "You lost him?" She seemed genuinely perplexed. It was a wonderful performance.

"Should we sound the alarm?" Darren asked. "This sounds like a situation."

"Not a situation," Michael said, lifting one finger. "Just give him back."

"We should alert the director," Melissa said, handing Maya to Darren and shuffling quickly toward the steps. She did not look back to smirk, did not look back to gauge Michael's reaction. She just walked out of the water and stood there dripping, talking fast to the head counselor, whose red face deepened in color before she yelled for the counselors to get up, to go, to fan out.

Michael was up and out of the pool and running. He was out of the gate, scanning for Sal. His brother couldn't have gone far. Michael expected to see his wheelchair spun out in a grass-ringed mud patch or stuck between two saplings. He expected to see Sal in the doorway of the Great Hall, waiting for Michael to find him and apologize.

He looked across the parking lot, across the bridge over the creek, and started to sprint. Someone activated the siren. The air was getting a little thin. No time for a panic attack, but Michael took a breather anyway, hands on knees. The counselors dashed around him in every direction, flashing the white bottoms of their feet. If anything happened to his brother, his mother would murder him. She'd goad him into elaborate suicide: *hari-kari*-sword-through-gut, Drano-drink, lotus-pose-gasoline-match. *Deep breath.*

Michael peered across the deep-pooled creek and the white bridge. He stared down the road that led to the highway. No. Sal, that stinker. Probably hiding in the barn, waiting to see Michael's face. Had someone checked the barn?

Just then, a golf cart flew by with an enormous man stuffed into it, a clown car for one. It was the camp director, gunning it toward the bridge. He screeched to a stop, reared back his giant head, and said to Michael: "Get in."

I
TRICK OR TREAT

1

Hannah's neighbor asked if there was something wrong.

Like what?

With that one. His arms and all. His head—it flops. Had he been checked out?

He had been checked out.

Hannah's babies sat in a double stroller made by the Swiss—an engineering marvel, really, its frame hollow yet strong like bird bone. But the infants perched inside had a few kinks: Sal up front with his tight arms, his lolling head; Michael bringing up the rear, bug-eyed and fetal. Both cautiously bundled, tiny bodies wedged in a nest of blankets.

Their neighbor, Mrs. Snavely, specialized in unsolicited advice. Since the birth, she kept bringing Hannah casseroles that looked like dog food. She terrorized them with cookies as hard as rocks. She pointed to the back. "He's the healthy one?"

Hannah nodded. Right. It wasn't obvious.

"That's good," her neighbor said. She smiled sweetly. It was a condolence. Hannah knew what she meant: *You can give the other one away.*

Hannah tried to smile back. "I love both my babies," she said.

"Of course," the neighbor said. She pinched Sal's cheek. "Cute."

Jesus. Mary. Joseph. "Say bye-bye," Hannah told her babies and pushed forward. *Keep your kindness. Keep your cookies.* Next time, she'd give them away. Or fling them over their shared fence like frisbees.

Before the twins, Hannah had taught middle school English, supporting her husband, Gabe, waiting patiently for him to go to med school, to quit med school, to freak out and reevaluate and earn his PhD in anatomy. When he began his postdoc, they started trying. After four years and two miscarriages, it finally happened. She got her unit on Shakespeare ready for the sub. Then in class ... she thought she'd peed her pants. God, she'd never hear the end of it. What else could it be? It was too soon.

And then.

She knew how strangers fawned and humiliated themselves before strollers, suddenly fluent in some idiot dialect. But when they saw her babies, they paused. Their eyes darted up (*I'm sorry*), then back down. "How cute." *There's something wrong.*

The uneven sidewalk needed repaving. The Swiss should've made shocks. She didn't want to be crying when her husband came home. Sal cried so much, a mewling wail that gave her shivers. On the phone to his mother, her husband said *postpartum*. But it wasn't like she didn't have a reason. And Gabe was far from fine. When he got home from work, he smoked cigarette after cigarette on the deck like he'd rather go off by himself and get cancer. He slipped away and went walking in the woods.

Gabe wouldn't show her Sal's brain scan, but she heard the doctor mention the white patch. It was behind her baby's eyes. The doctor told Gabe it was the worst bleed he'd seen. He said maybe vegetable. But Hannah was a gardener. She would lay Sal in the soil, cover him in peat moss, and wait until he grew into something else. Her husband said the baby was plastic. His brain would grow back if given enough. Hannah asked herself, *Can I give enough?*

When she got home, she laid their little bodies on knitted blankets. Her husband was still at the lab where he worked as a neuroscientist. Even after six months, he still referred to his sons as Twin A and Twin B. *Did you feed A? Did you burp B? A's diaper is dirty, and B's puked on himself again.* To call the babies by their names meant you had to hold onto them, plan for them, reimagine your own life. This way, they could still be one of his experiments, subject to funding, starring Twin A and Twin B. They were deep in debt from the month in the NICU. As long as they paid ten dollars a month, the hospital wouldn't alert the debt collectors. They were currently enjoying the doctor's "twin discount": thirty bucks per checkup on two babies, a savings of nearly one half-baby.

As she undid Michael's diaper, he laughed and kicked his legs. This was Twin B, their "normal control," their small known quantity. His brain had hemorrhaged too, but the blood reabsorbed. With every delayed milestone, she thought: *Not you too*. But he smiled, rolled over, scooted forward on his own sweet time. Soon he would crawl. All in the shadow of what Sal wasn't doing. She wanted to tell Twin B to take a timeout, to wait until his brother caught up.

Twin A gurgled, his arm stiffening, then writhing to the left. *Primitive movements* her husband called them, the medical term, her baby's brain not yet driving his body. Might never. Sal had those fat pinchable cheeks and looked so sweet in his blue jumper. She clutched her scapular necklace, her silver image of Mother Mary, as she prayed: *Let me forget the white patch, the petal.*

She tickled their feet and sang their names: "Sal. Mich-ael. A...A...A...B...B...B." At first she thought it was just an odd grimace during baby gas, but then Sal's lips angled up, a divot in his cheek. A dimple.

The boys turned one, two, three, four, then five. One morning Hannah walked into their bedroom and found them intertwined in their red-and-green pajamas, like some Christmas ornament made of children. They were forehead to forehead, so she couldn't tell where Sal's mop of light brown hair began and Michael's ended. She cleared her throat. Michael loosened his grip and sat up.

"What are you doing?" she asked.

Michael looked at her toenails, the red polish already chipped. "Nothing."

"Well," she replied. "Looks fun."

Michael nodded, his eyes still downcast. "We were just talking," he finally said.

"About what?"

"Not telling." He looked up, his big brown eyes peering into her.

"Okay," she said. "Just keep your clothes on."

One minute Michael would be playing quietly with his He-Man figures, and the next he was in the buff with his pink skin and slender shoulders, his penis pointed at her like an accusing finger, clothes crumpled like snakeskin. It was fine when no one was watching, but he'd started stripping in the corners of his preschool, the teachers' aides still smirking at pickup as they warned her that this little streaker might have to go elsewhere. She asked moms in her support group for advice, but they laughed, said it was *just a phase* in a tone that meant *the least of your problems*. She started pulling Michael out of preschool once a month for a "special day with Mommy," letting him bask in her undivided beam of love.

On one of these days came the grand question. Michael asked: "Why is Sal in the wheelchair?" They'd explained before that Sal had a disability, but now Michael wanted a reason why. Hannah was a practicing Catholic, had returned to the Church when the boys were born. She preferred to do her praying to Mother Mary but why not trot out the Lord when you needed Him, in his moldy robes and omnipotence? God was love, she said, God loved Sal, loved them both very much, but this was just the way God wanted it. She mumbled something about the mystery of fate. Not her most philosophically sound argument, though it did the job. There were no more questions.

Michael was a sweet kid. He woke up singing and paid such good attention to his brother. But he was also anxious and clingy. He worried about the welfare of inanimate objects: the hurt feelings of discarded wrappers, the inner turmoil of a burned-out lightbulb. He couldn't fall asleep unless she was right outside their door with a flashlight and an *Exceptional Parent* magazine. Sometimes she wanted to give Michael a good shake: *Jesus Christ. Just be normal.*

On their beds, Hannah laid out different clothes for each boy. In the past she had hunted in thrift stores for near matches of all their clothes—as much as their single income would allow. She didn't see the harm. It was the fun of being a twin. There's your double—not just for age and experience, but (why not?) down to your very DNA—staring back at you, promising: *You'll never be lonely.*

No matter how many times her husband explained that Michael and Sal were not identical—not from the same egg—Michael wouldn't believe it. "Very funny, Dad," he'd say. He claimed to remember when they were the same and shook his head, said they never should have separated, because that's when Sal *got hurt*, which would have been cute if he hadn't hissed it.

When Michael started stripping, Gabe thought it best to stop matching their outfits. "He's confused about who he is," he'd said. "I know it's cute, but I don't blame him for wanting to be his own man."

Gabe had shaggy brown hair and a sheepish grin that she still found handsome. He often neglected to shave and wore faded jeans, Rolling Stones t-shirts, and white Nike Cortez that made his feet look like they were encased in footballs. "You're a brain scientist," she often reminded him, and he'd repeat it as if he also found it improbable: "I'm a brain scientist!"

He was still stuck at project staff, doing another scientist's dirty work, but she knew he would get his own lab someday, especially if he kept working weekends. That morning, a Saturday, before he left, she'd said, "Get a grant. Change our lives." And he'd laughed. "No pressure."

He'd kissed her cheek, and she sent him on his way with a loving shove.

Now she said, "Let's start our day, shall we?"

"Mmmmm," Sal said.

He stretched within his range of motion. They were on Sal's mattress, in the room the boys shared in their small house. Hannah had plans to buy them beds but never seemed to have enough left at the end of the month. She got a diaper from the closet and lifted his legs to peek under what they called the "disaster zone." As she worked, her necklace dangled down, and Mother Mary said, *Be careful with his hips*, but Hannah told her to *Shhh* and tucked her into her shirt. She had to make sure Sal, with his mighty bite reflex, didn't snap off the Blessed Mother and swallow her whole.

"Get ready," she said.

Michael bent into a crouch position, wonderful form for a five-year-old, all set to sprint if she shouted, "Number two!" But she said, "False alarm," and he relaxed. Sal was just soaked, the diaper puffed out, but thank God it hadn't leaked through.

Sal's midsection was tight as a drum, his belly button jutting out as if he hadn't quite wanted to let go of the cord. Who could blame him? He was not a good eater. His chubby cheeks were gone. The doctor wanted to insert a feeding tube, had said "failure to thrive" like an indictment. But it was *her* time, Hannah countered. Her ticks off the clock. It sometimes took an hour and a half to feed him, but it felt like the closest they'd come to a conversation: the give and take, the dip of the spoon, his mouth open to receive, and the scraping of his front teeth against the metal.

She balled up his wet diaper, still warm, and handed it to Michael, who walked it to the trash can. He threw it in and then raised his arms and waited.

She was already exhausted from getting up with Sal in the night. She wanted to snap, *Must we make everything into a game?* But no, she was the mom. She was the children's show host. She made her voice into an announcer's: "Two points! For the win!"

Michael did a victory dance, wiggled his butt. His pajama shirt crept up over the belly that came from too many canned raviolis in front of the television. For him, food was easy. *Eat this, I love you.* But if she let Michael eat all he wanted, he'd eat until he threw up, surprised as he gagged over the toilet. Their pediatrician started emphasizing the need for healthy options or at least some tee-ball. They no longer got the twin discount. He was more than one whole child.

She cleaned Sal with wet wipes, finished with a puff of baby powder, and slipped a new diaper underneath. The doctor insisted on hip surgery. There'd be a prolonged stay in the hospital. A month in a body cast. Changing his diaper in that thing would be like solving a Rubik's Cube. They wanted to cut him up so he'd sit better in his new wheelchair, this clunky thing with powder-blue leather pads. It was all scheduled: He'd have surgery in six weeks.

Sal went into one of his long whale-like sonar calls that ended with a laugh. She was still waiting for words. They'd almost gone bankrupt hiring speech therapists, but they got him to say "Eh" for Yes and "Eh-eh" for No. The next year, he added, "Momma," and then, last winter, "Mike-a" and "Da-da." Still she waited for more.

Sometimes she dreamed that Sal had grown enormous, with hairy legs and arms, rolls of belly fat and salami-sized nipples, but he still had his adorable little-boy head. She'd climb his body, endlessly Velcroing and buckling him into this gigantic wheelchair. He'd say, "Great job, Mom." He was sarcastic, like Gabe when Hannah had first fallen in love. "Real nice. Oh, I'm so comfortable. You're really looking out for me. I would clap if I could but . . ." She wanted him to speak so badly, but maybe not if he took that tone.

Hannah wedged Sal's stiff left arm into his t-shirt and helped him guide his good hand through the sleeve. Then his overalls, being careful not to catch his toe as she scrunched the cloth like an accordion and guided his foot through, then white tube socks up to his knees. She felt a sharp stab in her wrist, her carpal tunnel acting up, and shook it off. She wedged his ankles and his stubborn feet into his cream-colored AFOs and stuffed the braces into his white sneakers.

Then she sang to him. She was no great vocal talent. The choir director in middle school told Hannah she sang like she'd been stung by a bee and her throat was closing, but she'd later budded into a middling mezzo-soprano. She sang Gloria Estefan: "The rhythm is gonna get Sal. The rhythm is gonna get Sal. . . . This morning." And how about some Carly Simon: "You're so Sal. You probably think this song is about you . . . don't you . . . don't you . . . Sal?" Sal tried to drown out her voice with his own blasted *Ahhhhhs*, but he smiled too, which belied more comedy routine than musical criticism.

Michael complained from his own mattress. "What about me?"

"The rhythm is gonna get Michael. The rhythm is gonna get Michael . . . sometime later."

Michael danced into his shirt. They were late for everything. Sal was their free pass, because of course you'd be late with a son like Sal, with all the dressing and feeding and damning of fate. They'd never imagine she was late because of singing.

Sal *Ahhhh-ed* again, went into another whale call, laughed, and then let loose with a long string of vowels: I-O-E. It was almost words. A couple more consonants and we might have a winner. She smiled. "What are you saying, sweet pea? What are you telling Mommy?"

Michael sighed. "Don't you hear him?"

"What?" she said.

Michael walked to Sal's mattress, crouched down, turned his little ear to Sal's lips, and whispered: "Listen."

Michael pushed Sal down the grocery-store aisle. He could barely see over Sal's headrest, but he wanted to be a help. Pushing Sal made him feel big. Their mother was behind with the cart, studying her coupon and staring at boxes of pasta.

Sal said, "Brother."

"What?" Michael said.

"How about now?" Sal asked.

Michael stood on his tiptoes and peered over Sal's nest of brown hair. The old lady ahead was shuffling out of the aisle, took a left toward the meat section.

"I think the coast is clear," Michael said. He looked back at his mother, who had moved on to the jars of pasta sauce and was fishing through her purse for another coupon. Michael glared at the Wheat Chex in her cart. He'd begged for Lucky Charms.

"Don't be a baby," Sal said.

"I don't know," Michael said.

Michael had seen it on TV a few months ago in the 1988 Winter Olympics, the men in weird suits and helmets running on ice and leaping into their little sleds. Sal said it looked like fun. When Sal got his new wheelchair, he wanted to try it. They'd practiced, but Michael always chickened out and hopped off early. He would be braver this time. He looked back at his mother, still pondering the sauce. "Okay," he said.

Gripping Sal's foam handles, Michael ran forward with one step, two steps, three, and hopped onto the back bars and then they were gliding together past the cans of tomatoes and the Chef Boyardees, past the vinegars and olive oils, past the canned beans and corn until they'd traveled almost beyond the aisle, and then Sal's chair started listing left and Michael tried to lean right but too late. Sal's footrest crashed into the sauerkrauts, sending three jars rolling. They shattered on the floor. Michael hopped off. The limp cabbage was leaking onto the tiles like pale seaweed, the vinegar burning his nose.

Their mother came running. "What happened?"

"We were playing," Michael said.

"Jesus Christ," she said. "Can't I turn my back for one second?"

Sal was stiff—in his startle reflex—his arms curled into his chest. He laughed and said, "Again!"

"You all right, baby?" Their mother inspected his feet. "What did your brother do?"

Michael didn't tell her what Sal had said. He wasn't sure, but his parents could be idiots. Michael had sung a rendition of "Born in the USA" into his Fisher-Price microphone, complete with breakdance number, and Sal yelled, "More! Bravo! Bravo!" That was English and Italian—two languages—but their parents couldn't even hear Sal speak one. Michael didn't remember a time when he couldn't understand Sal. It was always. It was in the womb.

He would have to take all the blame. He said, "Sorry, Mama."

She cupped his face and said, "Just be more careful, okay?"

There was a call for cleanup on aisle five. A clerk appeared with a mop. Their mother offered to pay for the kraut, but the clerk said, "Lady, you've got enough on your plate."

Back home, Michael and Sal were in the living room, lying on the shag carpet. Sal had scooted his face off the blanket, and Michael tugged him by his legs to put him on a fresh section with no slobber. Sal smiled and said, "What can we play now?"

"I don't know," Michael said. "Not bobsled. Let's think." He took Sal's stiff and sweaty fist and wedged his finger through.

"How about Lego knights?" Sal asked. The knights who lived on Sal's chest were at war with the ones who occupied Sal's legs.

"No," Michael said, because the last time they'd played, Michael lost a guy's peggy head in Sal's diaper and got a talking-to, was taught the phrase "pressure sore."

Sal thought for a second, arched his back, and yelled: "How about dogs!"

"Okay," Michael said. "But don't eat yours anymore."

Their father had come back from a conference with identical stuffed dogs. They had great fun dipping their dog heads into a water bowl and squeezing out the drops, making them slobber. The dogs mauled Sal with their plush muzzles until he squeaked. Sal had chewed his dog's left paw and made the fabric crusty. It was the only way to tell the difference.

"Let's growl," Michael said and Sal *Ahhh*-ed down low, did the sounds he made for their parents. Michael looked forward to when they were older and could live on their own, having a conversation that never ended. Once, he said to his little cousin: "I can't wait until my mom and dad die so I can take care of Sal myself. It will be so fun." He meant by natural causes, much later, but she took it out of context, called out: "Aunt Hannah, Michael wants you to die!" and his mom said, "Michael, that's not nice."

Their real dog sniffed his way to their stuffed animals. "Get away," Michael said and shoved Batey by his neck, but Batey lunged toward Sal and raked his tongue across Sal's cheek.

"Batey!" Sal yelled, gagging and tightening his fists. The dog galloped away. Batey was still a puppy and had a dirty mouth. Their mother said they had to be careful to tell the difference between Batey's toys and Sal's. Both liked to chew, both liked the texture.

"Why does he always try to lick you?" Michael asked.

Sal smiled. "Maybe I just taste good," he said. "Want some?"

Michael gave Sal's arm a good lick, and they laughed.

Their mother came into the doorway, her hands on her hips. "What's all this commotion?"

Sal said, "Batey was getting me."

"What's that, Sally?" their mom asked. "You've got a lot to say today. Ooo-whau-whau."

She was pretty enough to be a TV mom and Michael had told her so. Her hair was a blonde helmet that protected her high cheekbones and beaklike nose. Michael knew enough to keep his Sal secret. "We were just being silly," he said.

"Come on, Sally," she said as she kneeled over him. "We need to get ready for therapy."

"But I'm playing," Sal said. "I don't like that lady."

"That's right, honey. You love Ms. Diana, don't you?"

When the therapist arrived, she helped their mother move Sal's arms and legs. They tried to get him to roll over. They worked on his grip with his good hand. They made him do a never-ending push-up. Michael was supposed to watch TV and behave. As they moved Sal's joints, Michael made soft squeaking sounds like Sal was just rusty, like all he needed was a little oil.

After Ms. Diana left, their mother ran the vacuum and set out the chairs, getting ready for her group.

Michael asked, "Can we play tank outside before they come?"

Their mother glanced at her watch. "I suppose so," she said. She peeled off Sal's long-sleeved shirt. "Say, 'The sun's out.' Say, 'I don't want to get too hot.'"

As she lifted Sal into his chair, Michael got the old lampshade from the living room floor. He put it on Sal's head, his armor. He got the whiffleball bat from the closet and wedged it into Sal's wooden wheelchair tray.

"Sal," their mom said, laughing. "You're alright with this?"

"Eh," Sal said from under the lampshade.

"Okay," she said. "But no Wheelchair Bobsled." She eased Sal over the front step. Their dad hadn't started building the ramp. "When is your father going to do something with those boards?" she asked, glaring at the mound under a blue tarp. She squeezed Michael's hands over Sal's chair handles. "Hold on tight," she said and took her seat in the sunlight.

Michael and Sal ran down the sidewalk through enemy fire, blasting beams of good-guy blue. They fought their way to the boss. Sal yelled, "Come out with your hands up!" The door swung open to Mrs. Snavely in her bathrobe, with a cigarette dangling from her lips and varicose veins snaking up her calves, proof of some inner evil. She flicked her cigarette, said, "Hello sweeties. Having fun?"

Michael and Sal fired, turned, and ran, and when Michael looked back, she was smoldering in smoke.

Up ahead, Michael could see the next boss, his mother watching from the stoop, waiting for him to make one wrong move.

One by one, the Moms arrived. They pulled their kids up the step past the goddamned not-done ramp. Kids with wheelchairs and walkers, kids with canes, kids with stiff gaits. The Moms arrived asking, "Who brought the wine? Where's my martini?" when they knew there was no wine, no martini. The Moms needed their wits. They needed hot tea and brownies from a box, cookies and zucchini cake thrown together in between feedings and chasing children, all laid out on a table in Hannah's cramped living room.

Hannah sat next to Sal, who was listening closely, holding her hand. Michael played on the floor with Becky's blind son, manipulating crusty puppets that really should've been washed, saying, "It's soft, right?"

The Moms were sharing. Hannah's best friend in the group, Ashley, wore her trademark leather jacket, sitting next to her daughter, Tina, who was even more disabled than Sal. Ashley had informed Hannah about her biker days, but she'd long since traded in her Harley for a van and Tina's wheelchair. She was telling a story about buying pants. "So there I am at Macy's, standing with Tina in line, and this old woman is just staring at us. She looks like she's on the verge of tears, and I'm like 'Can I help you?' and she just blurts out, 'God gives special children to special mothers.'"

"*Boo*," the Moms said. "*Hiss*."

"And I'm like, 'Lady, we're just trying to purchase these pants.' She won't leave. She keeps staring. I'm about to tell her off. But then she reaches for her purse, and here's this crisp twenty-dollar bill."

"You didn't," the Moms said.

"Um . . ." Ashley said. "Free pants." She extended her foot, modeling her white denim, her pity pants. The Moms laughed. Ashley made it funny, even though she'd called Hannah in tears. She'd recently separated from her husband. Lately it did not take much to tip her over.

Tina moaned. She was low functioning. She looked sweet, with raven black hair and a button nose, but her eyes never focused, and her laugh was free-floating, not pinned to anything outside herself. Maybe she had her own jokes, Hannah thought. A private world no one could access, but her laughter seemed no more voluntary than a cough. She was so unlike Sal, who lived in this world, whose eyes flashed with purpose, his brain humming behind them no matter how clumsily his body carried out the orders. It was one of the reasons Hannah liked hanging out with Ashley: to watch Sal shine in her daughter's shadow. Hannah wasn't proud of it, but she figured they all had similar shameful thoughts: *At least my kid can talk, at least my kid can walk, at least my kid can think, at least my kid stays put. At least, at least, at least . . .*

They brainstormed: "What do you say when they make you into a saint?"

Sandra held her son, rocking him on her lap as her daughter lay at her feet. She said, "I try to take it as a compliment."

Hannah rolled her eyes and Ashley smirked. Sandra had adopted her special needs kids, had actually chosen to raise not just one severely disabled child, but two. It was admirable, sure, but she also seemed insane, like this was her backup plan after getting kicked out of a cult. Ashley and Hannah sometimes wagered on who would cry first during a meeting. Sandra was always a safe bet. If Hannah or Ashley cried first, they'd have to pay up.

Hannah said, "You say, 'It doesn't take a saint to love my child.' You say, 'Hello. I do have thoughts and feelings.' But if there's money..."

They laughed. Sal *Ahhhhh*-ed in agreement.

At Hannah's first meeting, the Moms had offered advice: "You might buy dog toys for the texture." And Hannah kept thinking: *I do not want to be in this club.* Old Hannah had friends from school, fellow teachers with whom she cracked jokes in the teachers' lounge and went out for after-work cocktails. She'd been friends with the wives of Gabe's colleagues, went camping and skiing, went out on the town. After the boys were born, she would phone these women about her day and they'd say, "I can't imagine." Those old friends mostly fell away. With the Moms, she didn't have to explain so much, especially about things that defied explanation: multisyllabic medical terms, hip surgeries, feeding tubes. Medical emergencies were just part of their lives. The Moms didn't pity her, which was the one thing she could not stand. They knew exactly what she was going through, even the ugly thoughts.

One of the Moms asked about Hannah's speech in front of the county board. Ashley said, "You should have heard her. She was awesome." Hannah was head of the PTA at Tina and Sal's school, and they needed a new roof. Whenever it rained, the aides had to play "dodge the buckets" with the wheelchairs. This had been going on for years. Hannah had stood before the board as they pleaded lack of funds. Hannah stared daggers at them, asking, "Would this be good enough for your kid? Why, then, is it good enough for mine?"

"I used my teacher voice," Hannah said. "I still have it."

Ashley smiled. "I also don't think they liked the phrase, 'Legal action.'"

"I was bluffing," Hannah said. "But we got the roof."

The Moms clapped. Hannah took a small bow. She said, "You want to know my secret?"

The Moms did.

"I was so nervous that beforehand . . ."

"What?"

"Explosive diarrhea."

The Moms cracked up.

Ashley said, "God gives special children to special mothers."

The Moms howled.

As Sandra launched into a battle with the insurance company, Hannah's mind wandered. *Special mother.* On the mantel was a photo of Gabe and Hannah fresh out of college, on their honeymoon, just stupid kids camping on Virginia Beach in a borrowed tent. Gabe, her goofball, choking himself with her hands, his tongue lolling, Hannah's head cast back in laughter. They'd go to the mall and speak in a made-up language, have a whole conversation about shoes—"Smorgen borgen. Koola-ya!"—as the old people stared. It was nonsense, but it was like she knew exactly what Gabe was saying. In another frame Hannah was standing with her eighth-grade English students. How proud she'd been to be in charge of her own classroom at twenty-four. And now *that* Hannah was *this* Hannah, age thirty-seven, less silly with no job, stress going straight to her intestines. Irritable Bowel Syndrome. She'd been diagnosed before the boys, but after their birth it came on stronger.

On the wall beside the mantel was a cross with a skinny anguished Jesus, a reminder that God died for our sins, but with the Moms there, it looked like some physical therapy device they'd have to subject their children to. Next to it were the four-pronged antlers of a deer's head, Gabe's sad trophy from his first hunting trip a few months before. She needed to redecorate.

Special mother. When Hannah was growing up, her family was famous for being sick. Her older brother had been born with bum kidneys. He collected coins, loved Kennedy, mailed bad jokes to the Smothers Brothers, but the year he became an official adult, she watched him yellow and wither. It was a long expensive battle, complete with humiliating fundraisers and optimistic newspaper profiles. Hannah's mother quit her job to nurse her son. For all her mother's hardness, for her cold and distant demeanor, her devotion to Hannah's brother was unimpeachable. If you asked her how much she loved her son, all she had to do was raise her shirt, show the long scar cut across her abdomen. Hannah wished it were that easy: *I love you. In fact, here's my kidney.* If it were, she'd cut it out herself. Anything. Which organ did they want? Instead, there wasn't enough of her to go around. Not for Sal, and not for Michael.

Other times she really did feel special. She'd been so lost before the boys were born. She'd put too much time into lesson plans and grading papers, trying to help kids who struggled in class, but she'd also pined for a more glamorous life, especially when she'd travel with Gabe to scientific conferences in New York or Madrid. Now her days had a shape: three-feet tall in a wheelchair, looking up at her and listening. He needed all she could give. He needed someone to face down the county board post-diarrhea. He needed someone special.

Sandra asked Ashley how she was holding up. "You know," Ashley said. "Been better." She picked up a washcloth and wiped the drool from Tina's mouth. "Give me that."

"Any word from *he who shall not be named?*" Hannah asked.

"Nope," Ashley said. "Ugh. I could murder him. Isn't that right, Tina? She's heard all about it. Say, 'We don't need him.' Say, 'Run him over with my wheelchair.'"

Tina moaned at the sound of her mother's voice, seeming to agree. Her mother laughed. "That's right."

Her husband's infidelity had shaken the group to their core, made them question their own husbands. But Gabe was thrilled. In comparison, he was a hero. It allowed him to say, "Well, at least I'm not that guy." *At least, at least, at least.*

"Shoot," Ashley said and dabbed at her eye. "There they are. It's hard. It's just . . . you're the only ones I can really talk to."

Hannah squeezed her hand.

"Thanks, Han," Ashley sniffed and whispered, "Can I pay up later?"

Hannah patted her back. "It's on the house."

The conversation stalled. Sandra coughed. Across the living room, Becky's blind son said, "Your house smells funny," and Michael said, "Thank you." Michael took a few steps towards the cookies, glanced back at Hannah, and she shook her head. He'd already had three that she knew of. He retreated and picked up a moose puppet.

Hannah did not want to share her ugly thought—she was the strong one, the one who doled out advice but didn't ask for it—but Mother Mary on her neck was being pushy. *Come on, be honest with the Moms.* Hannah usually saved her confessions for the priest, but she began: "I have something..."

"Look at you," said Sandra, smiling.

She started with the surgery. "I think what's bothering me is he'll be in such pain, and he won't be able to tell me where it hurts. He'll just scream. The not talking..." She touched Sal's cheek, rubbed his hair. "It's the one thing I still grieve about. I want to hear him say 'Mom, I love you' just once." Hannah's voice broke.

Sandra nodded. "Did you read the Holland essay?" Her son bucked on her lap, and her daughter moaned at her feet. She wrapped her arms around the boy, put him in a squeeze box as she caressed her daughter with her toe.

"I did," Hannah said. Last month, Sandra had passed around this essay, which provided the following analogy: To have a disabled child is to think you're going on a trip to Italy, but instead it's a trip to Holland. At first you're sad about missing the cafés and the Sistine Chapel and the gondolas, but then you realize Holland has windmills and tulips and even Rembrandts. Hannah couldn't help but take it literally. She thought Rembrandt overrated, tulips dopey, and the windmills, well, she agreed with Don Quixote. They were good to fight with.

"You need to focus on little Sal's Rembrandts," Sandra said.

Ashley said, "Sal's more of a van Gogh guy."

Sal smiled. He knew they were joking.

Sandra clucked. "If you guys aren't going to take this seriously." Her son pinched her leg and jumped up. He hurdled his sister and ran into the kitchen.

Sandra rubbed her thigh. "Well, at least your son doesn't do that."

"It's not a competition," Hannah said.

"If it was," Ashley said, "I win."

"Hannah, dear," Sandra said, "God only gives us what we can handle."

That was Hannah's mother's famous line, repeated during their weekly calls almost without fail. It should have been a comfort, but Hannah felt her intestines roil. She looked down at Michael, who had dropped the puppet and was staring at her with those big eyes again. She said, "I'm okay, honey. Keep playing."

After the meeting, Michael petted Batey under the dining room table. Michael had eaten too much again, three brownies and two cookies when his mother wasn't looking, and now he could hardly move. He felt like a snake who'd swallowed a whole mouse. Batey kept trying to lick him, as if he knew Michael was full of treats. Meanwhile, Sal relaxed in his red foam seat. Their mother had ordered it special so Sal could sit up with his legs separated, something about "positioning." Sal did not eat too much, had the opposite problem, and now he was wiggly, trying to pop out of his seat belt. "Help!" he said. Michael couldn't move.

Michael didn't understand everything the Moms talked about, but he knew Sal was going to the hospital. He knew it would hurt. His mom was sad that she didn't know what Sal was saying. Michael had told her to listen, but she didn't listen. What else could he do? Batey stared with his furry eyebrows bunched in concern, like he was also trying to work out the problem.

Sal called for his Cookie Monster. He looked toward the shelf, where his favorite stuffy was in a box, its two googly eyes peeking over the rim. "Cookie! Cookie!" Their mother came in from the kitchen and bent over him. "Cookie!" he called.

"What's wrong, bubba?" she asked. "Do you have a spasm? A hurt? That doesn't sound like a pain cry." She touched his cheek. "What is it?"

Her lips were pursed, her eyes scanning him for hints. "Do you miss Dad? He'll be home soon."

Then Sal was bellowing, his face flushed. "No! Cookie! It's there. Give it to me!"

Michael watched his mother guessing when it was so clear what Sal wanted. She held up a picture book. "You want me to read to you? What is it, baby?"

Sal screamed back, "No! I want Cookie!"

She paused and looked at the box where Cookie was staring back at her with its white plastic eyeballs. For a moment, it seemed like she had heard Sal. But then she walked right past it and grabbed the tape player. "Music? You want your tape?" Then, like a dummy, she pressed play for Bruce Springsteen, and "Born in the USA" blared from the speaker.

This made Sal even angrier. "No, not him! Cookie!" He arched his back, pressing against the foam, trying to burst his seat belt.

Michael couldn't stand it any longer. He got up from under the table, walked to the shelf, pulled the monster up by its eyeball, and placed it in Sal's lap. Sal was breathy with relief, his smile bouncing up between his gasps. "Thank you thank you thank you."

"Was that it?" their mother asked. "Did your brother get it right?"

"Eh," Sal said.

Michael shrugged. "Sal was saying he wanted his Cookie."

Their mother stood above them, her face blank. For a moment, it seemed like she traveled somewhere in her mind. But then she leaned down and cupped Michael's face. "You're such a help," she said. "I love how you pay such good attention to him."

"Okay," Michael said, because sometimes he wasn't a help. Sometimes, when she left him at Mrs. Snavely's to take Sal to a doctor's appointment, he cried into the chalky gravel of their neighbor's driveway. Sometimes he bothered her when he should have let her sleep because she was up and down with his brother all night. "Here are some paper and pencils, now go." Sometimes he needed to behave, to not wander off, to think of someone other than himself. He'd rather be a help.

Sal let out a long whale call. "I love you," he sang. "You're the best mom...."

She smiled, then looked toward the drone of the kitchen television. There was applause. The show would begin. She glanced back at Michael.

"Do you want me to say what he said?"

"Okay," she said. "Tell me."

2

As soon as Gabe drove home the nail, he knew. It was uneven. The boards didn't kiss up against each other. Gabe had measured carefully. Used math. Carried the one. Double-checked. Watched countless hours of *This Old House*. His calculations, the very laws of the universe, said these boards should conform. And still, there was a bump.

Hannah would complain. Not right away. She'd say she loved it and walk down the ramp to the sidewalk and up again, pushing Sal in his new wheelchair. She'd say, *VIP entrance*. She'd say, *I knew you could do it*, though she'd told him to hire a guy. But Gabe was right to build the ramp himself because they were tight on money, and he'd taken shop in high school. He'd watched a kid saw off his finger, which rolled into the wood dust like another scrap. He wasn't exactly skilled, but he also wasn't that kid.

When he unveiled the ramp, he'd do the moonwalk down it and up again. She'd laugh and kiss his cheek. She might even forget about the bump. Then, days or weeks later, she'd trip, or Sal would catch a wheel on the crooked board, or Michael would trip (he was clumsy as hell), and Gabe would come home to her mad. He glanced at the flowers his wife had planted on each side of the step, some kind of lily drooping up from their beds, their stamens pointing at him like tiny boom mics, part of a floral production team recording his failure.

"Shit," he said. His kids were listening, watching from the stoop. Sal was safe. Sal wouldn't tell a soul. Mum's the word with Sal. But Michael repeated it in the specialized way of a five-year-old: "Shit... shit... shit," he sang, and then he caught Sal's eye and they both laughed.

"Guys... Let's sing a different one."

It was a balmy Saturday. June could be nice in Cleveland, but Gabe was sweaty; his t-shirt clung to his back. Hannah had parked the twins out here with him so she could take a power nap. She felt guilty just staying home, but by the end of the week, she was exhausted, her nerves frayed. She was looking forward to Michael starting kindergarten at St. Marks a few blocks away, Sal doing longer days at his special school.

When Gabe peeked inside, Hannah was lying on the floor with her feet up on the couch. She was too young for her back to hurt like that. With this ramp, she wouldn't have to drag Sal up the step. And it was just the beginning. Gabe would build a whole house for him.

Sal sat up high in his new wheelchair. He swiveled his head, scanning the neighborhood. Gabe wished he could afford a better view, but they were stuck on this dreary block in Cleveland Heights, with its old fixer-uppers that needed new paint jobs, the cars driving by too fast with rattling bass. His wife wanted a better street, a better life.

You could tell the chair made Sal feel important. For the percentage they paid out-of-pocket, it should also fly. And Sal wouldn't even be able to sit in it after the surgery, which was in three weeks. But for now, Michael's hand rested on Sal's handle. He kept touching it, always asking to help push. Momma's little helper, Hannah called him. The kid wore those striped overalls. Gabe didn't know why Hannah dressed him like a train conductor.

When the boys were born, Gabe called his parents, two states away in Illinois. His father was having a bad spell and was a little off his rocker. Gabe told him that Sal would have severe disabilities, yet his old man kept complaining about the plumber. "Can you believe he left the pipes leaking?" Gabe could not believe. Gabe's mother took the phone and had one question: "Will you send him away now, or will you wait?" As if it were only a matter of time. That's what her generation did with children like Sal. They saw it as a judgment upon them, Old Testament revenge tactics. And if you pretended it never happened, it almost hadn't. Just don't speak its name. Just don't let it into the house. For all he knew, he had an older brother like Sal somewhere, in some dusty corner of an institution, some minimum-wage stranger wiping blender meat from his mouth. That was not where his son would grow. You make one good, hard decision, and then everything after comes easier. It didn't feel hard at the time. They were just babies then. You wrapped them up and took them home.

Gabe got out a cigarette and flicked his lighter. Mrs. Snavely peeked from behind her curtain. She'd already complained about the hammering. He belched smoke and waved the hammer, which seemed both friendly and threatening, the tone you had to take with her.

"Michael, can you hand me another nail, buddy? The big one?"

Michael peered into the shoebox, knelt, and almost toppled over. He had a problem with depth perception, with his fine motor. They should probably start playing catch, but the kid would surely get a baseball in the face. Gabe wanted to take him hunting, but worried Michael would shoot a hole through his own foot. Yet he was a constant reminder of what Sal wasn't doing. In the lab, they would call Michael the "normal control." If this were an experiment, which it wasn't.

When Michael had asked why Sal was in the chair, Gabe said, "Because he's not in the stroller. " Ha ha. But Gabe knew. The doctor had paid him the professional courtesy, had taken him back into the radiology suite and shown him the scans. Periventricular bleed. The motor neuron almost completely wiped out. The ventricular zone, the germinal matrix, that part of the brain right below the two little cavities where your motor neuron starts—it was toast. He'd seen a map of the bleed, seen that ruined country. He couldn't describe it to his wife. So he'd said, "We'll see." He noted recent studies on brain plasticity and made fun of the doctor's Australian accent. The doc had said *vegetable*. He'd actually said that. Thanks, mate. The scans translated into severe cerebral palsy, into severe mental retardation, but Sal was growing into someone who tracked you with his soft eyes, who laughed when you burped. Still they waited for Sal to steady, to stand, for his moans to make sense. Say: *No, I can't do that yet.* Or ever. No more questions. Let's play airplane. This is your captain speaking.

Michael was still looking. "Buddy," Gabe said. "It's the biggest one. It's right there."

Sal moaned, and Michael said, "Sal says he can't see it either."

Gabe laughed. "It must really be lost then." Cute. It was classic twin stuff. Cryptophasia, they called it: secret language. Gabe could play along, though sometimes he questioned if Michael could tell the difference between his brother and an imaginary friend. Anyway, they were both wrong. Gabe stood up and could see the nail he needed. Michael's hand was on it. *Grip it. Grab the freaking nail.* He dropped the hammer. He breathed. *Be careful with the boy. One wrong word. Who knows what he'll remember?*

Michael plucked out the nail and lifted it over his head like a Cracker Jack prize. Gabe yelled, "You got it!" Thank God. The boy stumbled down and handed it to Gabe, who settled the point at the pencil mark. He still had to put up railings and stain the wood, but soon the ramp would be done, bump and all. Good enough. "Ready?" He raised the hammer.

It took his wife a week to notice. She said, "I nearly broke my ankle." She tripped coming down, almost lost control of Sal's chair. Sal almost rolled into the street, she said. She kept catastrophizing.

"But you didn't," Gabe said. "But he didn't." He snapped her out of it. "Now you know about the bump." He went baritone, cribbing a line from Michael's *G.I. Joe* cartoon: "And knowing . . . is half the battle."

She couldn't help smiling. "Boy. Do you want me to shoot you, or would you like to shoot yourself?"

"No, I got it." He put his finger to his head and fired. After he reanimated, he said, "Look. I'll redo it if you want."

"Forget it," she said. "It'll take you another month."

He sighed. "It's not perfect, Han, but it works." *Just like us*, he wanted to say. He grabbed her arm and felt her rock-hard bicep from repeatedly curling Sal's thirty pounds. "Jesus. You should make a workout video," he said. "Toning with your disabled son."

"I'll put it on my to do list. But it'll be way down."

She offered up her forehead. He brushed her blonde bangs away to clear a space and gave her a kiss, tasted the salt of not showering.

She still looked good in a leotard, if a bit stuffed in. He was proud of how she'd adapted to her new life with the boys. They'd met in college when she moved in next door, laughing as he carried her desk in from the moving truck on his head. He wanted to carry a desk on his head forever just to hear that laugh. They traded family troubles: Hannah's dead brother, Gabe's crazy father. They'd both been through something, and now they deserved some good luck. He used to love listening to her talk about books he'd never read, political ideas he had no opinion on. He'd enjoyed the gossip from her teaching life: whose kid got caught drinking in the bathroom, which teacher lost her shit and threw a chair. He'd loved exploring a new city with her, finding that hole-in-the-wall in New Orleans that somehow had the freshest oysters. They'd loudly slurped one after another, as if they could inhale the whole sea.

Now Hannah's world was all Sal and Michael. The boys couldn't ask for a better mother, though sometimes she was too good. She could barely be persuaded to take a vacation anymore, given how expensive and inaccessible everywhere was, though if Gabe were being honest, he preferred to work anyway. Sometimes she'd want to go to war with Sal's school, fight the doctor for suggesting Sal get a feeding tube, or kill the insurance rep for approving only a few measly hours of speech therapy.

Last week it was a guy at the carpet store. The man told her if she'd accept Jesus as her Lord and Savior, Sal would walk. The man told her to repent. "The sins of the father," he kept saying, but Gabe put up his hands: "Don't look at me. . . ." The man raised his arm, started mumbling to Lord Jesus. Usually his wife would just roll Sal away from the scene, but she wouldn't let it go. "Stop it," she said. Squaring her shoulders behind Sal's wheelchair as if she'd charge, assault via footrest, she waited for Gabe to do something. Fine. He got in the man's face. "Hey, save yourself," Gabe said. The manager put his hands up: "Not in my store. Not in my store." They hightailed it into the station wagon, high-fived, had a good laugh.

Every battle took its toll. Sometimes she acted like the whole world was a poorly written paper she had to correct. Sometimes she got so worked up, she gave herself the shits. IBS. A gift from her mother, though it came on stronger when the boys were born. Maybe that was just motherhood: The beings who gave you the most joy also made you run for the toilet. All that stress didn't leave much time for her husband. Sometimes Gabe wanted to say, Hello. *I am still available to be the love of your life.*

But she no longer mourned for Sal, at least not like that first year. They agreed: He was now on his own path and they just wanted him to be happy.

With her salt still on his lips, he pinched his wife's necklace. "Don't squish my Mary," she said. "I'm surprised she doesn't burn your skin."

He laughed and let go. There was also her cross with a nearly naked Jesus on the wall. And she said his deer antlers were morbid. They'd had long pot-fueled conversations about religion, agreed they were both atheists, but then the boys were born and she backtracked. She wasn't annoying about it. It wasn't Gabe she was trying to save.

Cans of vegetables and soup waited by the basement steps for him to take down. She was always preparing for some imminent natural disaster. He wanted to say: *It's already happened.*

The next week, in the lab, he stared into his microscope at the MS lesion. Multiple sclerosis was a medical mystery. It typically hit you in your twenties or thirties, right when you started to doubt your own invincibility. One day you were in control, and then the pratfalls added up: catch a foot on the stairs, bite your tongue, drop a glass, start to slur when you've had nothing to drink. It was a slapstick festival. Pretty soon, you couldn't get out of your chair. The doctor ran tests and broke the news: Your body had betrayed you. Your white blood cells had gone rogue, jumped the blood-brain barrier, and were starting to eat away at your brain, nibbling at your myelin sheaths. You had lesions. You had pockets of cell death. And suddenly it stopped. You went into remission. Your brain compensated, but for how long? One year? Five? A lucky twenty-five before you started to trip again, before the words fumbled in your mouth and your arm curled at your side? And still. Life went on. As a myelin expert, Gabe was supposed to illuminate the ruins. He was cartographer of sister cities to his son's brain.

Of course there were differences between multiple sclerosis and cerebral palsy. With CP, you were injured in the womb or right after. You developed around the damage. It was not progressive. It did not progress.

He turned his attention to the mouse in its cage, its web of whiskers and bald little feet, its squeaky, desperate song. He spent a good part of his day murdering mice: suffocating them in a glass container with a generous helping of dry ice, guillotining them with a razor device like they were rich people in the French Revolution. A few times, when he was in a rush, he blew protocol and just snapped their necks with pliers. He was always sorry. He whispered little condolences: "I know. But you'll make beautiful data."

Here was a nice white one. For this little guy, Gabe the Merciful chose dry ice. He picked up the mouse by its tail and gently placed it on a plate with a smoking ice cube and sealed him under glass until it was still. Then he slid a needle into its heart, snipped its right atrium, and turned on the formalin pump, *click, click, click*, until the blood drained from its body and clear liquid seeped out between its tiny mousey teeth. He was profusing its little grooved bean. Later, he'd slice the brain paper thin, hoping for a dark patch, a gray petal, a lesion they might study.

He heard a hoopla in the hall. "Tenth! Tenth! He's in the tenth! Frank's funded!" Fuck. Frank got a top score from the NIH, in the tenth percentile. Gabe's grant application had been rated thirty-third. He was still far away from running his own lab. "To the bar!" his boss shouted. Gabe sighed. Nothing was so awkward as a group of scientists out on the town, but he got up anyway.

He rolled into their driveway well after eight. Hannah wouldn't talk to him when he came through the door. His sons were getting ready for bed. He bent down to embrace Batey and did his best "bad dog" impression.

"Sorry I'm late."

"You could have called," she said. "You've been drinking."

"We were celebrating. Frank got a grant."

"Good for Frank. Where's yours?"

"Very funny," he said. He didn't want to fight. It was too dark to go for a walk in the woods to cool off. He'd actually come home early—his colleagues were just getting started. He was being good. He deserved credit. "One day, I'll make more money," he said. "It won't be so hard."

"Maybe I'll make more money."

"I'm telling you. Toning with your disabled son. It'll sell." He squeezed her arm. She smiled. That was better. He wolfed down a few bites of overcooked pork chops and jarred sauerkraut. Before he was through, his wife threw a book at him.

"Go," she said. "They're still up. They demand a story."

He heard Michael yell: "Sal says 'Get a move on, Dada! Arriba! Arriba! Andale!'"

"I didn't know Sal spoke Spanish."

Hannah raised an eyebrow. "You should hear his Italian." She extended her arm like a game-show host.

He'd give them a story: *Once upon a time, you all shut the hell up and let me eat....*

Michael and Sal were under the covers on Sal's mattress, whispering in what sounded like a foreign language. "Hey," Gabe said in a stern voice. "Who's in there?" He tickled their feet. "I think I see an ishy-mo!"

Sal laughed, and Michael said, "I'm not an ishy-mo!"

What the hell was an ishy-mo? Gabe had no idea. His kids were so cute they turned him into a sputtering, second-rate Dr. Seuss.

Gabe tickled again, but Michael said, "Ouch."

Gabe said, "Oh, come on." This kid was so sensitive. Gabe worried Michael was too much like his own father, who sometimes needed to spend a few restful weeks in the psych ward.

His wife stood smirking in the doorway. She walked to Michael's mattress, sat down with her back against the wall, and opened a magazine. Even when she could have a moment to herself, she chose to watch over them.

"Look," Michael said. He showed off Sal's latest trick: his open mouth on Michael's cheek, a slobbery stamp of a kiss. "Wanna try?"

Sal opened his mouth and Gabe pressed his stubbled cheek to his son's lips. "Awww," Gabe said, before he felt the outline of teeth. "Don't you bite me!" He pulled away. Sal smiled and gurgled and they all laughed. *Stinker.*

Gabe and Michael sat against the wall, with Sal lying on the mattress under the tunnel of their knees. Gabe looked at the book cover: *One-Minute Bedtime Stories.* He opened to the first one and blew through it in a minute and a half, reading slow. He looked at his wife, sucked his teeth. "They enjoy this?"

"It's more for me," she said. "If the stories were any longer I'd fall asleep."

Sal said, "Ahhhhhh."

"Sal said, 'One more minute,'" reported Michael. "He said, 'If you love us.'"

Gabe glanced at his wife, who looked at him with her chin down, giving herself a goiter, threatening to stay ugly if he didn't behave. "Okay, then," Gabe said. "I love you," and it was true. This sorry mattress on the floor, with his legs draped over Sal, was where he wanted to be. He turned the page. As he read the one-minute version of poor Humpty Dumpty, he kept looking at Sal, who also had a broken head.

But Michael kept goddamned doing it. "Why did Humpty Dumpty fall? Sal wants to know. And he asked what's an egg doing on a wall."

"I didn't put it there," Gabe said. "These are fairy tales, bud. Best not to overanalyze."

"Because that's the way God wanted it?" Michael smirked. "Sal says he doesn't buy it."

"Well, Sal, that's all I'm selling." He closed the book. "All right, bedtime."

"Ahhhh," Sal said, and Gabe saw Hannah listening, waiting for Michael to translate. Her grief wasn't gone. It had just changed shape. It was here in the way she waited, staring at Michael's mouth to make Sal's words.

When Sal made those sounds, Gabe interpreted too. But his Sal was much simpler. Sal was saying, "I'm hungry. I'm thirsty. That sounds nice. I want my mother." Sometimes, Gabe suspected, he was just feeling the sound in his throat, high here, low there, how it tickled, how it felt to fill a room with his voice. Those are the thoughts you could have with a brain like Sal's. Sal was severe. Gabe did not wish more on Sal like his son did, like his wife. He loved Sal for who he was, broken brain and all.

Michael said, "Sal says, 'Again.'"

"Michael," Gabe said, "time for bed. I've had a long day."

Sal let out an "Ahhhhh-mmm."

Michael shrugged. "Sal says, 'One more.'"

"I said no."

"Sal says—"

"Goddamn it!"

His whole family turned to look at him. He'd said it harder than he meant to. His wife stood. Sal's mouth tightened into an *o*, his arms rigid, his body electric in alarm, what they called "stranger alert" because, yes, right now Gabe was a stranger. Michael's lip trembled, his eyes filling, and then the tears dropped, one, two, on the blanket. *Jesus Christ.*

"I just mean it's late, buddy," Gabe said. "You have all day tomorrow to say what he's saying." Gabe had a death grip on the book, and Hannah walked across the room to take it from him.

She sighed. "Just go."

He shut the bedroom door behind him. Through the wood he heard his wife say, "It's okay, baby. What did your brother say?"

While Sal was in the hospital, their bedroom was too quiet. Michael had to turn on the humidifier just to fall asleep. His father let him eat Lucky Charms for dinner, let him stay up late to watch a kung fu movie where the bad guy gets his heart eagle-clawed out, let him have an early birthday with cake and too many candles, let him have a sip of beer that made Michael mash up his face. Sweet at first, but then too sour.

His father acted strange, as if he'd been replaced by a more fun and dangerous dad, a "von Dad," which is what his father insisted he call him. His old father mostly said no, but von Dad was more of a yes man. Von Dad, can we make a WrestleMania mat out of the living room couch cushions and break a lamp? *Ja.* Von Dad, can we go to McDonald's and eat Chicken McNuggets and those little sauces until we throw up? *Ja.* Von Dad, can we play tug of war with Batey, fight over socks in our mouths and not care which end is dog's or man's? *Ja,* said von Dad. *Wunderbar!*

During long walks in the woods, they let Batey run, and his dad would show him the jagged muddy stamp of deer tracks and the ghostly white antler sheds lying on the leaves.

Michael missed his brother, but he wondered whether his dad did.

After their first visit with Sal, his dad asked him: "All right, buddy. What did he say this time?"

Michael smiled, appreciating the question. "Well, he said, 'It hurts.'"

His father nodded. "That makes sense."

Michael swallowed. "He said, 'It hurts it hurts it hurts it hurts it hurts it hurts—'"

After that, his dad didn't speak a word about Sal.

When they visited the second time, his twin was doing a little better. He was still up to his waist in a white cast, like a shell he carried with him.

Michael said, "Sal is a snail," and his mother said, "Sort of. Less slimy."

They had cut Sal's bones and put them back together with a pin. Michael saw the X-rays: his secret skeleton brother glowing with a bolt in his bone. He wrote his name on Sal's cast with a felt-tip marker, drawing a jagged face that was supposed to be smiling, but the plaster was too rough. The smile was more of a smudge. Not his best work.

It was their annual Fourth of July BBQ. Their mother had invited too many people, and their father was worried they'd run out of sauce. They spent the morning making an extra batch, wheeling Sal into the kitchen in his loaner chair that he could fit in with his casts. Their father did hand-over-hand, squirting the ketchup from the plastic bottle into the pot in little farts, which made Sal laugh. "Sally," their father said. "Don't you laugh at my sauce! Wait . . . you don't think it sounds like . . ."

Their mother said from the doorway: "If you get ketchup on his casts, I will kill you."

Sal had been home for a few weeks, and now their mother had something called "cabin fever." If she couldn't go out, she'd invite the world in: the neighbors, her support-group moms, their dad's colleagues, even her divorced brother from Illinois and their cousin Charlotte.

Sal said, "I feel good today, Momma."

"Sal says he feels good today," Michael said.

"I'm glad." She grinned at them and lifted Sal's hips back so he sat better in his chair. "Let's keep it that way."

The guests arrived, including their uncle and Charlotte, who was two years younger than Michael and Sal. She was no fun. She was an only child and had her hair in pigtails and was mostly concerned with her new Baby Feels So Real. "Here, baby, take your bottle. Oh, baby, it's time to burp." She tried to baby Sal, but Michael told her to get lost. His father fired up the grill for chicken and brats. Even Mrs. Snavely was there, invited so she wouldn't knock to complain about the noise. It was sweltering, too hot for Sal to sit outside in his casts, so he reclined on the living room floor, his casts propped up on pillows. Tina lay beside him for a while. Michael tried to listen to her like he listened to Sal, but he couldn't hear anything. He was relieved when she started fussing and her mom brought her outside. The kids drew hearts and get-well-soons on Sal's rough plaster, but then someone turned on a sprinkler in the backyard and they ran off.

Last week, Sal had been sitting in his wheelchair while Michael colored a picture beside him. Looking down at his cast, Sal said, "What kind of face is this?" He wanted a new one. "Draw it right this time."

"Your cast is too rough," Michael said.

"Then somewhere else," Sal said. "That wall."

Michael made perfect swoops with red crayon.

His mother thought the story was funny, kept saying, "Sal, did you get your brother in trouble?" which made Sal laugh and Michael feel better, especially after his father forced Michael to scrub the crayon until his elbow ached.

Now Sal had another idea: "Let's kidnap Baby Feels So Real."

Michael went on a spy mission, saw the baby abandoned on a kitchen chair. He scooped her up and brought the doll to his brother. Sal reached with his good hand to wrap his fingers over the baby's arm.

"Does it feel real?" Michael asked.

"No," Sal said. "It's squishy. Not even fat babies feel like that."

"How's it held together?"

Sal said, "Let's see if there's a bolt in its bones."

Michael peered out the window. Their mother was lighting sparklers for the children, with Mrs. Snavely conducting them with her fingers. No chance his cousin would come in. He got a steak knife from the kitchen, and the operation began. He slid the blade along the baby's hip until it oozed caramel. It made Michael's fingers sweet. He dabbed some of the baby doll blood on Sal's tongue, and Sal smacked his lips.

"Yum," Sal said. "You could put it on pancakes."

"Or chicken," Michael said. "Might be better than Dad's sauce."

They laughed.

Michael wiggled his fingers inside the doll's skin to scratch at its skeleton. It was smooth, hard plastic, with no pins or bolts. A complete fake. So Sal said, "Get out all the gunk." This required more incisions before

Sal counted down, "Three-two-one!" and Michael jumped with both feet. The goop shot out in all directions, splattering the carpet, the couch, the wallpaper, Sal's shirt and right cheek. Sal fluttered his eyelids, stiffened in startle reflex, and then he laughed. Michael stood triumphant on the deflated baby body, the last of the syrup oozing between his toes.

The screen door slid open. Someone was coming. He panicked and threw the flat baby behind the couch. When he peeked into the kitchen, it was only his dad, coming in for the sauce. "Chow time," he said. "Your mom saved you guys some sparklers." Michael nodded. As soon as his dad was gone, he grabbed a fistful of paper towels. He tried to mop up the mess but it only spread the slime thin.

Charlotte came looking. "Have you seen my baby?" she asked the guests until she started to cry. A search party was sent out to shut her up. Batey was made an honorary bloodhound and sniffed his way into the living room. Michael tried to shoo him out, but the dog scrubbed the carpet with his tongue. "Who spilled here?" became "What spilled here?" and the family detectives deduced. The body was discovered. His uncle dangled it in the air by its foot, its face caved in, covered in dog hair and dust.

Their mother was horrified. "Oh my God," she said. "Am I raising a Ted Bundy?" But their father laughed and said: "At least now we *know* what makes it feel so real."

Michael got some serious time-out. He sat with his face to the living room wall, the exact spot he'd scrubbed the week before, staring into the dappled blue paint. He listened to the guests leave one by one. His dad brought him a plate of cold chicken with extra cookies. "In my book," his dad said, "that baby was asking for it."

Michael asked, "Why isn't Sal being punished too?"

His father ruffled Michael's hair. "He's sort of always in time-out, buddy."

When Sal got his casts off, Michael and Sal did something that neither parent found funny. Sal said, "Take the matches from the drawer." He was the one who wanted Michael to hold the match under his nose so Sal could watch it spurt alive and curl black under the flame before Michael threw it with a hiss into the toilet. He was the one who said, "Again." When

Michael missed the toilet and hit the shag bath mat, Sal was out of ideas, especially when the rug started to smolder and then jumped with flames. Michael flicked toilet water on the fire, but that just seemed to make it mad as it filled the bathroom with smoke. "Uh-oh," Sal said, and when they started coughing, Michael pulled Sal into the hallway and pushed him to safety, past the smoke alarm that screamed and past their mother (also screaming). He was a hero, but all his mother could talk about was the hundreds of dollars in fire damage—that Michael was getting fire damage for Christmas.

"It was Sal's idea," he told her.

"Michael," she said. "Please."

When his father came home, he announced a spanking. "A spanking?" his mother asked, but his father was sure. He put Michael over his leg, pulled down his pants, and gave him three solid whacks, gave him a burning butt, made the pain radiate down to his toes and up again. Michael thought he'd never walk again, that he'd have to ask Sal to move over and make room.

Sal watched it happen from his chair, watched his father's hand come down. Michael waited for a "Stop!" or a "Hurts? You think that hurts?" but Sal said nothing.

After Michael stopped crying, his father said, "Enough. You don't speak for Sal. It's not cute anymore. It's getting creepy. You want attention, fine, but you don't blame your brother."

"Mom," Michael said, but his mother just shook her head.

"I'm sorry, baby. No more."

His parents had come to an agreement, a unified front. He was not, under any circumstances, supposed to say what Sal was saying.

When Michael started kindergarten, they took him to see the school psychologist. The man wore a dress shirt without a tie and laughed in between sentences. He kept folding his hands. It was a fun game to imagine what Sal might be saying, wasn't it?

"Yes," Michael said.

"You seem like a smart little guy," the psychologist said. "You know the difference between real and pretend, right?"

Michael nodded.

"Your brother isn't really saying what you say he's saying, is he?"

Michael was quiet. He knew the man didn't believe him. He knew the man thought Sal was severe. He bit his bottom lip.

"Is he?"

"I don't know." Michael turned away, staring into the dusty cream slats of the window blinds. He was angry that he'd started to cry. He wiped his cheeks with his shoulders.

"That's okay," the psychologist said and folded his hands. "That's perfectly all right."

3

Michael kneeled over Sal and pinned down his wrists, mock-socked him in the gut and jabbed him in the sides until Sal was soundless and shaking, until Sal gasped like he'd been held underwater and laughed again.

He wedged his arms under Sal's back and rolled on the living room carpet, pulling his brother on top of him, Sal's mouth open and drooling on Michael's chest until his brother's forearms found the floor and hoisted himself up. Hovering over Michael's face, Sal's head drooped and wobbled until Sal steadied, raised his head, and roared: "Ahhhhh!" His mouth was open wide like a baboon flashing fangs. He meant: *Now I've got you*, or something.

Michael pleaded toward the kitchen tiles: "Help! Momma, help!"

Their mother walked into the living room, wiping her hands with a dishrag. "Be careful," she said. "Watch his hips."

The bolt was under the red line of raised skin under Sal's diaper. He was all better. Sal only cried at night now. He was back to his old self.

"No, he's beating me," Michael said.

"You want help?" she said. "Okay I'll give you both help." She tossed up the dishtowel, and before it hit the carpet she was over them, wiggling her long fingers into both their sides. Sal collapsed onto Michael's chest and bit his t-shirt as they shook together, as she took both their breaths.

"I'll pee," Michael said. "I'm peeing."

"Bet you wish you had Sal's diaper," she said.

When she retreated, Michael pushed Sal back on the blanket. He dabbed at the slobber marks on his t-shirt. Wet blotches. Damp wounds.

It was Halloween. The twins had just turned six. When their father came home, Sal would be a ship. Michael would be a pirate. They had a patch left over from Sal's bout with a lazy eye. Michael wanted to be a devil, something really evil, but his father said, "Pirates are plenty evil. Plus it's one less costume piece to buy."

Their mother fried ground beef to violins from a horror movie. Someone screamed. As if to match the sound, Sal let out a howl that ended with an "Eh-eh." Michael asked him to please repeat. He hadn't heard him clearly, which was happening more often. He called into the kitchen: "When is he gonna get here?"

Their mother said, "He just called. He'll be late."

They ate dinner—Manwich night—without their dad. Batey whined and barked from the basement as three groups of trick-or-treaters came to the door, with better fathers who loved their children more and were not late all the time. Michael's mother fawned over their costumes and dropped peanut butter cups into their buckets. She sat back down beside Sal and held a triangle of Manwich between her fingers. She said, "Do you want more? Tell Mommy. Eh or eh-eh?"

Sal sat in his wheelchair with his hands splayed out like a praying mantis. His brown hair was framed by a sky-blue cushion, and a gray chest strap covered his striped shirt like a plate of armor. A plastic bib was draped around his neck: pastel dog paws. His wooden tray was covered in peeling orange pumpkin stickers and sparkling black bats. After his hands tightened into fists, he raised his head ever so slightly, as if it held an incredible weight, and grunted: "Eh."

"That's my boy," their mother said. "That's my baby. You tell Mommy. You're still hungry, aren't you?" She didn't glance at Michael to interpret. Michael scowled. All his parents seemed to do was try to make Sal talk in that grunting idiot's code. She shoved the grease-stained triangle into Sal's mouth, and he smiled before pressing his bottom lip to his front teeth, pinching off a bite.

"Mom," Michael said from across the table. "I'm still hungry. I'm really hungry."

His mother wore a headband with cat ears, her nose black and her face streaked with whiskers. She said, "I know, Mikey, but you've already had a whole one. What did we talk about?"

They'd talked about Michael being a little on the husky side. About switching potato chips for carrot sticks. About what the psychologist said.

"And you're going to eat all that candy. For now, honey, have some corn." She passed the bowl of golden nubs still swimming in their can water. She fed Sal another bite and tipped a hard plastic cup to his lips before glancing at her watch. "Jesus Christ."

More trick-or-treaters came to the door, kids from the neighborhood who waved at Michael. Every knock, every doorbell ring was torture. It seemed their father would never come.

"All right," their mother said. "We have to get ready without him."

Michael ran to their bedroom, threw on long underwear for the cold, and assembled his costume: a red-striped seaman's shirt, a black vest with sewn-on crossbones, and some ripped knickers. When he came back into the kitchen, his mother said, "Let's get on your peg," then wrapped his leg with brown construction paper and shipping tape. She handed him his hook, rubbed his chin with charcoal, scarred his cheek with lipstick, and then snapped on his eyepatch, making half the world dark. She rubbed and scarred Sal too. She took sheets of cardboard, onto which she'd drawn wooden slats with black marker, and tied them to the sides of Sal's wheelchair. She duct-taped a plastic whiffle bat (the cannon) to his wooden tray (the deck). She emptied the black leather bag from the back of Sal's chair, dumping out its wet wipes and spare diapers, its sunglasses and bug spray. "You're gonna fill this up," she said.

Finally their father pushed through a cluster of kids, his briefcase a battering ram.

"Hi," their mom said. "It's six-thirty."

"I know. I couldn't help it."

Their mother clenched her jaw. Michael worried she'd start throwing canned goods down the basement steps again. They were still trying to eat the dented ones from last time. His mother had left the canned goods on the steps for his father to take down, but then he didn't and he didn't and he didn't until she yelled, "I'll take them down myself!" and she went bombs away with corn and the beans and the tomato soup, each landing with a clanking thud and rolling against the wall. But tonight, she just sighed. "I can't believe you're not coordinating with them. You could've been a monkey. Or a white whale. You guys could've gone as *Moby-Dick*."

"Nobody would get it," he said. "Besides nerds like you." She finally cracked a smile. He kissed her cheek and inspected his sons. "Michael, you're looking quite evil. Sal, a bit more duct-tape and you're seaworthy." He flung off his tie as he jogged to his bedroom and returned in a blue sweatshirt with a rubber wolf mask over his brown curly hair. He stuffed his face with Manwich, beef crumbling from his mouth. "I'm ready."

They descended the ramp, his father easing Sal over the bump. Their mother yelled, "Get me some gumdrops!"

His father sighed. "Yep!"

"Are you guys fighting?" Michael asked.

His father smiled, lowered the wolf mask, and lit a cigarette, smoke wafting out of his muzzle. "No. Sal, let's speed it up a few knots." His father leaned into Sal's wheelchair handles.

Sal creaked forward. Sal set sail.

It was almost dark when Mrs. Snavely opened the door, saw the tandem costume, and said, "Cute." She walked down her stoop and dropped crinkly golden-wrapped hard candy into Michael's plastic bag, and their dad swung Sal around to receive cargo.

"She doesn't have a costume," Michael said after she closed her door.

"She doesn't need one," their dad said.

A few houses over, the Zeigenhagens pronounced them "adorable." They wore cloth devil horns and put their hands up at the sight of Sal's cannon. "Don't shoot. Take our treasure."

"Okay," their father said. As they turned around, he whispered, "We're gonna get this all night."

They did get it all night, but people also seemed happy to dump extra fistfuls into Sal's roomy sack. After one particularly large haul, their father swung Michael up by the armpits onto his shoulders, holding Michael's peg leg while pushing Sal with his other hand. Michael felt like he had climbed on top of a towering mast. His father yelled, "We're cute! We're adorable! Now hand over your freaking candy!"

"Arrrr!" Michael yelled.

"Ahhhh!" Sal yelled.

"Or you'll walk the plank!" their dad yelled. He was von Dad again. As Michael swayed, he held tight to his father's rough chin and looked down. Sal's bag was half-full, the wrappers glittering in the streetlight.

Then Michael saw a kid staring at Sal and heard him ask: "What's he supposed to be?" The kid was dragged forward by his mother, who told him to shush.

A few houses over, the door opened to a man with brains oozing out, patches of brown hair mixed in, and blood dripping in rivulets from his forehead. He stumbled toward them, his arms stiff, eyes rolled back. He said, "I've got a bit of a headache. Perhaps I hit my head." Michael ran down the steps and jumped behind Sal's chair, whimpering.

"All right," their dad said. "We get it." He nudged Michael with his foot. "Mike. Come on out. It's a costume. Thanks, buddy."

"Look, kid. It's a pump." The man held a green plastic ball sloshing with dark liquid, attached to tubes that ran up his plaid shirt. "Jeez. I'm sorry. I have peanuts."

"You're gonna do that and then hand out peanuts? You're sick."

"I'm a dentist."

"Then candy's in your economic interest."

"I've thought about that."

They turned around. His dad rubbed Michael's head. "What a jerk. But you're about the wussiest pirate I ever met."

"I am not," Michael said.

"I haven't met that many." He straightened Michael's eyepatch.

Sal *ahhh-ed*. His eyebrows were relaxed, his lips slightly parted. Sal had seen the same brains and blood as Michael. Why wasn't he scared too?

It grew darker. Michael could see their breath in the cold. Their father tugged mittens onto Sal's fists and rubbed Michael's hands in his own. "Warm 'em in your pockets, buddy. Sal can hold your hook."

They came to a nice brick house with flickering electric candles in its windows. Someone had smashed a pumpkin in the lawn, its wax nub poking out from a bed of slimy pulp. Toilet paper hung from a tree like Spanish moss. Michael had a bad feeling climbing the steps. He looked back at his dad, who nodded. Michael adjusted his patch and pushed the glowing button.

To Michael's relief, the door opened to a grandma, or at least a fat woman with gray hair. The doorway was dark behind her. She was stooped over but seemed too young for it. The skin wasn't loose enough on her face. "Hello," she said. "What do we have here?" She laughed sweetly and held a tray of caramel apples, their sticks as straight as soldiers at attention. "Take one," she said. He reached out, but his hand froze. The apples looked like they were covered in his cousin's baby-doll blood. Then he saw a flash of neon from the lady's left, and a glowing skull appeared above her head and growled. Michael screamed, knocked the tray out of her hands, and ran. He saw Sal stiffen in his chair, and when he looked back at the house, a whole glowing skeleton stood in the doorway, howling, with bony hands raised like claws. And he just knew it was coming to steal Sal's bolt for its own bones. To make his brother fall apart. Now Sal was yelling, and for the first time in a long while, Michael heard him clearly. Sal said, "Ready the guns." He said, "Fire." He said, "Get away from us, you dickbreath, you fuckface." Michael interpreted at the top of his lungs.

At the dining room table, their mother poured them juice, and their father twisted open a beer. "Sal was upset because Michael was so hysterical. I have no idea where he learned those words."

Their dad scooted his chair closer to Sal, who was still in his wheelchair, though they had untied the cardboard. "Did you really call that guy a dickbreath?"

"All right," their mother said.

Sal smiled.

"Can we not talk about this right now?" their mother said. "How can you be this unhappy in front of this much candy." She spilled Sal's bag of candy onto the table, as if she had busted a piñata. Michael thought that very TV-mom of her.

"Fine," their father said, rummaging through the pile.

"Pick out the Tootsie Rolls. It's the only thing soft enough for Sal to eat." She spread the candy with the back of her hand. "Where are my gumdrops?"

"It's trick-or-treat. It's basically begging," their dad said. "It's not like we went to the store."

Michael couldn't sleep. It wasn't just that he'd eaten too much candy. It wasn't just that Sal was snoring at exceptional volume on the mattress across the room. It was that when he closed his eyes, the skeleton appeared as he'd first seen it, glowing in the darkness of the doorway. He kept looking at the closet, thinking he'd see toes illuminated under the door, right before the thing jumped out and fell upon Sal, wiggling its fingers inside the scar on his hip, leaving Sal a mess of parts and goo.

Then there was the guilt. Because as they separated out the candy, as his parents poached favorites for themselves, all he could think about was his brother's sad little hill of Tootsie Rolls. He hadn't even liked Tootsie Rolls before, but as soon as the candy became Sal's, he wanted it. He thought about the candy so much that after taking a pee, he'd gone to the kitchen drawer where his mother had stashed the Tootsie Rolls and ate two pieces. His spit now tasted like chocolate, and for a moment that made up for the fact that his parents loved Sal more. Though Michael had his Special Days with Mommy, his mother washed Sal in the bath and held his head to her chest as she soaped him while Michael had to shower alone or with his father, shivering until his dad stepped sideways and let the warm water hit him. Most of all, Michael worried that his dad and the psychologist were right. He worried that Sal had not said what Sal was saying.

Michael checked the closet door for glowing toes one more time and swallowed hard. He peeled back his covers and crawled across the carpet. Sal was breathing like Darth Vader, but in the moonlight Michael could see the whites of his eyes. Sal's pupils flickered over Michael's face. His neck was hot and sticky. Their mother put on too many blankets again, so Michael ripped one off.

"Hi," he said. He pushed Sal toward the wall, crawled under the covers, and slid his arm across his brother's back.

Sal kept his steady rhythm, his back heaving up and down. His face was slack, with his mouth open and tongue still.

"Can I have some of your candy if I don't let the skeleton get you?"

Sal's snore broke. He closed his mouth, hissed air through his nose, and swallowed. "Wa," he said.

Michael shut his eyes and concentrated, but it was so quiet. "Do you forgive me?" he asked, though he wasn't sure for exactly what. He waited. Sal's cheek was flush against a pillowcase with a damp balloon of drool around his mouth. "Can you talk to me?" Michael pulled the pillowcase forward, giving Sal a dry section. He folded over the slobbered cloth and scooted closer so their faces almost touched, so that Michael could feel Sal's warm breath wash over his lips. "Can you say something, Sal?"

Sal's head moved. Michael heard the springs creak. Sal said, "Ehh-uhhh-eh." Michael shut his eyes to let Sal's sound enter his ear and vibrate in his brain until it signified in a voice like his own but different. Michael didn't dare move, not even to disturb a spring, and held his breath so long he could hear his own heart thumping. But the voice didn't come.

After school the next day, he only meant to eat one Tootsie Roll, but he kept coming back to the drawer when his mom was out of the kitchen until only a few pieces were left. He thought if he took it all she'd forget where she put it. But the dog screwed him again. Batey pulled a wrapper out of the trash, took it to the living room, near his mother's feet on the couch, and licked the wax paper.

Michael told his mother that Sal said he could have some, but his mother asked if Michael thought she was stupid, and Michael paused too long by accident, which made her angry. What had he been thinking? She didn't know what to do with him. "Wait until your father gets home."

He had not been a help. He had proved he needed to see the psychologist, for that man to nod and scribble, to whisper to his mother behind closed doors. He had proved he was a fat-ass.

Michael, Sal, and their mother were waiting at the table, spaghetti sauce simmering on the stove, when the door creaked open. "Hi," their father said, tired but smiling. He looked at their mother. "What's wrong?"

"Your son is doing it again," she said. "And he ate all Sal's candy."

"He said I could have some," Michael said as a reflex, and because now he actually wanted to be punished.

Their father set down his briefcase. He massaged his jaw. "Interesting . . ." He dished himself some pasta, pulled up a chair, and sat down. "Guys? Can we eat?" he asked as he showered his plate with parmesan powder.

Their mother looked disappointed. Getting up and grabbing plates, she cut Sal's spaghetti into little pieces, and then they ate in silence.

Their father cracked open a beer. He said, "Sal, did you say Michael could have some of your candy? Eh or eh-eh?"

Sal clenched his fingers, tilted up his head, and said, "Eh-eh."

"There you go, Michael. That's Sal speaking for himself. No."

Michael dropped his fork. Sal had never contradicted him before. He felt his stomach drop. Not his twin. Not him too.

Michael sat at the table watching everyone chew and stayed there after they got up. He reached in his pocket and put the eyepatch on again. He wanted a second one to cover the other eye. He wanted to disappear.

Eventually, their father called Michael into the kitchen. "Okay, buddy. Quit moping." He sat in the old wicker chair, holding Sal in his lap and watching football on the counter television. Their mother leaned against the stove reading a magazine.

"I'm sorry," Michael said.

"Don't apologize to us, matey," their father said. "Apologize to your brother." He held Sal under the armpits, hips balanced on his knee. Sal's head was on his father's chest, his hands loose and splayed out, his mouth hanging open. He hadn't covered for Michael, but was he angry? Did he care? Sal's face was still. He wasn't giving anything away.

"I'm sorry," Michael said to him.

Sal stiffened and flexed his eyebrows. He said, "Ahhh-rah," and turned his head.

"Oooh," their father said. "He's mad at you." Their father grasped the ends of Sal's fingers, curving his wrists and bobbing them in the air. "He says, 'I'm gonna kick your butt.' He says, 'Put up your dukes.'"

Michael stood with his hands at his sides. He looked at his mother, who put her fingers to her lips. Was that a laugh? It was a joke then, but his father said, "Come on."

So Michael raised his fists. He bounced like he had seen boxers do on TV. Sal's hands floated in small circles, and Michael moved from side to side. Then Sal swung, and Michael weaved out of the way. "All right," his mother said, but laughed again. It was all very funny. Sal's hands kept bobbing. Michael didn't know what his father wanted. Did his dad want him to punch Sal in the face? Or pretend to, as a joke? Michael stepped forward.

He saw a flash with his masked eye, felt a burst of pressure, and his head snapped back. Then he was sitting on the linoleum. Half of the kitchen was so bright.

His mother said, "Hey, that's too rough."

His father said, "He walked into it."

Michael's patch had shifted above his brow, leaving his eye bare. He squinted, adjusting to the light, but he couldn't see his father. He could only see Sal and his hard wrist, Sal's soft eyes looking down.

He finally heard Sal clearly. "Be careful," Sal said. "Even I can hurt you."

II
ALL IS FORGIVEN

4

In first grade, Michael made a new friend, Carl. Because words came to them too slow, they were taken out of reading and brought to the trailer beside the bell tower, where a lady with horse teeth and too many bracelets encouraged them. "Good job," she said. "Yay. Keep going." Their eyes crawled through every page.

At recess, they were picked last for football so often that they made up their own games—with fewer demands on coordination and overall movement. They threw a football back and forth over a telephone wire, aiming for the lowest clouds, with Carl saying every time: "To the moon!"

Michael's favorite class, by far, was religion. He liked learning about the saints, their good deeds and gruesome deaths. He started thinking maybe he was normal and Sal was not because Michael was meant to be a saint. He'd have special conversations with God and talk to dogs and deer. He'd heal the sick—tell Sal to get up, kick over his wheelchair and walk. He'd at least hear Sal clearly again. Someone might murder Michael, but that'd be fine. For saints, getting killed came with the territory, and it wouldn't matter anyway, because Michael would be at a party in heaven while people prayed to his bones. All he had to do was wait for grace to come, to be filled with the Holy Spirit.

In the spring, they got ready for their first communion. Maybe this was it. Maybe by ingesting God's grace, Michael would gain his holy powers.

Michael tried to be extra holy before their big day. He started a prayer in the morning and never said "Amen" so he could technically pray all day, as if he'd found a cheat code in God's video game. He thought of God as a dad who was watching him and keeping score. Every time Michael did something nice for Sal, every time he kissed his cheek even though it was slobbery, or sang to him when Sal was upset, Michael got a point. Every time he told Sal to be quiet or stole a sip of Sal's milkshake when their mother wasn't looking, he lost a point.

The night before, as they were eating dinner, his father said, "Sal, you better not spit out the body of Christ. You'll go to H-E-double-hockey-sticks."

"Stop," their mother said. "Say, 'I'm not going anywhere.'"

Sal smiled, forced his elbows down against his tray, and said, "Ahhhh." Michael watched his brother's eyes, and then came the meaning: *I won't spit it out. No hell for me.* He still often knew what Sal was saying, but his twin's meaning arrived in Michael's brain in a voice that was softer and slower than before, and sometimes Michael had trouble, like he was trying to hear someone talking underwater. Other times the voice was so loud that Sal might as well have shouted it. Of course, Michael wasn't allowed to claim direct knowledge. That's what he'd worked out with his parents, why he was allowed to stop seeing the psychologist. Michael had to use metaphors *as if* he couldn't be sure, *like* he couldn't exactly understand. Now he said, "It's like he's saying, 'I won't spit it out. No hell for me.'"

Sal smiled again and said, "Yeah," his new way to say "Yes." Saint Michael was right.

That Sunday, their mother dressed them up in new gray suits, husky for Michael, baggy for Sal. Both sat with Michael's class in the first two pews, sweating in their itchy fabric. All the girls wore gauzy white dresses and fancy lace gloves.

When it was time, the priest gave the signal. Michael stood, grabbed Sal's foam handles, and pushed his brother forward, his whole class marching behind. His feet felt slow, as if there were something heavier than pennies in his loafers. He looked back and saw the church ladies with tight smiles, whispering to their husbands. Yes, they saw him being so good, pushing his twin brother to God. He was ready for his holy life to begin.

As they approached the old priest in his gold vestments, he raised the paper-thin wafer and said, "Body of Christ." He cracked the host in half, placed one piece on Sal's tongue and the other half in Michael's cupped hands. Michael wanted to say, *Wait. I need a whole one*, but the priest was already looking over Michael's shoulder at the next kid. "Go," someone whispered.

Sal smacked his lips and swallowed. No hell for him. Michael popped the host in his mouth. As he made the sign of the cross, he felt the wafer's ragged edge on his tongue, felt it turn to mush. He grabbed Sal's handles, swallowed hard, and walked forward. As they made their way to the back of the church, he waited for a warmth to wash over him. He waited to hear Sal clearly again.

Nothing happened.

In second grade, their mother started talking about Sal getting a powerchair. Sal's therapist thought Sal was too spastic to control the joystick, that it wouldn't be safe. "So he's on the edge of ability," his mother argued to his father. "Why can't we at least try?"

"Honey," his father said. "Let's not alienate his entire care team. Plus, you really want to do that to our drywall?"

"He's getting that chair," she said.

Michael liked thinking about Sal driving a powerchair. He'd seen a Steven King werewolf movie called *Silver Bullet*, where the kid drives a powerchair as fast as a motorcycle. How much power would this powerchair have? He hoped a lot. It could be very useful for Wheelchair Bobsled.

They'd found a loaner for Sal to practice on at school. For months he came home with scuffed sneakers, and once, a bruise on his shin where he crashed. The chair broke and wasn't fixed for several weeks. It seemed like maybe the therapist was right. Michael tried to cheer Sal up. "You don't need to drive," he said. "You've got me."

Sal's pinched his lips into his pensive look. Sal was underwater. His meaning did not arrive. Something like *Okay. Thanks.*

Michael should've known what was up when his father drove away in their rusty brown station wagon and came back with a new van. It was blindingly white, with teal stripes and a turtle top that his dad could almost stand up under. It had a hydraulic lift near the side door with a metal platform to scoop Sal up in his wheelchair. No more dismantling the chair and stuffing it into the station wagon and lifting Sal into a car seat. Now they could strap Sal's wheelchair to the floor. If they got in an accident and flipped over, Sal would hang down like a bat.

Michael rode the lift, wiggling its yellow switch up and down, up and down, as if it were a not-very-exciting carnival ride. He cheered when he saw the framed box above the driver's seat and asked when they were getting the TV. His mother said, "We're not that kind of family," and bricked up the space with spare diapers.

The next week, their parents unveiled the powerchair like Sal was getting a first car: red bow on the teal tubing. There was a black joystick with a console that went from speeds of turtle to rabbit, and a black foam seat fitted to the curve of his scoliosis. When Sal saw it, his arms locked back and his feet strained against their straps. He stuffed his tongue between his teeth and squealed in spaz attack, and Michael understood him loud and clear: *Thank you thank you thank you.*

Their father drove the family to the church parking lot to watch Sal cruise around. It was fun at first, Michael running beside his brother. Thank God he was still faster. But Sal kept spinning away from him. "Tag, you're it," Michael said and tapped Sal's shoulder, but his brother didn't give chase. Eventually Michael just watched with his parents, who stood huddled together, dabbing at each other's eyes. "I knew this would happen," said his father. "You started, and now I've started."

Finally his mother realized he wasn't happy. "Oh, Michael," she said. "What's wrong?"

He bellowed, "I won't be able to push him anymore!"

His father pointed at Sal making a wild turn. "I know, buddy. But look at him go."

Michael pouted about Sal's new powerchair for weeks, until their uncle's wedding. They drove the eight hours in the new van to Illinois and stayed with their grandma, their mom's mom. There was a cross in every room of the house. One had a Jesus so detailed you could see up his nose. And on her mantel was a huge picture of his uncle who died, forever eighteen, his cheeks weirdly pink like someone had colored him in. His grandma glanced at the picture and said, "God only gives you what you can handle." His mother pulled her in for a hug. Michael wondered what he could handle, what God would give him. He hoped it was a lot.

Michael liked his grandma. She dyed her hair so that it looked dipped in ink. She sent them birthday cards stuffed with McDonald's gift certificates. And when she visited, she took him out for secret ice cream and called him her "special little boy." But now, in her living room, she leaned into Sal's wheelchair handles with her veiny hands. She said, "You say 'Grandma.' You say 'Grandma,' you silly goose!"

Sal gave his nervous smile. *Help. Her breath.*

Michael was understanding him pretty well on the trip.

"That's okay," she said. "He'll practice." She took his hand. "Oh, Sal, you're an angel. You're God's little lamb."

Sal smiled at Michael. *Did you hear that? I'm not even trying.*

"I don't know about that," their father said. "Sal's actually a stinker. He keeps running over our feet."

"Eh-eh," Sal said. *Not true, Grandma. Keep those McDonald's bucks coming.*

"Oh, I don't believe him, Sally." Their grandma's gaze settled on Michael. "And Michael, you're such a sweet boy, such a big help. I wish we lived closer."

Michael beamed. He'd take what he could get.

At the wedding, their cousin Charlotte was the flower girl. She had not forgiven them for her Baby Feels So Real, had made her father lock up the dolls and kitchen knives. Sal was the ring bearer, driving the two rings up the aisle as the church "awww-ed," delivering them to their uncle and new aunt in her puffy white dress. It was supposed to be Michael pushing Sal, but with Sal's new powerchair, Michael opted to sit. As the cameras clicked, Sal swerved a little but managed not to crash into a pew. Michael tried his best not to die of boredom.

At the reception, the adults were drinking. Even his mother had two glasses of wine. And then they started dancing: bouncing on their toes, waggling their arms, chopping the air like malfunctioning robots. Their father was the most embarrassing, doing great big kicks over his head. He tried to do the splits and had to be helped up. When their mother jumped into his arms, he pretended to hurt his back, and she swatted him and laughed. They kissed right there in front of everyone. Michael made gagging sounds from his seat.

His mother tried to pull him out on the dance floor. "Come on! You're too young to be this embarrassed." He got to his feet and swayed a little but felt all those eyes on him. All his movements seemed mistimed. He squirmed like a slug in salt. He sat back down.

Sal was having no trouble, zooming across the dance floor in his new chair. He spun in a circle to Journey's "Don't Stop Believin'," almost bursting out of his straps during the guitar solo. Their father offered the toddlers free wheelchair rides on Sal's lap. Then Sal was surrounded by bridesmaids, two of them shaking his hands to the beat, Sal smiling with his dimple. *Hubba hubba.*

If they had Sal's manual wheelchair, it would be fine. Michael would know what to do with his body. He'd be behind Sal's handles, popping wheelies, moving him left and right to the beat, tipping his footrest up into dancing people's butts. But Sal didn't need him. Now the only thing to do was be embarrassed and stuff himself with cake. He took a big old bite.

Sal cut away from the bridesmaids and stopped in front of Michael, leveling his gaze. *What's wrong?*

"I'm fine," Michael said. "Go. Blow a fuse."

Sal turned his chair. Michael thought he would speed off again, but he just sat there. *Come on, brother. Wheelchair Bobsled. All aboard.*

Michael took another bite of cake. He could refuse to join, just sit and eat until he felt sick. Or he could find out who exactly was this new brother. He swallowed and climbed onto the back of Sal's chair, balancing his feet on the rear of the battery box, and then they were off. It felt so good to be behind Sal's handles again. They spun, nearly taking out a bridesmaid. He yelled, "Sal, I'm full of cake! Don't make me throw up!"

The chair stalled, Sal laughing in spaz attack. *But that's our first stop!* He punched the joystick forward. Michael tried to guess where they'd go next.

By third grade, Sal had old-lady bones. He needed to dense them up. For half an hour each day, their mother strapped Sal into a device he used for standing. One Sunday they were playing in the living room, where the stander rose from the floor with a wooden plank for Sal's feet and a long, almost vertical padded board for him to lean on.

Sal hated his stander. Michael was sure. When their mother carried him to the contraption, Sal did his stiff routine and said "Eh-eh" all the way. Michael waited for the voice and here it came: *Let's think about this. Let's reconsider.*

Today, like every other day, she planted his Nikes into the footrest and leaned his body against the gray leather of the board, which went up to his chest and then jutted out into a wooden tray where he parked his elbows. Two gray pads pressed into his rib cage to keep him centered. She pulled tight the gray Velcro straps over Sal's shoes and shins and lower back, then turned a crank at the stander's base to angle him upright. He had no escape.

"There," she said and kissed his cheek. "You know you need it." She patted Michael's head. "Entertain him," she said and walked into the kitchen.

Michael stood on his tiptoes, but Sal still hovered over him, two heads taller. It made Michael uncomfortable. He was used to Sal down low. Sal had his elbows on the tray, his forearms tight against his biceps with his wrists locked down. On the tray was a picture book that involved apples, but it was for babies. Sal stared at Michael, his dark eyebrows digging into the bridge of his nose.

"Do you want to get out?" Michael asked.

"Eh," Sal said, jerking his trunk for emphasis. *Ding Ding Ding. Great guess.*

"Too bad," Michael said. He ran a circle around Sal, his captive. "It's because you've been bad," Michael whispered. "It's because you broke the law."

"Eh eh," Sal said. *I didn't do it.*

"You lie," Michael told him and threw pretend tomatoes and cantaloupe parts until Sal was sticky with pretend pulp. "Guilty," Michael whisper-screamed. "Put him on the rack."

"Eh-eh," Sal said and smiled. *You've got the wrong man.*

"Liar," Michael said. "Read that baby book. Die of boredom." He tapped Sal's calves with a Nerf baseball bat. Sal stiffened and cried out, "Ahhh!"

"Confess," Michael said. The crowd yelled, *Tighter! tighter!* and Michael reached down near the base and gave Sal a good crank. "Ahhh," Sal yelled. *Oh, the pain. Oh, the suffering. My legs, my back.*

Michael said, "That's right." The deer head on the wall was their witness. It wasn't impressed.

Their mother yelled from the kitchen: "I don't think Sal likes whatever you're playing."

Sal, mid-slobber, grinned. *Actually, Mom, I love it.*

"We're playing confession," said Michael, who was set to make his first confession in two weeks. Sal wasn't. This was the closest he would get. "He likes it. He smiled like *I love it.*"

"Okay," his mother said. "Just do it nicely."

Michael stuck a finger into his ear canal. It was itching again. His father said he was just prone to ear infections, pink eye too, but Michael worried it was something more. "That's it," Michael said. "If you won't confess, I'll sentence you to opera. You will listen to me sing."

"Eh-eh," Sal said. *No. Anything but that.*

Michael cleared his throat, did his best kid-baritone. "Fiiiig-a-rowwww! Fiiiig-a-rowww! Spa-ghetti! Meat-a-balls-aaaa!"

"Ahhhhhhh!" Sal yelled, all drawn out, really suffering now. *Okay. Okay. I did it.*

Michael put his face close to Sal's ear and whispered, "What did you do?"

Sal looked left, contemplating, remembering, keeping Michael in suspense, until he arched his back, bit at the air, and roared: "Ah-uh-ahhhhhhh!"

Michael crowed and ran around in another circle, because Sal had confessed to everything. He had done it all.

5

A week later, on Monday, Michael and Carl were waiting in line for recess when Carl turned around. "You're bleeding."

"I am not," Michael said, pinching tighter his maroon clip-on tie.

"You are," Carl said. "It's like a tear, but blood."

"Shut up." Michael pretended to glance at the clock and dabbed at his tear duct.

"Psych! You checked. He checked."

"I had an itch," Michael said, but it was too late. All his classmates were craning their necks and staring, smirking with raised eyebrows. What a Judas. Michael should've never asked Carl to check if his eyes or ears were bleeding.

"Gentlemen," Mrs. Stecker said from the doorway. She shushed and held up two fingers like a den mother. Carl faced forward, and they quieted.

Michael leaned in and whispered in Carl's ear: "You pee your bed," and Mrs. Stecker nodded, as if she agreed. Carl's head tilted down, and then the line shuffled out of the classroom.

Michael had finally figured out his eyes and ears. They were getting worse. This week his father dropped the pink-eye theory and said Michael kept sticking in his grubby fingers and should leave himself alone. *Yeah right.* No medical tests would reveal the truth: that Michael had escaped, but now God was claiming him, marking his brain like He had marked his brother's. The bleeding would start any minute. Friday would be his first and last confession. It needed to be a good one—with all the absolution he could get.

At recess Michael and Carl played one of their games: The Nerf football was a time bomb. Carl kept getting blown up, but then he'd refuse to die. The rest of the third-grade boys played actual football farther down the parking lot.

Michael heard a boy call, "Hey, Michael." He turned. It was Rob Wilkoff and three others, including Tyler Casey. Rob stopped a few feet away and waved. "We just came to see if you wanted to play."

"You did?" Michael asked.

"Yeah, because Neil's absent," Rob said. "We thought maybe you guys could sub in."

"Really?"

"Yeah," Rob said. "Wait. What's that?" He cocked his curly blond head and squinted.

Michael stiffened. "What?"

"Oh my God! You're blee-ding!"

Michael couldn't help but dab at his eyes and ears. The boys laughed, high-fived, doubled over. Even Carl cracked up. Michael stood glaring. Then the laughter died, and they seemed out of ideas.

Finally, Tyler said, "Hey, Michael. You're a retard."

"Thank you," Michael said.

"You're a retard like your brother."

The boys howled.

Michael felt far away, like he was watching himself in a movie. "Say it again," he heard himself say. "See what happens."

Tyler stepped forward and smiled, flashing the gap in his two front teeth. He said it slow: "Like... your... bro-ther."

Tyler Casey's legs buckled. He squirmed on the blacktop, wheezing and holding his neck. Michael waited for the other boys' fists, but Rob and the rest stood gaping, as surprised as Michael, and backed away when the volunteer moms knelt down. The nurse came running. Tyler Casey seemed broken, as if he had suddenly stopped working, but the boys said, "He punched him. He punched him in the throat." When Michael looked at his hand, his fist was still clenched.

He was suspended. Mrs. Stecker said they'd pray for him, told him he could come back Friday to make a good confession. His mother sent him to his room, where he stared into the mirror and stretched his eyelids to see if the blood cracks had grown bigger.

When his father came home, his parents sat Michael down in the kitchen. His father said that people might deserve to get punched in the throat, but maybe we should aim for the more solid sternum or opt for the underused open-hand slap. Or better still, his mother said, turn the other cheek. "I don't recommend it," his father said.

Michael wanted to know if Tyler was okay. His mother said she had talked to Tyler's mom, who said he was fine, a little sore maybe, and certainly sorry for what he'd said.

She went to finish making dinner, ketchup-topped meatloaf and instant mashed potatoes, which Michael viewed as further punishment. *Dear God,* he prayed to the cross on the wall, *let this not be my last supper.* Michael set the table as his father sat with Sal, giving him sips of thickened milk from a hard plastic cup. Their red-checkered tablecloth still had last night's stir-fry crusted into its fabric, and Michael couldn't remember where the knives and forks should go.

His father asked Michael how he was feeling.

"Bad," Michael said.

"Where does it hurt?"

Michael didn't want to say eyes or ears, so he just said, "On the inside."

"How specific," his father said. "Say 'Ah.'"

"Ahhhh," Sal said and stuffed his tongue between his teeth.

"Oh," his father said. "Sal beat you to it. You want to be sick, Sal?"

"Yeah," he said. *If I get to stay home.*

"Okay then. I'll feel your glands in a minute."

"You're a scientist," Michael said. "You're not a real doctor."

His father whispered, "Your mother isn't a real cook, but we still eat her food. Now give me your glands."

Michael offered up his throat to his father's rough fingers and yelped.

"Sorry," his father said. "Not a real doctor." He released Michael and gave Sal another sip. "I think I know what your problem is."

"What?" Michael asked and leaned in.

"You're ugly." Their father smiled at Sal, who choked on his milk and splatter-shot it across the table. Sal's face was already turning red, his chest heaving up and down under his chest straps.

"I know, Sal. He so walked into that. Breathe, buddy, breathe."

Sal gave a last cough and finally sucked in enough air to howl "Ahhh-hhhhh!" *Oh my God. Classic. I'm dying over here.*

The next morning, their mother called the principal, the only nun at the school. Michael listened in. The reason she sent her son to a good Catholic school, paid all that money for a loving, Christian environment, was so children wouldn't say things like *retard*. "So what are you going to do about it? What do you expect when you let children torment him?" Michael had never heard someone talk that way to a nun. His mom had lost some heaven points, for sure. After she hung up, she said, "You're going back to school tomorrow, and Sal is coming for show-and-tell." Would there be others doing show-and-tell? "No," she said. "Just us."

When Sal came home, their mother laid him down on a blanket in the living room. She changed his diaper. When the plastic strip was yellow, that meant dry, like sand, like sun, but really it was the color of pee. Deep blue meant dirty, pee or poop, but it was the color of clean water. Michael didn't get it. He held Sal's hips while their mother did the dirty work. Sal's aide at school had marked in his notebook that Sal already had a "really good BM!" Their mother pulled on his pants and wedged a teddy bear between his legs so his knees didn't rub, then left to take her "power nap."

Michael lay on his stomach with his chin on his hands, facing Sal. It started with a staring contest. They had the same light brown hair, the same deep-brown eyes with little flecks of gold. That was the only similarity besides their thick, cowlicked eyebrows. But everyone still asked if they were identical.

"Mike-a," Sal said. *Blink.*

"Sal," Michael said. *You first.*

"Mike-a," Sal said. *You're such a bitch.*

"Sal," Michael said. *Takes one to know one.*

Sal thought for a second, planned his next move, filled his lungs. "Miiiike-aaaaaa!"

"Saaaaal-aaaa!" Michael yelled. "Salad."

"Eh-eh," Sal said. *Looks like you don't eat much of that, big boy.* "Momma," he said. *You know I'm her favorite, right?*

"BS."

Michael blinked, and they laughed. Their father called it "ping-pong," and they played it on road trips, volleying each other's names back and forth, slipping in mistakes and calling each other out. To the outside world, it was mostly just their names, but to them it meant much more.

Sal had a dimple. Michael closed his right eye. *Show. Tell.* He wished he could show Sal just from the neck up, have him be all head. He thought of telling his classmates about ping-pong, and the game where you asked Sal who's ugly, and he tells you, but they wouldn't understand. They'd just see the rest of him. Even when Carl came over for a playdate, he seemed afraid to talk to Sal, though he did like the ugly joke.

Sal put his finger in his mouth, chewed thoughtfully. Michael pulled it out, but Sal put it back in.

"Fine, but don't get mad when you bite yourself again. You know why I got in trouble? You know what they called you?"

Sal flashed his squirrel teeth like *Let me guess.*

Michael pulled Sal's finger out of his mouth again and wedged his own hand inside Sal's fist. "I'll miss you," he said. "When I'm gone."

Sal watched him, knitting his eyebrows. Michael waited for the voice, but it didn't come. If he had to guess, Sal was thinking something like *What are you talking about? Stop being weird, you weirdo.*

Michael didn't want to trouble him. He was sure the bleeding had started again. Not like his great uncle who'd smoked those cigarillos, who'd had a brain bomb go off in his head and was found on his kitchen floor in California. Michael imagined his own bleed as more gradual, as though God had stuck in a finger and was slowly scraping, starting a seep that would build pressure, that would soon trickle out of his ears and ooze through his eyes. Because Michael had proved not good enough and didn't deserve his luck.

Maybe later, after Michael was gone, when science developed enough to make Sal really talk, Sal would tell their parents about this moment. Maybe Sal would tell them how Michael loved him when no one watched.

At dinner, Michael begged their mother not to come to school. "Please," he said. "It's fine."

"It's not fine, honey. Everyone should meet your brother. What's the big deal? Are you embarrassed by him?"

"No," Michael said, which was only partly true. He looked at Sal chewing cut-up spaghetti in his wheelchair. He wouldn't be embarrassed if Sal acted like he did when they played ping-pong, or if someone burped or had to go to the bathroom and Sal laughed. But if Sal yelled for what seemed like no reason, or if a string of drool crept down his chin, then Michael would have trouble.

His father shoveled pasta into his mouth. "I told you he'd be better off in public school."

His mother said almost to herself, "He'd get stabbed."

His father shrugged. "Even that'd be less expensive."

She fed Sal a bite of ground beef and then glanced at Michael. "I'm worried about you."

"Okay," Michael said, because he already knew that. More than once, when he was supposed to be in bed, he overheard them talking about him in hushed tones. At least when he was gone, they wouldn't fight as much about money. It'd be one less mouth to feed, and even Michael would admit it was quite a mouth.

"Do you need to see the psychologist again?"

"I'm fine," Michael said. Anything but the man with folded hands.

The next morning, their mother cradled Sal in her arms as she climbed the two flights to Michael's classroom, with Michael at her heels. Sal's powerchair was too heavy to lift up the stairs, so they brought his manual, which came last, courtesy of the janitor and the gym teacher, both swearing softly as it banged against the walls. Between flights, his mother said, "I'll write the pope for an elevator."

When she rolled Sal in, Michael's classmates stared: the boys in wrinkled white dress shirts with maroon ties and gray slacks, the girls in white blouses under brown-and-tan checked jumpers. Everyone wore penny loafers. As he was taking a seat in the front row, Michael's eyes met Tyler Casey's. Tyler sneered, flashing the gap in his teeth.

Michael saw how his classmates looked at Sal in his wheelchair, at his immaculate white tennis shoes stuffed into the footrests, at the plastic AFOs Velcro-ed to Sal's shins with white tube socks folded over the top, at his blue shorts that hid his diaper but not his skeleton knees, at his fist clamped tight in "stranger alert," the thumb laced under two fingers as though it had grown that way, at his mouth hanging open, at his eyes staring back.

Hey, Michael, your brother's a retard.

I know. Though the doctor was the only one allowed to say it: "severe retardation."

Their mother said it was his classmates' lucky day. They got to meet a very special person: Michael's twin brother, Sal. They might remember him from their first communion, but that was two years ago. So here's Sal. "Can you say hi, Sal?"

Sal smiled just barely.

She said it would take him a while to warm up. She told them the story about his premature birth and how Sal had hurt his brain, the part that lets you walk and talk. She said, "Sal sits in this special chair. He has an even more special chair at home that he can drive himself. He goes to a special school, but he understands everything and has his own special way of communicating." She was saying "special" an awful lot, which Michael thought they'd use later. *Your brother's special. You're special. Your family's very special. When you guys go out to eat, do you order the special?*

Rob Wilkoff raised his hand. He asked, "How does Sal go to the bathroom?"

Their mother reached into Sal's black leather wheelchair bag and grabbed one of his diapers. Michael cringed. It was like she was holding up Sal's underwear, but Sal didn't seem to mind. Michael thought they'd also use this later, that he'd go to the cloakroom and find his coat pockets stuffed with baby diapers.

Their mother said, "Sal, you're being very quiet. Can you show them how you talk?"

Here we go, thought Michael. Sal would "Uhhh" and Tyler Casey would laugh and Michael would have to jump on the desk, roundhouse him in the face, and choke him out with his own clip-on tie. Michael stared down at his desk.

Carl raised his hand. "I know. Sal, can you tell them who's ugly?"

Sal smiled and then lurched against his straps. "Mike-aaaa!"

The room erupted. Everyone laughed. Good old Carl. Sal had made a joke, and he squirmed in his chair, flashing his dimple.

The girls said, "Awww. He's so cute."

They said it like Sal was some puppy, but Michael breathed.

Then their mother got down to business. She said, "Sal is a lot like you. He doesn't like to have his feelings hurt. Sal has a mental disability, but he is *not* retarded. That's a bad word. It hurts him and his family. We don't use the *R* word, do we, Sal?"

Sal smiled. *Of course not. We're civilized.*

His classmates shook their heads at the thought of people still uttering those three syllables.

Michael's mother asked if he'd like to say anything. He wanted to tell his classmates that Sal was better than any of them, better than all their brothers and sisters combined, but his face felt hot, his lungs shallow. He couldn't find the words. "That's my twin brother," he finally said. "Sal."

Mrs. Stecker started to clap, and everyone joined in, even Tyler Casey.

When Sal and his mother left, Michael thought his classmates would start with the taunts, which would roll off their tongues like French: *re-tar-ded*. He thought they'd comment on his eyes and ears. But they were so nice. It was disappointing because he wanted to have his suspicions confirmed, but all they said was that his brother was "cool." Michael was even invited to a birthday party, told to bring his brother. What was wrong with these people?

Then, thank God, on a bathroom break, while Michael was peeing,

Tyler Casey stepped in front of the urinal beside him. They were alone. Michael kept his eyes on the bathroom wall, focused on a single brick, and held his breath. Now he would hear it. He was ready.

"Look," Tyler said. "I'm sorry." Michael turned his head. Tyler Casey was smiling with his gap tooth. His eyes were soft. He actually wanted to be forgiven.

"Apology accepted," Michael said and turned the rest of his body. Tyler Casey's pant leg grew dark with piss.

After recess, they were back in the classroom for religion. Tyler had not told on him, had scrubbed his pant leg with pink liquid soap. Maybe you don't tell people when you get peed on, Michael thought. Michael waited all recess for a push from behind, but Tyler kept his distance.

Standing beside a priest, Mrs. Stecker scanned the desks, extending her flabby arm like an over-the-hill game-show model. "Ladies and gentlemen," she said, "any last-minute questions for Father Tierney?"

It was the priest who'd given him first communion, who'd given him half. Father Tierney stood with his stooped back to the blackboard, his hands folded at his waist. He had rosacea, which made his skin look spanked. He didn't bring raccoon and moose puppets like Father Bishop or speak in a whispery baritone like Father Jacobs, whom they all agreed sounded like Jesus. Father Tierney just answered their questions in his gravelly voice and, when he got too close, smelled like moisturizing lotion infused with frankincense. He seemed very tired, like it hurt to move, like he could barely forgive himself let alone other people. For all Michael knew, Father Tierney would only half forgive him. But Michael bet he could damn with the best of them. Who knew what penance he would prescribe? Pray all day? One hundred push-ups and a thousand Hail Marys?

"No questions?" Mrs. Stecker asked again. She and the priests had done a good job of explaining things. The children had reached the age of reason. They could tell right from wrong. They knew mortal sin from venial sin. With venial, you just weakened your bond with God, but with mortal you completely severed yourself from Him and had to make a good confession or else. They tried to downplay the "else," but everyone knew it was Hell, eternal damnation, the worst pain you could imagine, breaking your arm times a million forever. Michael swiped his ear canal with his finger and looked: no blood, but he didn't have much time.

"This is your last chance before the big day," Mrs. Stecker said.

Carl raised his hand. "If you want to go behind the screen, can you still confess?"

Even Michael rolled his eyes. Mrs. Stecker had explained this several times already. The penitential grille was so you could confess anonymously, but the Fathers encouraged you to walk past the kneeler with the screen and sit at the chair facing them, since, hey, we're all sinners with no need to hide.

Father Tierney nodded. "You can kneel behind the screen if that's more comfortable."

"Awesome," Carl said.

Michael would choose the screen for sure. He had a long list of sins, so many he'd written them down. It was longer than his Christmas list. With luck his eyes and ears would hold out till he was done.

Thinking about his brother, Michael raised his hand. "If you mortal sin, and you can't confess, what happens?"

"And why can't you confess?" Father Tierney asked.

"Because . . . you just can't."

Father Tierney nodded. "You have to be as honest as you can. You have to be honest with yourself and the priest and God. And it helps to be sorry in your heart."

Michael sat back, and Mrs. Stecker scanned the desks. "Any other questions?"

Carl raised his hand.

Someone said, "Here we go again."

It was "shitty dinner night." It was the only time Michael was allowed to say "shitty": once a week in a dinner context. His mom made powdered macaroni and cheese with sliced hot dogs. The dish was one of Sal's favorites, but their dad was not a fan. He cooked himself a venison burger from a deer he'd taken last season. It looked like shoe leather, but he kept *Mmmmm*-ing loudly and offering Michael and Sal a bite. Michael would not miss his parents fighting about his dad hunting and being away from home. Maybe when Michael died, his father would have him mounted on the wall too.

Sal chewed too quickly, the mashed-up macaroni dropping from his mouth. He had shitty dinner all over his face, blotches of yellow caked to his chin, with half his meal in the well of his bib. Though he hadn't swallowed, Sal opened his mouth for more. "That's good eating," their mother said. "Bravo." She hovered close with his spoon and his cup of thickened milk.

Their dad said, "We can just put his bib in the fridge for leftovers."

In response, their mother belched—more of a roar, really. Sal cracked up, and then they all laughed. As a family, they were allowed to engage in a burp competition within the confines of their own home. His parents had educated Michael on the appropriateness of belching: only for Sal's entertainment, and if they weren't at home, then *sehr verboten*.

"Mom," Michael said. "How come Sal's not getting confession?"

She glanced at his father, who looked down at the sesame seeds on his bun.

"Well, honey, because he doesn't need it."

"Why not?"

"God knows what's in his heart, baby."

"He's special?"

She winced. "No, but he's already forgiven."

"Why? How do you know that? How do you know Sal won't go to Hell?"

"Okay," his father said.

Sal spit out his macaroni and made his squirrel teeth. *What do you mean Hell? Am I going to Hell?*

"No one is going to Hell," his mother said firmly. "Not you and not Sal. You're good boys. What could you possibly do to get sent to Hell?"

Michael said nothing. He had a whole list.

Their father threw down his burger. "I told you to send him to public school. I said the nuns would mess him up."

"There's only one nun!"

His voice softened. "Look, Michael. You can't be such a worrywart. You're too young to think about this stuff. Go play outside, for Christ's sake."

Michael glanced out the window. "But it's dark."

"Not now. I mean in general. Don't worry." He smiled at Sal. "That is, unless Sal is a grave sinner. What have you done, Sal? Out with it!"

Sal grinned. He had no comment. Only Michael knew Sal's mortal sins. If Sal wasn't getting confession, it meant they thought he was innocent, an angel like his grandmother said. It meant he couldn't sin because he wasn't smart enough to know right from wrong. A vegetable can't commit a crime. There were no carrots in jail, no cabbages serving time. But Michael knew Sal was smarter than that.

That night, after their mother turned out the light, Michael flipped on his flashlight and went over his list. It was about two hundred sins long, ending this afternoon, when he had peed on Tyler Casey's leg. In between was everything he could remember. He had some good ones. There was wrath when Michael punched Tyler in the throat. There was greed when Michael shoplifted candy from the grocery store. There was gluttony (just look at him). He talked back to his father and mother, and he told Sal to shut up. He took toys from Sal, and no one saw but God.

Sal lay snoring on a mattress on the other side of the room. He was no angel. He'd stolen candy with Michael. At the checkout, Sal stabbed his good hand at a Three Musketeers bar—*This one, please*—relying on Michael to smuggle it out. Sal too had talked back to his mom and dad, had screamed at them. He monopolized their mother's time, refusing to eat for anyone else. He'd bitten his mother on the arm when she tried to put him in his stander. He'd rammed his footrest into Michael's shin.

Michael turned off his flashlight and tried to fall asleep, but all he could think about was his brother crying in Hell, his wheelchair metal glowing hot. He could see Sal's skin bubble and break, see his face blotched scarlet like Father Tierney's. He pictured Sal's face like Jesus's face, the Jesus on his mother's cross, twisted in anguish. He knew exactly what Sal would sound like, wailing like he did after the surgery: *It hurts it hurts it hurts.* Michael cradled his stomach, trying to find comfort in Sal's steady snore. He started a Hail Mary. He knew what he had to do.

The next day after school, while Sal was in his stander, Michael got a step stool and spread the stander tray with sheets of white paper, colored pencils, and a jar of red paint. On each piece of paper, Michael had sketched Sal's sins, stick-people style. He dipped Sal's finger in the jar.

"I'll have Father forgive you from long distance," Michael said. "It's the best we can do." The red paint dripped from Sal's digit. It looked the way Michael imagined his own fingers would after a swipe at his eyes and ears. "Sal, you have to sign these. I won't be around to do this again."

Sal grinned. "Mike-a," he said. *Are you serious?*

"Do you want to go to Hell?"

Sal looked sideways. *Uhhhhh . . .*

"Do you know what Hell is like?" Michael pinched Sal's inner bicep and twisted. Sal yelled out, balled his hands into fists, and gnashed his teeth. *You dick. What's wrong with you?* He lurched his head toward Michael and snapped his jaws. Michael said, "I'm just showing you. It's like that but much worse."

Their mom called from the kitchen: "Are you boys playing nice?"

"Yes," Michael said.

"Eh-eh," Sal said.

"Then sign it. Hurry up." Michael raised the paint can to Sal's finger for a fresh coat and put the pictures under Sal's hand, which hovered above Sal shoplifting, the store items labeled, his wheelchair clearly visible. "Here, Sal." Michael pointed to a white space.

"Mmmmm," Sal said, pursing his lips. *I don't know.* His finger twitched once, twice, and then dropped onto the paper, smudging his fingerprint. Michael turned to the next picture and tapped. "And here."

On Friday Michael sat in the pew, eyeing the confessionals along the wall. It was almost his turn, but he had a problem. Mrs. Stecker had divided them into three lines outside the three confession booths. The other kids had Father Bishop and Father Jacob, who smiled and waved as they walked into the booths, but Michael was in line for Father Tierney, who hobbled into his booth without looking at the students. Michael's pocket was thick with Sal's painted pictures and his own list. Would Father Tierney be up for the job? Would he be powerful enough to forgive long distance? Michael thought of switching lines, but Mrs. Stecker stood sentinel by the altar.

Five pews in front of Michael, in the Father Bishop line, Carl walked into the wooden booth and pulled the velvet curtain shut. Good. He'd confess to being a Judas. Get that out of the way. Carl also shot cats with BB guns. He'd be in there a while. Ten pews up, Tyler Casey exited Father Jacob's booth, smiling. Only Tyler Casey would smile after confession, but it must have felt good to no longer be such an asshole. Michael decided not to hate him anymore. He felt serene as he approached the end of his short life. He looked at Jesus on the cross. Sometimes Sal looked like Jesus, in his stander with his splayed hands and open mouth. His mother said Sal's wheelchair was his cross to bear, but that made no sense. Sal's wheelchair bore *him*.

Michael's eyes and ears felt okay. He would make it to the end of confession, though maybe he'd be struck down right after. That'd be fine as long as he and Sal were forgiven.

When it was his turn, Michael chose the grille. Father Tierney was on the other side. The perforations in the screen reminded Michael of the lamp shade he used to put on Sal's head when they played tank and raced around the neighborhood. In the darkness, he could just make out Father Tierney's pink lips.

"Bless me, Father, for I have sinned," Michael said. They went through the spiel and then Michael began listing his sins, but after one minute, Father Tierney said, "Kid, you can just summarize. You don't have to tell me every one."

"Okay," Michael said. "Hold on." He had lost his place.

"You're reading them?"

"Yes."

"All right, let me see." The priest's liver-spotted hand stuck out of the screen's edge, and Michael fed him the folded pages. Michael heard him uncrinkle and smooth the paper. His pink lips mouthed the words. He said, "Jesus." It was bad. The priest was already praying.

"I also have my twin brother's list, if you can do that real quick," Michael said. The hand came again from the edge of the screen and snapped like it was hungry. Michael dug Sal's pictures from his pocket and fed them to Father. He heard the pages uncrinkle and tear. The paint must have made them stick together. He hoped they were still legible.

"He can't talk," Michael said, "but that's how he signs. That red mark. That's him in the chair. He's really sorry, so please. Just do it from long distance." Michael heard Father Tierney breathing, almost like Sal snoring. His lips were still. Had he fallen asleep? "Father?"

The chair creaked, and the lips were gone. Father Tierney emerged from behind the screen and stood before the velvet kneeler supporting Michael. He was breathing heavy under his black collar, his eyes wide and his face blazing with red splotches. Michael stared up at the white gap in his throat and didn't know if he should run or start begging again. But then Father reached out, grabbed Michael's fat face with both hands, and shook it. He said, "Stand up."

Michael stood. Father's hands felt like wax paper, but they held him tight. The priest pressed Michael into his chest. Michael smelled the lotion and frankincense and something else, a sweet rotting. He wanted to scream, but his lungs wouldn't fill. He loved his father and mother. He loved his twin brother, Sal. Carl. Tyler Casey. He was sorry. The priest's forearm dug into Michael's neck like a vise, and he stroked Michael's hair with his other trembling hand.

He said, "All is forgiven. Everything. You're free. You, your brother. You're forgiven forever. You get a pass, understand? You're forgiven forever." Then he shoved Michael through the velvet curtain and out of the booth, and Michael forgot his lists. He forgot to ask how many Our Fathers, how many Hail Marys.

He ran down the aisle and through the double doors, and he didn't stop until he reached home, where he let himself in with his key. He rushed into the living room, climbed the footrest into Sal's stander, and leaned into the leather. He barely fit. As he folded the Velcro straps tight along his own back, he breathed in and felt the gray pads squeeze his rib cage. No one was there to crank him tighter. No one saw but God. He would stand until his eyes and ears did not ache, until he believed Father Tierney. He would stand there until his mother laid Sal down on the blanket below, and he could tell him the good news.

III
WHISPER WOLF

6

As they toured the shitty Victorian, Gabe watched his wife fawn over the ornate tile on the fireplace and the flowery wooden cornices above the doorways. He watched her ignore the obvious creak and sag in the too-narrow steps up to the bedrooms. He looked on as she pretended to be interested in the unfinished basement and its dungeon-like coal room, where a small, fossilized turd of carbon had been left in the corner. He smiled as she swooned at the garden, which had huge stupid sunflowers as tall as Gabe and raised beds of flowers that looked as folded and fancy as origami. He heard her try to imagine how they'd convert this place for Sal: build a wing on the first floor for his bedroom and bath, add a graded incline up to the kitchen and a ramp out the front door and back, which would both have to be widened. The house fit their main requirement: It was in a good school district that always passed its Special Education levy—but it was already on the edge of their price range. With all the necessary modifications . . . he crunched the numbers and his head swam.

"It's not going to work, Han," he said, and she grew quiet. This was their twentieth failed house in six months of searching.

Hannah said, "But it has a foyer . . ."

"Is Sal gonna sleep in the foyer?"

She stared into the foyer, where Sal was not going to sleep. "Okay," she said. "I just want to look at the garden one last time."

"It's a nope?" asked the realtor, who'd lost faith in a commission long ago.

"It's a nope," Gabe said.

After years of struggling with his research and publishing low-impact papers, Gabe had finally been awarded major funding from the NIH. One and a quarter million. He'd gotten his own hoopla in the hall, his boss taking the whole lab out for an awkward night on the town. All his early mornings, all his Saturdays had paid off. He'd been promoted and now had his own lab, with the salary and perks of being an Assistant Professor. He no longer had to murder his own mice. He just saw their beautiful data. But he still came home to his family's cramped and boxy house in Cleveland Heights, the boys soon going into seventh grade and still crowded in their same bedroom.

When Gabe was growing up, his parents could barely make rent off his mother's secretary job and his father's military pension. He wanted to give his sons the life he never had. And Hannah was on board. She wanted a nicer house in a better district, in an outer-ring suburb where maybe Michael and Sal could go to the same school. But now, as they got in the Taurus and started back home, it felt like they'd never have a house that would work for their family.

Gabe pushed in the dashboard lighter and got his cigarette ready, but before the lighter popped, he remembered an empty lot on the edge of town he'd seen advertised. He pulled over to take a quick peek at the map.

"Where are we going?" Hannah asked.

"You'll see," he said, and stuck his cigarette to the glowing coil.

He stopped in front of a field with patchy grass, about a full acre all around, a few maples and shrubs, and far from neighbors and prying Mrs. Snavelys. It was a blank canvas.

He said, "Imagine for a moment. Imagine one place in this godforsaken world built just for him. Hallways wide enough for his wheels. Every doorway flat with no steps. A driveway large enough for his van. A new blacktop so the lift never stalls. Michael and Sal each with their own room, Michael on the top floor, Sal with us on the bottom so you can always hear him."

Hannah stared into the field. He thought she'd complain about how it was too far from town, how there was nowhere to walk to, how building was such a headache. But she said, "And a bathroom with a walk-in shower. So we don't have to lift him into the tub."

"Yes," he said. "We'll have tracks on the ceiling to slide him around. Or maybe a hydraulic lift."

Suddenly, she was hugging him, and he draped his neck on hers like they were geese. He meant: *And for you, my love, not another sore shoulder or strained back, never another creaky hip or burning hand—less fatigue, more intimacy, more of our old selves.* It didn't matter that they'd be mortgaged up to their ears, leveraged for life, because: *Imagine a house for him.*

They went home, bought the lot, and found a builder. The house was ready by the following summer, just in time for Michael and Sal to start eighth grade.

Hannah busied herself with furnishing the rooms and preparing her new garden. She got a pile of hot mulch dumped in the driveway and put in beds of bulging zucchini and tomatoes, of flowers with petals as soft as mouse ears, their perfume sweet enough to make Gabe stop while he was mowing the lawn and sniff. Did the deer take out their fair share of flowers and produce? Yes. But Hannah's boogers were black, just the way she liked them.

At night, they clung to each other like when they were first married, except now they had central air and could hold each other longer. They still made love, if not as often as he'd like, but hey, she scheduled him in. Her stress was under control, her IBS at bay. They didn't travel, but Gabe hardly had any time to hunt, so maybe they were even. It was 1997. They were getting older together, forty-six now. They sometimes joked about getting divorced just for the government benefits. "Oh, as a single mom with Sal?" she said. "The checks would roll in."

"But then who would you have to laugh with?"

"I'd hire a guy." She patted his cheek. "No, you're right. I'll keep you around."

At dinner, Gabe watched her feed Sal bite after bite. She'd change his diaper for the ten thousandth time, inspecting his loins for any errant speck. It was a kind of prayer. She talked to Sal like she was talking to an extension of herself. "We have to go pick up your brother, Sal. Why isn't there anything good on TV tonight?" Sal smirking like a sphinx. Sweet Sal. Funny Sal. He was hers in a way Gabe struggled to fathom. Gabe worked so she could stay home. That was his gift to her. But Gabe wasn't sure if Sal required this much attention, or if Hannah just convinced herself he did.

It was fine. As Principal Investigator, Gabe loved the lab even more than before. He started going in earlier, coming home later. He loved slipping on his white lab coat, feeling his shoulders relax and his mind sharpen, as if he were donning the costume of an analytical superhero. He loved the humming fridges and freezers, full of brain samples sliced razor thin, swimming in their solutions. They looked like little pieces of snot yet contained the keys to consciousness. He loved the animal facility on the next floor, those brave mice breeding themselves stupid in the name of scientific progress, the air pungent with their pheromones and turd pellets. He loved the lab itself, its black counters so clean, its white tiled floor immaculate, everything sterile, disinfected against any outside life. He loved the electron microscope that let him see the world up close, examine it down to its very grain. He loved disappearing into the tiny world of neurons and synapses, time slipping away like sodium channels firing down an axon. As soon as he looked up, he felt lost. People were too big, too complex, with all their curveball emotions. If he could just cut open their heads and go cell by silent cell, maybe he'd begin to understand.

The boys turned fourteen. The cold returned, and the trees broke into technicolor death, into wild hues of red, orange, yellow as their chlorophyll degraded. Gabe spent his long morning commute admiring the show and blowing smoke out his window with the heat blasting. One day, he came home to Hannah pouting at the stove.

She said, "We have another problem."

"What?"

"The boiler."

"No."

"Yes, and last week the faucets. I'm thinking this builder was no good."

"He had connections to the Amish," Gabe said. "They're craftsmen."

"Who don't use electricity."

"Not true. They're just careful about it."

"I can't even shower Sal."

"Doesn't need it," Gabe said. "My son smells great. He gets it from me."

Sal smiled. After two appeals, he finally had a shower chair. His hydraulic lift, the Hoyer, had come last week after only one appeal. It didn't matter what Hannah asked for, the insurance company said No. All paths led there, a clusterfuck maze with a multitude of corridors winding to the large white patch of No. This last year, for Sal's powerchair replacement, the insurance only paid half, leaving Hannah and Gabe to cover the other four grand. The company made the decisions seem rational with their "careful deliberations" and passive-voice "it has been decided" bullshit. Some asshole with a tie, some Stan or John, had decided against their son receiving help. Writing appeals, begging on the phone, was a part-time job. Gabe was worried that the stress would go to Hannah's gut again. Why did they make you work so hard for help? If this was the "good" insurance, what was it like to have the bad?

Hannah put a chicken breast in the grinder with applesauce for Sal.

"Are you actually staying for dinner tonight?" Gabe asked.

"Oh shush," she said. Hannah had volunteered to be the local parent rep for the Cuyahoga County Special Education Center, reporting back to the local moms about services they could apply for. That was on top of the night class she was taking at Case Western, something about women's fiction.

"Where's Young Werther?" Gabe asked.

"Michael's locked himself in his room again. He's still upset about moving. I think the teenage angst has finally arrived."

"Finally?" Gabe said. "That kid was born angsty."

"So, about the boiler. Should I call a repair guy?"

Gabe said, "I'll fix it."

She laughed. "What have you ever fixed?"

Gabe looked at the wall. There was her new cross featuring a Jesus levitating with arms raised. He didn't look like he'd just been tortured. He seemed happy to be hanging out, had a little muscle on him. "I like it," he'd said when she brought it home. "It's suburban Jesus. He looks like he plays tennis."

Now he asked, "How much did that cost?"

"That's between me and Jesus." She looked over at his new deer head, the six-point buck he'd taken last season, its marble eyes watching them age. "How much did *that* cost?"

Gabe laughed. "Where's old Jesus?"

"I gave it to Michael," she said.

"Just what he needs," Gabe said. " A teenage angst Jesus."

He got a beer from the fridge. Sal was staring into the plaid tablecloth, a string of drool down his chin. Gabe took the washcloth from his bib and cleaned his mouth. "There," he said. "More studly."

Hannah sat down with Sal's plate. "Sal wants to show you something. Are you ready?"

Sal smiled and said, "Eh." He stretched his neck. He was warming up.

"Sal," she said, "what do you think of your dear old dad?"

There was a delay, but then both eyes jerked up into his sockets. Sal had learned to roll his eyes. "Oh God!" Gabe said. "We've got a real teenager here too."

Sal stuffed his tongue between his teeth. A little nonverbal communication. Sal hadn't learned to say a new word in years. He'd topped out at eight. Hannah was trying to get his school to set him up with a new augmentative communication device, but they were dragging their feet.

"Tell Michael dinner is ready," Hannah said.

Gabe nodded and climbed the newly carpeted steps to Michael's room. At least the builder hadn't fucked that up.

The move had been difficult for Michael. Though he had his own bedroom, he'd wanted to sleep on the pull-out couch in Sal's room. It took him a whole week to finally sleep upstairs. Gabe thought some space from his twin would do Michael good. He still spent most of his time after school talking to Sal, telling him every detail of his day as if they were still six.

Gabe knocked on the door. No response. The handle wouldn't turn, so he took his fingernail and twisted the divot in the lock. Bingo. He opened the door and choked on incense. The boom box was blasting some kind of mumbled dirge. He saw the band posters: Green Day and the Red Hot Chili Peppers and Woodstock '94. It was if a set designer had clumsily decorated a room for a script that read: modern teenager. The only element that seemed off was Hannah's old cross on the wall, Jesus wincing in pain. Though now his expression was appropriate: The music was truly terrible.

Michael was on the bed, staring up at the ceiling. He had this idiotic haircut, shaved underneath and parted down the middle in long strands, framing his face like a curtain does a stage. Gabe had made *one* joke, said it looked like a vagina. Big mistake. He had to apologize, take him out for a burger and fries, Michael's stomach still giving reliable access to his heart.

"You in here, Young Werther?"

"Stop calling me that," Michael snapped.

The kid was hair trigger. Gabe would stumble into one of Michael's insecurities and uncover an endless well of rage and resentment. Where did that come from? Who put that there? Gabe studied the kid's acne, wanted to run his fingers over it like braille, as if it would finally tell him what was wrong with his son.

"You got a science test tomorrow, right? I'll help you."

Michael was working something in his mouth. He flipped his retainer upside down so the metal loops over his canines hung down. "F-anks," he said, then flashed his metal fangs.

After dinner, on the couch, Gabe explained the biology of a cell and saw Michael's eyes light up. *There I am. There's my boy.* Thank God he was done at the Catholic school, with all their prayers and magical thinking. Now he was learning the proper curriculum.

A few days later, when Gabe came home, he found a test at his place on the table, a big fat A scrawled at the top. Michael was usually a C or B student. This was a curious development. Underneath was an essay on how power corrupts the pig characters in Orwell's *Animal Farm*. B. Yes. Science for the win. He put his hands on Michael's head and said, "Bzzzz," as if he were being electrocuted by his brain.

In November, he took Michael deer hunting, letting him play hooky from school. In the ride over to the camp, Gabe offered him his old hunting knife, the one Gabe's father had given him but never taught him to use. It had a white pearl handle and a silver blade. "This is for you," he said. Michael said, "Sweet" and ran the blade against his palm. Gabe thought for sure he'd slice himself open, but Michael sheathed it back in its leather case.

Gabe took a buck in the late morning and then staked out with his son, made sure he got a good shot. Right at dusk, a beautiful six point came broadside. *Take him take him take him*, Gabe whispered. It would happen. His son would feel that ancient rush and make a nice memory.

But what did his kid do? He sat like a mushroom, pretended he didn't see it. Jesus Christ. It was right there. It was so right there, so freaking close that Gabe couldn't help himself. He ripped the shotgun from Michael's hands, aimed, and fired. When the deer ran thirty yards and stumbled, he smiled at his son and said, "Good shot."

"You shot it," Michael said, and Gabe said, "Not if anyone asks." There was a one-buck limit.

Gabe wanted a picture. He stuck his fingers inside the bullet wound and brushed the blood on the boy's face. Michael jerked away. "Stop!"

"Come on," Gabe said. He got in another good swipe. "German hunting tradition."

"Of course it is," Michael said. "Only Nazis would think of this."

Gabe shrugged. "That was later."

It was at home that Michael's eyes welled up, and Hannah asked, "What did you do?" Gabe confessed, but what was his crime? Attempting to bond with his boy, who refused to see what was in front of him? He should have taken Sal, who knew how to keep a secret and needed Gabe to shoot for him anyway.

Gabe tried to win Michael back. He apologized. He took him for a burger and watched him wolf down fries like he wanted to choke on them. One night, Gabe was trying to engage the boy and asked him how his day had gone. Michael started explaining something he learned in honors science, something about cell mitosis.

Sal, meanwhile, yelled "Ahhhhhh!" from his chair. "Dada. Ahhhhh-rah," he said.

"Sal," Gabe said. "Can it for a second."

Sal smirked, flashed his dimple, and said even louder: "Ahhhhh!"

"Sal," Gabe said. "Stop heckling. What do you want? You want to play soccer?"

Gabe got up from the couch and retrieved the blue bouncy ball, set it up in front of Sal's footrest, and backed up three paces. He got in a wide stance.

"Actually," Michael said. "You want to know what he's saying?"

"I'd love to know," Gabe said. He didn't finish the sentence. *But I can't.* There was danger in filling Sal in with yourself, overwriting him, making him into this articulate person when what you've actually made is a mirror. It was as if you looked into a microscope and saw your own eyeball staring back. He couldn't believe that Michael was still doing it after all this time. Still living in a land of magical thinking. He didn't see what was right in front of him.

Michael asked again, "Do you want to know?"

"All right," Gabe said. "What's he saying?"

"He's saying you broke the law," Michael said. "He saying you're a poacher and should be in jail."

Gabe swallowed. "Well, Sal, that's a bit harsh."

Sal smiled with his hands splayed out. He laughed and said, "Yeah!" and then let out another whale call. Sal cranked his joystick forward and rammed his footrest against the ball, which bounced to Gabe's left and ricocheted off a chair.

Michael raised his arms and yelled: "Goal!"

7

The Wolf whispered, *Eat.*

The Wolf whispered, *Drink.*

It whispered, *Mom-my, Dad-dy. Mich-ael.*

Michael sat next to Sal at the dinner table and was supposed to feed him. But he couldn't stop watching the Wolf whisper into Sal's ear through the small plastic pillow speaker Velcro-ed to his headrest. His parents didn't know why Sal's new computer was called the Whisper Wolf. It was just the one the therapist recommended, that insurance would pay for.

The worst kind of snow fell in fat flakes outside the sliding glass door: not enough for no school but enough that he'd have to shovel. It was December. The Wolf had arrived two weeks ago, and now Sal's hand was perched tight in front of the block-shaped red switch suction-cupped to his wheelchair tray.

Before the Wolf, Sal had a picture board that he stabbed at unreliably with his good hand. He'd experimented with computers at school, but his fine motor wasn't great. They never found the right one. At his new school, they were convinced the Wolf would work.

Now a black metal arm extended up from his wheelchair frame, holding a computer screen in front of him like a platter presenting lit-up icons: a wavy glass of water, a plain hamburger, a dopey grinning cartoon boy. That last one was supposed to be Michael and looked nothing like him, unless Sal's speech therapist was trying to say something.

The Wolf whispered, *Milkshake* and *Talk*, *Done* and *Back*. It was scanning the Dinner page made for dinner conversations, and Sal's hand was hovering over the red switch, ready to strike in his patented slo-mo when the Wolf whispered something he actually wanted to say. Michael knew his brother wanted to say far more.

His mother whistled in two tones from across the table: *we-wu*. "Earth to Michael," she said and pointed to Sal's empty mouth.

"Sorry, bro." Michael raised a spoonful of butter-sopped mashed potatoes and made an airplane sound. "Quick," Michael said, "emergency landing," and dive-bombed toward Sal's mouth. Just as the metal slipped past Sal's teeth, he snapped them shut, capsizing the spoon, spilling its contents down his chin. "Come on," Michael said. "You murderer."

Without taking his eyes off the television news, their father made mouth explosions and whisper-screams.

"Mom," Michael said. "I quit."

"Sal," she said. "You stop teasing your brother."

"Yeah," his father said. "Even if it's fun."

Sal grinned around his clenched teeth: *Ssssssucker*.

Sal had been putting the screws to his family all evening. Their mother tried to feed him, but she was stonewalled. Their father lasted a few bites before he threw down the spoon and said, "Next batter." With Michael, Sal cooperated for a few bites too, even opened his mouth for more and glugged milk, building Michael's confidence before he got that light in his eye and locked his jaw. *Guess what? Also . . . fuck . . . you.*

Then there was the coughing, the bits of food that flew at Michael like birdshot, that stuck to his cheek, lodged in his hair, clung to his t-shirt. Sal didn't cough on purpose, but aiming was another thing. Batey sat like a gargoyle next to Sal's wheelchair, waiting for dropped food. Sal was by far his favorite person.

Michael mumbled, "Stop making me look bad," but was interrupted by the Wolf, who whispered, *Eat*. "Yeah," Michael said. "Listen to your Wolf."

His mother reminded him: "He does better from the corner of his mouth." Michael recalled her other tips: Sips of thickened milk from plastic cup with the big lip smoothed the swallowing. If he coughed, give him a moment. Maybe several. Make regular trips to the microwave for reheating. Wipe with a washcloth or his chin got chapped. She was letting Michael help more. But that didn't mean Sal would always accept it.

Michael loaded the spoon again, this time with baked fish, and steered it to his brother's mouth. "Open sesame," he said. Sal made his squirrel teeth. Michael waited, studying the lay of his eyebrows, the wrinkle of his lip, but the voice did not arrive.

When he explained to himself how he could often "hear" his brother, it sounded silly, but deep down, understanding Sal felt true. Sal's brain damage was undeniable, but Michael felt like his own brain was damaged in a way that no one noticed. The damage connected them, like two cups on a string. Sal's brain spoke into one cup, and sometimes Michael, with the other cup to his ear, could hear him, especially when Michael concentrated and got in a certain altered brain state. But Sal's voice was growing weaker and less frequent. Michael feared that one day he would never hear Sal in his head again.

The speech therapist said there was a large gap between Sal's receptive and expressive. No computer would ever close it. Sal's words had topped out at eight: "Eh," "Eh-eh," "Hi," "Yeah," "More," "Mom-ma," "Da-da," and "Mike-a." But the Wolf would give Sal more to say. You had to make the least dangerous assumption, the therapist said: Presume competence, assume communicative intent even when it's not clear. Michael repeated that phrase like a mantra: *The least dangerous. The least dangerous. With Sal you make the least dangerous.*

The Wolf couldn't fix Sal's intelligence test, which said Sal was six months to six years, even though Michael and Sal were now fourteen. How could Sal be all those ages at the same time? *Scattered skills*, said the docs, which sounded like some rap group. And okay, sometimes Sal was six months, still wore diapers and couldn't even hold up his own head for more than a few seconds, had to wear that black foam strap around his forehead like some disabled ninja, slobber dripping like a faucet set to trickle so the pipes didn't freeze. But other times he was ten or more. He laughed at Michael's jokes, laughed harder than kids their own age, which Michael thought very mature. Sal even smiled when Michael showed him the old moldy copies of *Playboy* he'd found in a garbage bag down by the creek. How old are you if you smile at bare breasts and airbrushed vaginas, even if they're waterlogged and from 1988? If Sal were truly six, he'd cringe or look away. Sometimes Sal could be an old man, especially with pain tolerance. He already had osteoporosis, took calcium for his old-lady bones, laxatives for his constipation, so why wasn't he also sixty-five? He had the patience of the elderly, could sit three hours in his chair, just listening to the birds singing or watching old Batey twitching in his sleep. So why didn't they put that on the report: six months to ninety-six? His mother said the doctors couldn't tell the whole story about Sal. But she needed to realize the Wolf wasn't much better.

Sal didn't want what the Wolf offered. He clicked because that's what *they* wanted—for Sal to speak through that electronic fuzz box. It was a robot call-and-response, Sal a shitty Steven Hawking without the theories and the physics.

The speech therapist wanted Sal to be a cheeseball. Sal could say "Hi" well enough with his voice and his direct eye contact, his body stiff in excitement. But the Wolf wanted Sal to say "Howdy, pard-ner" like a cowboy who'd been kicked in the head. The Wolf had Sal saying, "I love you, Mom-my." What eighth grader says *I love you* to his own mother? The ones who got punched. Not that they'd punch Sal, which was worse: He'd never learn.

Michael had his own animal interference—another voice in his head. He imagined it to be more of a Boar, and it whispered like Sal's Wolf: *Eat* and *Drink* and sometimes *T-V* but mostly *Eat*. Sometimes it whispered, *Steal* and *Take*. Sometimes it whispered, *Shut Up*. Sometimes it whispered, *Head Down* and *Hide*, especially when his parents were fighting. Sometimes it got stuck on one option with no choice but to click. And sometimes he had to just listen as his Boar let him have it: *No one likes you. Awkward and fat. A fatty with little bitch boobs. You needed to live for two, and now look, you little disappointment.*

Michael said, "I think Sal is sick of his Wolf. Can we turn it off?"

"Or at least turn it down," his father said. "I can barely hear the TV."

"No," their mother said. "His therapist wants us to use his computer at home. How would you like it if I turned you down?"

Their father whispered, "I'd be fine. See?"

Their mother smiled. "I could actually get used to you like that."

Michael waited, wondering what kind of night this would be. If his father laughed, he might talk ridiculously quiet for the next half hour ("*Pass me the salt. . . . Sal, how was your day at school?*"). His mother would roll her eyes, but they might end up snuggled together on the couch, legs intertwined, even kissing as Michael and Sal gagged. But if his dad didn't laugh, if he walked to the fridge for a beer and followed that up with a little whiskey, and his mother asked him to clear his plate from the table and he ignored her, then they'd start in on each other. *Are you even here right now? You've barely talked to Sal all evening.* And his dad would come roaring back: *I don't need this shit from you. Do you know how much pressure I'm under?* And his mother would respond, *You're under? You?* Michael held his breath.

His father laughed.

Michael relaxed and once again dipped the spoon into the potatoes. He got one bite in before Sal clenched his jaw again. "Eh-eh," he said through his teeth, and this time the voice arrived slowly: *You . . . cannot . . . pass.*

"Use your computer," their mother said. "Use it to tell us."

The family sat frozen until the Wolf whispered, *Done.* Sal's hand flinched forward and clicked the switch.

The Wolf boomed in its robot voice: "I am done with din-ner."

"Sal," his mother said. "Look at your plate. You have at least three more big bites."

Eat, the Wolf whispered, as if to agree.

His mother looked at Sal. "You don't want to eat for your brother? Is that it?"

"Eh," Sal said.

He breathed in, turned his head, and coughed, blasting milk-wet specks of fish and potato onto Michael's cheek.

"That," Michael said, "was on purpose."

Michael woke up covered in sweat. He'd had the dream again.

A black hole was spreading across Earth, coming to swallow Sal. It was the Nothing. It had already engulfed their middle school and classmates, their father and mother. The only safe place was the water, the creek behind their new house. So Michael unstrapped Sal and carried him down, waded up to his ankles, arching his back to take on Sal's full weight, but the rocks were slick with algae, and he slipped.

He dropped Sal onto the stones. His brother's head cracked open like a shell, and inside was Kraft macaroni and cheese. He knelt down and tried to pack his brother back in noodle by noodle, but they kept slipping through his hands, drifting downstream. When he woke up, his sheets were stuck to his skin, his heart hammering, his stomach twisted.

He crept down the stairs to Sal's room, to comfort himself with Sal's steady Darth Vader snore. On the shelf above Sal's hospital bed, the baby monitor glowed with its single red eye. Michael turned the wheel to off, and the eye went dark. The little bulb plugged in under Sal's bed made it seem like he slept on a box of light. Michael crawled over the safety bar onto the mattress. Sal was lying on his stomach, his face on a pillowcase. His eyes batted open.

"Are you okay?"

"Mmmm," Sal said. Michael waited. It took a second. *I . . . was sleeping, . . . you weirdo. What . . . is it?*

The voice was very quiet, but Michael still heard it. "Sorry." He grabbed his brother's hand, his spindly fingers. "Go back to sleep."

Getting up from Sal's bed, he pulled the mattress out from the couch and tucked himself in. He listened to Sal's slow breathing, and the steady hiss and wheeze sent him to sleep.

In the morning, he rode the bus with Sal to their middle school, then watched his twin through the cage as the lift lowered like a tongue from the roof of a mouth. The driver pushed Sal onto the icy blacktop, smiling with his gummy mouth and doffed his cap. He often didn't wear his teeth.

"There," Michael said. "You're free, Willy."

Sal smiled in his puffy coat. He liked the killer whale movie. "Eh-eh," he said. *Shut up.*

Michael walked Sal to his special-ed classroom. Their new school was massive compared to Michael's tiny Catholic school. He'd gone from a grade of twenty-five Christians to two hundred upper-middle-class heathens. The walls were decorated with pictures of Santa Claus but also menorahs and generic Happy Holidays placards.

Michael cut a swath in the crowd of students for Sal to follow. He unzipped his coat, hoping his new yellow tie-dyed Grateful Dead shirt would make a good impression. He looked down at his too-tight blue jeans to make sure he didn't forget to zip his fly again. He missed his old uniform. Almost everyone here wore Abercrombie and Fitch, as if they spent their weekends yachting and playing polo on horseback instead of watching MTV. His first week, he'd witnessed a girl walk up to another girl and pull up the tag on the back of her dress. "Off-brand," she said. "I knew it." Michael felt like he was off-brand too. After four months, he still had no friends. He'd hung with Carl a few times, but now they lived too far away to get together often.

When the hallway of seventh graders refused to part, Michael went around to the rear of Sal's powerchair and balanced on the back. He whispered into Sal's ear: "Charge." Sal smiled before he cranked his joystick forward, and then Michael was riding Sal though the crowd. "Look alive!" he yelled. "Watch your ankles!" The students hopped out of the way as the twins plowed to the elevator.

When they arrived at Sal's classroom, Michael checked to see if anyone was looking, then said, "Give me a kiss." To the outside eye, it would look like a twin brother make-out, but Sal was in effect giving him a hand slap, a fist bump, an *It's all good*. Sal paused for a second, considering, until he scraped his bottom lip against his front teeth. *Bye, brother.*

Going to school with Sal had initially been exciting. Michael had heard of the twin trick, of twins switching places and waiting for people to notice the difference. With Sal's CP and bone-thin frame, no one would mistake him for Michael, a certified fat-ass, though Michael thought it would be fun to try. *Sal, did you gain a little weight? Michael, you seem a little stiff. What's with all the lying down?* But as Michael walked to honors science, he lamented that Sal wasn't smart enough to be in his classes. Or the Wolf wasn't smart enough, which was the same thing: Sal was stuck in Tard Alley, which was what several kids had called the wing before Michael asked them to please repeat, before they saw his forehead vein, before he went full Boar. At school, Michael barely saw Sal, just for lunch and choir and once a week for Buddies!, a club founded at his mom's suggestion.

When he and Sal had first come to school, his classmates wanted to know what happened to Sal. Michael told them Sal was disabled from a freak trampoline accident, had been struck down on his Huffy when a beer truck jumped the curb. He made up exotic diseases: Finkenstein disorder, moose-calf meningitis, Glockenspiel syndrome. He wanted them to feel unsafe, to look for themselves in Sal's face. But it was difficult to keep track. His classmates conferred, found his stories contradicted. They surrounded him, put him against a wall. What really went wrong? *He was born, okay? Breathe a sigh of relief.*

Michael knew what his classmates said behind his back. He saw it in their eyes, that word: *retarded*. In the beginning, he tried to fight people who said it aloud, but it was everywhere. His parents enrolled Michael in kung fu classes so he'd have a place to put his anger, or at least get his ass kicked less often.

Michael even tried the word himself for a day, felt it roll off his tongue—*re-tar-ded*. "What a retard. That's retarded. What a retarded retard. An el Re-tard-o." His classmates said, "Okay. We get it." He came home and before going to lie down with Sal in the hospital bed, he washed his mouth out with Listerine. He was afraid Sal would smell the *retard* on his breath.

In honors science, Mrs. Steuben passed back the quizzes on population genetics. She placed his quiz face down on his desk and patted it like she was tucking it in. Michael held his breath and peeled up the right corner where the grade should be, expecting to see at best a B, but scrawled in hurried red ink was an A minus. He could show it to his parents, get the *Bzzzz* again. Michael was starting to accept that he wasn't so bad at this science stuff. He could map the systems in his mind, imagine the networks of a cell, their tight nits of nucelli and chunky mitochondria selected through infinite divisions to help you survive. He could imagine how a bottleneck effect might put a stranglehold on genetic diversity, hear the painful death-groans of a prehistoric bison herd that lost the gene lottery. It was not that different from how he imagined God and all those saints, all Catholicism's tidy cause and effect. Evolution actually made more sense with its hard, cruel math. Even Darwin looked a little Godlike with his draping beard you could wipe a counter with. But what was all that evolution for?

As Mrs. Steuben went over common mistakes, he raised his hand. "So the strong DNA gets passed on, and the weak genes die?"

"That's about the gist of it," she said, clutching her chalk.

"But what about people?" Michael asked. "Why do the weak ones survive? What's the point of all that pain and suffering?"

"That isn't really in my pay grade," she said. "You might want to bring it up with your religious professional."

Michael ran his tongue across the plastic palate of his retainer. Sal wasn't strong. They both weren't. They were damaged from the premature birth and would be dead if not for the incubators. Sal was so weak he wasn't even allowed in the classroom, but Michael was let in. They couldn't tell just yet with Michael.

Michael knew what a priest would say: Suffering was a teacher that brought you closer to God. Or suffering was like the wrong side of a tapestry, looking ugly and chaotic with no pattern or meaning, but when turned around you witnessed the whole beautiful picture, the plan. God just hung it wrong, is what they were saying. He was a bad decorator.

"Okay, how about this?" Mrs. Steuben said. "People are different. We're special. We've got civilization. It's animals we're talking about."

Michael pretended to sneeze and mumbled, "Bullshit." He looked around. Only one kid in his class, Gregg, was laughing. Good enough. He wanted very badly for Gregg to be his friend. Gregg had the same split-down-the-middle haircut as Michael and was as skinny as Michael was fat. Like Michael, he'd also transferred that year, but from a Hebrew school. He seemed more adept at fitting in, sitting at lunch with Shawn who smoked pot behind the rec center. Michael had mentioned that he was studying kung fu and told Gregg he should check it out sometime. But so far, he hadn't shown up.

Mrs. Steuben said, "Now it's time, people, to start brainstorming for your science-fair experiments."

Michael groaned. His only idea was feeding Batey different kinds of dog food and seeing what happened, but Michael was sure he'd fuck it up and get sent to remedial science. He could ask his father, an actual freaking scientist, and hope the experiment wouldn't end with his dad rubbing deer blood on his face again. He had to think of something. School was getting easier. He'd always tried hard but now he was seeing results. He needed to not waste his chance, to not disappoint, for his parents not to wish that Michael would've been the one in the wheelchair.

During lunch, he ate with Sal's special-ed class more often than not. It was Steak-umms day, and Sal's aide, Mrs. Bridgewater, was feeding Sal too fast again. Mrs. B wore floral dresses and had a gland problem that threw off her balance and made her walk into walls. She said that's why she got along with Sal: They both drove a little crooked. She talked endlessly about low-fat foods like frozen yogurt and burgers made from bison, which, if they weren't endangered, would be soon. But most of all, she talked about her cat: "Do you know what Pretty did last night? She was so naughty, Sal. She keeps leaving birds on the neighbor's doorstep. And with some of them she forgets their heads. I said that's not my Pretty doing that, but they swear." Sal was polite, smiled at her like *That's nice*, but Michael couldn't imagine listening to her all damn day.

"You should go slower," Michael said. "He's coughing more." Sal's spasticity had increased with puberty, and he was having more trouble swallowing. Their mother worried he'd aspirate.

"Sorry," Mrs. Bridgewater said. "We're just trying not to be here all day, right, Sal?"

Sal smiled. "Yeah." *I can take it. Speed it up.*

Michael took out his retainer and set it on a napkin. He looked at Gregg eating at a table with Shawn, who laughed and looked over. Was he laughing at Sal? Michael looked behind him. Two girls were play-fighting, holding each other's wrists. False alarm. Michael's Boar chimed in: *Don't be paranoid, you little freak.*

Quincy, a boy who had CP like Sal, started telling jokes between bites. He was more mainstream than Sal—in all normal classes—but still needed help. He had a voice grounded in his sinuses. As a hall monitor, he cruised the corridors with the squeaky morality of a school marm: "Get to class. You'll be late!" He was a narc, and no one liked him, but he also happened to be in a powerchair, a sleek, black electric cruiser he controlled with his giant head.

"Why was six afraid of seven?" Quincy looked around. "Because seven ate nine." The table erupted in laughter and groans.

On cue, Sal rolled his eyes. *What? Did you get that from a popsicle stick?*

"Ohh," said John, a kid with Down syndrome. "Sal is heckling you."

"I think Sal wants to know," Michael said, "if you got that from a popsicle stick."

"Yeah," Sal said, and the table laughed harder.

After lunch, Michael was late to Buddies!, which happened on Wednesdays. It was about as much exposure to mainstream students as Sal got. These students—Buddies!—were not popular, and most of them were in it for the free ice cream. Michael thought some of them belonged in the special-ed wing themselves. When he arrived, the club was immersed in an art project. A large gray table was covered in paper and feathers, markers and glue. The room smelled strongly of pine, so clean it stung his nostrils. As Michael sat next to Sal, he nodded at the teacher, who nodded back. Being late was a brotherly privilege.

One blonde girl with the meaty face of a Ninja Turtle leaned toward his brother and sang: "Hi, Saaaaaalllll. How are you-ooo?" Then Michael saw it: She looked over to her friend to see if she was watching—not kindness, but a performance of kindness.

"He's not deaf," Michael said. "You can talk normal."

The girl stood up. "Sorry," she said. "I was just being nice. God." She moved to a different spot at the table.

Mrs. Bridgewater had already set up the Wolf. Its computer screen hovered before Sal's face on the metal arm, lighting up with ghostly gray icons as it started scanning through the options in the Buddies! page. As Sal's arm hovered over his red switch on his tray, it whispered through his pillow speaker, *Tur-key. Rain-ing. Ice Cream. Stu-pid.*

That last one was Michael's only contribution. When Sal had first gotten the Wolf, his mother asked for suggestions, but Michael didn't want to help. "This is stupid" was all he typed. It became Sal's favorite button.

A new girl who'd just joined Buddies! took up Sal's hand. She said, "Sal, do you always let your brother scare away the girls?"

Sal smiled. *Not always.* She put his hand flat on a piece of paper and traced his skinny fingers with blue marker. Michael recognized her from his history class. She knew all the answers, was *Jeopardy!* smart. She wasn't afraid to talk back to the popular boys who made fun of her weight: *When are you getting the surgery to suck your own dick?*

"Bobbie, right?" Michael asked.

"That's what they call me," she said. "It's a boy's name, but I rock it." She wasn't bad to look at, on the bigger side like Michael, with boobs about as large as his. She had excellent bone structure and a laugh that got away from her. She wore long sleeves and pants even when it was hot. Probably ashamed of her body, Michael thought. He already liked her.

"Twins, huh?" she said. "Who's older?"

"Eh," Sal said. *Me.*

"Yeah, I'd have guessed you're older, Sal," she said. "It's the way you carry yourself."

"You mean the wheelchair?"

"No," she said sharply. "The confidence."

Sal smiled. *Burn.*

Michael inhaled her vanilla lotion, which almost overpowered the pine. Sal clicked right on time: "This is stu-pid."

Bobbie laughed so hard she had to cover her mouth. "Oh my God," she said. "I wasn't going to say anything, Sal, but I think so too. Look at my hand." It was covered in wisps of orange feathers. She clucked and pecked at the air and flapped her elbows. Her sleeve rode up, and Michael saw her skin covered in thin white slashes, with one line rusted over. Fresh.

"What happened to your arm?" Michael asked.

"I've got an aggressive cat," she said, and yanked the sleeve back down. So she loved animals. Another outstanding quality.

The Wolf whispered, *Raining,* and Sal clicked: "Look out-side. It is rain-ing. Psych." The Wolf didn't even pause for them to look out the window, flatly delivering the punchline.

Bobbie frowned, tilted her head like a puppy, and Michael's palms started sweating.

It was as if Sal was on some annoying children's show with terrible writers and no sense of timing. Sal cycled through again. The Wolf whispered, *Tur-key*, and Sal clicked. The Wolf said, "Did you have tur-key for lunch? Be-cause you are a tur-key!"

"Oh!" Bobbie said and laughed. "These are jokes! Not bad, Sal."

Sal's whole body stiffened in excitement, as if he'd burst right out of his wheelchair straps. He smiled wide. *Thank you. The Wolf and I will be here all week.* But Michael's Boar whispered: *You're blowing it.*

"Whoops," Michael said. He pressed the power button and the screen went blank. "Now we can have a proper conversation."

"You have proper conversations?" Bobbie grabbed Sal's hand. "Sal," she said. "How do you put up with your little brother?"

Sal rolled his eyes. *I have no idea.*

"Ha! Yeah, exactly."

She did not look to see who was watching.

At the kitchen table, his mother peeled the foil top off Sal's tiny cup of applesauce and readied the spoon. She got the pill-crusher, placed a white Valium pill inside the plastic well, and twisted the top like she was turning up the sound on a radio dial, though it had the opposite effect. Michael called it Sal's "volume" because it turned Sal down. It relaxed his muscles, but also had a sedative effect. She sprinkled the powder onto the spoon of waiting applesauce.

"Okay, Sal," she said. "Time for your volume."

"Time to get zombified," Michael said, and laughed like Boris Karloff.

Sal didn't open right away, made his squirrel teeth. *Guys. . . not today.* But then he grimaced, accepted the spoon.

"That's my good boy," his mother said.

"That's *my baby*," Michael said.

Sal glared and spat out the sauce.

Their mother caught it with a washcloth and expertly scraped it again onto the spoon. "Nice try," she said and slid it back in. She cupped his jaw shut until he gulped.

"If I did that, he'd bite off my finger."

Their mom shrugged. "It'd only work a few times, then. Only so many fingers."

On the couch, Michael watched Sal's eyes begin to droop. His arms relaxed. The electric current that ran through his body was now damped down. He was barely awake. The zombification was complete. "You still there, Sally?" Michael asked.

"Mmmm," Sal said from very far away. The voice didn't arrive.

After an hour, Sal started to liven up. As Michael lifted him back into his wheelchair, their mother got a call from her friend Ashley, something about Tina's school not letting her get out of her chair. "All right," their mom said on the way to her bedroom. "Here's what you need to do." God. She was already worked into a lather, into Special Needs Super Mom mode. Michael wished she cared that much about his C in Math.

Ashley was one of his mom's only real friends. His mom claimed people didn't invite her places because they thought she was too busy with Sal. When his father said that *she* could invite people places, she smiled. "I'm too busy with Sal."

They were watching a TV show about alligators, their habits and habitat, how they ate every few months. Thick-forearmed men flung raw chickens that the gators snatched out of the air. At an interesting fact, Michael said, "Hmmm. How about that, Sal?" and Sal smiled and stuck out his lower lip. The voice was still far away but Michael thought it was like *Yes. Indeed.*

When he first heard it, he hoped it was the house, a floorboard creaking with premature age. But then it came again, unmistakable: "*Grrrt.*" Sal was grinding his teeth.

"Stop," Michael said, trying to focus on the gators. Three seconds later: "*Grrt Grrt,*" like Sal was saying, *Stop what?*

"It's annoying," Michael said.

"*Grrrt. Grrrt.*" *What's annoying? This? This is annoying?*

"*Stop,*" Michael said. One second, two.

"*Grrrt. Grrrt.*" *Is this what I'm supposed to be stopping?*

"Shut . . . up," Michael said.

"Mike-a," Sal said.

"What?"

"*Grrrt. Grrrt.*" He grinned as he gnashed his teeth, like *You so walked into that.*

"Why are you being a dick? What have I done?"

Sal thought for a second, said, "Mike-a" sharply, like *For starters: You were born.* Then for emphasis he added: "*Grrrt. Grrrt.*"

"You know what?" Michael said. "If you're going to do that, you can do it by yourself." He toggled Sal from the living room into the empty and dark dining room and turned him to the lightless window. He put the chair in manual mode, killing the battery, and then locked the breaks. "There you go," he said. Sal said, "Eh-eh," but Michael said, "Too bad," and walked back to the living room. The gators were losing their habitat. As he sat back on the couch, he said, "Hmmmm," loud enough for Sal to hear.

From the dining room, faintly, Michael heard "*Grrrt. Grrrt.*" He flipped the channel to the moment in a movie where someone gets shot, and then back to gators. From the dining room again: "*Grrrt. Grrrt,*" like *You think I can't be annoying from over here?* A few seconds later, still louder, "*Grrrt. Grrrt,*" like *You think you can break me? I'll wear down my teeth first!*

Michael turned up the volume and waited a minute that felt like five.

"Mike-a," Sal said softly, like *Okay. I'm sorry.*

Michael said, "Did I hear something?"

"Mike-a," Sal said with more edge, like *I said I'm sorry. Seriously, come get me.*

Michael turned up the volume again and waited. His brother needed to be taught a lesson.

Sal said, "Ahhhhhhhh," like *You will regret this.* Or like *You'll get bit at the next opportunity.* Michael started humming. "Ahhhhhhhh," Sal said again. "Mike-aaaaaa!" like *This is solitary confinement.* Michael started to get up but thought better of it. He wouldn't be pushed around anymore, not at school and not by his disabled brother. He sank back into the couch. Then Sal was the loudest: "Ahhhhhh-eh-ahhhhhh!" Sal's yell broke into a high-pitched scream, like *You asshole. You fucking asshole.*

Michael leapt up, ran to the dining room, unlatched Sal's breaks, turned back on his battery. By then, Sal was crying his "hurt feelings" cry, less rage, more moan.

His mother walked fast from her bedroom. "I'm *trying* to talk on the phone," she said, her hand cupped over the cordless mouthpiece. "What did you do to him?"

"He was grinding his teeth again, so I put him by himself."

"Let me call you back, Ash," she said to the phone. "In the dark?" She walked to Sal and stroked his cheek. "Oh, my baby. What happened?" She laid her hands on top of his tight fists. "Come to Mommy." She put her forehead to his and rubbed the back of his neck under the foam headrest.

"He was being so annoying. He was grinding his teeth!"

"Oh, wow," she said. "How awful. What psychological warfare. You know what? That's what he has to tease you with."

"He *knows* I hate it."

His mother raised one eyebrow, clenched her jaw, went "*Grrrt*."

"Fine," Michael said, throwing up his hands. "He's always right and I'm always wrong. He never does anything."

"Michael, don't be so sen-sit-ive. Take a chill pill. You know how he hates to be excluded."

Sal's crying died down, and he let her wipe the tears from his face and trace his eyebrows with the pad of her finger.

"That's better," she said. "There. Can I please call my friend back? Your father should be home any second."

When she walked away, Sal drove back to the television but he became his black-hole self. He wouldn't look at Michael.

Michael said, "I'm sorry."

Sal just blinked.

"Fine," Michael said. "Punish me." Sal's mouth was slightly open, and Michael slipped in his pointer finger, lodged it along the ridges of Sal's left molars. "Do it."

Sal bit down lightly, a love tap. He smirked.

"See?" Michael said. "I knew you weren't really mad." Then Sal clamped harder. "Okay. So you're angry," Michael said, and Sal increased the pressure until Michael felt the ragged edges of his crooked teeth. "Ow. All right. I get it. You can let go." Sal's face softened and his jaws relaxed. Michael started to pull his finger away, but then Sal's eyes flashed and he clamped down with a new crushing fierceness, bulging his jaw muscle, his body spastic with concentration. Michael no longer felt pressure, just searing pain shooting up his hand and down into his feet, curling his toes, making him grind his own teeth. His finger was breaking. It was broken, and through the pain he received Sal's voice loud and clear: *You knew the rules and you broke them. You used my chair against me.*

Michael screamed like Sal, "Ahhhh-eh-ahhhh!" He slapped Sal on the head lightly with his free hand. Sal fluttered his eyes but held fast. Michael slapped harder. " Let go!"

The back door opened, and their father appeared in the doorway holding his briefcase. "What's going on here?" he said.

Sal released, and Michael withdrew his finger. Below the first knuckle were two valleys of flesh seeping a pink of blood and spit. Sal had broken his skin.

"What happened?" his father asked.

Michael whimpered and wrapped his finger in his shirt. "Sal bit me."

"And how did he get your finger in his mouth?"

"I put it there."

He scratched his beard. "Why does this sound like your fault?" His father took off his coat and leaned down to pat Batey's sniffing head. "Who's a good boy?"

"*Grrrt*," Sal said, like *Me*.

Later that night, at kung fu practice, Master Steve put flute music on the boombox. He said, "Focus the mind."

The studio was located at the edge of a strip mall. Its windows were lined with trophies featuring tiny blank-faced androgynous figures frozen in sidekicks. Master Steve's followers comprised of middle-aged cubical monkeys trimming their computer paunch, lean high schoolers learning to kill between wrestling seasons, and unathletic middle schoolers working on their anger issues. Michael was in this last category. There was one girl, who was seventeen with a caveman forehead but otherwise quite attractive. It was getting uncomfortable. Master Steve kept adjusting the girl's punch angles and giving her too many tips for what to do in a rape situation.

The English translation of Master Steve's fighting style was "Foot from the North, Fist from the South." It had something to do with China's terrain. Michael didn't know exactly where his own foot and fist came from. Foot from the cul-de-sac? Fist from the Doritos bag? All he knew was that now, thanks to Sal, it hurt to make a fist.

Michael felt like the most out-of-shape student, like all his movements were a bit off. He'd confessed this to Master Steve, who reassured him: "There is an animal for everyone. You've a body type best suited to boar form, and I don't mean that as an insult. It's a respectable form for the stout and hearty." Michael already knew his animal was a wild pig, but it was nice to have confirmation.

Master Steve described boar form as having a lot of punches and rushing, some head butts, elbow strikes, and short kicks. Were there any neck breaks, Michael asked, and Master Steve said, "Oh, yes." It was best fought in a phone booth.

Before they got started, Gregg walked in. Michael felt like there was a bird in his chest. Master Steve introduced the class to Gregg, who shuffled into line next to Michael. "What up, player," he said and nodded.

They did horse stance, legs apart and slightly bent, dropping lower until their thighs burned. They went into a twist stance and longbow, cat stance and crane. Gregg mirrored Michael, trying his best to keep up. By the time they got to punches, Michael's legs were pure Jell-O. Master Steve did the stances with them, barking changes over the flute music. He had receding gray hair and a small potbelly, but Master Steve considered himself more of a vessel than anything else, concerned mostly with chi and its flow. He spoke methodically, so that every syllable seemed full of wisdom, even when he said, "Yes . . . you may go . . . to the bathroom." When he did strikes, the air whistled through his nostrils. Michael leaned over to Gregg and whispered, "Imagine that nose whistle as the last thing you hear." Gregg laughed.

During break, Michael asked Gregg why he was studying kung fu. "I want to learn the touch of death," he said, "and try it on my sister."

Michael smiled. "There are worse reasons."

When they broke off to work on their individual forms, the senior students seemed to disappear into the animal. The man imitating a tiger smashed the air with his hands stiff as claws and roared, and the girl imitating a praying mantis tucked down her wrists like Sal and writhed like an insect as she stung at vitals with two fingers. Master Steve said over the rustling uniforms: "Set aside your human ego. Be the animal."

Michael wished he could be all Boar instead of his puny human self, but when he practiced his form, all Master Steve did was nod and say, "Go slower. Concentrate on your chi."

After class, Michael asked Gregg if he'd like to come over to his house that weekend. "We could practice."

"Sure," Gregg said.

Michael came home and showed Sal his finger. "Your kung fu is strong, brother. You want to do some wheelchair form before bed?"

Sal gave a weak, "Eh." It was progress. They went into the living room for more clearance. The scenario went like this: They were at a high school football game. A boy in a group of kids would laugh, and they'd hear that word: *re-tard-ed*. They'd turn. *What'd you say?* And the boy said: *Hey Michael. You're a retard like your brother.* Cue the techno music. Michael used Sal's handles as a platform to launch kicks, and Sal charged forward to do the "footrest of fury." He narrated for Sal: "You take out their shins, and I punch them in the face. You spin around for handle attack and I sidekick. And then you blind them with your food-milk cough, and I run in front with a dragon strike." Sal was already dressed appropriately, his head in the ninja strap with nylon loops over the foam, a good place to hold throwing stars.

Concentrating on his chi, Michael saw Sal's smile creep up. He made his breathing slower until the voice came through: *Apology accepted.*

That Saturday, Gregg came over. He had seen Sal in the cafeteria but never up close. Michael was terrified about what his new friend would think. Would Gregg concentrate on Sal's tight arms, his skinny knees, his baby bib, the cavernous gape of his mouth, the string of drool rappelling down his chin? Or would he wait to discover the person who laughed when you burped, who rolled his eyes, who heckled Michael with his name: "Mike-a!" It was like show-and-tell all over again.

They walked over to the kitchen table, where Sal was eating lunch, and

Michael introduced them. "Hi," Gregg said, looking nervous, then turned to Michael. "Does he shake hands?"

Michael's mother said, "You can ask him."

"Do you shake hands?" Gregg asked.

"Eh," Sal said, and Michael said, "That's a yes."

Gregg picked up Sal's stiff fist as though it might break. Sal flashed a smile. Gregg was breathy with relief. "Yeah," he said. "What's up, Sal?"

His mother said, "Watch this. Sal, what do you think of your twin brother?"

It took a second, but Sal delivered. His eyes flicked up into their sockets.

"Was that an eye roll?" Gregg laughed. "Oh, Sal. Good one!"

When they were alone in the basement, Michael answered all of Gregg's questions: What happened to him? Will he ever get better? Is that all he can say? How much does he understand? Do you have to change his diapers? Only now had he felt comfortable enough to ask.

Michael was feeling comfortable with Gregg too, so much that he told him about Sal—how sometimes he could still understand him, like knew what he was thinking. Michael expected Gregg to laugh or call him crazy, but he just smiled and nodded. "I'd believe it," he said. "You guys seem like . . . really close." Then Gregg revealed a certain embarrassing fact about himself: his on-again off-again relationship with his mother's vacuum cleaner.

"Like the hose part?" Michael asked.

"Yes, the hose part," Gregg said.

Michael was honored to receive this information.

On Sunday night, when his parents were watching TV in their bedroom, the Boar whispered, *Pour out half the Sunny Delight.*

The Boar whispered, *Fill it back up with vodka.*

The Boar whispered, *Bring it to school. Make them like you.*

Michael told it to *Shhhh*, but it would not shut up. He wanted so badly for Gregg and his friends to like him, he went to the fridge and did as he was told, then spent half the night worrying about getting caught: his mother weeping, his father in a huff. *Why can't you just be normal?* But he didn't want to just be normal. He wanted to be special.

In the morning, he packed the bottle along with his ham-and-cheese sandwich, grapes, and Doritos. When lunch rolled around, he walked to Sal's table, where Mrs. Bridgewater was already loading Sal's cut-up spaghetti onto his metal spoon. He bent down and said, "Is it okay if I eat with Gregg today?"

Sal thought for a second. "Eh," he finally said.

Gregg was sitting with Shawn, who wore a spiked wrist cuff and a shirt with holes even though the rumor was he lived in a huge house. Michael pretended he was on his way to somewhere else until Gregg caught his eye and smiled, flapped his hand. "Sit with us," he said.

Michael sat and looked back toward his brother, searching Sal's face for sadness. He couldn't find any.

Michael unzipped his lunchbox and made the offering. "Who wants some of this?"

"What's in it?" Shawn asked.

"You know what's in it," Michael said.

Shawn took a sip. "Holy shit."

"See?" Gregg said. "I told you he was cool."

The boys passed around the Sunny Delight, taking sips and silently nodding, and when it got back to Michael, he took the last glug, almost all alcohol. It burned in his belly, and a warmth washed over him. Yes, he felt lighter in his own body. When he went out to recess, he extended his arms and locked hands with Gregg and Shawn and they ran through the parking lot like they were flying, their breath fogging ragged in the cold.

8

Gabe swiped his ID badge on the card reader and heard the lock click. "Open Sesame," he said, holding the door for his son.

"That's still so cool," Michael said.

Gabe shrugged. He had pulled strings, cleared it with his boss: approved use of his world-class multimillion-dollar laboratory for Michael's science fair experiment. That meant access to microscopes with 63x magnification, to pipettes that measured microliters, to pristine and sterile workspaces, but after two visits, Michael was most impressed by the card swiper. Gabe would take what he could get.

They were doing the final count of the cancer cells. It sounded like the worst game ever: Count the Cancer by Hasbro! But that was the experiment they'd come up with after Gabe brainstormed with the boy for two whole hours. Michael's big idea: "We could feed gunpowder to a goldfish." The other scheme involved giving Batey different kinds of dog food and seeing what happened, but who wanted to collect that data? Gabe reminded himself that Michael was only fourteen, with a pubescent brain and worldview, but he still wanted to shake him: *You've got a whole laboratory, kid. A whole life. Let's use it.* Gabe finally designed a simple experiment himself, tracking the growth rate of cancer cells when compared to a normal control. He'd get the cells from a colleague. Done.

It was February. They needed to stain the cells for the final count. Last Saturday, they'd fixed the tissues with formalin, but it had not been the bonding experience he'd hoped for. Gabe had to practically pry Michael from his bed with a crowbar, and his son spent the car rides to and from the lab compulsively stabbing at the radio buttons while complaining about missing his martial arts practice. In the lab itself, Michael sleepwalked through the protocol, was like an absent-minded and lethargic robot: *What now? What now?* The kid acted like Gabe was making him earn the world's most boring Boy Scout badge instead of giving him a front seat to catastrophe, an exclusive viewing of the worst disease known to man. How cool was that? Apparently not enough. But that card swiper...

Gabe watched his son lope down the hallway, his jeans looking overstuffed. The kid already wore a size thirty-four waist. Was he getting fatter? He was getting fatter. They'd have another sit-down about healthy choices, about going out for soccer instead of martial arts, which as far as Gabe could tell was a glorified dance class. Meanwhile, Sal was skinnier than ever, his knees as knobby as baseballs. If only Michael could donate some of his fat to Sal, like one snowman giving to another.

They took the elevator up to Gabe's floor. All Gabe wanted right now was another cigarette. Last year, he'd switched to Ultra Lights, which meant low tar, a more complicated filter, and less guilt about killing himself. It was a gesture to Michael, who wrote him overly earnest pleas to quit, full of inflated cancer statistics and warnings he'd never live to see his grandchildren, always ending with hastily scrawled professions of love. Gabe's response was to look deeply into his son's eyes and say, "I smoke because I am weak." That usually freaked him out for a while. Gabe had liked getting the letters, because when they stopped last year, his son was in effect saying: *Actually, drop dead.*

Maybe it was natural for fathers to feel distant from their sons. His own father was a machinist when well, a gentle person who never talked about the war. What Gabe knew came from his mother. His dad had been studying to be an engineer when the war came. He joined the navy and had been tasked with locating enemy planes for a destroyer, calling out coordinates for the gunners, which took some mathematical chops. He could calculate most men under the table. He was off the coast of Japan when his ship got sunk. Floating in the Pacific, he'd listened as his shipmates bled out or got picked off by sharks. So many men went under, did not buoy back up. It could have been an hour or a day or more. Eventually he was pulled out, dried off, and shipped back, but that water got into his blood, his bones, his brain, logged him for life.

No wonder Gabe had gone into brain science, fascinated by cognitive decline. Still, he didn't quite feel equipped to raise sons of his own. *I'm not crazy*, he wanted to say. *Isn't that enough?*

As they walked down the hall to his lab, Michael kept running his grubby hands along the wall, touching the expensive equipment, contaminating their surfaces. Then he tripped over his own feet, barely recovering. The kid was pathologically clumsy, military-grade clumsy. Got a rogue state developing nuclear weapons? Parachute his boy into the lab armed with nothing but a banana peel, and done, a big *Whoops* for America. Gabe's goal was to finish this experiment without Michael ruining years of research.

"Don't touch," Gabe said, but Michael let his hand hover over the giant centrifuge next to the refrigerator, smiling at him.

"I know you think it's funny . . ."

Michael smiled, doing his retainer routine again, flipping it upside with the metal loops over his canines. "But it's not?"

Gabe rolled his eyes but laughed anyway. "It's not," he said.

Michael flashed his fangs and hissed.

The first thing Michael did was almost drop the petri dish with the cancer cells, spilling a bit of the solution over the side and onto other samples in the fridge.

"Watch it!" Gabe yelled.

"Sorry," Michael mumbled and then walked to the lab as if on a tightrope, clutching the petri dishes like they would explode. Michael had asked if he could catch cancer by getting it on his hands, and Gabe responded no, but he should probably not eat it. After Michael set the samples on the lab bench next to the microscope, they snapped on latex gloves, and Gabe waited for Michael to say, "What next?" even though the protocol was right in front of him.

Everything went fine as they stained the nuclei, then Michael used the same pipette tip on the normal control as the cancer sample, and Gabe shouted, "What are you doing? Always change your tip. You could ruin your sample!"

Michael dumped the tip into the plastic bin. "Don't yell at me."

Gabe could see the impending disaster, Michael ruining weeks of work, and they wouldn't be able to run the experiment again before the science fair, which would result in a meltdown and the end of Michael's science career and his retreat into some monastery. "I'm not yelling," Gabe said. "We're just so close to finishing."

"Then you can be done with me." Michael stared into the petri dish as if it were a void.

"Come on," Gabe said. "Don't be like that. I'm sorry." A strand of hair had jumped to the wrong side of Michael's part. Gabe straightened it, and Michael let him.

When it was time to apply the wash, Michael picked up the pipette, and he was suddenly a natural, measuring milliliters of buffer with the gage. He expertly injected the petri dish with the wash solution before tamping down the disposable nozzle into the plastic bucket and putting both petri dishes on the rotator. He read the protocol himself and didn't ask, *Now what?* He was so smooth it was like Gabe had passed down his experience through their shared DNA.

"Keep track of which is which," Gabe said.

"Duh," Michael said. After washing the cells once more, it was time to look. They went to the inverted microscope room, where the Axiovert 135 was waiting, the lens underneath the platform with the condenser above like a spotlight. Last week, Michael needed Gabe's help to bring a petri dish into focus, but now he adjusted the knobs slowly, carefully, the light beaming down over the dish as he peered into the eyepiece. Gabe asked, "Do you see it?"

"Yeah," Michael said.

Gabe took a peek. His son had brought the cells into perfect focus. They were sepia from the stain, crowding the dish in a single layer, their nuclei like black knots dotting the space, the cell bodies larger and more jagged. He let Michael look again, and his son counted the cells and recorded it in his black marble notebook in uncharacteristically neat script. Gabe snapped a few pictures on the microscope's camera. Michael did the same for the less dense normal control, noting their softer edges, their more regular shape. They cleaned up, put the pipette back in its jar, dumped the petri dishes down the sink drain. "Bye-bye cancer," Michael said. "See you on the other side." Gabe would get the lab tech to develop the images. Done.

"You did it," Gabe said, and Michael shrugged like *No big deal.* "You gotta pee before we get going?"

Michael shook his head.

"Okay," Gabe said. "But—"

"Don't touch anything," Michael said. "I know."

As Gabe urinated onto the pink soap cake, he sighed. They hadn't exactly bonded, but they'd gone through the motions, and that was something. His son was just going through the typical turbulence of puberty. His thoughts wandered to his new project. He'd identified a group of proteins he thought had promise, that were perhaps instrumental in MS demyelination. It was either the Alpha, the Beta, or the Gamma. One or a combination. Overexpression or under. He didn't know yet. But up above in the animal facility he was breeding a knockout mouse, taking the gene away to see what happened, praying for pathology, hoping for a hitch in their little mousey step. Who knew what it would lead to? Maybe an article in the *New England Journal of Medicine*. The *New York Times?* Then translational research: pharmaceuticals that would relieve the suffering of millions. There might be fan mail. Did scientists get fan mail? What would be for certain was more money: a better lab at a better institution, consulting gigs, speaking fees. All that meant more help for Sal, more help for his wife. The experiment would take years. His boss said to run other experiments in case this one didn't work, but Gabe didn't want to waste time. He could practically see it.

He returned to his lab to retrieve Michael but it was empty. Gabe first thought was the fridge, where he kept the tissue samples. Would his son purposely ruin months of research? Gabe started to think anything was possible.

He peeked into the hallway. He fast-walked through the corridor, trying locked doors. He found him in Yin's lab, staring at the zebra fish, a jar in his hand, the fish under the glowing light in their tank.

"What did you do?" Gabe said, grabbing him roughly by the neck. What was in that jar? Did he dump chemicals into Yin's tank?

"Ow," Michael said. "Stop. I fed them."

"You fed them?"

"Or that's what this is, right? Fish food?"

"Fuck. Let me see it." There wasn't a label. Gabe sniffed. It smelled fishy enough, but he couldn't be sure. "Do you have any idea how much these fish cost to make? They're genetically modified. They're phosphorescent. I told you not to touch. Why can't you listen?"

Michael flexed his jaw, obviously trying not to cry.

"All right," Gabe said. "It's probably fish food. And if they die, it's what Yin gets for leaving his door unlocked. Let's go, buddy."

"I'm not your buddy," Michael said.

"Hey," Gabe said. "Don't be like that."

Michael didn't move. "You said you'd show me. You said we'd look at a lesion."

"We don't have time," Gabe said. "We've got to relieve your mother."

Michael stared at him.

Gabe wanted to pull his own hair out. "All right," he said. "But real quick." He returned to the fridge and grabbed a white box that held the slides.

He picked a slide from a MS brain containing dark patches in the white matter, the ventricles widening out into atrophy. He'd encased the brain tissue with paraffin wax and cut it on a microtome into ribbons so thin they could blow away with your breath. He'd stained the tissue for myelin, which reversed the colors: the healthy tissue a web of black and the MS lesion lacking it, a white petal. Loading the slide into the upright microscope, he brought the section into focus, then backed away and let his son look.

"Where? I don't see it," Michael said.

"The white spot," Gabe said. "You'll find it."

As Michael twisted the metal nubs, Gabe was beginning to think he'd never see it, never see the damage right in front of him, but then Michael said, "I see it."

There was a moment, after they shot the deer, when they were dressing it on the ground, that Gabe found himself giving Michael a tour of the deer's insides—the steaming coils of small intestine and the disk-like liver and the balloon lungs and the purple bulb of heart, all the way up to the trache: a rubbery handle that would bring everything else with it. The wound was not just a wound. It was a window, and for a moment, Gabe had him. There were so many things to show him, to explain through the messy viscera—but then Michael had gagged and walked away.

Now his son was peering through the microscope, into another kind of window, and was finally seeing it.

Gabe said, "We're born into bodies, buddy, bodies that fail us." He put his hand softly between Michael's shoulder blades, and Michael didn't flinch. Through that touch, Gabe said all he needed to say: *You are no different than the mouse, the deer. You don't have to ask why anymore. It's all improvisation. That's what my father saw in that water, what drove him insane. We are animals to be picked off and pulled under. What's all this ceremony? Don't make your brother more than his body.*

Michael said, "Is this what Sal's brain looks like?"

"Maybe," Gabe said. "Sal might have fewer lesions. He might have a big hole. Atrophy."

"How do you know?" Michael said.

Gabe still hadn't described what he saw to his wife, but he told Michael now. "I saw the scans when you both were born. His brain was devastated. It was toast."

Michael stirred, his expression unreadable. "But it's grown back, or at least filled himself in around the gaps," Gabe said, squeezing his son's shoulder. "And look what he's done with it. Look how he's become himself."

Michael turned back to the scope and peered in.

9

In the mornings, from the second Hannah opened her eyes, every movement had purpose. Listen to the baby monitor for the quality of his breath. Crack open the door to see him blinking. Rub the small of his back and sing him awake. Give him Valium to loosen him up, with swallows of thickened apple juice. Watch him stretch within his range of motion. Change his diaper and pull off his jammies. Blast his pits with aerosol deodorant and shove him into his clothes. Make sure his chair was fully charged and raise him with the lift into his wheelchair seat. Yell as his brother up the stairs until you hear his feet. Hurry. They were always running late: oatmeal and yogurt, soft foods, soft bites.

Today was a Sunday in March. The crocuses were beginning their hopeful creep through the topsoil, their pale green shoots making Hannah hopeful too. She'd asked Gabe to go with them to church. The great outdoors was his church, he claimed. Mass, on the other hand, was torture. He'd recently won them a fishing trip at a United Cerebral Palsy charity auction. That would be torture for Hannah. She thought they should trade.

Now Michael was saying, "Can I just stay home?"

"What? You've got your confirmation coming up," she said.

"About that, Mom. I'm a man of science now."

"You weren't even a finalist at the science fair, Einstein. Now go upstairs and put on a proper shirt. We're already late."

"I've been ready for ten whole minutes," Michael said, and Sal said,

"Eh-eh," and Michael said, "How would you know?" and Sal bit the air. "You take that back," Michael said, and Hannah said, "Guys..."

They missed the liturgy but made the sermon, the meat of the mass. Father O'Neil stood at the lectern. He was too good-looking to be a priest, with wavy blond hair, fine cheekbones, and a breathy book-on-tape voice. He made the old ladies swoon. He was delivering a sermon about forgiveness. She liked to do some reverse engineering, figure out what the liturgy was by the sermon references. They must've read *let he cast the first stone*.

She looked at Gabe. What did he need forgiving for? She still loved him. But she wondered if he was working so hard for his career or just avoiding his own family. One part of him was always in the lab, thinking about his next experiment, imagining his mice. Sometimes she had to say: "Where are you right now?" and he'd look up, startled. "Hmmm?"

She grabbed Gabe's hand, sticky with sweat. His other hand gripped Sal's handle as though his wheelchair were a life raft.

Sal said, "Ah, Momma" loud enough to echo, and she whispered, "*Shhh. No heckling the priest.*"

During the Our Father, she held Sal's hand, giving his wrist a rough shake to loosen it. Aside from her, only Michael knew that trick. Michael crawled down the pew, in a proper red polo shirt, and whispered into Sal's ear. They both laughed, Sal with his dimple, Michael with his retainer teeth.

Then people came to shake Sal's hand: "Peace be with you." It was a one-way street. Sal stiffened into stranger alert during this part, like *Who are you?* But they were so nice, called him sweetie, honey, angel. She liked to judge them by how they did it. Who was afraid to make contact? Who lifted his hand by the back and dropped it down? Who stuffed their fingers into his tight fist, then *Oh ... it's wet. Spit or sweat?* But it was the way they looked at her after: not pity but admiration. Here, what she did with her life, caring for her son, felt holy. Sal wasn't a burden. He was God's work.

After she went up for Eucharist, Hannah lowered into the kneeler's cushioned leather and pinched the scapular at her neck. *All right*, her Mary said. *Lay them on me*. For Sal: *Let him have good health*. For Michael: *Let him feel more comfortable in his own skin.* For Gabe: *Let him not be an idiot.* But what should she pray for herself? *Let me stretch within my range of motion.*

After church in the social room, she saw the man with his powerchair and computer. His name was Paul, and he had CP like Sal but was what her son could probably never be. What if Sal had a little less damage? A bit more control over his pointer finger?

Paul's wife was wide-eyed and fresh-faced, not exactly beautiful, just unbearably wholesome. What was her name? Probably Betty or Alice. Paul's three sons ran a ring around him. Hannah secretly hated looking at him every Sunday, comparing him to Sal, but they had to speak with him. They were on the same team.

She followed Sal as he drove straight toward Paul, who toggled his powerchair toward them and smiled. His computer had all the keys, produced a sentence or two every minute as he poked them out letter by letter with that agile digit, articulating in a halting robot voice: "How are you Sa-l? God b-less. These kids . . . oh boy . . . wh-at a hand-ful." As he reached for his wife's hand, they shared a look, the kind Gabe hadn't given Hannah in quite a while. She was surprised, then surprised that she should be surprised, as if there couldn't be genuine love here, and what kind of person was she with her own son to be surprised?

Sal smiled back at Paul. He must've liked seeing someone in this great big church who looked like him, who had the same robot voice. Paul had a job, made money with his computer. And he probably had government help, not that anything was wrong with it. With all the everyday bullshit, the stares and comments, the curbs and closed doors, the too-narrow aisles and the too-tiny bathrooms, he deserved checks in the mail. So did Sal, but she'd have to die or have a mental breakdown before they'd help her family. The social workers loved a crisis, rushed to put out fires, but if there were no open flames, they let you smolder no matter how much smoke.

After they parted, Hannah motioned Gabe and Michael toward the donut line. "Okay, guys. Go get your quota of saturated fat."

Sal thought that funny and executed one of his epic screams. A little boy behind them stared, asked, "What's wrong with him?"

"He's happy," she said. The boy looked terrified, as if that's what happiness did to you.

Later, after dropping Michael off at home, Hannah took Sal to meet Ashley and Tina at the mall. As they cruised past the shops, she tried to ignore the staring and the looking away. In this sacred hall of commerce, the eyes said Sal wasn't God's work; he was damaged goods. She'd gotten a bad deal, and there'd be no refunds.

Having a partner in crime, someone to take on half the eyes, made it better. Ashley pushed Tina past a group of teens. They ogled rudely, slouched and misshapen, acne rashes blooming on their cheeks. But oh, *their* children were the weird ones. Ashley said, "Tina, say, 'That's right. I'm hot stuff. You can look but don't touch.'"

"Ma," Tina said. It was the only word she'd learned, but that was more than enough for her mom.

"I'm right here," Ashley said, and she was: still sporting the trademark leather jacket, her raven-black hair with those natural curls Hannah had always wanted, and her eyes with only a hint of laugh lines. Considering she averaged fewer than six hours of sleep each night, she was aging surprisingly well.

Ashley thumbed back at Sal, who'd stalled before another window, looking at a flashing row of wide-screen televisions. "Look at him. He's a shop-a-holic."

It was true. Sal loved to shop, loved being out and about, knowing there was a ramp or elevator to wherever they were going. He loved cruising past the displays of frozen mannequins who had even less range of motion than he did. He loved exploring the aisles, loved getting stuck and laughing about it. He even loved making trouble—driving past a rack of shirts with his left arm out and knocking a few to the floor, then smiling as the nervous clerk picked up after him.

Hannah, on the other hand, hated to shop. She felt exhausted by all the fashion trends. She pointed to a particularly absurd mannequin in a glittering purple sequined dress with a plunging neckline. "Let's wear that to our next IEP meeting. *Hello. Give us all the services.*"

Ashley snorted.

Hannah felt so comfortable around Ashley. She'd let three months go by without talking, but it felt like no time had passed. She realized how lonely she'd been in her new neighborhood. She hadn't connected with any of the special-needs moms yet, though she'd gone to a garden-club meeting and discovered that, in her new town, there were women who lunched. That's all they did. They'd put their kids on a bus, wait till lunch, and then go to it. The seafood place. The Italian. The spot with complicated salads. It was their biggest decision of the day: where to go and whom to go with and what to talk about while there. And they thought *her life* was tragic? She'd been feeling like an alien, and now here was someone from her same planet.

"Thanks for the advice about the PT," Ashley said. "She got reassigned."

"I also had her murdered."

"That really helped, then. Anyway, Tina has at least two hours out of her chair. They even bought her a couch." Ashley looked away for a moment, like she was going somewhere sad in her head, but then came back to her body. "I hope you got a good deal on the hit man."

In the department store, a young woman at the makeup counter was attacking people with free samples of perfume, cologne, and face creams.

"On the wrists," Ashley said, and the girl carefully gave Tina two spritzes. Tina, who tended to smell like used dental floss, was now all roses and lavender.

"Ma," she said, with maybe delight.

"Make a cloud," Hannah said.

The girl spritzed three sprays of the Tommy Hilfiger cologne into the air, and Sal drove through. They gathered and sniffed: a whisper of manliness and money.

"Watch out, ladies," Ashley said, and Sal smiled like *That's right*.

Now it was time for the moms. The girl dabbed depuffing cream under their eyes, babbling about Swiss doctors and secret formulas, kelp extract and essential oils. Hannah only knew how it made her feel: her face a desiccated plant that had finally been watered. But then the girl started talking about a very special sale. "For a limited time. Forty-nine ninety-nine."

Ashley laughed. "I don't know. For that price, I'd rather be puffed."

"Sorry," Hannah said. She could not bring herself to pay that much for eye cream, especially not in front of Ashley. They were not ladies who lunched.

On their way to the clearance rack, Hannah said: "Want to see if we can score some pity pants?"

"Shut up," Ashley said, laughing. "That happened once."

In the food court, Hannah tried to feed Sal the PB&J she'd brought from home, but he was having none of it. He eyed the soft and golden Auntie Anne's pretzel on Ashley's plate and the cup of vanilla Häagen-Dazs that Ashley was dipping it in before giving Tina bites.

"Oh, come on, Han," Ashley said. "We're at the mall. Tina and I are basically on welfare. You can buy the kid a pretzel."

"Yeah," Sal said.

Hannah threw down the sandwich. "Fine."

As she waited in line, she tried not to think about the economic gulf between them, especially after Gabe's promotion. But it had been cropping up all day: the clearance rack, Tina's shabby wheelchair seat, references to aides that Sal didn't qualify for, waiting for medical procedures that Gabe could just make happen. Hannah knew Ashley's life was harder than hers. She was still a single mom, and while her parents and ex-in-laws helped with Tina while she worked as a receptionist, she did much of her caretaking alone.

When Hannah returned with the pretzel and milkshake, Sal smiled like *Now we're talking*. She watched his tongue mash the luscious goop against the roof of his mouth, his face contemplating the rush of flavors.

Tina was contemplating too. "Ma," she said, and her daughter's words seemed to pierce Ashley.

Something was eating at her, Hannah realized. "Ash, what's wrong?"

Ashley shook her head. Eventually she said, "You know, they just see how much Tina takes. They don't see how much she gives back."

Hannah nodded. If Tina gave back, what did Sal do? He gave much more. She felt a pang of guilt for comparing him to Church Paul. She should not wish for impossible things. Sal was his own unique creature.

She gave him another bite of pretzel and watched him chew. "Say, 'That's right,'" she said.

After more shopping, Sal needed a diaper change, and Tina also came up blue. They commandeered the women's bathroom. Sal and Tina were too big for the changing table, so Hannah retrieved a beach towel from Sal's back bag and laid it on the grimy bathroom tiles. Ashley laid out Tina's as well. "Looks like you guys are gonna sunbathe," she said.

A woman opened the door, took in the scene, and quickly backed away. Ashley called after her: "They don't bite!"

"Actually, Sal does," Hannah said, "sometimes." And Sal said, "Yeah."

When it was time to leave, Hannah gave Ash a hug, said they'd do it again soon. Before they reached the exit, Sal stalled in front of a bookstore, studying the covers of books he couldn't read. "Come on, Sally," Hannah said. "We're going now."

He sat for a moment and then drove forward into the shop. "More," he said.

Monday, she was waiting for the boys to come home from school, the hands on the clock ticking by like they were trapped in syrup. Gabe sometimes acted like this house was all she needed—handicapped-accessible to make their lives easier. But what was she to do when Sal wasn't in it? Sure, she drove to the occasional meeting as a parent rep for the Cuyahoga County Special Education Center, to the grocery store, the bank, the post office. Otherwise, she was in this house. She could clean it only so much before she got distracted or depressed. She talked to the deer head: "What are you up to? Just hanging out? Me too." She talked to the Jesus statue: "Lord, give me the strength to dust you." She talked to Mary on her neck: "What do you think? Break time? Good idea."

She wrote a check to the credit card precariously close to its limit. God, they were in so much debt from the house, and insurance only paid for half of all Sal needed. She tried to scrimp, but that wasn't the same as receiving a paycheck. She'd thought about getting a job, but she never knew when Sal would need to be kept out of school if his aide was sick or if she'd need to haul him to another doctor's appointment. She couldn't rely on a sitter. She didn't trust a single soul with him, not even herself, and that's why he was still alive.

She tried to read for the extension class she was taking at Case Western. Catholic fiction. They were on Flannery O'Connor. She liked the stories, liked how weird everyone looked in them. (One of the old ladies complained that all the characters were misshapen and ugly. Hannah had raised her hand: "But that's how bodies really are if you look close enough.") Hannah liked less how quickly the plots descended into violence, though the instructor said that violence often led to revelation. Mostly Hannah just loved being inside a classroom again, even if it was with a bunch of old biddies. She thumbed through "A Good Man Is Hard to Find" and settled on the last page, where the Misfit says after shooting the grandma: "She'd be a good woman if there was someone to shoot her every day of her life." Hannah sometimes felt like Sal was that gun trained on her, that she had no choice but to be good.

She closed the book and turned on *As the World Turns*. She knew it was a particularly bad day if she started watching soap operas. She'd like to see those soft-focus women take a break from stealing each other's husbands and do some serious, hardcore caretaking. Get woken up in the middle of the night, their child crying and not able to tell them where it hurt. Beg the insurance company for a new wheelchair their kid could sit in without getting pressure sores. Take their kid out into a world with too-narrow department-store aisles and restaurants with no ramps, with all the staring and looking away. Why wasn't that on television? Those actresses wouldn't even have to use glycerin to imitate tears. "I can't do it!" they'd yell. "Call my agent!"

At least the soaps gave her something to talk about with her mother. She dialed, heard her mother's gravelly hello.

"Can you believe they challenged each other to a drag race?" Hannah asked.

"I know," her mother said, cackling. "Idiots. Of course they crashed."

When Hannah's brother had died, her mother never quite recovered. She helped Hannah's younger brother with little Charlotte and went to church, but she mostly filled her days with her "stories," living vicariously through the characters: their romances, their careers, their evil twins. She lived vicariously through Hannah too, listening to her narrate the soap opera of Sal's school, the insurance reps, Gabe's distance, Michael's teen angst, Hannah's ongoing bowel issues. She gave consoling *ohs* and *that's too bads*, but no matter what trouble Hannah related, it couldn't be worse than losing a child. Her mother would not be out-martyred. She'd conclude each conversation with her famous line: "God only gives you what you can handle."

When the boys came home, Michael collapsed on the couch and changed the channel to Ricki Lake's trashy talk show. He was in one of his moods. Sal drove in the living room to watch too.

The show featured two men fighting about a baby, and who was the daddy. Hannah said, "I don't know about you, Sally, but I'm rooting for the one with the most teeth."

"Yeah," Sal said.

Hannah thought that was pretty good, but Michael didn't even smile. On the TV, there was yelling. One of the dads charged the other and put him into a performative headlock. The bouncers pulled them apart.

"Awwww . . . No he didn't!" Hannah yelled. "Eh-eh!" Sal yelled back. Hannah felt a good belch brewing and let it fly. "*Uuuuu-rrrr-p!*"

"You're so embarrassing," Michael said, but she finally got a smile.

"I'm not, because your *poor* disabled brother thinks it's funny," she responded, and Sal said, "Yeah."

Loving Sal was so unlike loving Michael, who was humiliated by every hug, mortified by every kiss. Sal didn't pull away when she snuggled him, didn't squirm when she lay down with him and traced his eyebrows with the pad of her finger. Sal still let her mother him in all the ways that were worth it.

"You guys have much homework?"

"Sal never has homework," Michael said, and Sal smiled like *That's right*.

As Hannah coaxed Sal to the table and set up his computer, she thought: *Sal never has a lot of things*. She put his tray back on, having decorated it with sparkling shamrocks for St. Patrick's Day. She read his aide's daily report. *Dodgeball at gym.* How exactly was that adapted? *Sang in choir. Worked on academic readiness with computer.* Right. Not much progress there.

She'd battled for Sal to attend the mainstream school. They'd picked this district for its strong special-education program, this middle school for its whole wing devoted to special needs. And after their initial assessment, when the director of pupil services said he thought Sal should be bussed out, that Sal was too disabled to be educated even here, she'd gone into hell-beast mother mode. She cited the 1975 Individuals with Disabilities Education Act, the mandate for a free and appropriate public education. They countered with Sal's abysmal IQ test. She explained that it was difficult to get an accurate assessment on Sal. Though he could see well enough to drive his wheelchair (though watch out!), he lacked the fine motor to type or control a cursor with his joystick. And whether through cognitive deficit or dyslexia, he did not recognize words, only picture icons. When the psychologist noted, "Unfortunately the success of his efforts is very much determined by the interpretation of the listener at any given time," Hannah read between the lines: The mother was in denial, still unwilling to face that her son was severely retarded.

It was the speech therapist who'd saved them. A pale, short woman with a stringy red puff of hair, she overenunciated her words as if everyone else spoke English as a second language. She thought augmentative communication was being "underutilized" with Sal. What if he could use his computer full-time and learn to navigate it with more ease? She used infomercial words like "freedom" and "empower," implying that Sal's old care team had let Sal languish. She said Sal seemed capable but stubborn, that he'd learned helplessness. Hannah asked who'd taught him that, but the therapist didn't answer, which meant, of course: you.

He'd made some progress over the course of the year but not enough. He had five pages now, five options each. She knew he had more to say.

Sal clicked, and the computer said: "Can I please have some more?"

Yes, more of everything, my little cyborg son. Whatever you want, but what do you want?

She fed Sal his afternoon meds and snack, hearing the thickened milk catch in his throat. She did not like his cough. He'd passed his most recent swallow test with no signs of aspiration, but it was obvious that swallowing was getting harder.

Michael went to the freezer, got two Hot Pockets, and nuked them. He was eating his feelings again. He walked to the living room and collapsed on Batey. Hannah went and stood over his body. She had the urge to make a chalk outline. "Honey, what's wrong?"

He looked over to Sal in his chair and whispered, "I don't understand him like I used to."

She bent down and raked her fingernails gently through his scalp. "Maybe that's a good thing, Mike-a. Maybe you're just becoming your own person." She knew from her own brother, how when your sibling had medical issues, you could feel such pressure to make yourself small, sometimes so small that you disappeared. He needed cheering up. Instead of growing small, he could grow useful. She asked, "You want me to teach you how to give Sal a shower?"

He smiled. "Okay."

In the bedroom, Michael refused to use the Hoyer lift, having too much trust in his young body. "Lift with your legs," she told him, but he bent with his back. After he lifted Sal onto the mattress, they stripped off his clothes.

She'd wanted Sal to be a little boy for always. *Never grow up. You'll just make it more difficult.* But Sal's body wasn't listening. The fuzz above his upper lip was darkening, as was the hair on his legs. She counted: three hairs sprouting in the well of his right armpit. She could see the handsome man he'd become, even as he'd grow more fragile.

If not for his body, he could do so much; if not for his body, he wouldn't be himself. Sal and his body were hard to separate. He still felt like part of her in a way that Michael did not. His spit was almost her spit. His shit was almost her shit. His body fluids were not repulsive. Her brain still registered them as *mine*. He was so skinny with his six-pack and his little balls of bicep. She couldn't keep the calories on him. She prayed to Mother Mary to lessen his spasticity, Mary who also had to watch her son be crucified.

When Michael lifted him into the mesh shower chair, Sal settled open-mouthed around Michael's shoulder. "Oh my God," Michael said. "You wouldn't..." Sal laughed low, Michael's soft muscle in his teeth.

Hannah shrugged. "Told you to use the lift. Sal is teaching you an important lesson here. It's not a one-way street. You take care of him, but he can make it more difficult or less."

"Great," Michael said.

Sal let go, and Michael pushed the chair into the bathroom, where the floor heaters were blowing, the shower already running.

Hannah said, "First you test the water," and dipped her inner wrist into the spray. "Too hot." She turned down the temp and handed the nozzle to Michael. "It should be like this," she said. "All right. Let him have it." Michael let the warm water hit Sal, whose body relaxed like *That feels nice.*

She showed Michael how to work up a lather with the washcloth, to keep the water trained on Sal's chest so he didn't get cold. How to hinge him up by his shoulders and scrub his back, lift his knees and soap his thighs. Then the dirty work: Scrub his pubic hair, wash his undercarriage.

Michael hummed a sort of march, started to sing: "Just washin'... just washin'... just washin' my bro-ther's penis."

"Ahhhhhh!" Sal yelled like *You are such a dummy,* his voice bouncing off the walls.

For his hair: the tear-free shampoo. "If you get water in his mouth or eyes, he'll think that he's drowning. When you're ready to rinse, fold the washcloth in half and lay it over his eyes."

This was take-your-son-to-work day. This house was her lab; this body, this boy, her object of study. It was not less important than Gabe's work. It was more. And here she was, producing a kind of knowledge, all Michael needed to know: *Pay attention. This is a way to know him, a closeness that others do not get. Know his body but also know it is a flawed vessel for the soul. That's what broke my own mother. We need to keep watching him, keep hearing him. Don't stop listening for your brother. If he could leave us at any moment, we need to pay attention.*

Back in Sal's bedroom, they dried him off, but his undercarriage was still damp. Hannah got the blow-dryer. "I don't want him getting rashy," she said, and handed it to Michael. "Set it to low."

Michael laughed. "Are you serious?" He clicked it on and swept the nozzle back and forth over Sal's crotch. "What did you do last night?" he said over the hum. "Oh, nothing. Just gave my brother a blow job."

"Oh, stop," she said, then caught Sal laughing. "Salazar! How do you know what that means?"

The next week, Hannah went in for a kiss, and Sal tried to bite her face. When she tried to feed him ice cream, he barricaded his teeth. Maybe he wasn't feeling well. She put her hand to his forehead, but it didn't feel warm. Then he breathed in a long suck of air and coughed. Was it wetter than usual? Was it raspy?

She took his temp, which pissed him off even more. He was a bite risk, so a dab of Vaseline and—whoop—sorry, up the butt. The thermometer revealed a low-grade fever. She stared at the number like it was tea leaves, trying to predict the future. Last time he'd run a temp, it turned out to be a wicked case of constipation. At the hospital, Gabe had said, "Sal, I knew you were full of shit, but this is ridiculous."

Sal kept coughing. She listened to him breathe as if waiting for a radio station to come in through the static.

Hannah canceled her meeting, skipped her class to watch him. The next day, she called it, grabbed the dreaded blue spiral notebook from the shelf—the one in which she recorded all their medical interactions. At the emergency room, the culture confirmed pneumonia. In the consult, the doctor said Sal had aspirated, that they should consider a feeding tube.

Hannah held her scapular, rubbed it like it was a genie's lamp. Mary had messed up. She was supposed to protect him. *Enough, lady. Whatever lesson this is, we've learned it.*

Gazing at Sal on the hospital bed, a plastic semicircle hissing oxygen into his lungs, she knew that she was also sick. She was the one who saw disaster around every corner, guilt in every kind act. She could give her whole self, every minute of the day. She could dissipate herself into Sal until she had nothing left, until it was less like caregiving and more like annihilation. This love for her son could be too much for one body to hold, but she held it now.

Sal said, "Ahhhhh," and looked to the ceiling.

She froze. It sounded like song, like prayer, like Sal was saying in his own way *Your power made perfect in weakness. Your everlasting flesh.*

10

Michael squinted into the murk of Lake Erie, scanning for swirling, sharp-teethed fish, but the lake was a solid black block. It reflected the northeast Ohio sky, which was overcast—seemingly the sky's default mode.

His mother said, "Slow . . . slow . . . slow."

"I'm going slow," Michael said. "More slow is not moving."

Together, they pushed Sal's manual wheelchair along the dock. The powerchair was broken and in the shop, but they probably would've needed the manual anyway. Michael gripped its foam handles while his mother shuffled backward, guiding the wheels over the slats. Michael felt good pushing Sal again, but these were not ideal circumstances. There was only a foot of dock on each side of Sal's back wheels before the two-foot drop into the water.

Sal turned his head and looked down. His face was a white mask of SPF 50, even though it was April. The sun wasn't even out.

"Mike-a," Sal said softly. The voice didn't come, but if Michael had to guess, it was like Sal was saying *You know . . . we don't have to go fishing.*

"Don't worry, bud," Michael said. "I won't mess up."

"Uhhh-moa-mmm," Sal said, like *Don't get cocky . . .*

Their father waddled behind, carrying the cooler. "I'd push him, but apparently I'm drunk, so—"

"Stop," their mother said.

"We might have to pause for me to puke."

"If anything happened, I'd never forgive you."

"I had one road soda. One. That's what you do when you fish."

"Except we were still in the van. And it was two."

"Then it was prep work. Why have a van if you can't drink in it?"

Their father looked slightly homeless. He'd let his beard grow out, so that it looked overtly masculine and bedraggled. He wore a faded, wine-stained t-shirt featuring bug-eyed fish that read: *Life Is Full of Important Decisions*. Michael knew that was not true for this trip, because they had no choice but the ugliest: walleye.

The Mitchell family was embarking on a fishing trip with Captain Phil. They rarely went on real vacations. His father hated taking time off work, and his mother dreaded the expense and inaccessibility. But this time they were the only bid in the UCP silent auction, where they won the services of Captain Phil for only forty dollars. Over the phone Captain Phil said he'd hoped the winning bidder would be Shirley Cavanagh from News Channel 5, because she'd called him up and twisted his arm with her honey voice to donate the trip, implying that she'd more than likely be on that boat herself. But she wasn't, and now Captain Phil was pissy.

In the van on the way to the dock, they'd had a family argument. Michael asked whether fish was meat. "No," his father said. "Fish is fish." His mother agreed, said, "That's why we're allowed to eat fish on Fridays during Lent. No meat, but fish." Michael said he thought it was because in medieval times, the pope cut a deal with the fisheries, and his mother asked, "Where did you hear that?" "A book," Michael said, and his mother said, "Yeah, a stupid book," and Michael backtracked, saying fish flesh was the meat of a fish—what was the difference? His father said that for one thing, fish didn't feel pain like other animals. They didn't have the cortex for it, the brainpower to suffer. Michael asked, "How do you know?" His father said, "Because I'm a freaking neuroscientist." He took a pull of beer, said, "And another thing, fish is fish and meat is meat. So shut it." Michael chewed on that a while.

As they approached the boat, Captain Phil waved. His face, neck, and forearms—all his bare skin not covered by his "Capt. P" embroidered blue polo shirt—were pale white. Michael didn't know if he should trust a fisherman without a tan. A much younger and darker man in a sun-kissed

Hawaiian shirt hopped around on deck, lurching from task to task, loading fishing rods in their holders and spraying out a cooler with a hose.

"This is my first mate and no-good nephew, Tony," Phil said.

Phil's boat was called *The Beauty*, a.k.a. OH-4570-HB. Michael thought the second name was more fitting to the vessel, which looked mostly made of tin stained a sickly green by algae and whatever had made Cleveland's river catch on fire.

They shuffled Sal next to the boat, locked his brakes, and introduced themselves. Sal was often stingy with greetings, but he gave a big "Hi," making his family laugh.

Captain Phil smiled, said, "Well, hello to you too." For a moment, Sal seemed to make him forget about Shirley Cavanagh. "You all need help loading him?"

His mother squinted, sizing up the boat and the dock, settling her eyes finally on Sal, modeling in her mind Sal's body through space.

Their father put down the cooler. "Will you just let me lift him please? He's getting heavy. You'll hurt your back again, I'm telling you."

A seagull splashed down in the water, cawed.

"Okay," she said.

Michael followed his mother into the boat, both taking Tony's calloused hand while his father undid Sal's seat belt and straps. Sal stiffened, making squirrel teeth, like *This could go badly*. What if their dad miscalculated, caught his shoe on the wood, and stumbled? Who'd be the first to jump in after Sal? Maybe they'd all dive in at the same time and bump heads, a fitting end to his family.

Their father laughed. "Relax." Scooping Sal out of the chair, he strode toward the boat, graceful as a dancer with Sal as his stiff-fisted partner. He propped a hairy leg against the side and leaned in, momentarily suspending Sal over the gap, over the water, and here he came. Then at the last moment, he lost control—Sal was falling, dropping fast for a few inches, until their mother caught Sal's back while Michael scooped Sal's legs, yelping as their bodies bent to receive him, the boat rocking with Sal's weight. Sal was an open mouth, like *Holy Crap*.

"Look at you," their mother said. "You're on a boat!"

"He's on a boat!" their father and Michael yelled, hype men all.

"Okay," their dad said, closing his eyes and spreading his arms like wings. "Now someone catch me."

When Michael had visited Sal in the hospital a month earlier, Sal was masked, a plastic semicircle hissing oxygen into his lungs—Darth Vader for real this time, gasping in and out. All he wanted to do was make Sal smile. He whispered into Sal's ear: "Sal, I have to go to the bathroom." He waited for Sal's mouth to curl up under the foggy mask but there was no movement, just Sal's eyes fixed on the ceiling.

If God existed, this didn't make sense. Maybe God was less a Yahweh, more a Melvin or Steve. Less like an all-knowing father and more like a feckless uncle, sweaty and nervous, who threw up his hands and mumbled, "Sorry. Couldn't be helped." Standing in the hospital room, he knew that he wasn't all forgiven. The priest had lied. When he got home, he took his mother's cross off his bedroom wall and put Jesus in the dresser drawer next to his father's hunting knife.

He told his mom he didn't want to get confirmed after all. When she asked why, he said something about not really believing. She said his faith only needed to be as big as a mustard seed, went to the spice drawer to demonstrate, but they were all out.

The only good thing to happen in the hospital was that Bobbie came to visit. She brought Sal a card signed by all the Buddies! She said, "Sal, we miss you. Who else is gonna make terrible jokes? Quincy? No way. And Michael is even more awkward without you. He needs your help. Come back." She got Sal to smile.

Michael bobbed his plastic lure and concentrated on the horizon, which is what his father recommended for a churning stomach. He'd forced himself to eat a turkey sandwich, and it was not sitting well.

"Looking pretty green, boy," said their father. "You sure you're okay?"

"I'm fine," Michael said. "But my arm is gonna fall off."

"This is fishing," his father said. "You jig. You seduce. You entice the fish." He smiled, said ruefully to Captain P: "Only my son would get seasick in a lake."

"It's a *Great* Lake," Michael said.

"That it is." Captain P inhaled the lake air. Michael liked how he wasn't making a big deal about having Sal on the boat. He said he had a cousin with CP. "Good fisherman" was all he said about him.

It had taken a half-hour to run out to the "super-secret honey hole." It was just a patch of water off an island, but Capt. P raised his eyebrows to make it gross, like they'd be fishing above some giant underwater vagina. After accusing his father of almost dropping Sal, his mother retreated to the cabin to read a novel with Sal's head on her lap, as he reclined on a lounge seat. Michael wondered why Sal didn't feel sick. He was the one with the crap stomach, the acid reflux. He was the one who'd had pneumonia, who might get a feeding tube. Michael imagined the feeding tube cutting through the water, closing in like a shark, leaping into the boat and biting into his brother's belly with little eel teeth, which did not help with nausea. His Boar whispered, *To take his taste away.* His Boar whispered, *Don't puke, little piggy.*

Captain Phil grinned. "You go ahead and hurl. We could use some chum in this water."

Tony laughed. "Common knowledge: The great walleye is a sucker for re-gurged turkey sandwiches."

"That's good," his father said. "Because I did not donate forty dollars to disabled children to *not* catch any fish."

Captain Phil glared into the distance at Canada.

"Okay, Gabe," his mother said from the cabin. "Maybe it's time for that beer."

"I'm fine," he said.

"Someone has to change this luck," Tony said. "Puke or drink. Pick one."

"I'll do both," Michael said.

From the cabin, Sal said, "Eh," like *Me too.*

"Good men," Tony said, smiling with his stained teeth.

Peering out the cabin door, their mother frowned at a darker set of clouds. She pulled on a sweatshirt and draped a jacket over Sal. "Are you sure the weather will hold?"

Captain Phil looked up. "It always looks like this."

"That's not true," Tony said.

His father looked at the pixelated blobs on the fish-finder screen. "Is this deep enough? Can't we fish over some shipwreck? Some sunk lake frigate?"

"Fishing, like everything else, is all probability," Captain P said. "This honey hole here deserves the name because in my vast angler experience, we have a high probability of catching fish. Sometimes it don't pan out. Sometimes you're wrong. There're currents and temp changes. Bait problems. Magnetic field fluctuations. You never know. Just like there was high probability that this boat would be full of *News Channel Five*'s Shirley Cavanagh, but here you all are."

"Touché," his father said.

Captain Phil shrugged. "I'm a high-school math teacher most of the year."

"Yeah," Tony said and looked out over the water. "And I actually just got out of prison."

His father smiled. "Really?"

"Who just got out of prison?" their mother asked from the cabin.

"Tony," their father said.

"Oh," she said. "Congratulations."

"Thank you. Nonviolent, of course. I was intoxicated. Robbed a bank. A friend, now former friend, told me all you needed to rob a bank was a little note, which I found so hilarious that I decided to try it. As a joke. Handed the teller a slip of paper that read *I have a gun. Give me the money.* Made a frowny-face under my sunglasses and had a little hand bulge under my sweatshirt. I was ready to laugh, to let everyone know *Just kidding*, but then they handed me so much cash I forgot what I was about. Anyway, the problem was with my getaway plan."

Captain Phil chuckled. "You tried to take the bus!"

"A felony." Michael whistled. "That's big time." He felt his stomach rumble and braced himself against the hull, concentrating on how he'd tell Bobbie about the felon who took them fishing. Ever since the hospital, she'd started calling for Sal at least once a week. If Michael made her laugh hard enough, maybe she'd call for him too.

"Got ten, served five," Tony said. "My record renders me unemployable.

But when Phil retires, I'll be the new Captain P. He'll just hand over his gear and embroidered shirts."

"I promised your mother nothing," Capt. P said. "Anyway, probability again. We could've been fishing with a rich man. Instead, you took the bus."

Sal yelled from the cabin, like *Hurry the hell up*.

His father turned to Captain Phil and said in a low voice, "The boy demands fish."

"I'm doing all I can," Capt. P said.

"Surely you have another . . . honey hole." His father raised his eyebrows.

Michael felt an onslaught, a groan from deep within his plumbing. He scrambled to the side, his mouth filling with spit.

"Quick," his father said, jumping to his feet. "It's happening. Where's the camera?"

Sal cheered from inside the cabin: "Mike-aaaaa!"

But the puke did nothing. Captain Phil pulled up anchor, attached the trawling boards, and switched the bait to feeder fish, venturing away from the honey hole. Sal was back in his chair on deck, watching the lines. The rods bobbed against the waves. Michael wondered why kung fu had no fish form. Boar. Snake. Tiger. Crane. But no fish. Probably because flopping on land was not effective in an attack situation. He'd tried.

As they waited, Michael secretly fondled his fat. At least the turkey sandwich wouldn't stick. But his father noticed, ruffled his hair, said, "You hate your body like a girl."

"Good to know," Michael said. His father smiled. Michael wasn't sure who his dad would be from one day to the next—the guy who rubbed deer blood on his face, or the one in the lab who wanted to show him the true nature of reality.

Just then, the line dipped down. Tony yelled, "Fish on!" Capt. P killed the engine, and Tony set the hook, gave the rod a crank, and then held it in front of Sal.

Sal laughed with his body stiff in fish alarm. "Ahhh-ah-ha-ha," he said, like *We got Moby-Dick! Get yer harpoon!*

"Michael," his father said. "You want to help him?"

As his mother crouched with the disposable camera, Michael wedged the bottom of the rod into Sal's leg divider and helped Sal crank.

Sal squealed, like *Faster, you idiot.*

"Slower, slow, slow," said Capt. P.

The fish seemed like it would never surface. How much line had they let out? Michael's arm ached. He was relieved when he saw the flash of scales, the darting circles coming closer to the boat. Just as he thought he'd drop the rod into the lake, Tony swooped down with a net and pulled up the fish, dumping the writhing spade of muscle on the deck.

His mother looked at the back of his father's shirt, then at the fish itself. "It's uglier in real life."

His father held the fish to Sal's face as it wiggled in his hands. "Give us a kiss," he said in a Cockney accent.

"Come on, Governor," his mother said, joining in.

Sal delivered a plosive smack, like *Goodnight, sweet prince.* They cheered.

Their father tossed the fish onto the deck like it was a piece of wood. The fish thrashed, slamming itself against the metal nubs. It couldn't breathe. Michael saw the fish gasp like Sal had in the hospital, its jaws opening and closing. *They do not suffer like us,* Michael tried to tell Sal over the damage. *They barely feel it. They barely feel.*

Sal watched the fish, knitting his eyebrows, his arms tense. His eyes darted to Michael, like he was saying: *Help him. Do something.*

The fish thrashed so hard it threw its hook. Tony raised the mini–Louisville Slugger for a stunner, but before the bat came down, Michael put his body in between, grabbing the fish by its slimy tail and hooking his thumb in its gills, which fanned out like some exotic ruby flower.

"What are you doing?" Tony yelled.

"It hurts," Michael said as he heaved the fish into the lake with a splash. "It's suffering."

The fish flapped on the surface and then wiggled down into the black water.

"Yeah," said Captain Phil, looking down. "That's how it ends up on your plate."

They were quiet. His father went to the cooler, fetched a beer, and slicked back his hair with the ice water. "What can I say? My son, he's sensitive."

Capt. Phil said, " Just so you know: This boat don't do catch and release. You do that again, I throw *you* back."

"Okay," their father mumbled. "Let's not threaten him."

When Michael sat back down, Tony winked at him. "Do it again," he said. "It'd be great for Phil's blood pressure. And my career." He put his hand to his chest and mimed a heart attack.

Michael wanted to say it was Sal, but he knew they wouldn't believe it. They had no idea what was under Sal's surface. It wasn't just probability. He felt like he had a scanner, and even if he no longer always caught Sal's meaning, he could see it swimming down there, glimpse the flash of it.

Their father finished the beer in a few gulps and cracked open another one. He said, "Sal says, 'No fair!' He didn't get to keep his fish. Sal says, 'Redo!' Right, Sal?" Sal did not protest.

When their father helped Sal reel in the next fish, Sal squealed as the fish surfaced. And when Tony netted it, and it started thrashing and gasping as the sun spilled over its scales, Michael waited. He would do it if Sal gave the signal, but Sal's eyes did not meet Michael's. Sal only stared at the fish. Tony brought the bat down on its head as if in payback for the other's escape, splattering blood onto the deck.

Sal squealed again, his arms tightening.

"Yeah, buddy!" his father yelled.

Michael realized he'd been wrong. He'd imagined Sal incorrectly. He thought he'd glimpsed the flash of Sal's meaning, but he'd only mistaken it for his own reflection.

As their father posed for a picture with Sal and the fish, the sky grew darker.

"This does not look good," their mother said.

Capt. P looked up through his fighter-pilot sunglasses. "There's only a thirty percent chance of rain."

"That looks seventy-five to me," their mother said.

Capt. P shook his head. "You really want to stop at two fish?"

"I certainly do not," their father said and cracked open another beer.

"Yeah," Sal said, something like *Can we get on with it? I was enjoying myself.*

Their mother swore under her breath.

Fifteen minutes later, the spare rods at the top of the boat started buzzing as the waves rocked the vessel with higher peaks. And then Michael felt the first drop. Tiny rings bloomed on the surface of the lake.

"Goddamn it," his mother said. "Help me get Sal in the cabin."

"We didn't come all this way to give up," their father said. And then the rain started coming down in sheets, and they all ran into the cabin. "Whoo!" said their father. "Now this is fishing!"

His mother said, "If we capsize . . ."

"We're not going to capsize," his father said. "Phil here is an experienced boating professional."

"And you're drunk," their mother said.

"Here," their father said. He opened the cabin door, wiggled his way to the fish well, and came back with the zombified walleye. "Kiss this fish. That's what you need. A cold smackeroo." He resumed the Cockney accent. "Give us a kiss. Wha' you think, Sal?"

"I'm so unhappy," their mother said. "We're in a real situation and you're intoxicated and here I am again basically by myself with Sal."

"Ah-hem," Michael said. "What about me?"

Their father, still holding the fish, shrugged. The rain tapped the roof of the cabin. He raised the fish, moved its jaws back and forth, and played fish ventriloquist: "So you don't want to keep fishing?" He looked around, waiting for laughs, but his mother knocked the fish out of his hands. It fell to the cabin floor with a dull thud.

They all stood still as statues. His mother looked wild, like if they said one word, she'd hijack the boat and drive them into rocks. Sal was in stranger alert too, his lips bunched up as he watched her, as they all waited for her to make the first move.

"Give me one of those beers," she finally said. Their father opened the cabin door and got pelted with rain as he dashed to the drink cooler. He returned with the can and cracked it open. His mother took a gulp. "God, this is gross. How do you stand it?"

"Pretty well," their father said. He climbed into the first mate's seat and stared out into the horizon. "What can I say?" he said. "My son, my wife, they're sensitive."

"Okay," Capt. P sighed. "We're going in."

Michael caught Sal's eye. Sal smirked, like *We tried, brother.* But then he held the smile for too long, so it became *Maybe you need to barely feel it, to barely feel.* Michael could no longer be sure.

Capt. P drove them back towards his dock, but when the rain died down, he killed the throttle and turned back to Sal. "You want to drive?"

Sal thrust his elbows against his armrests, said "Eh."

"Affirmative," their father said and sat Sal on his lap on the captain's seat, steering the wheel hand-over-hand with Sal's wrists hooked at ten and two. "Look at you," their father said. "You're driving a boat!"

"He's driving a boat!" Michael and his mother yelled, and Sal Chewbacca-ed back, "Ahhhhh-ew-raw!" like *I'm driving a fucking boat!*

Michael's mother patted the seat next to her, but Michael sat on her lap. "Ooof," she said. "Hi, baby."

Michael whispered, "Are you really unhappy?"

"I don't know. I'm just feeling like my life is passing me by." She patted his leg. "K. You're cutting off my circulation."

Michael slid into the seat. "I'm sorry I'm not getting confirmed," he said.

"There's always next year. Maybe you'll find that mustard seed yet."

Together, they watched Sal drive, and Michael tucked this moment away as "sweet" in case he needed it later. His father wiggled the steering wheel and warned Sal away from the icebergs and pirate ships. Michael didn't want to reach the dock that led to the van and their house and the rest of their lives, because right now, they were a family, and Sal was driving over every wave.

11

On Tuesday, Hannah walked up the ramp to Ashley's townhouse in Cleveland Heights and rang the bell. She finally knew what had been bothering Ashley that day at the mall: She'd moved Tina up on the wait list for residential care, and now a space had opened up. Sal was on the wait list too, because you had to sit on the wait list for a decade or more. Hannah wanted to wait forever, but now Ashley was done. In the doorway, Ashley's eyes were bright, and her dark hair was combed back in a coif. Hannah was surprised how together she looked for the worst day of her life.

"Thanks so much for helping us finish," Ashley said, offering hot tea. "My parents just left. Tina is moving out early tomorrow."

"I wouldn't miss it," Hannah said, taking the chipped mug. Her first sip was scalding, but she swallowed it anyway.

Tina was lying on the couch, open-mouthed and listening, her eyes slowly oscillating in their sockets. Her nose was upturned like her mother's. She was still so little, but was growing up too, the outline of breasts under her Mickey Mouse t-shirt.

"Are you ready, Teen?" Hannah tried to say cheerfully but sounded hysterical.

"I explained it to her," Ashley said. "She knows something's up." She turned to Tina. "Say, 'I'm not letting my mom sleep.' Say, 'I'm punishing her.'"

"Ma," Tina said, as if she were approving the message.

"But you know what?" Ashley said, "I can love you better this way."

Tina had nothing to say about that.

Hannah held open a trash bag for Tina's carefully folded clothes. As they packed, Ashley kept talking about how great the staff was. "There's a nurse twenty-four-seven," she said. "They'll check on her every fifteen minutes."

Hannah nodded as she surveyed Ashley's house: the junky dream catchers scattered on the walls with their feathers dangling down, the dusty framed photo of a Harley, the used furniture, the ratty carpet, the medical supplies. This was the life she and Gabe had joked about, small and fragile. The benefit checks obviously weren't beneficial enough. For all of Hannah's complaints, she didn't have to make this choice.

"What are you going to do after?" Hannah asked.

"Drink?" Ashley laughed. "But then maybe nursing school? Tina taught me all these skills. Might as well cash them in."

Hannah nodded. Ashley would re-enter the world, a civilian, untethered to her daughter except for a few visits a week. There it was: a tinge of jealousy. *Hello.* Because sometimes didn't Hannah want solid nights of sleep? Didn't she want to travel without wondering who would keep Sal alive? Didn't she want to stop juggling doctor appointments and med schedules and feedings, let all the balls drop, and just sit with herself? Yes. But she wanted to keep going more. Because what would be her point? *Because they don't see how much she gives back.* What happened to that? She glared at the dream catchers. They'd dropped one.

Tina blew a spit bubble. Okay, maybe she wasn't as charming as Sal. But there was still someone home in there, a soul that deserved a loving hand, and now she would not get it. Hannah wanted to shake Ashley. *You're giving her away. You're fucking quitting. You're kicked off the team.* Instead, she opened the garbage bag wider.

"I didn't want to tell you," Ashley said. "Because I knew you'd try to talk me out of it. But I've been doing this mostly alone. I just reached my limit. I'm tired, Han."

Would Hannah have bullied her? Was she really that overbearing? She felt like Ashley had picked up a rock and found Hannah's ugliest self squirming under it. "It's okay," Hannah said, dropping the bag. She reached out for a hug, and Ashley went limp in her arms.

Hannah climbed into her van and sped all the way, trying to outrun her friend's disaster. When she arrived at the house they built for him, she was relieved. Soon her son would be home, where he belonged.

Later that week she ran into one of her old teacher friends at the grocery store, who was now running a tutoring company. She asked: Would Hannah think about applying? They always needed good people. It was in an office in one of the inner-ring suburbs, where she'd meet clients and have the camaraderie of coworkers. She could still be a parent rep, still have mornings free for Sal's doctor appointments, but she had to work afternoons.

For Sal's after-school hours, Hannah looked into hiring an aide out-of-pocket, but she'd barely make enough to cover the aide's salary, and Gabe made good money but not good enough. It was an awful math problem. She could apply for the Medicaid Waiver to pay for aides but there was a long waiting list for that too. And she'd heard Ashley's horror stories: how aides sometimes didn't show up, how they lied about hours, how they quit without notice. Hannah cringed at the thought of a stranger caring for her most precious person. After the offer, she unloaded all these concerns to her mother on the cordless, with Michael and Sal sitting on the couch watching TV. She'd hoped for encouragement, but her mother said, "Han, nothing's wrong with a woman staying home and caring for her children." Thanks, Mom.

When she hung up, Michael turned to her. "I can take care of him," he said.

"I don't know, Mikey," she said. He was fourteen—but there were old fourteens and young fourteens. He still picked his nose and wiped his boogers on his bedroom wall, but he often helped without her asking, giving Sal bites or changing his diaper. Sometimes he seemed like a mini version of herself, marshalling anxiety into vigilance. Sometimes he was even too mature. She'd caught him trying to smuggle alcohol to Shawn's house, a small and nasty Schweppes bottle full of vodka, whisky, gin, and whatever else he'd skimmed from his father's collection. Could he really be trusted?

"I've watched you take care of him my whole life. Who better than me? Right, Sal?"

Sal thought for a second, doing a math problem of his own. "Yeah," he finally said.

She went to Sal's end-of-year Individual Education Plan meeting at the middle school. The whole team was there: Sal's teacher, the director of pupil services, the speech therapist, the physical therapist, the occupational therapist, the parent-mentor, all convened to discuss Sal's progress and plans for next year. Hannah came armed with her "IEP cake"—a sheet of apples, flour, butter, cinnamon, and sugar—to get them in a good mood before she started with her demands.

She smiled at the director of pupil services, who had wanted to bus Sal out, and waved to the speech therapist.

Sal's teacher began the meeting by stating what a joy Sal was in the classroom. "He's always cracking us up," she said, and then went through the IEP line by line, starting with Communication and Socialization. She read, "'Sal demonstrates the ability to use a switch to activate his communication device.' He's got five pages now, five options each."

They acted like this was progress. "It's May," Hannah said. "It's been nine months. He should have more options, be able to do more with it. That's what you said last August. So why does he still only have five pages?" Hannah could sense the goodwill in the room plummet. Their sugar high was wearing off. "All I'm saying is he's got more to say."

"Of course he does," his teacher said, and then she read the next goal. "Sal will make his speech options more age appropriate."

The speech therapist said, "Maybe his brother could help with that one? We haven't really used this feature, but the Whisper Wolf can record human speech. What if we ask Michael to give Sal his voice, say what Sal wants to say?"

This was their old game made real. Maybe Michael was mature enough to finally handle it. "I'll discuss it with them," Hannah said.

His teacher continued to Self-Help and Transition, Daily Living and Physical Therapy, Academic Readiness. It was hard to hear the meager goals set for him. *He will walk in a pool. He will participate in range-of-motion exercises. He will use a switch to turn on the radio and change the stations. He will recognize more numbers. He will drive his chair without crashing. He will not startle with strangers. He will demonstrate a need for help.* She read the reasons he wasn't reading, wasn't writing. *Cognitive limitations. Too difficult motorically.*

When his teacher brought up Sal's next year, there was an awkward pause. The director of pupil services cleared his throat. "There's just not a lot that Sal can efficiently participate in, given his physical and mental limitations."

Hannah said, "I don't expect him to go to algebra. But what about more social ones?" She didn't want him to just sit there, being ignored, on the sideline of life.

The director glanced at the teacher, the parent-mentor, the speech therapist. They had a secret, and now it was time for telling. "Mrs. Mitchell," he said. "I know integration has been your goal since Sal started here. But Sal deserves a program that better fits his needs. Our high school special-ed program is great, but it's mostly focused on job training."

"I don't want to bus him out," said Hannah. But that's what they were recommending. Were they dumping him? Or was this really his best option? She could fight it. Or she could sign.

The boys unloaded from the bus. Today was the dry run, the final test. It was still not too late to call it off. Sal pushed his joystick forward, and the motor propelled Sal up the walkway.

Hannah said, "Pretend I'm not here."

"I can't," Michael said. "You breathe too heavy."

Sal smiled with his dimple and his jagged teeth. She would've gotten him braces like his brother, but he already had them for his feet. You could only tame a body so much.

Inside the house, she said, "What's first?"

"Our afternoon cigarette," Michael said.

"Shut up."

"Take off his coat."

"Right. And then?"

Michael tapped his temple. "Meds and snack."

She watched Michael's rough hands handle Sal. He clasped a bib around Sal's neck, peeled the foil off the applesauce, stirred the powdered

Thick-It into Sal's milk. Hannah had persuaded the doctors to delay the feeding tube in favor of a baclofen pump, which would lessen his spasticity and help him gain weight. This summer, just under his skin, they would surgically implant a small hockey puck, which injected muscle relaxers into his spinal cord without the drowsy side effects. But for now, Michael pulverized the Valium in the crusher and sprinkled the powder onto the spoon of waiting applesauce, and with his finger twirled it all into a cloud. She couldn't have done it better herself.

"Zombie-time," Michael said, and steered the spoon to Sal's face.

Sal grimaced, opened up, took a swallow.

"That's a good baby," Michael crooned, and Sal spit out the rest. "Damn it," Michael said.

"That's what you get for goading him."

Finally, Michael lifted Sal onto the living room couch and reluctantly put his nose to Sal's loins. "What you got cooking in there?"

Sal gave a weak laugh.

"Oh no," Michael said. "It's shit. That's his shit laugh."

"Mike-a," Sal said, tightening his arms and gurgling out an "Ahhhhh," like *Ha ha. You gotta change me.*

"Oh, screw you," Michael said. "He knew I was training today. He set me up. Can we pretend you're here just for this part?"

Hannah took a peek. It was a ten-wet-wiper for sure. Thank God. Sal was constipated, going on day three. She did not foresee her well-being so closely tied to her son's bowel movements. "Watch," she said and wiggled her fingers. "Learn from the master...."

Hannah waited for Gabe until 5:15. When he still hadn't come home, she walked out into the garage, turned around, and walked back in. She said in a deep voice, "Hello, boys! I'm your father. No one is dead? Great! Sal, how are your girlfriends? Wonderful! Michael, how are your boyfriends? Kidding! My job here is done. Tough day. Where's my beer? Glug glug glug. Science is hard!" Russian accent: "I am strong like bear! Glug glug glug." She collapsed on the couch and promptly started snoring.

Michael clapped. She cracked one eye. Sal was smiling. "Whoa," Michael said.

"He deserves it," she said. "He's late."

Gabe stumbled in a few minutes later. "Sorry," he said. He put his briefcase on the floor and kicked off his sneakers.

"It's got to be at five," Hannah said. "They can't be left alone longer than that."

"I know," he said. "Sorry."

Then he went to the fridge and expertly chopped the onions, mushrooms, bell peppers, and was soon sautéing, a natural at the stove, a better cook than she was. She was surprised he'd even offered to come home early to relieve Michael. She thought he wouldn't sacrifice his own career for her midlife crisis. But he was trying.

As he added the Prego pasta sauce, he asked, "How'd they do?"

"Good. Until Michael had to change Sal's poop diaper."

"Oh, bravo, Sal. Way to give it to your brother."

Sal smirked like *Thank you*.

Just thinking about leaving them alone put a knot in her neck. She placed Sal's cups in the sink. Gabe must have read her face. He came over and massaged her delts. "Don't worry, Han. We'll be fine." She relaxed. "Or Sal will die and you'll never forgive yourself." She reached back and pinched his belly fat. "Help," he said. "Domestic violence."

Monday, Hannah drove to her first day of work. She wondered: Am I fucking nuts? She could barely handle all of Sal's needs as a housewife. It was like having two jobs and asking for a third. She felt like she was pretending to be a different person with a different life. And leaving him with Michael, who was only fourteen, who was so absentminded he sometimes walked into traffic?

She decided to make a quick stop at the mall, to that makeup counter. She could allow herself this indulgence. She found the girl, the same one from the month before, and asked for the depuffing cream. It was still $49.99. She put it on her credit card, added some expensive lotion too, and in the van she anointed herself, rubbing the cream under her eyes, massaging in the lotion. She felt herself depuff, the anger and resentment leaving her body. She admired herself in the rearview.

As her old friend showed her to her new desk, Hannah's skin felt like it was glowing. She was ready for whatever the day would throw at her. Sitting down with a mumble-y high school boy, she got straight to work. He had a thin mustache and wouldn't look her in the eye. His five paragraphs on the *Catcher in the Rye* were all jumbled. She explained topic sentences, taught him how to quote and how to analyze: "Now you say what you think those ducks stand for." His eyes lit up. How had no one taught him this before? When it was over, he said, "Thank you, Mrs. Mitchell." He meant it. She wished Michael would talk to her like that. Was she still good at this? Maybe. She tucked her hair behind her ears and called the next one in.

In the break room, they were talking about some kid's idiot parent, who teetered almost daily between threatening to sue and telling them what miracle workers they were. She laughed too loudly. The day-mares only came in flashes—imagining all the ways Sal could die. Choking on cut-up fruit, Valium overdose, driving his chair down the basement stairs. A student asked if she was okay. "Yes," she said. *Just murdering my son....*

She raced home. When she pulled into the driveway, there were no flashing lights, no ambulances. In the kitchen, Sal's applesauce container was overturned next to a plate with burned and fossilized burrito cheese, and there was a wet spot on the floor she didn't even want to examine, but Gabe was whistling by the stove, wearing an apron, playing Mr. Mom. And Sal was very much alive on the couch, a pillow between his legs, his braces off, Michael knelt over him as if in prayer. Sal had his shirt up as Michael listened to the white drum of his stomach.

"Hey, Mom," he said. "Listen. *Squish. Ehhhh. Um...uhhhhm...blu-urp!*" He was singing the song of Sal's gastric juices.

Sal smiled and said, "Mike-a!" like *You idiot.*

Michael was giving voice to Sal's inside sounds, and Sal liked it. Maybe this was a good time to talk to them about Sal's computer. She said to Michael: "You know how Sal's computer voice can be a little off-putting?"

"Yeah," Michael said. "We might as well put a metal box over his head."

"Right. So at his IEP, we discussed how Sal could sound more like a fourteen-year-old. If Sal agrees, maybe you could record some of his options."

"What do you mean?"

"Like record yourself into his computer. Give him your voice. Would you like that, Sal?"

Sal took a moment, his lips in pensive formation.

Michael said, "We'll think about it."

12

The Wolf whispered, *Chow*.

The Wolf whispered, *Beverage*.

It whispered, *Mom. Dad. Mike.*

The school year was almost over, and Michael couldn't wait. His summer plans involved getting stoned and drunk with Shawn and Gregg when he wasn't busy watching Sal, which wouldn't be that much. Sal was signed up for day camps half the time, and with school out, his mom's work schedule would be flexible.

The Wolf whispered all through dinner, Sal's hand perched in front of the switch, hovering, ready to strike.

Sal coughed milk in Michael's direction. Michael tried to duck but got blasted on his left cheek. "Let's be quicker with that washcloth," he told their mom.

"Maybe you need to work on your reflexes," their mother said. "What am I paying that maniac kung fu teacher for? Bob and weave out of the way. Hi-ya!" She made a series of ducking movements and hand chops.

Michael rolled his eyes. "His name is Master Steve. And 'hi ya' is not kung fu. It's karate."

"What does kung fu say then?"

"Whatever it wants."

"How about 'Yeee-ow!'" their father asked.

Michael sighed, took another bite of burger.

"Sighing is not kung fu," said their father.

"Bruce Lee never sighed," said their mother.

"Are you guys done?" Michael asked. They caught each other's eyes and laughed.

It was a wonderful performance. They were acting like everything was normal, but in the past two weeks, they'd been bickering more than ever. At the same time, their mother seemed happier since taking the tutoring job. She regaled them with humorous stories about her coworkers. "Today in the break room they had a debate about which municipality has the best-tasting tap water. I'm like, 'Is this what I was missing?'" But she was. She'd been missing it, and her complaints took on a whimsy that wasn't there before. She'd even gone out for a happy-hour gathering and come home with this weird smile on her face.

The Wolf whispered, *Milkshake*, and Sal clicked. "I am hank-er-ing for a milk-shake. Plea-se, Mom-my, plea-se?"

Michael laughed. "That's what his speech therapist thinks is age appropriate?"

"You could help," their mother said.

"I *do* help," Michael said. He'd been looking after Sal three days a week, for two hours after school, and doing an excellent job, he might add. Sal could make it more difficult or less, and so far he was choosing more.

Their mother said, "I know you help. Just consider what we talked about. The school year is almost over."

"Okay," Michael said. Over the summer, they wouldn't have the therapist's help, and Sal would have fewer people to practice on. But Michael hadn't heard Sal's voice inside his head in weeks, and he'd gotten him wrong on the fishing trip. He worried he'd lost him for good.

Their mother leaned over and whispered into Sal's ear. He smiled open-mouthed. She said to their father, "Sal wants to show you something." She pressed his computer screen until the Wolf whispered, *Rain*.

Sal clicked, and the Wolf boomed: "What a glor-i-ous feel-ing, I'm sing-ing in the ra-a-ain."

"What the hell was that?" their father asked, and Sal slammed down his arms on his tray, like *I know!*

"Sal has a solo in the end-of-year choir concert," their mother said.

Michael rolled his eyes. He was not looking forward to it. All those people would hear the Wolf sing, would "Awwww" and clap. It'd be a sentimental puke fest.

"Cool, buddy," their father said.

"You're coming, right?"

"I think so," their father said. "I'm trying to finish this grant."

"Shut up," she said, and then smiled at Michael and Sal. "We're coming."

The phone rang. Michael saw Bobbie's digits on the caller ID and picked up.

"It's me," she said.

"What's up, girl?" he responded in his most confident drawl, even though his stomach seized. Sometimes she discussed what a douchebag Ben Stanley was or the oppressiveness of the Latin her mother made her take—before asking for Sal. But today she wasted no time. "Is your brother there?"

"Sure," Michael said. "Unless you'd rather talk to me?"

She laughed. "Maybe next time."

Michael's shoulders deflated. Sal lay on the couch watching TV, his head in their mother's lap. Michael said, "It's Bob-bie," and Sal started in on a spaz attack, his arms tight against his ribs.

"All right, settle," their mother said. "You'll give yourself a cramp." She looked up at Michael and patted his cheek. "They'll call for you eventually."

Girls were drawn to Sal. By default, he was a good listener. And then he had a smile that seemed to wrap around his face, punctuated by his dimple. Their father had often said to Michael: "Man, what Sal could do with your vocabulary."

Michael held the phone to Sal's right ear, and Sal let out a whale call: "Ahhhh-ah-mmm!" Michael was pretty sure about this one: It was like *Oh my God, it's so good to hear your voice.*

"Well, hello to you too. Hold on. My bitch of a mom's yelling at me. What!"

Sal laughed.

"I'm glad you don't judge, Sal."

Bobbie told Sal secrets. Like how she hated her father, who lived in Florida and seemed to drink more than Michael's. Like why she wore long-sleeved shirts and pants even in hot weather, why her arms were full of white slashes like she was counting time on a prison wall. She told Sal on the phone that she did it herself, that the pain made her feel something, which was getting harder to do. *To barely feel.* She didn't even own a cat.

"Is that crazy brother of yours listening?" she asked. "I think I can hear him breathing."

When they hung up, Michael asked Sal if he wanted to practice Wheelchair Kung Fu. But Sal said, "Eh-eh."

Michael asked him, "What's wrong?" Sal didn't respond. "Are you afraid they'll send you to the special school?" Sal stared off, looking past Michael's head. Michael asked, "What are you thinking, bud?"

Michael concentrated on his chi, on his breathing, and got slower, but the voice did not come. He opened his eyes. Sal bunched his mouth into squirrel teeth, let out a long howl of despair, and then switched to pensive, his eyes looking far away, followed by a smirk that folded up to a full smile before he flexed his arms and laughed. In less than ten seconds, Sal had gone through his whole facial repertoire, performing himself, playing his expressions like notes on a scale, mixing signals, like *Read it and weep, brother. Behold the mystery.*

Their choir class was where people who didn't have much talent went to get their music credit. Sal moaned during the songs but was by no means the worst singer. Michael himself wasn't half-bad, though he was never chosen for a solo. While everyone else lined up on the carpeted bleachers, Sal sat ground level in his wheelchair with Mrs. Bridgewater.

"Is everyone clear about the end to 'Singing in the Rain?'"

"Eh-eh," Sal said, using his emphatic tone, like *No. One question: Why does it still sound like shit?* The whole class laughed, though to them, the joke was simple.

"What's not clear, Sal?" asked the choirmaster. "When I give you the signal, you *do* your *thing*!" She pointed with double fingers.

Sal smiled and stuffed his tongue between his teeth.

"It's clear to me," Quincy said, writhing in his wheelchair. "I can sing it."

"That's great, Quincy," said the choirmaster. "But I think Sal has it under control. Right, Sal?" She didn't wait for his answer. "All right. From the top."

She started in on the piano, her upper body swaying to the beat. Mrs. B held the mic away from Sal's Wolf, but you could still hear it whisper "Rain" and "Back" over the speakers every three seconds, as if it were part of the song itself. Michael didn't sing, just lazily lip-synched. Then they got to Sal's part, and the choirmaster took her hand off the keys and pointed to Sal, her mouth open wide as if she were actually dying of happiness. Sal, on his typical delay, clicked his hand forward and, in its halting and flat robot diction, the Wolf arrived: "What a glor-i-ous feel-ing, I'm sing-ing in the ra-a-ain."

Someone gave the requisite "Awww," and they all clapped. Michael clenched his jaw, curled his toes. His Boar whispered, *Oh, how sweet. How freaking adorable. Someone call News Channel Five's Shirley Cavanagh.* The Boar was right: It was a moment fit for a fluff piece on the evening news.

Michael would rather have Sal yell in his normal voice, Chewbacca it out: *Ahhhhh-rah-uhhhhh,* which to the discerning listener, to someone like Bobbie, would be like *Listen to me in all my glory!* Instead, they'd get the Wolf, his brother adulterated, cut with switches and circuits until he was no longer Sal. And the worst part was that Sal loved it. He stiffened in spaz attack, smiling open-mouthed as he rocked off-rhythm to the piano.

As they were leaving, Bobbie said, "Man, Sal. You were great."

Sal flashed his dimple like *No sweat.*

Bobbie was wearing a black velvet dress that clung to her curves. Her hair came down in brown curls to her shoulders, framing the freckles on her apple cheeks, and her nostrils flared in an adorable way when she sang. Her smile put Michael at ease, made him think: *Don't worry, you're doing fine.* He saw why Sal liked her so much.

She caught Michael staring. "What?" she asked.

"Nothing," he said. "You look nice today."

She laughed. "Sal, where did you get this guy? He's the awkwardest wingman ever."

Sal shouted, "Yeah!" like *Tell me about it.*

Michael straightened his imaginary tie.

In English, Michael and Gregg sat in front of the class, staring into the pretend deep green pool of the Salinas River, performing the ending to *Of Mice and Men*.

Michael said in a slow, soft voice, "I thought . . . you . . . was mad at me, George."

"No," Gregg said. "No, Lennie, I ain't mad. I never been mad, and I ain' now. That's a thing I want ya to know."

His class was competing to see who was the best George and Lennie. Michael didn't like the book. Lennie had a petting problem. He petted everything to death. Michael could relate to loving things so hard you crushed them, but otherwise the book was boring. Lennie and George kept talking about buying some patch of land where they could live in peace, and then everyone wanted in on it—a guy who had no hand and a Black dude with scoliosis. And you knew the whole time that Lennie would fuck it up. He was "mentally disabled," the teacher kept saying. Sure enough, he'd death-petted that puppy and shortly after, the girl. Now it was time for a mercy killing. Whatever George would do to him, the mob would do worse.

Michael said, "Le's do it now. Le's get that place now."

"Sure," Gregg said. "Right now. I gotta. We gotta."

Michael felt Gregg's finger pistol rise to the back of his skull. They let the moment sit, and then Gregg's hand jerked and his mouth exploded. On cue, Michael jarred and then slumped forward, just as the book said. He imagined his brains clearing out, his lights turning off. He may have given himself whiplash. He didn't care. He was serious about dying. He wanted that A.

He did not reanimate until the class started clapping. When he opened his eyes and his teacher was standing, he knew that they'd won, that they'd be voted best.

"Dude," Gregg said. "You were a great Lennie. You sure you don't have a mental disability?"

Michael put his hand to Gregg's hair and pushed down hard. "Soft," he said in Lennie's voice, and Gregg said, "Ow."

Michael waited in the lunch line for his Mexican pizza. He blocked the cafeteria lady's sight line so Gregg could shove Gobstoppers and Sour Patch

Kids into his cargo shorts. "Thanks, bro," Gregg said, and Michael nodded. Gregg did feel like a brother, or like Michael imagined that weaker non-twin bond. They played hacky sack in the middle of town, where they spat and smoked and slouched. They slept over at each other's houses nearly every weekend and skimmed their fathers' liquor bottles to make a foul brown liquid that mashed up their faces and got them buzzed quick. At the same time, Gregg competed with Michael to see who could get the highest grade in honors science. They still did kung fu together, could spend hours sparring in one of their basements until they were out of breath with too many bruises. He felt like he could tell Gregg anything. So what if his best friend occasionally made love to vacuums? He was good with Sal, had no problem with Michael carrying Sal down to the basement to hang when they played video games, and would make fun of Michael until Sal laughed. "See? Even Sal thinks you're a little bitch."

Michael walked by Sal's table to give him a hand slap, then sat down with Gregg and Shawn, where Gregg said, "Mission accomplished," and threw down the stolen candy for the table. He doffed an imaginary cap to Michael, who took a bow.

Shawn asked, "You coming over today too, Mitchell?"

"My mom works today," Michael said. "I'm hanging out with Sal."

"So we're going over to your house?" asked Shawn.

"Um, nein," Michael said. "Verboten."

"Okay," Shawn said. "You don't have to get German about it." Shawn was tall and wiry and spent his time attempting "sick" skateboard tricks. He seemed too confident, sniffing out others for weakness, and wore both skating shirts and hemp necklaces as if he couldn't decide which subculture he belonged to but smoked enough pot for both. Although Michael liked Shawn less, Gregg was enamored, always inviting him along, and Michael worried they'd start hanging out without him.

Gregg said, "You take care of Sal a lot."

Michael shrugged. "Just for two hours. Not every day. We mostly just watch TV. We'd be doing that anyway."

Shawn, whose father worked in finance, asked, "You get paid for taking care of him?"

"No," Michael said. "He's my brother."

Gregg said, "You wipe his butt, though."

Michael shrugged. "Sure. But not if I can get out of it. I bribe him to hold it in."

"Nice. So you actually lose money," Shawn said. "You get shit on your hands?"

"Sometimes," Michael said. "We have special soap."

How could Michael describe changing his brother's diaper? It was gross, of course, but not that different from taking care of his own business. When he got shit on his arm, he'd yell at Sal in an Italian gangster voice, "What kinda shit-a is this shit-a!" and Sal would laugh and shout "Momma!" like *Compared to Mom you so suck at this.*

"Poop is poop," Michael said. "You can't get mad at poop."

"Shit happens?" Gregg said, holding up one finger.

"Exactly."

"Guys?" Shawn said. He looked down at his lunch. "It's hard enough to eat on Mexican pizza day. You think you can get us some of his pills?"

It was not the first time they'd asked. "I'll think about it," Michael said.

"You know what I love about your brother?" Gregg said. "He never gets mad or sad."

"Sure he does," Michael said.

"You know what I mean," Gregg said, brushing a wedge of hair out of his eye. "Every time I come over, he's always in a good mood. Like with everything he's got going on."

"Come on," Shawn said. "He's got to get depressed."

Michael looked over at Sal's table. Sal had his mouth open, waiting for Mrs. B to come at him with the spoon. Michael looked at Sal like his friends would, noticed how awkwardly he chewed, like his mouth was a trash compactor with bad wiring.

"I don't know," Michael said.

"Because if I was like that, I'd . . ." Shawn said, and then he stopped.

"What?" Michael asked.

He shook his head. "To never touch a girl? To never have sex?"

"He can have sex," Michael said. They looked at him weirdly. "I mean . . . it's technically possible." Michael had changed Sal's diaper when he had a boner. He had desire. Just look at how Sal spazzed when Bobbie called him on the phone, how he beamed at her in Buddies! That guy Paul at church, who controlled his computer with his one finger and had three little boys and a cute wife—that kind of future for Sal was possible if the Wolf would get its shit together and close the gap between Sal's mouth and brain, if it could just let the world hear Sal correctly. But his friends weren't listening.

"Uhhhh," Gregg said, staring into the tortured landscape of his Mexican pizza. "I can't imagine." He glanced at Shawn to make sure he also could not imagine, that they were united in this not imagining.

Michael wished they would just stop talking. What was so good about their little lives? Shawn had to smoke pot to fend off panic attacks, and Gregg had a long-term relationship with his mother's vacuum cleaner.

"You don't think about it?" Gregg said, and then glanced at Shawn. "I mean, if I were like that, I'd fucking kill myself."

"Stop!" Michael yelled, and was out of his seat with his fist clenched.

Gregg had sat in the soft foam of Sal's wheelchair, tried it out on his own body, and spun around the room until the room spun too. Michael thought those were moments of joy, of play, but now he knew what Gregg was really thinking: *Put him out of his misery.* The line of action was obvious: Lunge across the table at Gregg and get him into the phone booth. He heard the Boar's guttural snorting in his ears. He felt himself being taken over, going whole hog, his heart hammering. *Punch. Kick. Murder. Weeeee.*

He said to Gregg, "You vacuum fucker."

"Okay," Gregg said.

"You fucker of vacuums."

"All right," Gregg said, his head dropping.

"Wait," Shawn said, glancing at Gregg. "The hose part?"

Michael nodded. Yes, the hose part.

"Look," Shawn said. "We're sorry. Sit back down. We won't talk about it."

Michael stormed toward the bathroom. As he shoved open the door, he wondered what kind of life would be unimaginable. He often felt it was the one he was already living. But they'd picked Sal's. The life of the person he loved most. He thought of Bobbie. He went to the sink and turned it to hot. He let the faucet run, and then plunged his hands into scalding water. *To barely feel it. To barely feel.*

"You okay?" asked a pair of legs under the toilet divider, in crumpled jeans and black chucks with anarchy symbols sketched on the toe tips. "It's hard to go with you doing that."

That afternoon, Michael watched Sal descend from the bus, the metal grate blurring his body until, with a robot whirl, it lowered down flat for the big reveal: Sal slobbering in all his glory. In the house, Michael fed him his afternoon yogurt and meds. As he twisted the pill crusher, he wondered what it would be like to take the Volume himself. He wanted to feel what Sal felt. He shook the pill container and listened to its hollow rattle.

While Michael fed Sal, he practiced guitar. He only knew the basic chords, but it was enough to make up songs. "You smell so terrible, so bad," he sang. "I'm the best brother you've ever had."

"Eh-eh . . . Mike-a!" Sal said, like *Boooooo. Give yourself a whiff. You do that without a diaper.*

Michael paused, sniffed. "No seriously. What's that smell?"

Sal smiled, like *Belated birthday present.*

As he changed his brother's diaper, he thought of how he'd wanted to tell his friends that Sal made his family special, that in comparison, his friends' families were boring. Sal made every moment gleam with meaning. He pulled Sal's pants back up and studied his face. Was Sal depressed? He searched for sadness, but his brother wasn't giving anything away. Michael closed his eyes. Could he still imagine? Or was this the reason why he lost his shit at the lunch table? That he couldn't imagine either? That if he were like Sal he'd . . . *say it* . . . kill himself?

No. The Wolf could be a way to imagine again. Maybe, through the Wolf, he could finally get Sal right. "Do you want me to give you my voice? Like . . . record into your computer?"

Sal took a moment, his lips pressed together, pondering. Then his lips flicked up just barely, and then yes, curled into a smile. "Yeah," he said, like *We could do a trial run.* Or maybe Sal was just challenging him, like *Let's see how well you really know me.*

When they told their mother the news, her smile took up too much of her face. For a moment, Michael had to look away, staring into the tartan print of their couch. It would be different this time. Not like when they were younger, when Michael just spoke for him. Sal would have the choice. He could click or not. "I'm so glad," she said. "You guys think of what you want to say."

Later, with his brother on Sal's bed, Michael breathed deeply, tried to focus his chi. *Come in, Sal. Come in.* Michael put his forehead against Sal's forehead. He waited, but Sal did not come. Then Michael reached for the bottle of Volume on Sal's shelf. He wanted to know what it was like to be Sal.

He crunched the pill in his molars as he laid back down. It tasted like chalk and coated his teeth. God, he really should have just swallowed it whole. He feared there'd be the opposite effect, that he'd become spastic, but then he felt the first wave of relaxation, a pleasant buzzing that radiated from his head into his bones. His thoughts no longer raced. He felt his spit pool in his mouth. He put his forehead next to Sal's again, and suddenly through the static he heard something. *Mmmmmm.* Sal, just barely. Sal, from so far away. *Mmmmmm,* the voice inside Michael's head said, still underwater. *Mmmmmmm.* He closed his eyes, and then it surfaced: *Mmmmmichael!*

He scrambled off the bed and fetched Sal's Wolf from the powerchair. He engaged the edit option, and spoke—recording sound files, rough approximations of the speech in his head. And after each guess, he looked Sal in the eye and asked for the green light: "Is this what you want to say?" If Sal balked, he said, "Or how about this?" and tried again.

He spent the weekend with Sal's Wolf, filling it with his own voice. He recorded the prompts too, what the pillow speaker whispered into Sal's ear. It was as if he'd had transferred a ghost of himself onto the computer, a ghost Michael could no longer control.

13

On Monday in choir, Mrs. B held the mic away from the Wolf as usual, but Michael could hear himself whisper from the speaker: *Rain . . . Back . . . Rain . . . Back*. Near the end of the song, the choirmaster gave Sal her double-point. Sal clicked right on time, and it was no longer the cold robot coming through the speaker, but a warm human voice. It didn't sound like Michael, but like how Sal used to sound in Michael's head when he let out one of his long whale calls: "What a gloooo-rious feeling, I'm sing-ing, singing in the rain. . . ."

The music stopped. His classmates craned their necks to see Sal at the bottom of the bleachers. Everyone smiled. Sal clicked his switch again, and as their voice rose up from the Wolf, Sal glanced at Michael and stuffed his tongue between his teeth and spaz attacked, like *That's right. We sound not too shabby.*

Gregg turned to him and said, "Dude, that's awesome. Really."

"It was all Sal," Michael said. "But I'm still not talking to you."

"Come on, dude," Gregg said. "I'm sorry."

Michael turned away.

After practice, the choir director said she thought that at the performance next week, it would be "super neat" if Michael assisted Sal instead of Mrs. Bridgewater. "It's already sort of a duet," she said. "Let's make it official."

Michael turned to Sal. "What do you think?"

Sal smiled like *A twin act. I like it.*

The choirmaster said, "I'll take that as a 'Yes.'"

Bobbie came to congratulate Sal. She laughed. "There's something different about you. Did you get a haircut? A new shirt?"

"Eh-eh," Sal said like *Guess again.*

"Wait, I know. You sound different. Frankly, I thought your voice would be lower." She smirked at Michael.

"Good one," he said as she mussed his hair.

Over the next few days, Sal revealed himself through the Wolf. Instead of "Howdy, Pard-ner," he said, "What's up?" Instead of "I love you, Mom-my," he said, "Mom, you're a quality Mom." Instead of "I would like more food, plea-se," Sal said, "Place more food in my mouth hole." Instead of "I would like more juice, plea-se," Sal said, "Juice me." Instead of "I want to sit with frien-ds," Sal said, "Park me with the ladies. I'll take it from there." During Gym, instead of "Go team, go!" he said, "Run, you fatties. Run!" Instead of "Mis-sus B helps me," he said, "Mrs. B, my faithful servant." Michael continued to make minor adjustments to Sal's Wolf. If he was in a pinch, he'd pop one of Sal's Volumes, which made his twin's voice easier to hear.

By Wednesday at lunch, Sal had gained an audience. Michael was sitting at his brother's table again, instead of with Gregg and Shawn, and they'd drawn a crowd that was shouting requests. One boy said, "Hey Sal, tell everyone to shut it. And call Mrs. B your servant."

Michael waited to hear someone mutter *retard* under their breath, but instead the students all just stood there waiting for Sal to scan through the options. Bobbie was in the crowd, too, looking on. The other special needs kids enjoyed the added attention. Quincy laughed from his chair, and John covered his eyes and shook his head.

The Wolf took its sweet time, over fifteen seconds to scan through the Talking page, but when Sal clicked the switch, Michael's voice sounded over the speakers: "Please shut your mouth holes!"

His classmates doubled over in laughter.

"Oh my God," one boy said, raising his arms in victory. "So classic." Every time Sal clicked was further proof that Michael had gotten him right.

"Say something else," Bobbie said, grabbed Sal's non-switch hand, and held it.

Under no circumstances was Michael to have people over when he was watching Sal, so he made Bobbie promise to be gone by five, before his father got home. On the bus, Sal sat strapped in the back, so she sat next to Michael, who was nervous about what she'd think of his dad's taxidermied deer heads and his mom's weird crucifix and all Sal's adaptive equipment. Michael knew so much about her, but he had to pretend not to or she'd know he'd been listening. He played twenty questions. Her favorite band: No Doubt. Her favorite book: *Catcher in the Rye*. Michael received this information as if for the first time.

She asked, "What is it like to be a twin?"

Michael thought for a moment. "I guess you don't ever have to be lonely."

"That must be nice," she said. "I'm lonely all the time. That's why I call your brother."

Their thighs were touching, and she brushed her knuckles against his hand. Michael wanted to think it was on purpose.

She said, "I can tell you guys have a special bond. Just the way you are with him."

Should he tell her about hearing Sal? Michael looked down at her covered arms. She had damage too. She would understand. He didn't want to get too weird too soon. He found his hand in hers, and he let it sit there. He felt like a robot that was malfunctioning in the most wonderful way, feeling real emotions for the first time. He freaked out and gave her hand a small shake. Her palm was as clammy as his.

Bobbie oohed and aahed as the lift lowered Sal down onto their driveway. "Very cool," she said, clapping. As Sal drove his chair off the lift platform, he pursed his lips like *That's right. The latest in bus lift technology.*

They opened the door, and Batey furiously sniffed her. "Watch out," Michael said. "He's a dog-pervert."

"Oh, stop. He's sweet," she said, scratching behind his ears as Batey craned his neck and thumped his back foot.

On the wall, the deer head stared out through its marble eyes. "Sorry," Michael said. "My dad's hobby. I know you're a vegetarian."

She shrugged. "It's more ethical than the meat aisle."

Then he pointed to his mother's Jesus, levitating off the cross. "I'm sure you've met Mister J," he said.

"You're looking well," Bobbie said to Jesus. "Suspiciously well."

"Yeah, he works out now."

They followed Sal as he drove into the kitchen and pulled up to his port at the table. Michael offered her a Hot Pocket, which she declined.

"I know. I don't eat food either. Not sure how I got like this." He waved at his gut.

Bobbie laughed. "Okay, maybe I'll have some pretzels."

He took her through their after-school routine, feeling as if he were performing the role of "good brother." There weren't any manly bib options: Mickey Mouse, Thomas the Tank Engine, and pastel dog paws. His mom needed to update.

As Michael crushed the Volume, explaining that it helped Sal relax, he felt this wild urge to impress her. "You want one?"

Bobbie froze. "What?"

"Just kidding," Michael said with a strained laugh. "You need cerebral palsy first, right, Sal?"

"Yeah," he said, like *I'd recommend it.*

"Okay." Michael lifted the spoon of applesauce. "Here goes nothing." But Sal clamped his teeth. "Show off," Michael said, and Sal grinned.

"I think what Sal is saying is he wants me to feed him." Bobbie took the spoon and expertly swooped it into Sal's mouth. "I have a much younger half-sister."

"Here you go, buddy," Michael said. He gently gave Sal a sip of thickened milk and wiped his chin with the washcloth, more carefully than usual. Did Sal notice he was acting differently? His brother didn't clench his teeth, like *Poser.* Maybe Sal was performing too.

Sal drove into his room and stopped in the middle, looking up at the glow-in-the-dark stars dotting the ceiling. Bobbie said, "Whoa. Cool stars, Sal. Can we get a proper look?" They pulled down the blinds, turned off all the lights, and stared up.

Michael said, "I put them up myself."

Bobbie said, "You suck at constellations."

She held Sal's hand and then reached for Michael's. His Boar whispered, *Kiss her. First base. Second. Third.* But Michael told it to *Shhh*. He reminded himself she was here to see Sal, who would never forgive him if he made a move, not after what they'd put on the Wolf together in the Bobbie category. When he turned the light back on, he could tell the volume pill was starting to take effect, making Sal loose.

Bobbie picked up Sal's Wolf from the back of his chair and dangled it in its canvas bag. "I want to hear him say more stuff."

"Should we show her?" Michael asked, and Sal said, "Yeah." They set it up and Michael pressed the Friend page. Then Sal's hand hovered over the switch, waiting for the Wolf to scan. "Bob-bie," the Wolf whispered and Bobbie put her hand to her chest like *Aww. Me?* But Sal didn't click. Michael said, "Sorry, he's just a little out of it from the medication." They waited for the Wolf to cycle back to "Bob-bie," and when the icon lit up, Sal's wrist finally fell forward. "I love you," the Wolf said.

"Oh," Bobbie said and laughed nervously. "I love you too, Sal." She mussed Sal's hair like he was her little brother. Sal smiled but seemed unsure, his mouth bouncing up and down.

"Not like that," Michael said. "Like really. He wants you to kiss him."

Bobbie hesitated. "Okay," she finally said, bent down, and gave Sal's cheek a little peck.

The Boar whispered, *To never touch a girl. To never have sex.*

"On the lips," Michael said. "Like you mean it."

Bobbie got very still, and Sal went stiff in stranger alert.

"Michael," Bobbie said, rubbing her hands as if she were no longer sure where to put them. "I don't like him like that."

"Then how do you like him?" Michael asked. "Like he's your little buddy?"

"No," she said. "You're the one who calls him that."

"I know you understand him like I do."

"What?"

"It's like you hear him too."

Bobbie turned to Sal as if Michael was no longer there. "Your brother is getting weird."

"No one is watching you," Michael said. "You don't have to pretend."

Shaking her head, Bobbie walked out of the room, saying, "I'll call you later, Sal. It's been real. Cool house."

As she gathered her book bag and gave Batey a final rub on his ears, Sal followed her, saying, "Eh... eh..." like *Don't go. We were kidding.*

"Bye, Sal," she said, and then she was out the door.

Sal made squirrel teeth, like *Way to go, asswipe.*

"I thought that's what you wanted."

Michael had heard Sal say it last night—faintly, through static—when they were programing the Wolf. He swore it was Sal in his head, took an extra pill to be sure, and Sal hadn't *eh-eh*-ed the option afterward. Why was he backing out now?

Sal turned his chair to the drywall. He was shutting down, taking himself away. Maybe he knew she'd held Michael's hand, that Michael wanted her for himself.

"Fine," Michael said. "Punish me." He put his pointer finger in Sal's mouth, against his back teeth. "Do it right this time."

Sal clamped down. Michael felt the ridges of Sal's molars cut into his cuticles. He waited for the pain, for the punishment he deserved. He'd let Sal break his finger if he wanted. He needed to be forgiven.

But Sal released the pressure, like *Forget it.*

"What do you want to say, then?" Michael asked. "What do you really want to say?"

The next day, Bobbie refused to make eye contact with Michael, as if he were a chair or a desk, and not a particularly attractive one.

At lunch, more people gathered around Sal. Out of the corner of his eye, Michael noticed Gregg and Shawn. They were smirking. "Music?" Michael asked, and Sal smiled like a pitcher approving his catcher's call. Michael didn't want to keep the crowd waiting. He reached over and pressed the icon for the Hobbies page, and the Wolf scanned two icons before it whispered *Music* and Sal clicked. The Wolf said, "The Spice Girls sound like dying squirrels."

Everyone laughed, except one girl, who said, "Wait. I like them."

"Say it again," someone said.

"Sal," Mrs. B said. "You have to eat."

"One more," said Gregg, which Michael took as a peace offering.

"Last one," said Mrs. B. "Sal is not some jukebox."

Michael pressed Back and navigated to the skull-and-crossbones icon labeled Fun. He'd spent the better part of last night programming it. He'd taken extra Valium. It was the clearest, the loudest he'd heard Sal in months.

The Wolf whispered, and Sal clicked. The Wolf said, "Where are the ladies at?"

The crowd cracked up. Mrs. B shook her head. "Oh, gosh."

Then Sal's eyes flashed like an evil genius. Michael knew what he would press before he pressed it. He let the Wolf scan, and then he clicked. "Shit," the Wolf said. "Motherfucker."

"Sal!" Mrs. B said. The crowd laughed uncomfortably as Mrs. B leaned on the table, trying furiously to get up. Quincy and John said, "Oooooo" in unison, their voices rising like a siren.

Sal let it scan one more option, and then he clicked. "Mrs. B, nobody gives a shit about your cat." He smiled open-mouthed at Mrs. B like *How you like me now?*

Mrs. B wrote an account of what happened in Sal's notebook. Instead of the usual *Big BM at noon*, she wrote: *Sal's computer has become inappropriate! It has become hurtful!* Michael ripped out the page and buried it in the trash before his mother had a chance to see it. He'd already gotten in trouble with Vice Principal Fagan, who'd tried to give him a detention, but Michael claimed he couldn't make it. "How many days a week do you watch your brother?" Fagan finally asked, and Michael said, "All of them."

He thought he'd gotten away with it. That night, they were eating plates of mystery casserole that his mother had defrosted after several months in cryogenic stasis. She didn't even have to grind it up for Sal. It disintegrated under the lightest fork pressure. Sal had the Wolf mounted and was clicking: "Milk me," he said. "Place more food in my mouth hole."

Their mother sighed. "This is a phase, right, Sal?"

Sal smiled like *No. It's the new me.*

Sal navigated off the Dinner page. "Shit," the Wolf said, and Sal smirked, looked from his mother to his father, waiting for a reaction.

"Whoa," their mother said. "That's not appropriate." Sal squealed and slammed his elbows on his tray, like *I know! It's great!*

"It's age appropriate," Michael said. "I say 'shit' all the time."

"Yeah," she said. "And you're obnoxious. Erase it. That's not how my Sal talks."

"Shit, man," their father said. "My Sal says 'Shit.'"

"Gabe, please. You're not helping."

"Sorry. I meant 'Listen to your mother.'"

Their mother got up to get another glass of water, and his father smiled and whispered, "It's hilarious. Don't erase it."

The phone rang. Michael tried to get to it first, but his mother was right near the cordless.

"I'm sorry to hear that," she kept saying. "That *is* concerning." She did her syrupy voice, the one she used with doctors and therapists to get what she wanted. "Thank you, Mr. Fagan. I'll talk to him."

When she hung up, she paused to gather herself. Then she shouted, "Michael!"

14

Sal was edited. Sal was no fun. His mother had replaced half of Michael's options with her own options, her own voice. At lunch, the crowd gathered, waiting for Sal to say something dangerous. Sal clicked, and his mother said, "I want to hang out with some cool friends!"

Mrs. B said, "That's much better, Sal. I like you more like this."

"What the hell?" asked one boy. "Call Mrs. B your servant." But it wasn't an option. Sal's arm dropped onto his tray as he slowly chewed, like he was saying, *Show's over.* The crowd dispersed. Sal spit out the bolus of chicken fingers into his bib.

"What's wrong, Sal?" Mrs. B asked. "You don't want to use your computer?"

"I don't know," Michael said. "Maybe he doesn't want to sound like a forty-seven-year-old woman."

It was like Sal had been kidnapped. Michael wasn't allowed to fix him. Michael thew his burrito back onto his tray. He wasn't hungry—a first. All that work, all that Volume, all those moments with Sal's voice in his head again, were erased.

He picked up his lunch tray and walked over to Gregg and Shawn. Maybe they couldn't imagine right now, but they could learn.

"Can I join you?" he asked.

Gregg pulled his book bag off the table to clear a space. "You forgive us?"

"I guess," Michael said.

Shawn made a droning vacuum noise. "Look," he said. "He's getting turned on."

"Shut up," Gregg said. He squirmed in his seat and tried to laugh.

"*Hoover*," Shawn whispered seductively. "*Kenmore*."

"Come on, Shawn," Michael said. "Not cool."

"Sorry," Shawn said. "I'm a dick. Gregg's more a Dirt Devil guy anyway."

Gregg smiled. They all laughed. "Okay," he said. "That's pretty funny."

Michael took a giant bite of his burrito and said with his mouth still full: "You guys want to come over after school?"

As he prepared Sal's medications, they played a round of Iron Man Sal, seeing how long Sal could hold his head up off the headrest. Gregg bet five dollars that Sal could do twenty seconds while Shawn took the under. Sal held his head up, jutting out his crooked bottom teeth, his whole body tight in concentration, like *Look at my neck muscles*. Gregg shouted "Iron Man Sal! Iron Man Sal!" But at second eighteen, Sal's head dropped back onto the foam.

"Look at him smirking," Gregg said as he handed over the money. "He threw the match."

Shawn said, "I'll give you your cut, Sal, when he's not looking."

Sal smiled like *That's right, bitch. Pay up*.

They watched as Michael prepped the Volume. Predictably, Sal opened for Michael but then spit the applesauce down his chin. Michael frantically tried to scrape the flecks of white pill back into Sal's mouth. "Asshole," Michael whispered, and they all cracked up.

After Sal swallowed on the second try, Shawn said, "I'm next." He pulled up a chair beside Sal and opened his mouth wide, said "Ahhhh."

"You wish," Michael said. He reached into the container of Thick-It and pinched the powder. "If you want, snort this."

"Come on," Shawn said, rubbing his shoulder. "Skateboarding accident. Stiff muscles." Batey was suspicious, sniffing every inch of Shawn's blue jeans. "This thing is over-friendly."

"He's drug sniffing," Michael said.

"I wish, dog," Shawn said. He looked sincerely into Michael's eyes, as if Michael were a dad denying ice cream. "Just one pill? Sal has so many. We have so few." He batted his eyelashes, stuck out his lip.

Michael tried to think how many pills he'd taken over the last week, how many before his mother would notice. His Boar whispered, *Don't be a pussy.* He looked at Sal. "What do you think? Can they try it?"

Sal thought for a second, pursed his lips. "Eh," he said softly, like *I guess.*

"Yes!" Shawn said. "You're the best, Sal. And a beer to wash it down, right?"

Michael looked at the clock. His father wasn't due for another hour and a half, his mother even later. "Fine," he said. "They're in the garage." Michael would remain sober, but he could let them indulge.

Shawn asked, "You want a beer, Sal?"

"Yeah," Sal said.

"I don't know," Michael said, but Sal was smiling with his tongue in between his teeth, like *Don't baby me. Don't be Mom.* If their mother found out, she'd send Michael to Catholic military boarding school for sure. But he wanted Gregg and Shawn to see that Sal could have fun, that his life was imaginable.

"Can I give Sal a sip?" Gregg asked.

Sal's eyes lit up.

Gregg and Shawn got the tepid Black Label beer from the garage and washed down their pills. Then they stood in front of Sal with his beer.

"Careful," Michael told Gregg as he cracked it open. He said to Sal: "It won't taste good. But don't spit it out." Michael wasn't sure if he should add Thick-It, if it would make the beer fizz over. Gregg tipped the can, while Michael cupped a washcloth under Sal's chin.

Sal took a full swallow with no trouble and mashed up his face into squirrel teeth. He smacked his lips for a moment and let out a small burp. "More," he said.

The boys cheered. Gregg chanted, "Chug ... chug ..." as Michael gave Sal a second sip, and then a third. On the fourth sip, Sal's throat caught, and he coughed the beer down his shirt. "Party foul!" Gregg yelled.

Michael tried not to panic. If they just changed his shirt and threw it in the washer, his mother would never find out. They went to Sal's room, where Michael peeled Sal's shirt off. He waited for his friends to comment about Sal's bone-thin frame, but Shawn just pointed to his toned little ropes of bicep, his defined abs. "Dude, Sal's cut. Look at that six-pack." He poked Michael in the gut. "You could learn a thing or two, little bro."

"Fuck off," he said and laughed. He announced it was time to change Sal's diaper. They counted down three-two-one before Michael unstrapped the tape to reveal no poop.

Gregg said, "That was sort of exciting."

Michael demonstrated how to make Sal's hospital bed go up and down.

"This thing is awesome, Sal. I wish my bed did this," Gregg said, and then snatched the controller from Michael and elevated Sal's trunk so he was sitting eye-level. He raised Sal's legs so that Sal was almost crunched together in a folding mattress.

Michael took the controller back. "Okay," he said. "That's enough."

Gregg pointed to the Hoyer lift. "Let's do that one."

Michael attached the nylon netting and lifted Shawn's body off the ground, his big hairy limbs hanging over the edges.

"I feel like a fish!" Shawn yelled. "I could fall asleep in this thing. I'm so relaxed, man."

Gregg climbed on top of the crane neck and said, "What's the weight limit for this thing?"

Michael gave them a ride—up, down, up, down. With all of Sal's equipment, their house felt special, like they had coveted toys no one else could afford. Gregg was about seven feet off the ground, and Michael asked Sal, "Should we turn on the ceiling fan?"

"Eh," Sal said, like *It is a bit hot in here.*

"No!" Gregg said. "Sal. What have I ever done to you?"

"I don't know," Michael said. "I can't *imagine* what you've done. Higher Sal?"

"Yeah," Sal said, and Michael raised the lift until Gregg's back almost touched the spinning blades.

"Jesus," he said. "No higher!" He tried to rotate down to the underside of the crane, but the blades hit him in the upper ass. "Ow," he said as the blades stalled. "I can't believe you'd sell me out, Sal."

When Michael lowered them both onto the ground, Shawn said, "Hey Sal, can we ride your wheelchair?"

"Eh," he said softly, like *Don't break it*. He was feeling generous.

"Me first!" yelled Gregg. He hopped in and cranked the joystick forward, nearly running into the wall. Shawn hung off the back of the chair as Gregg lurched out of the bedroom and down the hallway. They both seemed a bit drunk, a little high. There was a crash, and Batey came running, cowering under Sal's bed. Sal's eyes grew wide.

"It's probably fine?" Michael said

In the living room, they sat with Sal as he lay on the couch, a pillow propped between his knees. His eyes were growing heavy from the Volume.

Gregg said, "Sucks about Sal getting censored."

"It's temporary," Michael said.

"Sal should get gangster," said Shawn. "Like 'Yo, Cleveland, suck my dick.'"

Gregg laughed. "Or how about Dr. Dre. Like, 'Deeez Nuuuts . . .'"

Michael imagined Sal rolling down the halls, flashing spastic gang signs, drinking gin and juice with Thick-It.

"How about"—and here Shawn growled— "This is Satan. Give me your soul!"

Gregg laughed. "Or"—Gregg pitched his voice high—"Red rum! Red rum!"

Michael imagined Sal going on a rampage, his powerchair turned up to full rabbit, his footrest a sharpened blade slicing through shins. "What do you think, Sal?" he asked.

Sal smirked like *I'll think about it*.

"Look," Shawn said. "That's a yes."

Maybe it was the way Shawn said it—so confident, no room for doubt—or maybe it was how they laughed a little too hard, but Michael realized Sal was absurd to them. He wasn't real. That was not how Sal talked, not how he sounded to Michael over the damage. It was Sal as a cartoon. They could not imagine.

Michael said, "We'll see, Sal, if that's what you want to say."

Shawn scoffed. "I thought you knew."

"What?"

Shawn looked at Gregg. "Isn't that what you told me, G? That he . . . what is it? Some kind of twin telepathy? Or like mind reading?"

"You told him?" Michael said.

"Sorry. It slipped out," Gregg said. "Sucks for people to know your secrets."

Michael tightened his fists. He couldn't believe he'd trusted them, let them back into his house, gave them Sal's Volume and let them play with his equipment. His Boar whispered: *Mortal Kombat*. But before he could click, he heard the garage door going up, the soft roar of the van's engine. Even before Batey looked toward the door and wagged his tail, Michael knew he was fucked.

He heard the doorknob turn, and there she was in her work clothes: a polka-dotted blouse and black skirt with hoop earrings. She looked so put together, so un-Mom-like, that for a second, he held out hope she was a stranger who'd just wandered in.

She walked slowly past each boy on the couch until she reached Sal. "Hi, baby," she said, knelt, and kissed his cheek. She glanced at Michael, and then turned back to Sal and sniffed.

After she sent Greg and Shawn home, she did an inventory. She examined Sal's every part—his cheek, his collarbone, his elbows, his hips—and finding him whole, she counted his Valium. Twelve pills missing.

"Twelve?" she asked. "He's missing almost a whole week. You want to send him into withdrawal?"

Michael couldn't meet her eyes. He'd forgotten about withdrawal. Was it his fault the Volume also helped him hear Sal again? He couldn't explain it to her. He knew, out loud, it would sound stupid, even to himself.

Later, from upstairs, Michael heard his parents arguing. His mother said she was quitting her job, and his father said, "I'm sorry, Han. But it's probably for the best."

His mother said, "Of course they were drinking. He watches you."

His father said, "Don't start that again."

"It's just as well," she said. "With Sal getting the baclofen pump this summer, I'd have to take too much time off anyway. It was fun while it lasted. I'm ready to want less."

His father said, "Don't put it like that," and his mother said, "Then how should I put it?" His father said, "You tried it out, okay? I'm proud of you. Come here."

When they called Michael downstairs, he said, "I know it was stupid. I don't need a lecture."

"Stop," his mother said. "I was waiting for a good time to tell you. I brokered a compromise for next year. Sal will go to the high school for a few periods in the morning, and then he'll be bussed out to Rosemary Center. It's really the best solution for him. His whole care team agrees."

"You're bussing him out? That's bullshit," Michael said.

"Sal needs more support," his father said. "You can see that, right?"

"Sal, you belong in high school with me." Michael said. "Tell them."

Sal looked left, and then directly at Michael. He said: "Mike-a," like *Give it up, brother.* Or like *What will be, will be.*

In the middle of the night, Michael snuck downstairs to Sal's room. The baby monitor glowed in the darkness, and Michael turned its wheel until its red eye went black.

Sal slept on his box of light, but the night light barely illuminated anything else. Michael squinted in the dark. He slid the pillowcase forward to give Sal a dry section. He repositioned the polar bear in between Sal's knees and adjusted the stuffed alligator, the seal, and the parrot, repositioned the whole menagerie guarding Sal so he wouldn't slip out. Sal stirred and his snore broke, his eyes opening. "Mmmmmm," he said.

Michael backed away until his calves hit something hard, and then he was sitting in Sal's powerchair. The chair didn't fit Michael's body because Sal had a curved spine and was so skinny. Michael had to wedge himself into the chair's soft cavity as the foam bulged into his back, but it wasn't unbearable. If he were Sal. He almost was. If his brain had bled a little more. It almost did. He felt his spit pool at his teeth and tip over his bottom lip, creeping down his chin. He hit the joystick forward, jammed the footrests against the bars of the hospital bed. "Hi, brother," he said.

If he were Sal, he'd be so angry. A few periods in the morning? Just so they could say he was participating? Just so they could feel better before sending him off to the center? Maybe that's what Sal wanted to say—to express not love, not jokes, but anger. He would let Sal howl and be all Wolf, and Michael would go full Boar to help him.

"Are you angry? Tell me."

Sal didn't answer for a second, breathing in and out. "Yeah," he said softly.

"Okay," Michael said. "Tomorrow, we'll tell them."

He reached into the back of Sal's chair and pulled out his computer. He couldn't risk taking anymore pills. He needed to just be Sal's true twin, to listen for him again, to finally get him right. The Wolf lit up the dark.

The Boar whispered, *Take the hunting knife from the dresser.*

The Boar whispered, *Stuff it in your pants.*

It whispered, *Make them listen.*

His classmates filed onto the stage and into the risers. Michael followed with Sal, guiding his brother down the ramp. The hunting knife was too big to fully fit in his front pocket, so he wedged the sheathed blade under his belt, the pearl handle cold against his belly. Standing behind Sal under the stage lights, Michael could barely see into the crowd. His classmates loomed above him but he felt relaxed behind Sal's handles. He was where he belonged. He could make out their mother sitting four rows deep. Their father had not yet arrived, but was coming, his mother said, if he knew what was good for him.

Before they went out to the risers, Bobbie had stopped to wish Sal luck, giving him a kiss on his cheek. "Hey guys, break a leg." She punched Michael on the shoulder. "Or maybe just you. Sal's got enough going on."

"I'm sorry about the other day," Michael said. "I'm a weirdo."

She shrugged. "So am I."

He now felt like an asshole for what they put on Sal's computer last night, but there was no time to change it. And the Boar didn't want to. The Boar didn't want to make *the least dangerous assumption*. It wanted the most dangerous.

The choirmaster stood in front of the risers and rhythmically waved her hands. They began with "John Henry," a song about a steel-driving man who raced against a machine. He won but his heart gave out. Michael looked at Sal. There were certain parallels. Sal sang in his natural voice: "Ahhhhhh-ehhhhh-ahhhhh," which got drowned out but could certainly be heard by Vice Principal Fagan, who sat near the front with his yellow tinted glasses. His arms were crossed, like *I'm watching you, Mitchell*. He sat next to Mrs. B, who was eating trail mix and clapping wildly between songs. The vice principal would probably be the first person up, the first person Michael would point at with the knife so Sal and the Wolf could say and say.

They sang "This Land Is Your Land." During a lull toward the end, Sal shouted "Momma!" like *I'd like to give a shout out to my mom*. The crowd wasn't quite sure what to do with it, whether to laugh or "Awwww," so they decided to do a bad job at both.

Michael sweated through a few more musical numbers until he heard his cue. As he set up the Wolf, he noted his father had still not arrived. In front of Sal's tray, the Wolf's screen lit up, flashing the icons with Sal's hand hovering next to the switch. The tray's St. Patrick's Day stickers were peeling off, leaving ghostly outlines of shamrocks. Michael bent down and turned on the Peavy amp, its red eye glowing back at the dads' camcorders. He pressed the icon for the School page and let the Wolf scan through the options. When the time came, he'd press the Choir button, put the mic to the Wolf, and let Sal *do his thing*.

The choirmaster shook a metallic screen to approximate the sound of thunder as their classmates squirmed into raincoats and fought with their hoods. Michael struggled into his old red rubbery coat. The knife was heavy in his pants. The Boar whispered: *Problem, little piggy? Don't cut your nuts off.* Michael pressed the button on the handle of Sal's umbrella, and exploded it open. He held it above his brother while the front row of classmates raised theirs and twirled.

The crowd murmured with delight as the front row spun their umbrellas slowly in an arc. As the pianist played the first few jangly bars, Michael felt a drop of cold sweat run down his side, as if it were actually raining. The Wolf whispered through the School page: *Reading. Math. Therapy.* Sal couldn't read. He couldn't do much math. But he knew what was owed. Where the fuck was their father? He should be here for this.

His classmates started on the first verse: "I'm singing in the rain, just singing in the rain. What a glorious feel-ing, I'm hap-py again." Another rivulet of sweat ran down Michael's side.

Michael lip-synched as Sal belted out for both of them in his natural voice: "Ahhhhhhh!" Their classmates sang, "I'm laughing at clouds... so dark up above. The sun's in my heart... and I'm ready for love." They sang, "Let the stormy clouds chase... everyone from the place. Come on with the rain... I've a smile on my face." They gave their umbrellas a solid turn. "I walk down the lane... with a happy refrain. I'm singing... just singing... in the rain."

What a choice for Sal's solo. *He never gets mad or sad. What an inspiration.* The real Sal was waiting. He had the choice. Sal could sing or he could say and say. They would know he belonged in the high school full-time even if Michael, after this, wasn't allowed there with him.

The choirmaster caught Michael's eye and pointed with her double fingers. Michael dropped the umbrella and moved out from behind Sal's handles. He pressed the Choir icon, turned on the microphone, and put it close to the Wolf.

The Wolf whispered, *Rain.* If Sal pressed the switch, he would sing like they wanted. He would be sweet. Michael's Boar raged in his ear: *Don't freaking press it.* Sal's hand flinched, but he let the cursor move on to the next option.

Bob-bie, the Wolf whispered. If Sal clicked, the Wolf would say, "Bobbie McGee is a bitch who cuts herself. Ah-whooo!" This was an unfortunate turn of phrase, but Sal, during their private rehearsal, did not object. Michael glanced at Bobbie, who was staring at them like everyone else. And Sal, the merciful, did not click.

Gregg and Shawn, the Wolf whispered. If Sal clicked, the Wolf would say, *Gregg Schwartz, the vacuum fucker, and Shawn Monroe, the drug addict. If I were them, I'd kill myself. Ah-whoo!* Gregg looked over, like Bobbie, waiting... wondering.

The choir director stood. She knew this wasn't how they'd practiced. Sal's hand still hovered next to the switch.

Mom and Dad, the Wolf whispered. If Sal clicked, the Wolf would say, *My dad ignores me, and my mom babies me. Ignore this! Baby this! Ah-whooo!*

One last time, Michael looked for the outline of his father standing in the back. He hadn't come. Michael would have to tell him how their mother's face had crumpled, how this was the real Sal, how he'd missed it, how he didn't see it. But Sal's hand only flinched. Someone coughed. The crowd was getting restless. The choir director started toward them.

Listen, the Wolf whispered. If Sal clicked, the Wolf would say, *Listen to me! Look at me! Fuck your prissy daughters and dull sons! I don't want to go to school with them anyway. Ah-whoooo!* The Boar was raging: *Weeeeeeeee. Whip it out. Let's get started.* Michael's heart pounded. They would finally be all animal. Any moment now Sal would click and the crowd would gasp. But Sal's wrist was still. Someone whooped.

The choir director was almost here. Michael retreated behind Sal's chair, slid the knife out of his pants, and held it in his hand. He'd tell her to back the fuck up, to let his brother speak. He'd make them promise to not bus Sal out. Sal did not need the least dangerous assumption. He needed the most dangerous.

The lit-up scanner shifted back to the beginning, and the Wolf whispered *Rain*. Sal glanced at Michael with his soft eyes, and before Michael's voice sang through the Wolf and into the microphone, before the choirmaster turned to face the crowd and smile, before he saw his father jogging down the aisle to finally take his seat, before the thunderous applause and the collective *awwww* of a hundred parents and siblings and teachers, Michael knew. He'd gotten Sal wrong. He couldn't imagine. Sal, in the end, just wanted to be sweet. He wanted to sing and sing.

Hey, Michael, your brother is a retard.

I know.

Sal's wrist hit the plastic.

IV
CAMP CHEERFUL

15

Gabe and Michael fought Sal's manual wheelchair over the sand while Hannah scoured the beach for an open space. "Can we stop here?" Michael asked as he pulled on Sal's front wheels, and Gabe, who was pushing Sal's handles, said, "Yep, looks good," but Sal said, "Eh-eh," and she kept going. One spot had too much seagull shit. Another was a burial ground for a dead crab, its shell caved in, flies doing laps. She wanted to get closer to the surf. "Mush," she told Gabe and Michael, flicking an imaginary whip.

There it was—a window of white sand in between a sunbathing woman and a family building an elaborate sandcastle. She spread out the towel for Sal, lathered him with SPF 50 until he looked shellacked, and wedged sunglasses onto the bridge of his nose.

"There," she said. "We're ready to have fun."

"I'm exhausted," Michael said, and Gabe said, "I think I pulled a muscle."

Hannah sighed theatrically. "This is nice."

And it was nice. It was the summer of 2001. The twins were seventeen. The Mitchell family was finally on a real vacation. For Hannah's birthday, Gabe had sprung for four nights in Puerto Vallarta. They'd taken a red-eye on a budget jet, loaded Sal into an adult sized car seat, and crammed it into a plane packed like a sardine can. After taking a taxi van to the resort, they'd spent all day at the pool, where Sal soaked for so long in his specialized life vest that his gnarled yellow toenail fell off in the water.

Now it was their beach day. "Relax," Gabe said, massaging her shoulders, and she said, "What do you think I'm doing?"

Gabe was definitely relaxing. She was surprised he'd agreed to take time off, even more when he brought no work with him. He still drank, but maybe not as much as a few years ago. He was a fifty-one-year-old scientist with a pale beer gut and a mop of wild brown-and-white hair. Hannah looked down at herself in her one piece, her spare tire bulging the fabric and blue-lightning veins on her thighs. They were well into middle age together, and it was okay. She still took classes and volunteered, still made time to garden and occasionally splurged on depuffing cream, and now she was in Mexico. She'd learned to stretch within her range of motion, even if the range was not as wide as she'd once wished.

Gabe scooped up a handful of sand and stared down at her weird flat feet. "What do you say, boys? Let's bury these monsters for good." She growled and attacked him with her toes, saying, "Hey, you're one to talk. You've got a pair of monkey paws." Gabe picked up a canvas bag with his toes. "You take that back," he said. They laughed. She let them bury her up to her knees, felt the sand weigh her down grain by grain, a half-casket of silica. The waves clawed toward them, collapsed, and were dragged back to sea. Sand fleas jumped at their feet.

Michael, glancing at a row of bronzed beauties sunning themselves, whispered to Sal: "You take the one on the left, and I'll take the one on the right." Sal smiled like *Deal*.

Michael had grown into his skin these past three years, as if at fourteen he'd gained all the fat he would need and spent the next few years stretching it out. He'd ditched kung fu for ice hockey, and Sal particularly liked to watch him bang his body into the boards and slip after some elusive black disk as if he weren't just clumsy but a master of well-crafted prat falls. He almost made straight As again last year and was getting a little cocky after scoring 1500 on the SAT. Yet almost every night in his room he blew pot smoke through toilet-paper rolls stuffed with Downy fabric softener sheets. *We know you're not doing laundry in there.* She'd warned him about bringing anything on the plane, and so far, he'd behaved.

Sal was growing into himself too. After his baclofen pump was installed, the doctors stopped talking about a feeding tube. He'd gained weight, and you could see less of his six-pack, his knees no longer so bulbous. He was also no longer stiff as a two by four. The doctors thought that with Sal's more relaxed tone, he might be able to say more words, but when those words never arrived, she didn't grieve. It didn't matter. Whatever had been eating at her before was now settled.

Sal's health had held, and now he was looking up at the blue sky in his shades, his brother holding his wrist, dancing it to the salsa music blaring from a boombox, and Sal smiled. Twin A. Twin B. They weren't as close anymore, not like when they were younger. These days it seemed the most they had in common was their infatuation with Bobbie. She was lovely and smart but troubled too. She'd spent part of the summer at a clinic for eating disorders. Sal still had a spaz attack every time she called. But after they were done talking, she'd ask to talk to Michael too, and Michael would run upstairs with the cordless like it was a flag he'd captured. Though they were both shit out of luck. Bobbie had a boyfriend.

Hannah shut her eyes. The sun was baking her like a lizard. She put her palm on her scapular necklace, and even Mother Mary was hot.

In a half-dream, she heard Michael say, "Sal, you want to hit the waves?"

"Yeah," Sal said.

Her eyes popped open. Michael had peeled off his shirt and was now bending over his brother, wedging his forearms under Sal's neck and knees.

Hannah sat up. "Hold it."

"We're going in."

She looked out at the water, imagining a mighty wave crashing against Sal's drum of a belly, dislodging his baclofen pump, Sal going into withdrawal. A rip tide could arrive like a wet hand, scooping her sons out to sea. Or Michael, still clumsy, could lose his footing, Sal going under with a lungful of salt water. They were lake people, and this was an ocean.

She shot to her feet. "Absolutely not."

"What do you mean?" Michael asked. "We're at the beach. This is what you do."

"Come on, Han," Gabe said. "They'll be fine." He put a hand to her calf, but she kicked him off.

"I said no. He's got an open sore on his foot."

"Salt water's great for wounds," Michael said. "Sal, you want to go in?"

"Yeah!" Sal shouted in Michael's arms and gave a whole-body flail for emphasis.

"I'm sorry, baby," she said to him. "It's my job to keep you safe."

"Mmmmmm," he said, pursing his lips. He blew her a raspberry like *Get another job.*

"Nah, we're going in," Michael said, and he took a first step towards the water.

"Stop!" she yelled, and then she was ripping Sal from his arms. "Give him to me," she hissed, but what she meant was: *He's mine.*

"Hannah," Gabe said. "People are staring."

Clutching Sal to her chest, she bent and returned him to the towel. "They stare at us anyway," she said.

Later, at the restaurant, Hannah had recovered her composure. "Sorry about the beach." She gave Sal another bite of his rice and beans mixed with applesauce.

Gabe shrugged. "It's your birthday," he said, and she said, "It's my birthday." Every night was her birthday, even though it was two days ago. Gabe had already whispered to the waiter, which meant soon the staff would sing and bring out free cake and a daiquiri the size of her head and a shot of tequila, which she'd give to her husband. She had not been drunk in eighteen years.

They were at a place called Tamale Annie's, and there was Annie, carved into the front and back of every chair, smiling with garish lipstick and hooped earrings, a flower in her black hair, framed by a wide-brimmed hat. The walls were painted in neon greens and reds and yellows, which gave Hannah a headache but also made her feel more alive. She savored the languages passing through the restaurant like electricity: English and Spanish but also French, German, Arabic. It felt so good to travel again, to move through unfamiliar space, to hear a tongue you did not understand but wanted to. God had made a wide world.

"Cheers," Gabe said and raised his Corona. Michael raised his can of Tecate and sipped.

"That's your last one," she said. He had to be watched. Sal coughed, but she caught it with the washcloth before it sprayed the next table. Though his coughing seemed to be getting worse, pneumonia had not revisited.

When the waiters gathered and the birthday song began, she blew out the candle on the cake and swore her fifty-first year would be different. Instead of giving the shot to her husband, she took it herself and slammed the empty glass on the table. "You'll put Sal to bed?" she asked, and Gabe nodded.

She downed the daiquiri in a few gulps and tapped her glass for another. A mariachi band seemed to pop up from a trapped door. She found herself clapping furiously. Men hooted.

When she woke the next morning, her head throbbing, her family seemed in shock. Sal, who miraculously was still alive, looked at her with stranger alert. Who was this person formerly known as Mom? She was told she'd danced on a table.

Michael pointed to her and said, "You're fun." He'd never said that before.

She clutched her head, took an Advil. "Fun feels terrible."

On their final full day, they went snorkeling, and she stared at whole cities of coral, with their strange underwater flowers and darting fish. She took a picture with an underwater disposable camera to show Sal, who had to stay on the boat, though later they stopped in a quiet bay so he could bob with his specialized life vest. As she watched him float, her chest swelled. He was in the sea and stronger than she'd imagined he'd ever be. They could keep going like this. When he turned eighteen in October, he would finally qualify for benefits, and they could have aides come into their home to help out. It would get easier.

When they got home from vacation, Hannah signed up the boys for Camp Cheerful the next summer, a place she heard about from one of the special needs moms in Sal's class. An overnight camp for a whole week, a "special place for special people," the brochure said.

The twins started their senior year. Sal spent the first three periods at Michael's high school working on "social skills," where he went to choir and hung out with Michael and Bobbie in Commons. After participating in what he could, Sal was bussed to Rosemary Center, where they had in-house therapists and a handicapped-accessible pool and an adaptive playground. He was the smartest one in his class—catching his aide's jokes, laughing when someone got in trouble. He listened to *Harry Potter* on CD and answered reading comprehension questions on his computer. He learned life skills: Activate the switch to turn on the paper shredder; deliver a letter from one classroom to another.

She felt at peace with his progress. He'd never solve a complicated math problem. He'd never read or write. His expressive language had peaked at eight spoken words, augmented by his computer, which had expanded to ten pages, seven options each. But he engaged the world, nonetheless. And when Hannah observed Sal's visits at Michael's high school, she watched the students gravitate towards him, let their guards down. With him, you could be yourself in all your vulnerability. He had a presence, a stillness that anchored people. He'd learned to stretch within his range of motion too.

In September, she was feeding him breakfast when she heard it. That cough. Wet and raspy, settled deep. She listened again, put her ear to his bony chest. "I don't like that," she told him, as if he were playing a bad song and she could tweak his nipple to change the station. She kept him home to be sure, and was feeding him a second round of breakfast, yogurt this time instead of oatmeal, when suddenly on the TV, a skyscraper was on fire, a plume of black smoke climbing the glass column.

She dipped the spoon. "You open up," she said. "You swallow."

Michael, with his shirt off, stared at himself in his bedroom mirror. He looked thrown together, as if God had been in a rush while making him and said, "Good enough." Skinny, delicate wrists. Fine hair he could do nothing with. A small tire of fat around his midsection no matter how many lunches he skipped or runs he went on. He fondled it, got it all in his hand and jiggled. He opened his mouth as wide as it would go, as if he wanted to jump out of himself or else swallow the whole world, and then he gave himself a shake. His face went slack. The smile went up. There. All normal now.

His mother called, and when he came downstairs, she said, "Your dad will be home by seven. Or maybe eight."

His dad was in the habit of working late again. The "big breakthrough" he'd been talking about hadn't broken through. He was trying to get more funding.

Michael said, "Sal will help me with my college apps, right?"

Sal smiled, said, "Eh-eh."

She gave Sal a kiss on his forehead and patted Michael's cheek. "You should shave," she said, then, when Michael rubbed his hand against his cheek: "Just kidding. Like a baby's butt."

After she left, Sal scanned through activity options on his new Dynavox. "Mu-sic," it whispered in its robot voice. "T-V. Out-side."

When Sal got his new computer, he'd chosen to erase all the sayings Michael had put in. He'd wanted his old voice back. *Fine. Sound like a robot. See if I care*, Michael thought, trying to read the arch of Sal's caterpillar eyebrows, his faraway brown eyes, his open mouth. Nothing. His brother was mentally disabled. Michael could admit that. Like his father said, it wasn't clear how much Sal understood. Michael still thought he knew Sal better than anyone, but there was no telepathic connection. He had to guess like everyone else. The Boar was also buried. What a crazy little boy he'd been.

Except for the occasional panic attack, and the rare day when he couldn't get out of bed, and maybe the compulsive pot smoking so he could sleep, he was mostly normal. He got good grades, which was proof.

Michael went to the fridge and fetched Sal's plate. Sal was on a new pureed diet. Their mother had used a food-shaped plastic mold to sculpt Sal's chicken into a gelatinous drumstick. Sal stared down at his dinner like *You are fooling no one*. Or something.

Every meal was like a last supper. After his bout with pneumonia in September, Sal had failed his swallow test, and in his lungs they'd found a black spot where he'd been inhaling food and drink. Their mother had finally agreed to the feeding tube. After next week, the table would be a docking station. His mother had wept. She told Michael, "Eating is how he socializes. Feeding him is like a conversation we've been having his whole life. Now there'll be nothing to say."

Michael dipped a spoon into the mold and brought it to his brother's face.

"Momma," Sal said.

"Right now, brother, I'm the only one you've got."

When Michael turned eighteen, he bought cigarettes. When Sal turned eighteen, he bought strangers—aides who came fifteen hours a week to shower and feed him. That's all his family qualified for, and the aides were often poor and had to drive in from the city and were not excited to be paid $8.50 for it. They often didn't show up, and even when they did, his mother found a reason to fire them. One woman she caught lying about hours. Another man she timed: forty-five minutes before he said one word to Sal.

Michael parked the spoon against Sal's teeth. "Come on. I'll make you a milkshake. And I won't put carrots in it."

As he fed Sal, he filled out his last college application. He had the packet to mail off, listing his accomplishments and extracurriculars. President of Buddies! Volunteering at Sal's school. Hockey. Newspaper. The Clinic's summer program for high school science students. His personal essay was printed and ready to be stuffed in. It was titled "My Brother, My Teacher," and here were the lessons: *How to look for ramps. How to shower and feed a grown human. How to sing while doing it. How to endure pain. How to laugh. How to say much with little. And ultimately, how to be thankful for all that you have and not waste it.* He said he wanted to become a doctor, to help people with disabilities, to treat every patient as if they were his brother. His English teacher had Michael read the essay out loud in front of the whole class, and when he looked up, there were tears in a girl's eyes. The guidance counselor said it was money.

When he'd read the essay to Sal, he'd gotten a lukewarm response, an open mouth of indifference. Did Sal recognize the brothers in the essay? Sometimes they were still like that, joking and giving each other shit, but other times he barely saw Sal. His mother would announce, "And remember, your brother is here." And he was: Sal sitting in his chair, waiting for Michael to make the first move. More often, they tolerated each other. And when Michael did take care of him, Sal made it difficult—refusing to open his mouth during feedings, protesting with "Momma." Michael would mock him: "What da madder, baby? Want Mama? Goo goo ga ga," and Sal would bite the air, like *Fuck off*. They had become uninteresting to one another.

The cordless rang. Michael glanced at the caller ID. Bobbie.

"Is your brother there?"

"He can talk when he finishes eating."

"Cockblocker."

"Fine."

He put the receiver to Sal's ear and watched his eyes light up. He did not come close enough to hear Bobbie's end of the conversation, but Sal said, "Eh." He said, "Yeah." He let out a half-laugh and then broke into an "Ahhhhhhh."

Michael asked, "Is she making fun of me?" and Sal just smiled.

Whatever she said next sent Sal into a spaz attack. He was shaking with laughter, about to bust out of his straps. Michael could hardly make him do that anymore.

He pulled the receiver to his own ear. "You coming over or what?"

"I don't know," she said. "I'm supposed to call Casey."

"He's probably at a party anyway. That's all they do at OSU. Tell him we're studying. We have a test. We're having test sex."

"He'll lo-ove that."

"Come over," he said, and Sal said, "Yeah."

"We'll see."

When she hung up, Michael said to Sal, "She wants me, right?"

"Eh-eh," Sal said.

He was correct. She was dating a college freshman who treated her like garbage, which she seemed to enjoy. Gregg and Shawn declared Michael firmly in the "friend zone."

Michael had never officially apologized for forcing Sal on her in eighth grade, but she was forgiving. They hated all the same things: shopping, quadradic equations, Snapple, their own bodies. She had a gimlet eye, could locate someone's flaw in record time: Gregg was secret-gay, Shawn despised himself, and Michael . . . what was his problem? "You're afraid to be yourself," she said. Michael slid into a Cockney accent: "That's bollocks!" She had a point.

In tenth grade, she'd lost weight and become nerd hot. Michael had slimmed down too but still had a boyish body. They were in honors and AP classes together. She said, "You can be smart if you want to." He wanted to be the person she thought he was.

Sometimes she could be a buzzkill. Sometimes, if she was having one of her depressive episodes, Michael got freaked out—how she'd shut down and stop talking and not commit to showering. How she'd take small trips to the bathroom after she ate. But even that was slightly charming. She needed help, and Michael liked to be a help.

When Sal heard her Jeep in the driveway, his body stiffened in excitement, and Michael wondered which Bobbie they'd get: the one who dragged herself around the room, on the verge of tears, or the goofy Bobby, the one whose laugh put them all at ease?

She opened the door, and Batey, whose eyesight was failing at fourteen, recognized her smell and attacked with his tongue. "Help yourself," she said.

It was the fun Bobbie, the one with those apple cheeks and a smile that took up her whole face. She looked like a beautiful shark. Michael admired the holes in her jeans where he could spy patches of honey skin, but then felt guilty ogling her. He knew what her body had cost her.

She sat down next to Sal and took his hand.

When Sal came home from the surgery, he was almost always hooked up to the machine. His stomach could only take small amounts of formula at first. His mother said it was "another level of care."

There were complications with the tube. Sal kept throwing up and had to go on antibiotics. He stopped sleeping, and their mother stopped sleeping. Their dad would get up with him a few times, but he needed to be up at work early each morning. Michael tried to get up with him, but his mother said, "No. You've got school." She relied on power naps that were never powerful enough and kept Sal home from school more often than not. It got harder to find good aides with the proper training. His mother said she felt abandoned by the agency, by her social worker.

To help out, Michael learned how to work this new Sal. He uncapped the gummy tube coiled inside his brother's shirt, drew the distilled water up in a syringe and flushed the tube clean, driving back the soft clouds that floated in Sal's stomach acid. He dumped the formula in the plastic bag hanging from the stand. It said Vanilla on the can but looked like cement. Then he set the machine to *click click click*, the tube shuddering as the formula pulsed through it. Their mother hoped Sal would still want to eat some, but he spit out whatever she offered him, even carrot-less milkshakes.

In March, Michael's college admission letters started to arrive. Part of him wanted to stay close and be there for his brother. Another part wanted to get as far as possible from him—to find out who he was without Sal. Michael chanted "Big money, big money" as he opened each envelope, as if he were on the *Wheel of Fortune*. It was never big money, but the letters kept coming. "Looks like you'll be in-state," his mother said. She seemed relieved.

Then a letter arrived from some place in Oregon they'd never heard of but that his advisor insisted he apply to. Hilyard College. He held the envelope to Sal's face.

"Kiss it. Come on," Michael said. "I need your luck."

"Sally-boy, come on," their father said. "Pucker up."

"Stop," their mother said. "Sal, say, 'I'm not feeling well.'"

Sal sat there open-mouthed, defiant, like *No dice*.

"We'll be here all night," Michael said.

But then Sal's mouth twitched into a half smile, like *I'm just fucking with you* or something. His lips came together, followed by a plosive smack. Michael tore open the letter, his eyes racing over the page. He expected the usual "We must reject many worthy applicants. . . ." but it didn't start that way.

Michael leaned over Sal and kissed him on the fuzz of his top lip. Sal startled, went into stranger alert, like *Whoa. Who is this weirdo?*

"It worked, Sally! Those lucky lips. Look!" He held it up for his parents to read. It was a full ride. A motherfucking full ride to study pre-med. Michael jumped up and down, playing an imaginary electric guitar. He danced with Sal's feeding tube pump, then fell to the ground and had a small celebratory seizure. Batey started licking his face, but he didn't care. He could feel his dead cells sloughing off, the new person he'd become emerging lick by lick. His father started jumping too, but his mother stood still.

"Are you going to accept it?" she asked. "It's on the other side of the country."

Their father did a shuffle, windmilling his arms, ignoring their mother. "What do you think about that, Sally? Your brother is moving to Oregon."

Sal's lips bounced up, his nervous smile. He did not toggle his chair back and forth, did not join in on the dancing. Did he understand what had happened? Or did he just not want Michael to leave?

Michael couldn't wait to tell Bobbie. She'd already accepted a spot at Case Western with a partial scholarship, was majoring in pre-law. "Look at you," she said. "You've come a long way, Michael Mitchell."

In May, Bobbie called for Sal. Her voice was shaky. "Is your brother there?"

Michael put the cordless to Sal's ear but kept close enough to listen. She'd broken up with her boyfriend, who'd been seeing someone else for months, just stringing her along as a hometown hookup. "I'm so stupid," she kept saying, and Sal said, "Eh-eh." He blew her a kiss and she said, "Sal, you're so sweet."

After another minute, Michael took the phone and said, "I heard."

"Well, as I was saying, I'm such a stupid piece of fucking shit."

"Tell me more," he said.

"I'm ugly. I have terrible taste in boys. I'm batshit crazy. I have a shitty family who doesn't care about me. I throw up for fun."

"Interesting."

"But it's not. It's so fucking boring."

She was in a tailspin. Michael wanted to tell her she was lovely, that he thought about her every night before he went to sleep, that he talked to her in his head when she wasn't even there, that he spent his days looking for things she'd find funny.

"Well," he said. "I like you."

"Thanks," she said, straining to brighten her voice. "Maybe you have worse judgment than me. Ugh. Now I don't have a date for prom. I already bought a dress."

"You couldn't pay me to go to that stupid thing. Unless it was with you."

"Are you actually asking me?"

And suddenly he was. "Yes," he said.

"Um," she said. "Sure."

* * *

They posed for pictures in his mother's garden. Gregg and Shawn with their dates, Michael and Bobbie on the end, framed by purple azaleas, the parents clicking away. Bobbie seemed uncomfortable in a shimmery too-tight green chiffon dress, like a mermaid who'd spent too much time on land, but she let Michael place his arm around her waist in a way that seemed more than platonic.

Sal watched from his wheelchair. Their mother had floated the idea of Sal going too. Maybe some girl who talked to Sal in the mornings? Or Bobbie could go with them both? Sal had his own dance at his own school, Michael said, and when his mother insisted it wasn't the same, Michael replied, "You care more about it than he does."

She stopped asking after that, but now here she was, wrangling the girls to pose for a photo with Sal, who beamed in his teal wheelchair as all three collectively kissed his cheek. Greedy for Sal's moment, their mother crouched to get more pictures.

Michael thought he'd wanted this for himself, but as everyone climbed into the limo, he knew he'd made a mistake. A better brother would've said, "Sure, he can come along." A better brother would've played matchmaker. But he was not a better brother. *Piece of shit. Piece of selfish absolute shit.* Gregg was passing around a flask of whiskey, and Michael put it to his lips and gulped.

He continued to sneak sips in the school gym, as he watched the idiots move their bodies to music. The only time he liked dancing was when he could hide behind Sal's wheelchair handles, like at his uncle's wedding. Otherwise with all those eyes on him, he felt like he had no skin, every nerve exposed.

He and Bobbie slouched against the wall, where he made fun of the serious dancers: "I think Cliff is bringing back the Mashed Potato.... And is that move called the air-sex?"

Bobbie said, "I don't know. Maybe we should get out there."

Michael allowed her to pull him into the balloons and streamers, but he flailed his arms and legs like he was possessed by a spastic ghost.

Bobbie rolled her eyes. "Just dance normal." When he didn't, her own limbs grew listless.

He saw Quincy and John dancing with their dates, Quincy driving in a circle. There was no reason why Sal couldn't have come.

When Gregg proposed they leave, Michael was the first to get up. And then in the limo, he snorted coke for the first time. His head got fuzzy. He did a lot of screaming through the sunroof, with Bobbie pulling him down. More beers. Vodka. At Shawn's house, Michael found himself with Bobbie in a bedroom. As he put his lips on hers, he thought: *I do not deserve this.* Then it all went dark, and he woke up in the hospital, his stomach full of glass, his memory of prom just a fever dream.

His mother told him they'd pumped his stomach. "What were you thinking?"

"I don't know," he said. "I didn't want to feel anything anymore."

"Well," she said. "That's stupid. You have to feel things. That's part of being alive."

His father said, "Sometimes it's like you want to ruin your own life."

Bobbie was freaked out. All she'd say was, "You're not good for me. I need some time to think." She didn't return his calls.

And then they graduated, and she left for Florida to spend the summer with her dad.

When Sal's stomach started acting up again, his mother fired another aide, and his father said, "Do you even want help? What are you trying to prove?" One Saturday night, Michael came home late from a party to find the lights still on. Sal's formula can lay overturned on the kitchen table, but the floor was spotless. Batey must have licked it up long ago. The dog was blind now but found his way to Michael's feet, sniffing and wagging his tail. The television was playing *Saturday Night Live*. Michael pressed the power button, and when the screen went black, he heard a faint scratching.

He went past the stairs and through the corridor, past Sal's closed door, and on to the bathroom, where his mother was kneeling on a single pink flip flop, scrubbing Sal's wheelchair with a toothbrush. Below her, the white bathroom tiles were smeared in blood. She did not look up. She said, "Sal was full. He said it, but I gave him too much."

"Mom," Michael said. "You're bleeding. It's one a.m."

She looked down, took in the gash on her knee. "Fuck," she said. "Look what I'm cleaning this with." She held up the bent bristles.

Michael stepped forward and took the toothbrush out of her hand.

Michael never wanted to see her like that again, so he got trained as a delegated nurse. It was incredibly easy. He enrolled in a weekend course on distributing meds, giving CPR, and not getting the agency sued. When he interviewed with Sal's agency, he was hired on the spot. After a day of onboarding at headquarters, he was on the job at his own kitchen table. He looked at his brother and said, "Hi. I'm your new aide. I think you're gonna love me."

Sal made squirrel teeth. "Eh-eh," he said, like *You're already fired.*

16

Click. Click. Click. In August, they were in Sal's room, just home from church, with Sal lounging upright on his bed, the tube coiled under his shirt, his pump clicking away. Hannah had waited until that morning to inform Sal that he and Michael were going to camp, and he was angry about it, icing her in his patent way. But if she told him any earlier, he wouldn't sleep, which meant she wouldn't sleep, and then there'd be no sleep.

Michael and Sal had been to camps before, but never an overnight one. She gave Michael one last tutorial while trying not to have a panic attack: "This bag is his shorts and short-sleeve shirts. Over here are his long pants and long-sleeve shirts, with a few sweatshirts and a light jacket. In this one I've got his diapers and chuck pads and wipes. This has his pillows and sheets and stuffed animals for positioning, and this laundry basket has his formula and medications. Let's go over the pills one more time."

Michael slouched with arms crossed. He was one month overdue for a haircut and could have picked a nicer pair of khaki shorts and maybe not that ratty Jägermeister t-shirt, as if he were auditioning to be an alcoholic.

She explained Sal's pills for constipation and bone density, for acid reflux and depression. Michael kept looking out the window as if there were a more interesting television program in its panes. "I didn't know that one was for depression. Why does he need that?" he asked. "Sal isn't sad. He's just been sick."

"Those two are connected," she said. "Mind, body. It's a problem."

"You're not sad, are you, Sal?"

Sal flashed a smile, but otherwise didn't answer.

It was Hannah's idea to dye Sal's hair. When Sal showed preference for the washed-out blond, Michael said that Sal lived in Cleveland, not California, that Sal was not punk rock. Then Sal wanted it all the more. "I think Sal is punk rock," she'd said. And Sal said, "Yeah."

She went over Sal's positioning again. "So for sleep, put these pillows under every gap. His hips, his knees, his shins, his shoulders."

Michael groaned. "You're acting like I've never seen this guy before."

"Think of this as a refresher course."

"Just say you still don't trust me."

It wasn't exactly true. Michael had worked as Sal's aide for the summer without any emergencies. Hannah had been so close to canceling camp, but then Sal's health rebounded, and Michael and Gabe begged her to follow through. Still, this was a trust fall. As she went into the finer points of pump recharging, Michael let his mouth hang down in his best impression of a dead person, and she did her best not to slap him.

She looked over at Sal, who was smiling. "Laugh it up, buster. He's the one who has to keep you alive."

They'd been patronizing her ever since "the breakdown." That's what Gabe and Michael kept calling it. She recalled being on her knees in the bathroom, trying to scrub Sal's wheelchair clean of vomit, and having a brief conversation with Michael. She might have been frazzled, at the end of her long rope, but it was by no means a breakdown. She wouldn't call it that. It sounded too Victorian, too much like "hysteria," the repressed housewife shaking and shrieking: "I will not wash another pair of underwear!" When really what she needed was a little help.

Michael had performed admirably as Sal's aide, with her supervision, of course. But it was not a permanent solution, especially with him going off to college next week. She had feared what would happen in the fall.

Gabe was the one to call it. "What if we make another good hard decision?"

"What are you talking about?"

"I love Sal. I love having him home. But I'm worried about you. You're falling apart."

"You want to give him away?"

"I want you both to lead sustainable lives. This isn't sustainable."

"You want to run away when things get difficult."

She wasn't like Ashley. She wouldn't just quit. Hannah fell asleep hating her husband but in the morning, she called her mother. She waited for the pep talk, for her to guilt Hannah to keep going, to cut out a kidney, for the usual "God only gives us what we can handle." But her mother just said: "You've taken such good care of that little boy. He's been so lucky to have you as his mother."

She called her social worker and told him maybe it was time. Sal needed another level of care, and maybe she could no longer do this herself, even with help. He said there was a waiting list for residential care. She said yes, they were already on it. "How do we jump the line?"

"Here's one thing that could help," he said. "Do you ever think about hurting your son? Or yourself?"

"Ha ha," she said.

"Hannah, I'm serious."

No. The insurance rep? Yes. An arrogant doctor? Flay him alive. But Sal? Even though he could be so stubborn, she only got truly angry at his body, never him. It went part by part. *You fucking hamstring. You damned esophagus. You bastard small intestine.* And with everything he needed, she didn't have time for self-harm. But she thought about the toothbrush, and the blood on the bathroom tiles, and added: "Though if we keep on like this, something bad is bound to happen." And that was all he needed.

So she went on tour. The first place she visited was near the airport and looked like it hadn't been renovated since the 1980s. The residents slept three to a room in what looked like wooden boxes and were crowding the hallway while the head nurse led her through the home. A young man in a wheelchair with a beagle on his shirt hissed at the woman: "You treat me like garbage."

"Now, Pete," she said. "You can't do what you want all the time. There are rules."

"Roll me outside for pickup. That would be better. Just so I never have to watch the staff stuff their fat faces with pizza I can't eat."

"I'm listening," the nurse said. "I'm hearing your complaints." When Pete wheeled himself away, she said, "I'm sorry you had to see that. Really, we're like family."

"Of course," Hannah said. "Of course you are."

Another place was closer and had an opening right away, but Sal would have to share a room with a large autistic man who had violent tendencies. The nurse said, "He's never hit another resident. Only staff, and no one went to the hospital."

"Oh good," said Hannah. *Next, please.*

When she walked into a place not too far from their house, they were all watching WrestleMania. The residents greeted her with loud hellos and a man with Down syndrome smiled wide and bent on one knee, offering her a giant bowl of popcorn. "What service," she said and he said, "My pleasure." There was a resident who seemed like Sal, bemused in his chair as he watched the oiled muscle men bounce off each other. He held the hand of a cute girl with a headband, also in a wheelchair, and they looked at each other like *Are you seeing this? That man is wielding a chair.* The director had a graying brown ponytail and chunks of wood in his earlobes. He talked about the group home like it was a commune and seemed actually interested in her son. She could picture Sal there in the corner, holding court, maybe stealing that guy's girlfriend. But they did too much: bowling nights, movie theater nights, trips to the amusement park. Their pace seemed relentless. And a nurse was only on the premises part-time. Sal was too fragile; he needed to go slower.

At the next one she didn't like how they parked everyone in front of the television all day. At another, it smelled too antiseptic, chemicals killing any form of life. She felt like a group-home Goldilocks.

Finally she drove out to this facility a half-hour away in the country. It had three wings, a doctor on staff, a team of nurses. The rooms were gleaming. There was a helicopter pad in case someone needed to be lifeflighted. The residents were not as high-functioning as in the group home, but their swirling neon art hung in the hallways. In one of the wings, a man in his twenties mashed his hand into his neck and made long warbling whale calls. Another laughed at a *Barney* episode on repeat. Okay, not as highbrow as WrestleMania, not as exciting as bowling night, but Sal would be safe here. If she wasn't going to take care of him with her own hands, she needed absolute faith in the hands that would replace hers. She had power of attorney and just signed him up. There were no openings, so all they had to do was wait for someone to die. She'd never wish anyone ill, but sometimes she thought if it was going to happen, would they please hurry up? Other times she wished that call would never come, that Sal would stay with her always.

In the kitchen, she asked Sal: "You want to use your computer one last time before camp?"

The Dynavox was staying home. It was too expensive to break, and he'd have his brother as his interpreter.

"Eh," Sal said.

As she set it up, she looked at the clock. Gabe was due home soon. This last year, with Sal's health failing, Gabe had been struggling too. His big project hadn't led to the discoveries he'd hoped for. He'd apologized to her one night, said, "Hannah, I'm sorry. I wish I could be here more. I'm trying to rescue this thing." When she woke up with Sal, Gabe would also be awake, tossing, turning, his feet sweating in the sheets. One night she found him in the kitchen with his head in his hands, a tumbler on the table filled with watered-down whiskey. The drinking was just another way for him to take his leave, to achieve that distance which was his true addiction. She fetched some water for Sal in a hard plastic cup and walked past him without saying a word. They'd built this life together, and she didn't want him to be unhappy, but when she thought of what she'd do without Sal, her daydreams did not include Gabe. Without Sal, who would she even be?

After she turned on the Dynavox, Sal clicked through the pages, looking for something. His brow furrowed. It seemed he had something important to say.

Finally, the Dynavox bellowed out in its synthetic voice: "Please bring C-Eight-y-five its food re-qui-si-tion please." Sal laughed. She had no idea why he found that so funny—maybe because it made him sound so much like a robot—but she was relieved. For Sal, teasing was a barometer of health. If he messed with you, it meant he felt good.

"Any last thoughts about camp?" She washed her hands at the sink as he scrolled through and clicked.

The computer said, "This sucks."

The cordless rang. The number was not one Hannah recognized. Holding the phone to her chest, she let it ring three times before picking up. "Hello?" The caller identified herself as a manager from the facility. A place for Sal had opened up.

Oh, my baby. Oh, my boy.

Gabe came home with a raw chicken. He was expecting Hannah to be excited about having a week to herself but instead she was in turbo mode. When she was anxious, she paraded it all over the house, acting like every domestic task was a must-win battle in a Martha Stewart–style military campaign. She'd clean hard-to-reach places. She'd aggressively make cookies. She'd yell at Michael for not vacuuming or attack Gabe for not taking off his shoes or decide she had to cut Sal's gnarly yellow toenails when really what she wanted to say was: *I'm terrified. I feel something coming.*

In the kitchen, everyone was fighting.

"I'm just reminding him," Hannah said. "It's a refresher course, and he's not taking it seriously."

"She still doesn't trust me," Michael snapped back. "She acts like I'll kill him if given the chance."

And Sal said, "Ahhhh!" like *Everyone shut up! I don't even want to go to this camp!*

"You're freaking him out," Michael said.

"He should be freaked out," she said. "Because you're ignoring me." She glared at Gabe. "Wonder where he learned that from?"

"Hey," Gabe said, raising the chicken carcass in defense. "Break it up. Michael, listen to your mother. Sal, you're going to camp and you're having fun. Hannah, deep breaths."

"Who the hell are you," Hannah said. "Ward Cleaver?"

"No, but I've got this chicken, and I'm going to grill it."

It was something he could do for them, something not related to the lab. The data was coming back soon, and he'd know for sure if he'd failed, but he wanted to enjoy this day. He heard a thud. Poor Batey had run his head into the bench.

Gabe bent down and rubbed the lug's head. Batey's eyes were clouds floating in the sockets. "Did your mother move the furniture again?" He looked up at Hannah, who was wearing white shorts and a purple top with the arms cut out. She'd let her hair grow to her shoulders. It was blonder than ever now that she dyed it. She had aged rapidly in the last few years, and sure, she'd put on weight. Even her arms, which used to be stacked from lifting Sal, had lost definition. But when he looked at the person who used to be the girl he fell in love with—aging into her fifties—the word that occurred to him was *handsome*.

So what if they didn't talk as much as they used to? He told himself that they had a mature relationship. He was looking forward to this next week with the boys away. He could make it up to her.

He nominated Sal as his sous-chef and took him onto the deck. When he got the bird hissing and covered on the coals, he turned to his son.

"Hi, Ishy-mo." Sal had a string of drool hanging down his chin. Gabe took the bottom of his t-shirt and wiped his son's mouth, saying, "I'll take that." They stared at each other. "So . . ." he said. He hated how awkward he sometimes felt around his own son. He never knew quite what to say to him, how high to pitch it. "You think your mom is acting weird? Got any intel on her, buddy?" Sal was silent. Figures. Momma's boy. "Maybe she's just worried about camp, huh? But you're not, right? You're just excited about the babes. You gonna get a summer squeeze?" He squeezed Sal's wispy arm and waited for his son to seize with laughter. Sometimes he could still get him going. But Sal just opened his mouth into a smile.

"You talking back to me? How about some of this?" Gabe fake-slugged him in the gut, careful not to mess up Sal's hardware. Sometimes Gabe felt like his son was a bomb about to go off, about to explode into ambulances and surgeries, while other times Sal was so strong, and it seemed that the feeding tube would finally stabilize his health so he'd live long enough to slobber into a graying beard. If Gabe believed in God, he would've prayed: *Dear Lord, let my son live long enough to watch me die of lung cancer.*

Sal gave a solid chuckle. There was his boy. Sometimes you had to wait for him to appear. When the aides started coming to the house, Gabe had watched them discover Sal, glimpse the person in there. Yes, he laughs when you drop a cup. Sure, he loves when you don't know how to brush his teeth. And when you ask him what he wants to watch on TV and flip through the channels, he'll say "eh-eh" every time until you realize he's just fucking with you. He opened up as much as he could. Sweet Sal. Funny Sal. His CP had toned him nearly to death but left him cut. If not for the bleed, he might've been the athlete Gabe wished for instead of Michael, the slip-'n'-slide hockey player, the kung fu interpretive dancer.

He turned to check on the chicken. Right before he pulled up the grill top, he imagined that instead of the chicken pieces, it would be his mice, scurrying along the low-heat zones, their naked feet gripping the grill grates, defiantly immortal and fucking fine.

He'd taken a big swing. He'd identified a group of three proteins he thought had promise, that were perhaps instrumental in demyelination and the mechanisms of multiple sclerosis. In the last five years, he'd knocked the protein groups out of the mice by knocking out their genes, delivering slimy rodent babies without the Alpha, then without the Alpha and the Beta, then without the whole family. He'd run memory and agility tests: trained the mice to swim to a platform in the middle of a tub of water. Submerged the platform so the mice couldn't see it, and recorded how long it took the mice to remember. How they swam, if their back legs stumbled, if they took longer than the normal control. Gabe held his breath, waiting for the phenotype, for the faulty wiring to manifest. He'd been so sure, could practically see the lesions, the atrophy, the damage.

And yes, his boss had warned him, told him not to be reckless, to get a Plan B in case this experiment failed. He told him to think of his family, of the sacrifices they'd need to make if he lost funding. But he *was* thinking of his family—he was thinking of consulting fees, a better job, biotech partnerships, and what all that money could do for Sal. He wrote other grants on the side but none of them got funded, which was a relief. He wanted to stay focused.

After the first series failed, he went the opposite direction and overexpressed. He bred mice with too much Alpha that performed like little athletes, braving the bucket, scrambling onto the plastic island in the middle, their neurons humming along as if Gabe, a hapless god, had no hand in their existence at all. And then Gabe went home to Sal, who had phenotype to spare. *What I'd give for just one little mousey version of you.* Five years of experiments and more than a million dollars of funding had produced two measly papers to tepid reception.

After he lost funding, the Clinic floated him for a year. He'd made a last-ditch effort, overexpressing the Alpha and the Beta. He'd get the last of the data back on Monday. It didn't look good. If Gabe could just get another year, he could overexpress all three and prove that he was right. Next week he would basically need to beg for his boss to have mercy, but today there would be chicken.

They finally sat down to eat. Gabe had made a beautiful bird, crispy skin with moist meat, juices running a little pink down onto the serving plate. Hannah set a place for Sal even though he mostly no longer ate, except for the occasional ice cream. Gabe made sure to let Sal smell each dish, something his son still liked to do. Batey sat sentry next to Sal's chair, hoping for dropped food that would never come, though sometimes Sal's formula dripped onto the floor and Batey's tongue erased it. There wouldn't be much time after camp before Michael left for college. This felt like a last supper: all four of them together, still living under the same roof.

Sal's pump went *click click click*, the new soundtrack of their lives.

Hannah was watching the wall as if she were trying to beam herself into the wallpaper. She seemed somewhere else entirely. Gabe cleared his throat. "This is nice."

Hannah came back into her own body. "Oh. Sure. Yes." She smiled.

Michael was the first to cut into the bird. "Ugh," he said. "The bones are bloody."

Gabe pulled the chicken toward him to inspect. "It's medium rare."

"That's not a thing with chicken," Michael said.

"It's fine," Gabe snapped. "Eat it."

The boy didn't seem to know what to do. Gabe peered into his face and saw the tell-tale eyes, glassy and bloodshot.

"Are you high?"

"I'm not," he said.

Hannah pursed her lips. She steered the serving plate to Michael and said softly, "Beep it for two minutes."

She was undermining him. She was making him seem insane. But he wouldn't lose it. He wouldn't yell. He cut into his chicken thigh. Okay, there was more blood than he thought. And the fucking mice were fine. He put the raw chicken into his mouth and chewed.

He watched Michael at the microwave. Why was he afraid of his own father? What was so awful about them that he had to be high? Gabe had been so proud when Michael had gotten accepted into the summer program at the Clinic. It was shocking how quickly he picked up basic concepts. He was full of questions, and he found the days that he brought Michael to work, they talked the whole car ride home, discussing immunology or how gene assays worked. The boy had a talent for imagining biological systems and all that could go wrong.

Of course Michael had his little blips. On prom night, he almost died. Bobbie would no longer talk to him, and that meant she no longer called for Sal, which was hard for Sal to understand. Gabe had checked Michael's room once when he was sleeping at a friend's and found no secret drug stashes, nothing illicit, not even tattered hardcore pornography, which was a little disappointing. Every father likes his son to be red-blooded. Instead there were stacks of black journals in which Michael scraped a cursive so tortured that it might as well have been code. He'd grow out of it. Another week and he'd be on his way.

When Michael sat back down, Gabe said, "You'll experience different disabilities at this camp. Could be valuable for your medical career."

Michael shrugged. "I'm not sure I want to be a doctor anymore."

Gabe clutched his chest and mimed a heart attack. "Please," he said. "You *are* high."

"Hey," Hannah said. "Easy. Maybe Michael will major in English. He'll write a memoir and we'll go on Oprah. We'll turn up the wet works. 'It was all true, every word.' Sal, will you cry for Oprah?"

"Eh-eh," Sal said.

Michael took a long sip of milk. "What are you two going to do while we're gone?"

"Run around the house naked," Gabe said. "That's first."

"We'll see," Hannah said.

"No," Gabe said. "The neighbors will see."

"Hey," Michael said. "I'm eating."

"Yeah," Sal said, and they all laughed.

Gabe said, "We're going to miss you boys. It's just a week, though, right? Sal, aren't you going to miss your mom?"

Gabe expected a teasing "Eh-eh," but Sal said, "Yeah." His body jerked against his chest strap, and then he turned to his mother with a look like *I love you I love you I love you*, and his wife gasped as if Sal's glance was a violence. Gabe had to look away, had to say to himself: *Breathe, buddy. Breathe.*

17

On Monday, when their mother turned the van off Route 42 and drove past a sign for Camp Cheerful, Michael scoffed and leaned back to comment, "Can you believe, Sal, that it's called "Camp Cheerful?"

"Eh-eh," Sal said.

"Well, I think the name is nice," their mother said.

"You would," Michael said, and Sal said "Yeah."

"Guys," she said. "You're going, and you're having fun."

Michael was still fuming. How were they supposed to have fun when she'd just told him Sal was getting sent to a facility? It would be all Michael could think about as he tried to entertain the world's crankiest camper.

They drove a quarter mile along the narrow road, past the long, arching maples and the ivy-colored house with a rusty swing set, until they reached a gray concrete bridge spanning a deep-pooled creek. They crossed into camp and arrived at a cracked tar-black parking lot. It was full of vans, the handicapped signs like flags of a rival nation state.

They unloaded Sal's laundry basket of formula and medications and his four garbage bags full of shirts and shorts and sweatshirts and long pants and stuffed animals and bedding. "Sally, Michael's gonna take good care of you," their mother said. "Don't you worry." She sounded like she really believed it.

They checked into the Great Hall, and then a counselor with shockingly red hair named Jim led them down the blacktop path to their cabin.

At the sight of their four trash bags, he raised his eyebrows. "Wow, Sal," he said. "How long you staying?"

"If you ask him," Michael said, "too long."

"Yeah," Sal said.

They opened the cabin door to chaos. There was a muscular man with hearing aids hanging from the cabin beam as two guys who reeked of cigarettes scream-counted his pull ups. "Eight... nine... ten!"

They spotted a man with Down syndrome dressed in a cowboy hat. He glared at Michael and then crouched slightly with his hands at his sides, as if he would charge. "Draw, you varmint," he said and wiggled his fingers.

"What?" Michael said.

"Too late." Then his hand flashed up into a finger pistol and he fired into Michael's midsection. "Sorry. Dead." He picked up a broom stick and galloped away.

An angry man in a manual wheelchair was yelling to no one: "Has someone been smoking by the windows?! Who was it, you bastards!"

And a Black guy laying on his bed shouted in a lazy drawl: "Quiet... this... foolishness. Damn.... It's... gonna... be... a... long... week."

Someone farted and someone laughed. A man rocking on his bed suddenly put on what looked like a hockey helmet and sprinted out the back door, as a counselor holding a walkie talkie followed in hot pursuit.

That guy was right, Michael thought. It would be a long week. He felt his cargo shorts pocket for his one-hitter and his small stash of weed.

Jim guided them past the bunks to a hospital bed for Sal. On the fireplace mantel were various industrial cleaners, including one that loudly advertised its ability to kill AIDS. Michael peeked under the bunk beds, wondering where the AIDS might be.

Jim helped them put sheets on the plastic-covered mattresses and crammed Sal's belongings into a meager cubby. As Michael laid Sal on his hospital bed and took off his braces, Jim asked if Sal had a girlfriend. "Eh-eh," Sal said and Jim said, "Well... we'll see if we can fix that."

Another counselor in a ratty hemp necklace was just lying in his bunk, not being particularly helpful, scribbling in a notebook. He eventually got up and introduced himself as Darren, the cabin team leader. "So you guys are twins?"

"Eh-eh," Sal said.

"Okay, so he's just your brother?"

"Eh-eh," Sal said, and Darren said, "Well, who is this guy then? Your aide?"

Sal let out a big "Yeah!"

"Wow, Sal, that's cold," Darren said. "That's what we'll call him, then. The Aide."

"The Aide!" said Jim, and then the two campers who were counting pull ups joined in: "The Aide!"

Michael took a small bow, claiming the nickname. Sal laughed at that one.

Michael thought his mom would stick around for hours, teaching a college seminar on how to keep Sal alive. But she just bent and kissed Sal's cheek and gave Michael a peck. "Okay," she said. "Mommy loves you both. Have fun."

And then she walked out the door. Who was this woman? Where was all her guilt? Michael and his mother had talked about facilities in hushed tones, felt so sorry for Ashley and Tina, for the kids at Rosemary Center who were residential and had been abandoned by their families. And now their family was just as bad. She'd probably cry in the car. She'd better.

Sal's eyes swam around the cabin, taking in his new surroundings. His body was tight with anxiety. And then he said it for the first time: "Mom-ma," like *Don't leave me with him!* "Mom-ma" like *Come back!*

Michael looked down at Sal, and his stomach sank. *If you knew what I know, brother, you wouldn't be chanting her name.*

Michael changed Sal's diaper and stuffed his socked feet back into his braces. As he fumbled with Sal's shoe, Sal was smiling for what seemed like no reason. "What?" Michael asked, and Sal laughed and looked down like *You idiot.* Damn. Sal's braces were on the wrong feet. "Good catch," Michael said. "Strike one."

They were running late for the first activity, something called flagpole, which happened before every meal. As they went toward the cabin door, they heard it, and it only grew louder as they made their way outside. They saw at least eighty people gathered in front of the flagpole in sneakers and wheelchairs and walkers. They were clapping wildly and swaying and smiling, and they were fucking singing. About a bear. Way up there. Michael whispered, "Where did Mom send us?" and Sal made squirrel teeth and caught Michael's eye like *We are in hell.*

Over the last months, as Michael had worked as Sal's aide, Sal had given Michael a hard time. He'd call for their mother until her will broke and she'd say, "Just let me do it." And in those moments, Michael dreamed of escaping to college. It seemed appealing, especially the not paying for most of it, which Michael still suspected was a clerical error. He'd signed up for a class called Human Aspirations, where he was hoping to learn what was up with that one cave in Plato so he could drop it into conversations and sound smart forever. He wanted to take mushrooms and talk about the universe with other sensitive upper-middle-class kids. He wanted to lose his virginity. He wanted to fall in love with a troubled-yet-gifted girl who was like Bobbie but hotter. And he had to hurry before they discovered the clerical error.

But he also wanted to stay home. He hadn't been the best brother for the past four years. He wanted a mulligan. Because there were other moments with his brother over the summer when he really felt closer to him, when Sal would lay off the "Momma" long enough to let Michael set up his pump and *click click click* through an entire meal, when Michael would get out his guitar and play a song about Sal smelling and Sal would heckle him with his blasted *Ahhhhs*, and Sal would even take an actual bite of ice cream for dessert, and then they'd go out to the movies and laugh together at raunchy jokes, and Michael could build up enough good will so that come bedtime Sal wouldn't even lock his jaw when it was time to brush his teeth. It even seemed like Sal was starting to forgive him for ruining things with Bobbie, who hadn't called all summer.

Michael liked getting paid for something he'd do anyway. The checks he received for Sal's care were vaguely exciting—like breaking the law, like stealing, but he didn't know from whom. Maybe from Sal, but at least from the government. In addition to his dishwashing job, he'd managed to save three grand. Taking care of Sal was familiar, something he told himself he was good at. He didn't want to go somewhere he could fail.

But that first day, Michael already felt like he was failing at Camp Cheerful, where Sal was not having the time of his life. Yes, their cabin mates seemed insane and during Art when they were tracing leaves, there was that infestation of ants, and Michael had not been so careful with the sunscreen, so Sal was already starting to burn. But something seemed to be eating at his brother, something more than just not wanting to be there. Once Sal had stopped his chair in the middle of the path and just sat there as if he wanted to put down roots and finally be that vegetable the doctors predicted. It took three minutes of Michael begging and encouraging for him to get going again.

Michael kept searching Sal's face, trying to read the lay of his eyebrows, the gap in his mouth. He stared at Sal's long lashes, the flecks of gold in his dark-brown irises. His eyes were the surface of a pool, and Michael watched for any ripple, any sign for what lay below. He wanted so desperately to feel closer to him, to know what he was thinking.

For the day's last activity, they went to Barn. The activity leader brought out a large rabbit, white with red beady eyes and dried dung stuck to its cotton tail. Michael remembered *Of Mice and Men*, poor Lennie with his petting problem. He announced to the rabbit, "If you scratch my brother, I will Lennie you." The scene he'd performed with Gregg in eighth grade seemed different now. If he did that scene at camp, he'd get booed. It was the campers Steinbeck was shooting. Maybe Lennie should've been sent to Camp Cheerful instead. But with all the singing, he might've shot himself.

Sal had initially been afraid, his arms stiff and curled into his body. Michael thought he'd start "Momma"-ing again, but Ron came up beside them, clutching a different rabbit to his chest.

"Oh my," Ron said in his husky smoker's voice as he stroked the bunny's back, following the grain of its fur. "I love this." He was over forty and wore Snoopy t-shirts and publicly picked his nose, but in that moment, Michael was jealous. After four years of high school irony, Michael found Ron to be a revelation: He had no jokes, no embarrassment about petting this downy ball of fur. He was not afraid to be himself.

Michael took a deep breath and pet the rabbit meant for Sal. Cradling it against his chest, he felt his self-consciousness melt away. It was like holding a cloud. He met Ron's eyes, and Ron nodded like *You don't even have to say it.* Michael focused on the rabbit's silky fur, its long fuzzy ears. Ron had shown him the moment, and now he was in it.

"Sal," Michael said. "Feel." He set the rabbit on the wheelchair tray and placed Sal's good hand lightly on its back. Sal's splayed his fingers and raked them across the bunny, the downy fur bulging between his digits.

Michael watched Sal's face relax, his mouth open, his tongue set at the edge of his crooked teeth. Then his lips bent into a smile at petting this living thing, feeling it tremble and breathe fast in his hand. Sal was inside the moment too, with Ron and Michael, and Michael felt like he could finally sense what his twin was thinking: *Oh, brother—how beautiful, how soft.*

18

On Wednesday morning, Gabe sat in his department chair's office, staring at the floor. The walls were studded with awards and framed newspaper articles announcing his boss's discoveries. Gabe would kill for a career like Nichols's. He had no one to blame but himself.

Nichols held Gabe's printout as he looked over the data.

"So it's not looking good," he finally said. "You know that."

"I know," Gabe said, "but there are some promising findings here that give me reason to believe if we overexpress all three proteins . . ." Gabe stopped listening to his own voice. Behind his thick glasses, Nichols's blue eyes were dissecting Gabe like a specimen open on the table.

Nichols tapped his fountain pen. "Look. I've always liked you. You work hard. You have a wonderful family. I can't in good faith recommend another year, but we'll take care of you. They need someone to help run the animal facility upstairs. It'll be a pay cut for sure. . . ."

Gabe didn't know where to put his hands. He parked them on his knees. "The animal facility?" He'd be a glorified zookeeper. He'd have to lay off his lab tech, his post doc. He'd have to run experiments for his former colleagues, be their lackey. "I can't," he said.

Nichols rose from his chair and put his hands on Gabe's shoulders. "It's okay," he said. "You're still a good scientist. Some of us just aren't meant for the major leagues."

* * *

It was early afternoon as he drove up the hill and over the rise. Maybe he and Hannah could go out for lunch. It'd been ages since they sat down at a restaurant not on Valentine's or her birthday. Maybe they'd see a movie in a theater, smoke some of the pot they'd confiscated from Michael a few months back. He saw in the paper that there was a dinner cruise on Lake Erie. That sounded like something she would like, right? He'd tell her about his job eventually, but he wanted to show her a good time first.

The house he'd built for his family came into view. No Hannah in the garden. No spots of dark wet soil around the flowers where she should've watered. The van was still parked in the garage. He opened the door and called, "Lucy, I'm home!"

He only heard Batey stir, wagging his tail to greet him with his lolling tongue and milky eyes. So she wasn't out for a walk. "Where's your momma?" he asked, but could not read the Morse code of the dog's tail. He strolled through the house, calling for her. No Hannah cooking lunch. No Hannah anxiety-cleaning the bathrooms. No Hannah on the couch with a novel. No Hannah in their bedroom. No Hannah. No note. Too early for Miller Time. He cracked open a Diet Coke and sat down at the kitchen table, opening the newspaper.

She'd been sort of a wreck these past few days without the boys, lost in her own head. When he'd come home and ask her what she'd done that day, she'd say, "Not too much" and refuse to elaborate. Did she want to go out to eat? No, she did not. And now she'd be devastated about the layoff. He'd been arrogant, she'd say. He thought he was always right, and now they were ruined.

He'd wanted the trappings of scientific fame, but he'd also wanted the financial windfall to hire a live-in aide, not one of those assholes sent by the agency who often didn't show up, and when they did, acted like they were doing you a favor. No wonder Hannah had cared for Sal herself, but now he needed too much.

Gabe detected a faint scratching, maybe an imperceptible squeak. Maybe the mice, who were fine.

In the living room, he looked at Hannah's cross on the wall. Maybe Jesus knew where she went? He'd laughed at her when she first bought it, called him "Suburban Jesus." It was such a drastic change from the old one, its outline of muscles under his robe and his placid face instead of bones and sinew, pain and anguish. Maybe Hannah just wanted a more optimistic God instead of what she got. The old one. The honest one. And there was his deer head facing Jesus, challenging the Lord to an endless staring contest.

He remembered when Sal had his big part in the middle-school choir concert, how Gabe had gambled with the clock, finishing up late in the lab and speeding all the way so that he arrived at the last possible moment to see their sons at the edge of the bleachers, stalling the big show as if they were waiting just for him. Gabe sat next to his wife right when Sal clicked, Sal singing with Michael's voice in front of the whole school, and the look of relief on her face when she was so ready to be disappointed in him, how fiercely she grabbed his hand and pressed her body into his. He had vowed to be better, but didn't get close enough.

Where the fuck was Hannah? It was almost two p.m. His heart started pounding. *She wouldn't. She didn't.* He walked to the closet. Her clothes were still there, her suitcases still open and empty on the floor. He laughed. What would she do? Drain their bank account, take a cab to the airport, leave them all behind, finally travel the world? Yeah right.

Then he saw Sal's bedroom door—shut. He cracked open the door, and in the dim light that cut through the blinds, he saw a lump in Sal's bed. "Hannah?" he asked.

"Go away," the lump said. "Leave me alone."

19

When Hannah got home from dropping the boys off at camp, she had big plans. She wanted to sleep like the dead and paint her toenails and fill her head with gossip magazines. She wanted to zap her meals in the microwave in five minutes flat and eat processed meat and mushy vegetables straight from a steaming box. She wanted to sit in a hot bath and secretly fart. She wanted to not pick up a single thing.

But she kept finding herself standing in the doorway to Sal's bedroom and staring at all that empty space. She did it over and over again, day after day. When Gabe came home, she tried to act normal, but no matter where she was, she was still staring into that blue carpet.

Some of the best moments of her life had been spent in that room, singing to him, making him laugh, reading him a bedtime story while they just lay together on his hospital bed, giving him rides by raising the head, then the feet, then both head and feet into what they called "trash compactor." That was their favorite. All the medications were not their favorite. Two in the morning with Sal throwing up were not their favorite. But that was time with him too.

What would she do with her time? For eighteen years, that question had been answered for her.

Of course she'd known families who'd placed their children in group homes and facilities. Maybe there was a divorce or the kid's health became more difficult to manage or they just ran out of money. You only got so much help. Maybe none at all. But secretly, she thought those families just didn't love their child as much as she loved Sal.

She'd run into Ashley last year at the mall. They'd lost touch after Tina went away. Ashley had told Hannah about her new life: her nursing degree, her job at the hospital, her work friends, her boyfriend, her book club. She'd said Tina was doing well, that she saw her every Sunday. It was like she'd cast a spell on herself. *Make me boring. Make me lose my purpose.*

On Wednesday, staring into Sal's room, Hannah put her hand to her scapular necklace, the one she'd been wearing for the last eighteen years. She did not pray to God anymore. How could a man who'd sacrificed his own son understand what she was asking for? She pressed her thumb on Mary's face, felt the metal hood cut into her skin. *You've done a wonderful job, Hannah,* Mary said. *You've taken such good care of that little boy. He's been so lucky to have you—* She yanked, and the necklace snapped off. What good had the thing done if they were just going to arrive here anyway? She crawled into Sal's bed and stayed there.

"Hannah?" Gabe called as he opened the bedroom door.

"Go away," she said. "Leave me alone."

"Come on," Gabe said. "Enough. Snap out of it. We've still got a few days. We could do anything. We could leave the state. We could try that new rib place."

She peeked at him.

He unfolded an ad from the newspaper. "How about a dinner cruise? I heard it's not terrible. Not a ringing endorsement but . . ."

"They called," Hannah said. "He's going."

"What?"

"A space opened up. He's going to the facility."

"Oh, Han," he said. He stepped forward and bent down, hugging her while she cried on the bed. "It's a good thing," he said.

"Then why doesn't it feel like it?" She blubbered into her husband's blue collar, three quick spasms of grief, and then she wiped her eyes with his shirt, and stared at the damp cotton as if she had lost her sadness and was looking for it.

He laid her back on the bed. He first took off her right sock, then her left, uncovering her flat feet. He slid off her khaki shorts past the storm of varicose veins, her stubby calves. He threaded her elbows through each sleeve of her purple shirt, then pulled it, scrunched up like an accordion, over her head. It was the same way they took off Sal's shirt getting him ready for bed. He tilted her shoulders to one side and unhooked her bra. It took a few tries before her breasts spilled out.

"This is so stupid," she said, covering her eyes. Through her fingers, she looked at him. His face was open and wide, his piercing brown eyes trained on her, so focused, as though she were a collection of cells under his microscope. But there was no glass, no lens between them.

"Hannah?" he said again.

"I'm here," she said, and uncovered her eyes.

Afterward, they took Batey for a walk in the heat. It was odd not to have Sal cruising by their side, driving himself off the path and laughing about it, but the sun felt good on her skin, and she reached for Gabe's non-leashed hand. There. That wasn't so hard.

They completed the loop, Batey panting violently, and sat on a picnic table, where they watched the high school kids slip into the forest as if no one knew what they were doing. Hannah and Gabe squinted to see if they recognized any of Michael's delinquent friends.

"It's Wednesday," Gabe said. "Don't teenagers have summer jobs anymore?"

"At least they're experiencing nature," Hannah said. "The fresh air will offset the pot smoke."

"Hey," Gabe said. "I have an idea."

They ditched Batey in the house and climbed into the Taurus. "Let's see if I still remember how to do this," Gabe said as he took Michael's baggie of pot from his jeans and fished out a piece of rolling paper. It took him two tries, but he managed to close the joint.

He lit it and took a puff, filling the car with smoke. He held it out to her. "You sure?" he asked before she grabbed the joint out of his hand and made the cherry glow. "What if camp calls?" he asked. "What if Sal needs help and you're stoned out of your mind?"

She exhaled, hacking, and punched him in the arm. "I will kill you," she said between coughs, "if you make me paranoid."

"Make you? That's you normally."

She took a second drag and said, "Drive."

They headed into the city and watched the sun go down over the Cuyahoga River, spreading the water golden in front of a skyline built for better days. As they came down off the pot, Gabe started in on a series of dramatic sighs.

"What?" she said.

"Hannah," he said. "I messed up."

"Oh?" she said. "What did you do this time?"

"The mice," he said. "They're fucking fine."

"The mice?"

"My big project. I was wrong about the proteins. I got the final data back. I struck out, Han. Nichols has lost faith. He basically canned me."

She always thought he'd pull it off. Or else why all those early mornings and late evenings in the lab, all her single parenting? What was it all for if he was just going to fail? "You didn't have other experiments?"

"I thought it would work."

"You thought? You *thought*." There was that confidence, that abiding self-regard. Even now he couldn't admit that he'd made a mistake. "You didn't *think*. You gambled."

He put his head against the steering wheel.

"Are we going to be able to keep the house?"

"I don't know."

Was he crying? She watched him cautiously. He was like an actor trying to inhabit a role that didn't quite come naturally. She peered at his eyes shut in shame, a face within his face. He'd become someone who needed her. It had been so long since he needed her.

She scratched the back of his head, felt his scalp slough off under her fingernails. God, he had a lot of dandruff. "Look," she said. "You have two wonderful boys."

"And they're both leaving us."

"Then we won't even need the house. You'll just have me." She opened the door. "Come on. Isn't there an Irish bar on West Ninth?"

As they walked, Gabe put his hand on the back of her neck. "Where's your Mary?"

"She was giving me a rash."

The bar was full of cigarette smoke, but she settled into it. He ordered a Guinness for himself and a Harp for her, and then they just sat in an old booth. He put his arm around her and said everything she'd been waiting to hear: *I'm sorry. I love you. Let's keep doing this.* They listened to an Irish band with elbow pipes, a much less annoying bagpipe, and when someone moved the tables to make a space for dancing, Gabe stood up and extended his hand.

20

In the golf cart, the battery whined briefly before Michael and the director lurched forward. When they hit the concrete bridge, Michael peered down through the wooden rails into the creek's muddy pool, wondered if fifteen minutes before, Sal had looked down too. He wanted to stay on that bridge forever, caught in between camp and not camp, before they were on that road and on their way to whatever was at the end of it.

But then the cart dipped down onto the road, and the director aimed it right over the double-yellow line. His giant hands gripped the steering wheel at ten and two, his knuckles white. The siren from camp was still blaring, but Michael could hear the director softly saying from the front seat *shit-shit-shit* like a mantra.

He stared at the back of the director's thick, mottled neck, counted the hairs sneaking out of his blue polo shirt. Michael shivered in his bathing suit, didn't know whether it was from cold or terror. His forearms stuck to his ribcage, his wrists stiff in praying mantis, and he was having trouble unlocking his jaw, as if he were trying to play the twin trick and pass as Sal.

Finally, he asked: "What happened?"

"I don't know," the director said. "I just got the phone call. He was on Route 42."

"But he's okay?"

"There was an accident, Michael," he said. "I'm sorry. That's all I know."

They drove past a ditch shielded by a steel guardrail, past an ivy-covered white house with a rusted swing set in its yard. Michael wasn't sure what his role required. When something terrible happened in the Bible, they tore their garments, but Michael only wore his swimsuit. If he showed up naked, he'd just make things worse. He tried to cry but his tear ducts felt constipated. Better just sit here stiff and shivering.

He desperately wanted to put on Terrance's self-harm helmet, to view whatever he was about to see through the perforated holes of its clear plastic visor. If anything happened to Sal, he didn't know what he would do.

He'd need to go big. Drano drink was out then. Even the harakiri-sword-through-gut was a little cliché. But maybe the lotus-pose-gasoline-match? So his parents would say, "Wow. Okay. I guess he really *was* sorry."

His mother said Michael would take good care of him. Sal didn't have behaviors. But then Michael tried to force Sal into the pool and he heard Sal say he hated him. He actually heard it. And now what did Sal do? What did Michael let him do?

They traveled past the long arching maples, the evening sun slicing through their leaves. No. This wasn't happening. It could still be a joke. The director would stop the cart, turn to him, and say, "Just kidding! The look on your face!" Sal was safe. Sal was eating ice cream. Sal was petting the bunny. *Oh, brother—how beautiful, how soft.* He listened to the camp siren growing fainter and farther away, to the gravel crunch underneath their tires. The punchline never came.

And then there was a bend in the road and finally Route 42 came into view. Just up ahead, Michael could see cars crawling slowly past the stop sign, their glossy paint reflecting the red-and-blue flash of police lights. If Sal was dead, would they crawl like that? They would stop. The whole world would.

Finally, they reached the Camp Cheerful sign, which Michael still couldn't believe, especially now. They turned right onto the apron of the main road. A cop was directing traffic, chopping at the air with glowing orange batons. Flares hissed on the ground. The golf cart squeaked to a stop, and then Michael was out of his seat and running. The gravel cut into his feet. "Go ahead," the cop said, waving him through. He'd been expecting them.

Sal had driven a whole quarter mile to Route 42 and then fifty feet along the apron, along the white line as the cars whooshed past. On the other side of the road, a white Subaru Outback was wrapped around a guard rail, its owner sitting on the ground, his large gray mustache damp with blood. In front of Michael, an SUV was parked with its left headlight crumpled, its driver nowhere to be found. But Sal's chair, the smallest vehicle involved, was mostly unscathed, on its side in the ditch, its footrest just a little muddied. And the cars continued to crawl past.

Michael saw him lying in the grass six feet away: the soft bottoms of his gnarled white feet, his hairy chicken legs, his guitar-themed bathing suit, the tight drum of his belly, and then his fists locked back into his praying-mantis pose. Sal was on an orange board, and two paramedics in navy-blue uniforms knelt beside his head: One dabbed at his caterpillar eyebrow while the other was talking fast, shining a flashlight into his eyes. They'd put on a neck brace. He had a cut-up grass-stained face and green streaks on his bare left shoulder, but they were not draping a sheet.

As Michael ran on the gravel, he thought: *Blink, you asshole. Blink.*

Sal blinked.

V
A CITY OF OCEAN

21

Sal was sleeping. An IV stuck out from his arm, and a catheter snaked out from his pale-blue hospital gown. A square plastic mask seeped oxygen into his lungs. His dyed blond hair was bandaged in white gauze from where he'd hit his head on the grass.

Hannah had been dreading a call all week, waiting for a malfunction: His baclofen needle had slipped out of his spine, or his feeding tube had popped out of place, or he'd fallen out of bed, or had a temp that wouldn't go away and a wet cough. She'd been waiting for this moment—to see Sal—in this hospital room, but she never expected he'd arrive here by his own hand.

The camp director was a giant man. When she'd dropped the boys off at camp, he'd been sitting at the check-in table, but now, on his own two feet, he towered above her. He held her hand in his sausage mitts, said Sal would be okay, would be fine, that he'd had so much fun until now, that she had great boys, both of them. She could tell he was worried they'd sue. She said thank you very much, told him she could take it from here.

Hannah looked to the corner of the room. Michael was sitting with his head in his hands. He'd ridden along in the ambulance with Sal, wearing nothing but his bathing suit, which was now draped over his chair. He was in a pale-blue hospital gown, the same as Sal's, as if she had planned it herself, still matching their outfits.

She said it slow. "You were supposed to do one thing."

"I know," he said.

"You were supposed to keep him safe."

"I'm sorry," he said.

"Well, that's not good enough."

"Hannah," Gabe said. "Come on." He put his hand on her shoulder but she shrugged it off. Gabe said to Michael, "Sorry we forgot your clothes. We rushed over. You cold?"

"It's fine," Michael said. "They gave me a blanket."

"Which they'll probably charge us for," Gabe said.

"I told you he shouldn't go to camp," Hannah said. "I knew he wasn't well enough, but you both talked me into it. And now look." She was so angry her face twitched. She wanted to put Michael in his own wheelchair and see how he liked it. But then she saw the tears drop, beads of dark blue on his hospital gown, and she knew that whatever she might do to him, he'd do worse to himself.

Her first thought after she got the call was *Of course*. God was punishing her. This year had been a test to see if she was good enough, and she'd failed it by deciding to give him up. She'd been prideful and ripped her scapular off. And now she'd lost her privileges. God was taking Sal back. She'd told Gabe this in the van while driving to the hospital. Gabe said, "No. Come on. Don't do that to yourself. Don't be so damned Catholic. This isn't your fault. No one's punishing you but yourself."

Now she turned to Michael. "What happened?"

Michael explained about their fight, how he'd gotten in the pool. "It couldn't have been more than fifteen minutes, Mom."

"You left him alone for fifteen whole minutes?"

"I—" Michael stammered and then froze. He was a little boy again, so ashamed to have disappointed her.

She looked back at Sal, at his eyeballs roving under his lids. *Maybe he knew.* She thought she'd been careful. She always talked to her social worker and the group home directors in another room. But was it far enough? Sal had excellent hearing. Had he caught a snippet of conversation? Had the baby monitor receiver picked up her voice over the airwaves of the cordless? Or maybe it was the way she touched him—like it might be the last time she brushed his teeth, combed his bed-head hair, changed his diaper, traced his caterpillar eyebrows with the pad of her finger, sang to him, held his hand. Maybe he sensed how tired she was getting and guessed. He was so smart. Maybe he'd figured it out.

Gabe stepped forward and cupped his hairy hand around Sal's cheek. "What a silly thing to do, Sally," he said.

Hannah looked at her husband embracing their baby. This was their old argument. He did not consider Sal capable of thinking on that level. After seeing the white patch on his brain scan, Gabe could only see Sal as simple. She knew he considered her simple too. All that old resentment came flooding back, eighteen years of it. He went out into the world, hid from her in his lab and his conferences and his tree stand while she stayed home, and her world got smaller and smaller, condensed down to the body of this boy now lying on the hospital bed.

About that small world: Not many people bothered to visit, but she had mapped it. She knew what grew there. She knew the gradations of his smile, from the slight smirk to the full open-mouth with spaz attack. She knew all the ways he used his eight words, how he could make her laugh with a well-timed "Eh-eh" or almost cry with the soft way he said "Momma." She knew how to be silent with him, too, how it used to bother her so much that he couldn't say more words, but now his silence was what she loved most, that in this loud world here was someone with whom you didn't need to say a single thing. She knew how to put him to sleep, how to set him up to survive the long hours without her, with stuffed animals in between the hospital bars and a teddy bear between his knock knees, how at age eighteen he still let her read to him and sing lullabies as he nodded off. He would never not need her. She had known how he liked bites out of the corner of his mouth, loved seared, soft scallops, loved every kind of cake mashed into ice cream, and though that part of his world was gone, there was still more to discover. There was even his sadness, his rage, this dark place in him she had avoided but where she'd arrived anyway.

And if he would open his eyes, she'd tell him that she'd found more of herself to give. She wasn't used up, after all.

She said to Sal: "Don't worry. You won't have to go to the facility." She turned to her husband, and it was like a soap opera right before the credits, right before they make you wait till the next episode. She felt the camera up close. She said very quietly, "And I don't want to be married to you anymore."

In the morning, Gabe shuffled out of bed and found no coffee, because Hannah had slept at the hospital. He looked around the kitchen. When he'd gotten home last night, he'd been too tired to clean. He and Hannah left their plates when the call came, and Batey had helped himself to the meat. Gabe was surprised he could still jump that high. He looked at the table, at the place without a chair, where Sal pulled up to eat. In the living room, Sal's plush La-Z-Boy sat empty in the corner, besides a tall metal hook for his pump. This week, Gabe had imagined a life without the boys, but what would he and Hannah do in here without them? Get old and wait for the ramps and lifts to come in handy again? But oh, yeah. His wife didn't want to be married to him anymore.

He rounded up the things for the hospital. Who knew how long they'd have to stay? He packed her book, *Angela's Ashes*, a story about another long-suffering Catholic woman. Maybe there was a well-meaning but complicated man that Angela found a way to forgive before . . . you know . . . the ashes. In Sal's room, he spotted her silver scapular on the carpet and picked it up between his fingers like a dead bug.

Michael came down while Gabe was shoveling Wheat Chex into his mouth. "What do you want? Cereal?"

Michael shook his head. "Not hungry."

Gabe said, "You don't have to let this derail you."

"I'm not like you," Michael said.

"What is that supposed to mean?"

"I won't just leave her with him."

"Excuse me?" Gabe said. "I've been here the whole time. I worked so she could stay home. I made it possible. Me."

Michael filled his coffee mug to the brim so that he had to sip at it and splash it with milk, again and again, each time saying "Ow." How would he survive at college? Eventually he said, "Are you guys getting a divorce?"

Gabe cleared his throat. "It's a difficult time right now." He felt like Brian Wilson. He wanted to go in his bedroom and not come out for a year. "We should get going."

When they entered the hospital room, Sal's eyes were open. There he was. There was his boy. Sal blinked once, twice, gave a little moan of recognition.

Hannah sat in a chair near the bed. "Look who's awake," she said.

"Morning, Evel Knievel," Gabe said. "God, you got your brother good." He pretended to punch Sal in the gut and waited for Sal to smile and confirm it, that this was just a joke gone wrong. But Sal lay open-mouthed, looking around the room.

He switched tactics. "Hey, guess what? I drank a bunch of coffee, and now I gotta go to the . . . bathroom." He waited. Nothing. Bathroom was usually a golden word with his boy, but Sal just took a deep breath. Maybe hurling yourself into traffic put you in a bad mood.

Gabe held up a McDonald's bag. "I got this for my wife, but if you don't want to be married to me anymore, I'll give it to that cute nurse at the desk."

Hannah glared at him, then grabbed the bag, unwrapped a McMuffin, and took a bite. "This means nothing," she said. She must have noticed the hopeful look on his face. He dangled the necklace in front of her, and she snatched it from him and clasped it around her neck.

The doctor arrived on his morning rounds and pulled Gabe and Hannah outside. He told them what they already knew: that Sal had separated his shoulder and sustained a concussion but had otherwise escaped from what could've been much worse. They would keep him another night to be sure, and if all went well, he could go home the next day.

Back in the room, Gabe leaned in and said, "Hey, buddy. We've been wondering. You want to tell us why you ran away?"

"He's tired," Hannah said.

"He's okay," Gabe said. "Did you know we were thinking about getting you your own place?"

Gabe studied Sal's expression, waiting for him to deny or confirm. Sal held his breath as if he were about to answer but then he puffed it out, his chest resuming its steady rhythm.

"Were you trying to punish your mother?" Gabe asked. "Your brother? Were you trying to punish us? Or—"

"You didn't give him enough time to answer," Hannah said.

"Or was this just a prank?" Gabe waited. His son had always been a daredevil, always scuffing up the walls, always putting his fingers in Batey's mouth. *Just say "Yeah" and let your mother stop torturing herself.* He didn't want her to carry this for the rest of her life.

"Were you trying to kill yourself?" Michael blurted out.

Hannah gasped. "Jesus."

Gabe threw up his hands. "Let's not get hysterical," he said. "You know what? He doesn't even need a reason. Maybe he did it because he could? Because for once in his life, no one was watching him. Isn't that why, Sally? Did your old man get it right? Say, 'Eh. You're right, Dad.'"

"You don't know that," Michael said. "You don't know anything about him!" Then he shoved his hands hard into Gabe's chest, where Gabe caught them and said, "You sure?"

"Oh my God," Hannah said. "Stop! Both of you!"

Sal moaned. They froze. Sal yelled through gritted teeth: "Ahhhh-eeeh-arrrrr!" It was one of his long whale calls. He was arching his back, his eyebrows furrowed.

Hannah turned to Michael. "What did he say?"

It was obvious to Gabe. "He's saying, 'Everyone shut the fuck up.'"

"I'm not asking you," Hannah said. "Michael, what's he saying?"

Michael didn't move.

"You could do it once," Hannah said. "Try."

Not this again, thought Gabe. Why couldn't she stop waiting for words that would never come?

But Michael shook his head. "I don't know," he said. All that anger had drained out of him, leaving like a ghost that had overstayed its welcome.

Michael was sitting in a chair in Sal's hospital room, watching his brother breathe and feeling sorry for himself, when suddenly Bobbie was in the doorway. She had a deep golden tan, wore a tank top and jeans shorts, as if she'd wandered from the set of *Baywatch* into a medical drama. She was shivering in the hospital air-conditioning, her teeth chattering. With freckles on her apple cheeks, she was more beautiful than ever, the faded slashes on her arms and legs looking merely like chic tribal tattoos. Brandishing a bouquet of daisies, she entered the room, put down the flowers, and placed her hands on her hips.

"What are you doing in here, Salazar?" she asked. "Your mother told me everything. What a stunt to pull. I can't believe you." She knelt before Sal, took his hand, and kissed the stubble on his cheek, eliciting one of the few smiles Sal doled out.

In the hallway, she gave Michael a hug and held it. "Jesus. Stay here for a second. I'm fucking freezing. Sorry I never called you back."

"It's fine," Michael said. "I left like two messages."

"More like five."

He shrugged. "I ruined prom. I threw up on you."

"It was more than that, Michael. You got scary."

"I know."

"Do you remember what you said that night?"

"Not really."

"You kept saying you thought you were retarded."

"I shouldn't use that word."

"You said nobody could tell, but they'd find out soon. You went to this dark place, and I couldn't follow you there. I didn't want to relapse. And then, I don't know. I was at my dad's."

"I get it," he said. It was wiped from his memory but sounded like something he would do. He wasn't normal, no matter how much he pretended. He could stop pretending now. He listened to her stomach acid jump into her mouth, heard her swallow it back down. "Do you still?"

"No," she said. "I've been good. I did a lot of thinking in Florida. I'm changing my major. I'm going to work with special needs kids. People like Sal."

"But you couldn't bother to call him?"

"I knew I'd have to talk to you too. I wasn't ready. But I am now."

"Well, you caught me at a great time." He explained about his parents sending Sal to a facility, about how Sal didn't know but maybe did. "I was supposed to take care of him. Instead, I let him drive into traffic."

"God," she said, and gave his shoulders a shake. "You love to punish yourself. That's really your fucking favorite."

"Debatable," Michael said. "But I'm not going to college anymore. I'm staying home."

"See what I mean? Wear a hair shirt while you're at it. How do you know he was trying to hurt himself? How do you know he wasn't just going somewhere."

"And where would that be? The gas station?"

She shrugged and peeked into his room. "I don't know. Somewhere. Anywhere."

In the van on the way home, Sal's lift creaked over the potholes. Their father drove with their mother sitting shotgun—Michael in the way back. Sal was in the middle, strapped in his wheelchair to the floor, his head still wrapped in a fat white bandage. Michael thought they'd travel in silence like this the whole way, but midway through, Sal said, "Mike-a."

"What?" Michael said.

"Mike-a," Sal said again. He wanted to play ping pong.

"Sal-a," Michael said.

After two more volleys, Sal mixed it up, said, "Momma."

"Momma yourself," Michael said.

"Eh-eh," Sal said. "Mike-aeeeah!"

"Saaaal-aaaaah! Salad."

Sal sputtered his lips, and they all laughed. It meant he was feeling better. Everyone played their roles. Their father turned around, said, "Pipe down back there! I'm trying to drive."

"Watch the road!" their mother said, and their father said, "Right. Guess I should keep my eyes peeled for surprise wheelchairs, huh, Sal?" Their father peeked at the rearview mirror for Sal's reaction. The lift squeaked again over the potholes. Might as well have been crickets.

At home, Michael waited for his mother to say to his father: "That's it. Pack your bags. We don't need you anymore." He waited for her to say, "You'll be hearing from my lawyer." But she gave no marching orders. Instead she rifled through the mail and inspected the garden for her ruined flowers, which had withered unattended in the August heat. After her initial declaration at the hospital, he saw signs of her second thoughts, but she was still difficult to read.

She spent the afternoon in Sal's room, then for dinner defrosted venison sausage and microwaved frozen bags of white rice and peas.

Michael got himself a glass of skim milk and joined the three of them already at the table. He dug in while Sal *click click click*-ed, Sal's Dynavox mounted on his chair, on the Family page, whispering into his ear through the pillow speaker. *Talk*, it whispered. *Mom. Dad. Mich-ael.* No one took its advice.

Back, it whispered and Sal clicked the switch. *Back*, it said in its robot voice, and then Sal was on the main page but didn't click. Maybe he meant back to the way things used to be. Back to when they were a family.

His mother took a long sip of Diet Coke and cleared her throat. "Michael," she said. "I wasn't thinking straight yesterday . . . about a lot of things. We think you should still leave tomorrow. You can still make orientation."

"How are you going to manage him? Those aides again? You can't do this by yourself."

"We'll figure it out," she said. "I'll try a new agency. Your dad has agreed to take a job in the animal facility. It'll be a pay cut, but he'll have more time to spend at home. You don't need to worry about us."

"It's what's best," his father said. "We'll load up the van tomorrow. I'll drive you. I mapped it out. We might have time to stop at the world's biggest ball of twine. Guinness certified. Of course it's in Kansas."

Michael had wanted Sal to stay at home, to be taken care of by his own family, but now they'd decided that family did not include him. "I'm staying," he said. "I've already decided."

His father winced. "You have a scholarship. We can't afford it now otherwise."

"I'll take a year off, then," Michael said.

His mother shook her head. "You need to go. You need to be your own person."

"Let's ask Sal," Michael said.

"It's not up to him," she said.

"*Shhhh,*" he said. "Sal, do you want me to stay? Eh or Eh-eh?"
Sal took two breaths, looked from Michael to his mother.
"Come on. Eh or Eh-eh?" Michael asked again.
Sal locked eyes with his brother, his lips bunched in pensive formation. He clenched his fingers, tilted up his head. "Eh-eh," he finally said, like *Listen to them.* Like *Now you're the one they're sending away.*

Michael spent the evening throwing his belongings into garbage bags. His father said to be ready to go early in the morning. Fine if Sal didn't want Michael taking care of him. Fine if Sal just wanted to be mamma's little boy. Their father wouldn't change. Their mother would baby Sal by herself until he had another health scare, and then she'd decide that actually no, she couldn't handle him anymore. And where would Michael be? Incommunicado. Sorry. Leave a message. His mom always called Sal the gravity of their family, bending their orbits to him and keeping them all grounded. But in a metaphor just as true, Michael was the glue. Without him, they'd fall apart.

He couldn't sleep. He lay in bed, imagining Sal at the pool under the green awning, staring at the back of Michael's head as he played brother to someone else, inflicting on Vince his care and worry and bad jokes. He imagined Sal cranking his joystick forward and hanging a left past the Obstacle Course with its balancing board, past the benches and blackened rocks circled for campfire. In his mind, Sal drove past the empty cabins and the Great Hall. He turned left out into the parking lot, past the rows of stick-figure handicapped signs standing at attention. He felt the bumps of the bone-white bridge and heard the water running over the rocks into the deep pool, and still no one was coming. Did he stall here, in the in-between? Did he think about turning back? Or maybe he kept going until he dipped down onto the other side of the bridge, and back on blacktop, gunned it down the tree-lined road, past the ivy-covered house with a rusty swing set, past the long arching maples that spliced the sun through their leaves.

Did he slow down as he got closer to the whooshing traffic? Did he take a last look at the pink sky, at the sun-kissed leaves, at all the beauty he could see? Did he pause at the edge of the road, thinking: *I'm free, I'm finally free.* Before he drove another fifty feet and swung his chair into traffic.

If I was like that I'd . . .

No. That Sal was too terrible. Michael didn't believe in that brother. Could he rewind? Make Sal funny? Maybe Sal really did mean it as a joke, an epic camp prank. Sal with his bleached blond hair. Sal as punk rock. Maybe he was trying to drive straight, to ride this punchline as far as he could, like *You're sending me away? Fuck you. I'll send myself.* But Sal, as usual, was a shitty driver, and like a true member of their family, he'd fucked up. He swerved over the white line before he bloopered it and face-planted into the grass.

Or were you going somewhere? Michael wondered. *Where were you trying to go?*

22

In the morning, Michael came back in from the garage. "All packed," he said, dramatically rubbing dust from his hands. "I'm ready." He spun the van key on its chain.

Their father was sitting at the table reading the paper, sipping coffee in his plastic traveler's mug. He looked at the clock. "Really? It's not even ten. I thought we wouldn't get you out of here till noon. Are you *gasp* growing up?"

"We'll see," Michael said.

Their father looked at Sal, who sat at his usual place, smirking. "Look at that. Sal says, 'Nahhhh.' Be nice to your brother, Sally. You won't see him for a while."

"I guess you guys better get going," their mother said. "Oh my God. Is this goodbye? Come here." She opened her soft arms, and Michael walked into them. "You're a good brother. And you'll always be my little boy." Michael felt her tears on his neck, and he inhaled her shampoo, tried to remember what it smelled like for future reference. She shoved something into his hands: a cell phone. "Anytime you want to talk to Sal, you can call. But not too late. And no drunk dialing."

"Ugh," his father said, wiping an eye. "I'm going to be too emotional to drive."

His mother rolled her eyes. "Call me too if you get sick of him. It's a long way."

"Speaking of," his father said. "I'm hitting the head. I suggest you do the same."

Michael bent down and patted Batey's big floppy head, kissed his furry cheek, and looked deep into his milky cataracts. "Don't die while I'm gone, okay?" He approached Sal and turned to his mother. "Can you give us a minute?"

She nodded and left the kitchen.

Michael stared into Sal's brown eyes and patted down the edges of the white bandage on his head. "All right, dude," he said. "This is it." He gave Sal a last kiss on his cheek and then walked slowly to the door leading out to the garage. He opened it and held it wide, showing Sal the van with the lift down and waiting. "You coming or not?"

Their first stop was the bank, where Michael withdrew his life's savings—three thousand dollars—everything from his gig washing dishes and working all summer for Sal. Michael hid the bills in an overhead compartment between the spare diapers. Inside his own trash bags and boxes, he'd smuggled Sal's clothes and formula, snuck his feeding tube pump and his powerchair charger and a month's worth of pills. He'd explained it to Sal earlier that morning, that if Sal was trying to go somewhere, Michael would take him. All he had to do was drive through that door.

On Route 422, Michael rolled down the windows. They were headed to Warren, whatever the hell that was. Michael had let Sal pick: "Toward Cleveland or Warren?" and Sal chose Warren. That meant southeast. Michael pressed the gas pedal until they reached cruising speed. He'd driven the van a few times but never on the highway. He'd forgotten how fun it was, how all the other drivers gave you a wide berth. Now the hot wind whipped through the open windows and the hair danced on their foreheads.

"Ahhhhhhh!" Sal howled, like *You bastards!*

"Ahhhhhhh!" Michael howled, like *You bastards!*

"Ahhhhhhhhh!" they howled together like *You fucking bastards! We're free! We're finally free!*

Sal laughed maniacally in his chair, his hands flexed back, a hysterical praying mantis with a bandage on his head. They would have kept yelling like this except the cell phone in the front seat rumbled to life. Michael rolled up all the windows and answered it.

"You guys having fun?" their mother asked.

"Yes," Michael said. He called back to his brother. "Sal, you having fun?"

"Yeah," Sal said.

"Great. Now come on back. Your father is getting pissed. You won't have time to stop at the twine."

"Dad can see the twine if he wants. But I'm not going." Michael hung up.

A whole minute passed before the phone vibrated again. "What?" he said into the receiver.

"Come back now," his mother said. "I'm serious."

"I'm fine," Michael said. "Sal's fine. We're just taking a little trip."

"Where are you guys? We'll come get you. We'll go there together—"

Michael hung up again. His parents would require time to adjust. It would be a shock not to be needed anymore. They could make it more difficult or less.

As the phone buzzed in the seat beside him, he drove through Youngstown. "Look at this shithole," Michael said.

"Yeah," Sal said.

"And we live near Cleveland. So that's saying something. But I bet it's cheap."

They had a choice to make. The exit was coming up quick. Continue east to New York or head south. He asked Sal: "East? Eh or eh-eh? Come on, Sal. Quick. East? New York?"

He pumped the brake, giving Sal an extra second to decide. Just as they were about to pass the fork, Sal said, "Eh-eh."

"South it is!" Michael lurched across the lane to the exit, cutting off a Honda Civic, which blared its horn. Sal's nervous laugh dissolved into a moan, and his smile bounced up and down.

"Sorry," Michael said. His heart thudded in his chest. They'd come within three feet of that asshole's bumper, three feet within Sal not trusting him anymore. He had to be more careful.

Down they went on Route 76. The flat Ohio fields grew craggy with an occasional hill, and then they found themselves headed into Pennsylvania. Not the state Michael would have chosen for a new life, but he wasn't exactly calling the shots.

Outside of Pittsburgh, at a rest stop, Michael bought a map. He laid Sal in the gray plush backseat. "Give your butt a rest," he said. He changed Sal's wet diaper and squirted a syringe of distilled water into his feeding tube—hydration and afternoon meds. He spread the map over his brother's body, the mid-Atlantic states covering the expanse between Sal's neck and knees. He said, "Where are we going? We need a plan. Where do you want to go? The beach?"

Sal thought for a moment, his eyes settling at the corner of his sockets. "Yeah," he said. Of course he did. The last time he felt good was Mexico. Michael scanned the eastern coastline, saw a city.

"Hey, how about Ocean City? An entire city of ocean?"

Sal smiled just barely. "Eh," he said like *Fine*.

"You thinking about Mom?"

"Mom-ma," he said like *I feel bad*.

"She'll be all right. Next stop we'll get you back in your chair and set up your pump."

He buckled the seat belts around Sal's chest and hips and tightened Sal to the seat, weighing the chance of an accident versus the danger of a pressure sore. The world was full of awful math.

Back on the highway, he looked at his phone. Seven messages. The first one, from his mother, was pretty simple: "Pick up pick up pick up pick up."

The third one was his father. "Hello, son," he said. "You couldn't let Sal have all the fun. I get it. You're twins. Competitive. Such an epic prank. You can be proud. But your mother is growing a tad hysterical, and if you don't come home soon, I will kick your fucking ass."

The fifth message was his mother's uninterrupted weeping. Jesus. They'd been gone less than three hours. When the phone rang again, he picked up.

"Thank God," his mother said. "Tell me you're bringing him back."

Michael spoke calmly. "We're on the road right now. We'll let you know where we land."

His father was on the other line. "After everything she's been through, Michael. This is unbelievable. This is cruel."

"Look," Michael said, "I'll take good care of him. This summer showed me I can do it myself. I took my eye off him for a little, but it let him tell us something. And I'm listening, Mom. I'm truly listening to him for the first time in a long while."

"He's medically fragile. Do you hear me? Bring him back, or I swear to God I will—"

Michael hung up and turned off the phone. "Enough of that," he said.

Sal looked at him with pinched eyebrows, like *What did they say?*

"They're taking it pretty well." He turned on the radio, found some punk rock on a local college station: three power chords, mumble-barked lyrics, something about not wanting to pay rent. It was awful. "You know how much I hate this, right?" He turned it up.

Sal smiled.

At two p.m., they hit 70 East toward Baltimore. Michael drove carefully, hands at ten and two. Would their parents call the cops? He kept his eyes peeled for flashing lights. Outside Hagerstown, he stopped at a Burger King and purchased a whopper and fries and large vanilla milkshake. He got Sal back in his chair and set up his pump. Michael pointed to his burger, "Fast food," and then to Sal's pump, "slow food."

Sal rolled his eyes like *Very funny*. He eyed Michael's milkshake, licked his bottom lip.

"You want some?"

"Eh," Sal said.

"If you cough, we're done."

Sal swallowed smoothly, his Adam's apple bobbing in a fluid motion. Maybe he'd finally figured it out. Michael *tap-tap-tap*-ed another strawful into Sal's mouth, but this one caught in his throat. Sal gasped and fell into a hacking fit, his face red. Fuck. Had he aspirated? Would it settle in his lungs? Then they'd have to go back for sure. When Sal regained his raspy breath, Michael said, "Okay. That's enough." He primed Sal's tube and set up his pump with a less tasty version of vanilla. *Click click click*.

They passed Baltimore and took 97 South to a long bridge across a bay with arching ships and all that blue. Michael rolled down the windows again and shouted, "Look at that water! Ahhhhhhhhh!" He glanced in the mirror at Sal, who smiled politely but did not howl back.

Two hours later, as the sun went down, they pulled into Ocean City. Each side of the wide boulevard was lined with hotels and condos and boxy stores selling t-shirts and surfing gear. They drove until they reached what appeared to be a boardwalk, with a Ferris wheel turning in the distance, glowing red in the night sky. To their right were yellow sands, the waves sweeping in. Drunks ran across the road, and teenagers on bicycles swerved in and out of traffic. The area seemed run down and seedy. It was perfect. Michael rolled down the windows so Sal could hear the quiet roar of the surf, get a whiff of saltwater.

"Smell that?" he called back. "It's the city of ocean!"

Sal smiled like *The city of ocean.*

Michael saw a sign outside a church: Free Spaghetti Dinner at 7. What luck. And praise Jesus: An open handicapped parking space waited for them. When they rolled in, dinner was wrapping up, but warm noodles still soaked in their crockpots, a few meatballs still stewed in red sauce. Michael set up Sal's pump, got a plate of free pasta, and then they sat with the homeless, the freeloaders, the church mice. A shaky Black man in a Terrapins hat pointed to Sal. "Isn't your man hungry?"

"He brought his own," Michael said, gesturing to Sal's pump.

The man watched the formula march into Sal's stomach. "It's a miracle," he said and smiled with two gold teeth. Maybe this was how things would be from now on. The kindness of strangers. An improvised life.

Their bellies full, they explored the crowded boardwalk. Michael had to help Sal steer to avoid hitting pedestrians. "Try to win," said an Eastern European man with hollow eyes.

"That's what we're doing," Michael said.

"No. Three throws for five. Best game on boardwalk." The man was holding darts, and suddenly the balloons on the wall behind him made more sense. Michael forked over the cash and threw enough darts into enough balloons to win a medium-sized plush Tweety bird. "We'll need this for your knees," Michael said to Sal. "I forgot your stuffed animals."

As they walked on, Sal stopped in front of a concession stand and looked longingly at a bag of cotton candy. "Eh," he said, like *Hook me up.*

"All right," Michael said. "But no coughing."

He tore off a piece of blue floss and placed the cloud on Sal's waiting tongue, where it melted into his spit. The cotton candy seemed to evaporate, like Sal had swallowed nothing at all, leaving behind just the blue saliva tie-dyeing his white shirt. Still, Michael held his breath. Sal wanted it, but did he know what was good for him? "Last bite," Michael said.

Standing in line for the Ferris wheel, Michael pulled a fuzzy sweatshirt from the wheelchair's black bag and threaded Sal's arms through. It was getting chilly. They watched kids their age stumble around to the attractions, drunk or stoned or both. Michael felt like he didn't need alcohol or drugs anymore, didn't need to be altered. He hadn't even brought any weed. For the first time in his life, he was feeling comfortable in his own skin. He was Mike-a, Sal's twin. Mike-a was all he had to be.

When they reached the carnie, the man waved away their tickets and said in a gravelly voice, "Naw. This dude rides for free." He helped lift Sal from the chair into the compartment, and then they rose, rider by rider, as the Ferris wheel filled. Michael held Sal against his shoulder to stabilize his head. They gazed down on the city and out across the ocean. They could see the ships in the distance lit up like constellations. Sal relaxed against Michael like he would rather be nowhere else in the world.

"You see all this? It's for us," Michael said. "We're special."

"Yeah," Sal said.

They rented a motel room not far from the beach. Michael had never rented a room before and felt nervous handing over so much cash at once, a hundred dollars for the night in addition to a two-hundred-dollar deposit because he didn't have a credit card yet. In the room, he brushed Sal's teeth. Sal gave him a solid five seconds before biting the brush. "Don't be an asshole," Michael said, and Sal smiled like *But that's what I am*.

Michael scooted their queen beds together and laid Sal down. He put the Tweety bird between his knock-knees and rolled the motel towels tight along his body for bumpers. He wedged the smaller towels under Sal's gaps. Sal was quiet, his arms tight, his eyes darting around the room.

"What's wrong?"

"Mom-ma," Sal said.

"I told you," he said. "She'll be fine. We need some space. We'll stay here for a while, then find some other place. Wherever you want, okay?"

Sal made squirrel teeth like *Have you actually planned this out?*

Sal had a point. They'd spent two hundred dollars on gas, food, a motel, and a stupid stuffed animal. What would they do after the money ran out? How would they live?

"If you're worried about money, I can always give hand jobs."

Sal rolled his eyes.

"We'll apply for benefits when we settle down. Sal, come on. It's just us now," Michael said. "I'm taking care of you."

Sal smiled just barely.

They watched an episode of *Cops*. Michael waited for the camera to roll up to their shitty motel parking lot, the cops kicking in their door. *Hands up! Drop the feeding tube!* But they were arresting mostly drug dealers. Michael watched until his eyelids grew heavy. He took off Sal's bandage to let the wound breathe and rubbed on Neosporin with a Q-Tip. It was just a little flayed strip, a little road rash, already starting to heal. Thank God for Sal's hard head. "How's your shoulder?" Michael asked, and took a peek under Sal's shirt. No sign of swelling. "Looks okay." He put his hand on the light switch, said, "Come on. Cough it up."

Sal scraped his bottom lip against his front teeth like *Goodnight, brother.*

Michael woke to Sal retching. He leapt out of bed and elevated Sal's trunk, making sure he didn't aspirate. He wedged himself between Sal and the mattress, holding his brother against his chest as he felt Sal's diaphragm lurch and lurch. "Shit shit shit," he said. "Too much junk today. Maybe just formula from now on?" He waited for Sal to admit defeat, to say "Yeah," but his brother just answered by gagging again. He could see the blue dye from the cotton candy in the upchuck soaking the sheet. They had to call the front desk for more bedding. Sal spent a good half-hour moaning in pain, maybe with a burnt esophagus.

"You're all right," Michael whispered in his best impersonation of their mother as he rubbed Sal's sweaty back. But Sal wanted the real thing.

"Mom-ma," he said. He called for her again, and it took all of Michael's willpower not to turn on the cell phone. He stayed awake for another hour listening to his brother breathe, listening for a lung rattle, praying to a God he didn't believe in for his brother to not spit up again, for them to not have to go back.

In the morning, after sleeping in, Sal was back to his ornery self, doing an extra-long round of Pick the Right T-shirt. Michael held up a surfing one. "We're at the ocean. Now is the only time it's not stupid."

But Sal didn't like how Michael put his head through the collar and yelled, "Ehhh-ah" like *Watch it.*

"Sorry," Michael said. "How's your tummy?"

"Mmmm," Sal said, like *It's been better.*

"You want to check out the beach?"

"Eh."

After meds and breakfast, they ventured out to the boardwalk. The sun was high, the sky a deep blue cut with white contrails. The wind kept the heat off their backs. Michael guided Sal down the beach walkway as far as the chair would go, then pushed it a few hard-won feet over the sand. He carried him the rest of the way to shore and laid down a beach towel. Old couples with beer bellies walked holding hands, knobs of lotion on their noses. Families camped out under umbrellas, their shit everywhere, their kids building shoddy sandcastles that wouldn't pass inspection. Two muscular twenty-somethings played overly aggressive Frisbee as their girlfriends sunbathed in impossibly tiny bikinis.

Michael took off Sal's non-stupid surfing shirt and squirted a maze of suntan lotion on Sal's body, even dabbing it around his tube. "I'll try not to get sand in your diaper."

They lay there listening to the rhythm of the surf, the caw of seagulls. One of the Frisbee men was apparently a "pussy." A boy's brother stomped on his wing of the sandcastle and now the kid was in mourning.

"Mom-ma," Sal said.

"It's another nice day," Michael said. "Not too hot."

"Mom-ma," Sal said again.

"Let's pick up some ladies. Smile and look extra helpless."

Michael watched for Sal's smirk, but instead he said, "Mom-ma."

"Enough about Momma. Remember in Mexico when she wouldn't let you go in the ocean?"

Sal was quiet. He looked up and pursed his lips, made his remembering face.

"We get to do that now. You're with *me*. Let's fight some waves. You want to?"

Sal took a second. "Eh," he finally said in a tone that meant *I guess*.

Michael cradled Sal to his chest and carried him to the water. They stepped into the carpet of foam. It was cold at first, and the shells cut Michael's feet, but they walked forward and adjusted to the temp. Another wave folded in and hissed around Michael's ankles. "You ready?" Michael asked.

"Eh," Sal said, more definite this time.

Michael walked forward until another wave rushed against them and he was knee deep. He swung Sal down, holding him under his armpits, and dropped Sal's feet into the water. "Tell me if this hurts your shoulder," Michael said. Sal gasped at the cold, but he did not "eh-eh" to get out, he did not "Momma." Michael thought he saw a jellyfish, but it was a grocery bag floating by. He said, "Your feeding tube isn't the only plastic in this ocean."

Sal smiled. They took another step forward. A few small waves lapped at Sal's legs, and then a larger one curled in front of them, the blue turning aqua then brown as it kicked up sand and broke into Sal's pelvis. Sal screamed, "Ahhhhhhhh!" like *It's freaking cold!* Or like *Shrinkage!* The foam hissed around their thighs, and then the surf rushed out again, sinking them deeper into the sand. They stepped forward. Another wave swept in, and Michael's body bent to receive the blow. The water hit Sal higher, up to his tube now as Sal yelled "Ra-a-aum!" like *I'm in the fucking ocean!* The water rushed back out, and Michael held onto Sal tighter as they sunk farther down into sand. He stabilized his footing and checked to see if Sal's feeding tube cap had slipped. It was shut tight. They had no leaks, not yet. Michael's biceps were burning. "Should we call it?" he asked, but Sal was electric in his arms, tight and quivering as he stared ahead at the next wave, bigger than all the rest, and here it came as it curled and crashed itself into Sal chest, and Michael stumbled and felt Sal slipping out of his arms, out toward the ocean as it tried to take him, tried to suck him out with the surf. Michael held fast as Sal screamed, "Ehhh-ahhh!" in full spaz attack, like *I'm getting my ass kicked by the ocean!*

Michael carried him out of the water and laid him back on the beach towel. "Holy shit," he said, panting. "My arms are falling off. You almost got swept out."

Sal, shivering in the sun, said, "More."

In the afternoon, they started walking back to the motel for Sal's afternoon feeding. Michael got a jumbo hot dog and a milkshake for himself. Sal eyed the shake, licking his lips.

"You can't," Michael said. "You'll puke again."

Sal got pouty. "Momma," he said.

"Would you stop with that?"

Sal halted in the middle of the boardwalk. "Mom-ma," he said again.

It was like they were back at camp. Didn't he realize what Michael had done for him? How much he was giving up? *My life for yours.* And Sal was having a tantrum about a fucking milkshake? Michael slammed the cup on the ground, spattering it across the wood.

"Watch it," a woman yelled, brushing off her shins. "Hey!" yelled a rollerblader, slipping into a half-split. Sal rolled forward without him.

"Sal," Michael called, but his brother wouldn't look back. Michael caught up and said, "Look, if you're sick of this place already, we don't have to stay here. We can go wherever you want."

"Mmmmmm," Sal said, still driving, like *And then? What will happen after that?*

"I'll figure it out," Michael said. "I said I'd take care of you."

After the feeding, they paid for another night and took a nap. Michael turned on the cell phone and deleted the messages without listening. He watched the news for reports of a twin brother kidnapping, of their weepy mother begging the public for help. He wished they could ditch the van, but where would they find another vehicle with such an awesome lift? After a while, he checked the clock. It was past five. They'd been lying on the bed for hours. His body craved motion. He asked Sal, "You want to cruise the boardwalk for chicks?"

"Eh-eh," he said.

"Another Ferris wheel ride? Try our luck at ring toss?"

"Eh-eh," Sal said.

"How about a movie? Get out of the heat?"

"Eh-eh."

"Deep sea fishing? It'd be better than Lake Erie. We can book a boat for tomorrow? Blow all our money?"

"Eh-eh," Sal said.

"Fine. Let's go somewhere else. Disneyworld? With your wheelchair we won't even have to wait in line. Let's Make-a-Wish."

"Eh-eh," Sal said.

"Then what? What do you want to do?"

"Momma," Sal said.

"You want to call mom?" Michael asked hopefully.

"Eh-eh," Sal said.

"You want to go back?"

"Yeah," Sal said.

He couldn't pretend Sal didn't say it. "You know what will happen if we go back home? They'll kill me. I'll be murdered. Fed to Batey. That's first. And then it'll be like before. She'll think she can take care of you and then something will go wrong and she'll lose her shit. Dad will check out. You'll go to a fucking group home. You'll have to live with other people and deal with all their crap. They have all kinds of stupid rules and idiots take care of you. It's like camp. Is that what you want?"

Sal didn't say anything. His lips got tight in his pensive formation. He knew Michael was right. Michael thought that was the end of it, had turned the channel and was a whole minute into *The Crocodile Hunter*, when Sal said, "Yeah."

"Yeah? But Sal, it'll be even worse. She'll send you to that facility. You don't even know what that is. It's like a hospital. And a prison. A hospital-prison—"

"Mike-a," Sal said like *You could explain. You could help me choose.*

Michael sat there in silence, waiting for Sal to change his mind. He waited for the surface of his face to break, for his mouth to ripple with doubt. For a moment, he could see the future he'd been planning: They were both ten years older, with respectable brown beards, not at all pube-like, and they lived in a first-floor apartment with ramps at every door and a walk-in shower. Michael got paid to be Sal's aide, and every month, they drove the van to cash Sal's sweet benefit check, laughing all the way. They had friends, girlfriends even, who thought it was strange that Michael... like... knew what Sal was thinking. And Sal was often thinking *You're an asshole*, though sometimes he mixed it up with *But I love you*. And Michael could always be Sal's brother. He never had to become anyone else.

Then Sal turned his head, locked his eyes with Michael's. "Mike-a," he said softly, like *Thank you for taking me this far. But I can't go where you're going.*

That night they slept together for the last time. They opened the windows to hear the low roar of the ocean, the surf in and out like breath. Tomorrow, anything could happen. But right now his twin brother was lying next to him. Michael studied Sal's face, the scabbing-over cut on his head, the constellation of little moles that ran down the end of his eyebrow. They were twins, but only their eyes were the same, set deep in different heads. And now they wanted different things: Michael grasping, and Sal the one letting go.

The mattress was too hard, the sheets grainy. They really could've picked a better motel. Michael scooted closer and draped his forearm across Sal's bony chest. He tried to imagine how their bodies were arranged in the womb. Were they like this, face to face? Or were they back to back, eyes shut in different directions? Were they turned around, Sal's ass in his face? Where did Sal end and Michael begin?

Michael opened his eyes to find Sal staring, his whites glowing in the dark. Maybe Sal wanted this night to last as long as Michael did. He listened to his brother breathing, in and out, in and out, melding with the ocean surf and the cars outside on the boulevard until he heard that old murmur, Sal's moans breaking into meaning.

In the dark, Sal said, "Hi, brother."

"Hi," Michael said.

"We're growing up," said Sal.

"What if something happens to you?"

"It will."

"They'll fuck up."

"They will. Or the pneumonia will come for me again. My body will break down. But that's how it works for everyone. In the meantime, though, I have shit to talk, people to make fun of, girls to flirt with. I'll have fun."

"How much did I imagine you? How much of you is real?"

"I was somewhere in the in-between. And you often found me."

Michael couldn't move. He was stalled in the in-between. He knew that he was dreaming, but it didn't matter because Sal was saying, "Mike-a. You can still be Mike-a even after I'm gone."

Back, they clicked. *Back*. They went back, and they were walking through their middle school hall, Michael looking left–right so no one would see Sal blow him a kiss, and then they were little boys on a blanket wrestling, Sal crowing in Michael's face, and then they were babies rumbling together over the sidewalk in the double stroller. They were sealed in the womb. They hadn't said a single word. Their cells were still blooming, getting ready. They would do it all over again.

23

On a Saturday in January, Hannah got the box of Hefty bags and started stuffing. Pack up the polar bear Batey chewed the ear off of, the Tweety Bird Michael had won during the kidnapping. Sal would be allowed only a single dresser at the group home, so she packed corduroy pants and thick fuzzies and light jackets and sweatshirts for layers. Stacks of adult diapers, his Ramones poster, his Mel Brooks DVDs. His stereo and tapes. His feeding tube syringes and cans of formula, his bags of medications, his computer and wires and switches. She labeled everything in black Sharpie: S-A-L.

In his bedroom, she showed him: "Your name. So nobody can jack your stuff."

Sal smiled with his crooked teeth.

She printed out his schedule, all the instructions for his careful handling. She thought if she was clear enough, thorough enough, they wouldn't mess up. It was seven single-spaced pages and still: How would she possibly teach them everything they needed to know?

No time to hyperventilate. She had to keep reminding herself: He wanted to go. He'd picked this place with Michael's help, and two weeks ago they'd called. A space had opened up. And now he'd watch Wrestle-Mania on Wednesdays. He'd go to bowling night. Movie night. A whole schedule of nights. So what if the nurse wasn't there as often as she liked? Or if a doctor wasn't on staff? Or that she'd smelled weed on one of the workers? Or that they weren't allowed to put the baby monitor in his room to make sure he was safe, because it would "violate his privacy"? He wanted to go.

It was relatively close. She would haunt that place like an annoying ghost. She'd intimidate the staff like a mafia member: Anything happens to my son and *skrit* (finger across the throat) I'll come after you. Horse heads in their beds. To make them pay attention. To make them look after her human.

When Michael came home from kidnapping Sal, she'd almost murdered him for the second time in a week. She inspected the other one, hair by hair and head to toe. He smelled like cheap motel soap, but Michael had managed to keep him safe, there and back. She gave him the highest praise she could: "You didn't fuck up." Then she looked into Sal's eyes and confirmed what Michael said on the phone: "Sally-boy, do you want to go to a group home? Because you can stay. I'll let you stay. Do you really want to go?"

"Yeah," Sal said.

She had imagined that when this day arrived, she'd be ready; she'd feel an immense loss but also a sort of relief, an optimism that she'd start to find her way, go back to teaching or help other parents with all she'd learned. Maybe that would come later. For now, she felt a particular kind of despair. Without Sal, they'd be just like everyone else.

Sunday morning, they climbed into the van. Gabe bent to crank Sal's chair to the floor, making the straps taut. He stood and asked, "You ready, buddy?" Sal's smile bounced up briefly, but he was nervous. They all were. As Gabe backed out of the garage, he said, "Say, 'Bye, house.'" He'd built a house for his son, and now he was driving him away from it.

"Bye, house," Michael said.

"Not you, dummy," Gabe said. "But I guess you'll be gone soon enough."

He watched Hannah for signs of emotional distress. She was calm and collected, more so than when she packed Sal for camp. She'd had months to prepare, and he supposed you could only say goodbye so many times.

But last night, Hannah did not crawl into bed until late. She might have spent most of the night holding him. But in the morning, she was once again nerves of steel.

He cut left, down a back road through the neighboring suburb. Here were the houses they'd drive by to pick him up on the weekends, the stop light they'd wait at and wonder: How would he feel today? Is he happy? Did they make the right decision? What kind of mood would he be in when they arrived? Would they find some unexplained bruise? Some traumatic event they weren't there to witness written on his face? Green light. Go.

After Michael kidnapped Sal, they'd both agreed the best course of action was to just call it quits on that genetic investment. He'd tortured his own mother, thrown away his future, played a game with his brother's life. When Michael had returned, however, all the fight was out of their son, as if he'd converted to a strange and bloodless religion. There would be no college for Michael, not right away, anyway. He'd lost his scholarship, but he didn't care. They had to let him complete this journey with Sal. He'd stay and take care of his brother until it was time.

Gabe rolled through a stop sign and turned down the road toward the group home. He counted the numbers. It had been humiliating to close his lab, to move one floor up with the other scientists who'd flamed out or never even launched. But once he was in the animal facility, he felt less pressure, less fear of failure. He could just focus on the science. He liked working with the mice, the rats, the dogs, the occasional monkey, even if he was the last kind hand to touch them. Maybe he'd been meant to be a veterinarian all along.

"It's there," his wife said, and he put on his blinker. Gabe took a deep breath and turned down the driveway. Hannah rubbed his arm, as though sensing his unease. Twin A was moving out, and Twin B would be gone soon. Hannah and Gabe would finally be by themselves again, but who even were those people anymore? They were getting to know each other again. It'd take more than a few months to fix what was broken. It might not work. But the experiment wasn't over. The results were still coming in.

He parked the van, and Hannah and Michael went in to smooth the way. Gabe bent at Sal's feet to unstrap him, then put his elbow on Sal's armrest and said, "One more wrestling match, Ishy-mo?"

Sal smiled like *Sure*.

Gabe laced his own fingers into Sal's stiff hand and wobbled left–right–left, Gabe huffing and groaning while Sal moaned in amusement. Gabe leaned dangerously to his right, Sal almost clinching victory, until Gabe unfurled Sal's pointer finger and put it to Sal's nostril. "Come on! This is no time to pick your nose!"

Sal's laugh shook his chest. They'd have to teach the staff this routine. Sal put his hand to his joystick. He was ready. Gabe helped him guide his chair to the lift platform and asked: "You want to do the honors?" He helped him lift up the yellow switch, elevating him over the van floor, and then together they pressed the red switch forward into this new life.

The home manager with the chunky wood in his ears introduced Sal to his housemates. "This is the new guy, Sal."

"Hi!" said a blonde woman lounging on the loveseat.

"Hello, new guy," said a Black man, looking up briefly from his sketch pad, where he was drawing a chicken with blue sprawling feathers.

An older fellow sat in his manual wheelchair in front of the big screen TV, watching *Willy Wonka*. "Ahh," he said, jerking his trunk in Sal's direction, like *What's up?*

A woman with Down's was talking into a cordless phone. She cupped the receiver, said, "Hello!" and then went back to gossiping. "Oh, I know. She sucks."

"I think everyone else is at church," the manager said. "Let's get you situated."

He led them down the hall, past photographs of all the group home members. They recognized the residents from a few of Sal's house visits, but their attention shifted to a picture of a guy with black hair greased and combed over his scrunched and smiling face. They wondered what his laugh sounded like, how he talked, if he was loved enough. They wondered when another family would look at Sal's portrait this same way. He was the space that had opened up.

In Sal's room, a hospital bed lay stripped and waiting, half the walls bare, half the shelves empty. The other half was taken up by Sal's roommate. He liked baseball and muscle cars and Disney films and sleep apnea machines.

"Jordan visits his family on Sunday but should be home later," said the house manager. "You guys will cause a lot of trouble together."

As Michael and Gabe stuffed Sal's shirts and pants and socks into his one dresser, Hannah cornered the nurse and gave her precise instructions. They set pictures on top of his dresser: Michael and Sal as undercooked babies on a blanket, looking shocked to be alive; Sal dancing at his uncle's wedding; Sal posing with a fish on Lake Erie; Sal swimming with his mother. The last photo their mother set down was a family portrait from their time in Mexico against an ocean sunset. The lighting was off. You could barely make out their faces, but they were wrapped in a band of golden light. "You can look at these when you miss us," Hannah said. "Because you will, right?"

Sal sat there open-mouthed, like *We'll see.*

Hannah looked at the aides. "He's teasing."

While she continued briefing the nurse, a resident wandered in and asked where they were from, if they liked Chinese food, if Sal liked to dance, and what was his favorite farm animal? A man with Down's took Michael by the hand and started gossiping about all the other residents: Someone was cocky. Someone was always on the phone. Another was crazy—eye roll, twirl of finger at his temple. The guy slurred, so Michael couldn't catch everything he was saying, but he paused in all the right places. He had perfect comic timing.

They stayed until they were no longer helping, just uselessly rearranging things.

"All right, Ishy-mo," their father finally said, leaning to kiss Sal's face. "Be good, but don't take any shit. Take out the biggest guy to send a message."

Sal rolled his eyes.

Their mother knelt and whispered, "Bye, my baby. I'm right up the road, okay?" She wiped her eyes and joined their father at the door. "I think I can make it to the van under my own power."

Then Michael was alone with him. He looked at Sal's new roommate's belongings. Who was this guy? NASCAR? A hillbilly. Or maybe his parents foisted the décor on him. Maybe he was more into Broadway musicals, into *Cats* and *Rent* but was just born into the wrong family. He'd have to get used to Sal's punk music, though if Michael wasn't there to be annoyed, would Sal even like it anymore? Would this guy get Sal's sadistic-fuck sense of humor? Would he be able to sleep through Sal's Darth Vader snore? "I don't know," he said. "We can still make a break for it. Me and you, the van, the open road."

Sal smiled. For a moment, it was possible: A nighttime raid, sneaking his brother out the back. But then Sal said, "Eh-eh," like *I'm good*.

"You always have to be first, don't you?" Michael said. "You can't help yourself." He picked up one of the roommate's bobbleheads and gave the doll's head a good flick. After he left Sal here, he'd have to figure out what to do with the rest of his life. His brother didn't need him anymore. He would never earn out his guilt, but he'd put it to good use. He'd applied to work at another group home in the area and was waiting to hear back. He'd learned so much from Sal, and now he might as well be poorly compensated for it. If he went to college in the fall, he'd switch his major. He didn't want to do pre-med anymore. Maybe his mother was right. Maybe he would write a book, not like the college essay, not just what they wanted to hear. He would write what was funny and sad, what was complicated and hard to explain. He would write what was true. It would be impossible to get right, but he might get close. He wondered: *What would Sal think of it?* He leaned in and fumbled with his brother's hand in a mock complicated handshake. He kissed his stubbled cheek and stood up straight.

Now all he needed was his name. "Can you give me one last Mike-a?"

"Eh-eh," Sal said, like *Um, no. Gross*.

"Who's ugly?"

Sal sat there open-mouthed, like *Nice try. I'm not falling for that*.

"Come on," Michael said. "I can't leave here without it. You know that. Tell me who's ugly?" He walked back two paces, but still Sal did not move his lips. He heard his father honk.

"See? Mom and Dad are waiting. Don't be a tool. Let's go. Tell me who's ugly."

Sal sat stone-faced, like *Stop whining. You've always been a little baby*.

God, Sal was so annoying. He couldn't just let them have this moment.

They were leaving each other for real this time, and still Sal had to fuck with him. Michael stepped back and was at the doorway. "Last chance," he said. "You'll regret it. Who's ugly?"

Sal seemed to soften for a moment, his lips twitching, but then he made his squirrel teeth.

Fine. Michael opened the door. "Bye, jerk," he said and walked through it.

Sal sat blinking in his chair for a full five seconds. He licked his lips and let his tongue retract. He said quietly into the empty room: "Mike-a..."

"Ha!" his brother yelled from around the corner. "Asshole. I heard that. Sal."

Sal listened to his brother's footsteps down the hall, heard the staff say goodbye, heard the spaceship whine of his van through the barely open window getting farther away and fainter until all that remained were the cars whooshing down the road, the wind through the trees, the low murmur of the movie, an "Ahhhh" and a laugh, a girl in another room saying, "Shut up."

The bedroom door was ajar, but he was alone.

He traced the four walls with his chair, driving slowly past his hospital bed with its wooden rail, his stuffed animals at attention peeking over the board. He paused at the paint-chipped dresser and its drawers stuffed with clothes. He looked at his family pictures crowded on top: Sal, at nine, out of his wheelchair and bear-hugged by Michael as Sal softly bit into his face; Sal, at fourteen, on the fishing trip, his father holding a dead walleye and Sal blowing a kiss; Sal, at sixteen, swimming in a pool with his mother as she gazed down at his floating head; the family all together in Mexico, wrapped in a band of fading sun. He cranked forward. He drove past. And turned toward the La-Z-Boy chair with the window above where the winter air seeped in through the dead ladybugs on the sill and beyond the glass the trees bled together, but he could still hear the birdsong and the hiss of wind between the leaves. He turned left, driving past his roommate's bed, almost identical to his own but with a NASCAR comforter and not as many stuffed animals, and on his roommate's dresser, fewer pictures of his family going fewer places, with no sign of a brother. He drove past the door cracked open, where he could hear a burp and a laugh,

I am grateful to my colleagues at the University of Oregon, especially Jason Brown and Betsy Wheeler. And a big shout out to my students, especially in Disability Studies, whose own stories inspire me every day.

Thanks to the organizations and fellowships that generously supported this book, including the Elizabeth George Foundation, the VCCA, the Centrum, the Taft Fellowship, and the Sewanee Writers' Conference.

Thanks to Michael Copperman, Nanosh Lucas, and Jeanne Shoemaker for your beta reading and friendship.

My gratitude to the special needs families, therapists, social workers, professionals, clients, and friends I interviewed for the book, including the Clawson family, Mike Burke, Kevin Berner, Sara Fenwick, Paul Mosley, and Dianna Bluso.

Thanks to everyone at Camp Allyn, LADD, and Camp Cheerful. Camp Cheerful gave me and my brother a place where we felt like true twins. Thanks especially to Ricky, Will, Mickey, Sarah, Jay, Tom, Leng, Laura, Klaus, Tim, and my favorite campers (you know who you are).

To my camper who really did escape in his power chair from a camp luau onto Route 42 (and was thankfully OK): I hope you got to where you were going.

I appreciate everyone who ever took care of my brother, especially Sue Englehart.

Thank you to M. for being my special person, and to my daughter, Ena, for being the special person we created.

Finally, to Dan the man: I miss you every day.

ACKNOWLEDGMENTS

When you work on a book for more than a decade, you have too many people to thank, but I'll try. First, I want to thank my parents for their love, support, and inspiration. You answered my endless questions and didn't ask too often how the book was going. Thank you for everything.

Thanks to my surviving siblings, David and Sara, for putting up with me. (Sorry I killed you off. . . .)

Thanks to my wonderful agent, Heather Schroder, for all those hours on the phone and for her vision, counsel, belief, and persistence. Thank you to everyone at Acre Books, including Sarah Haak, Barbara Neely Bourgoyne, and especially Nicola Mason, Nicola: You made my dreams come true with your faith and editorial brilliance.

To all my teachers, especially Elly Williams, Leah Stewart, Chris Bachelder, Patrick O'Keefe, Jim Schiff, and Michael Griffith. Michael, you believed in this story from day one. I grew up as a writer under your wing, and this book would not exist without you. Thanks, too, to my Cincy friends, especially Dietrik Vanderhill, Leah McCormick, Matt McBride, Tessa Mellas, Matt O'Keefe, Lisa Ampleman, Sara Watson, B.R. Smith, Ian Wissman, and Jason Nemec.

a dish hit the sink, a "Listen up?" and "Hey, I'm watching that." He drove past the TV with his box of DVDs stacked neatly underneath, and in the blank screen he saw his own blurry self staring back. He drove forward until his footrest tapped the front of his bed, and he came to a stop, his joystick at center, his hand hovering.

Soon someone would come to check on him. Soon the residents would file in. Soon an aide would be by with his afternoon meds. Soon his roommate would be in the bed next to him, breathing too loud. But right now, Sal was by himself in his new space, the space that had opened up. He turned his chair towards the door, toward the crack of light.

He took a deep breath and held it as he sat in his own stillness.

"Ahhhh-aaah," he said, like . . .

He said, "Ahhhh-aaah," like . . .

He said "Ahhhh-aaah," and it was like . . .